One Night at the C...

THE S...
who Loved Her

Three exotic and thrilling books by
three terrific authors:

Susan Stephens
Kate Hardy
Liz Fielding

THE SHEIKH WHO… COLLECTION

On sale 5th July

On sale 2nd August

On sale 6th September

On sale 4th October

On sale 1st November

On sale 6th December

THE SHEIKH
who Loved Her

Susan
STEPHENS

Kate
HARDY

Liz
FIELDING

MILLS
BOON

Mills & Boon, an imprint of Harlequin (UK) Limited, Eton House, 18-24 Paradise Road, Richmond, Surrey TW9 1SR

ISBN: 978 0 263 90731 5

027-0713

Harlequin (UK) policy is to use papers that are natural, renewable and recyclable products and made from wood grown in sustainable forests. The logging and manufacturing processes conform to the legal environmental regulations of the country of origin.

Printed and bound in Spain
by Blackprint CPI, Barcelona

RULING SHEIKH, UNRULY MISTRESS

SUSAN STEPHENS

Susan Stephens was a professional singer before meeting her husband on the tiny Mediterranean island of Malta. In true Modern™ romance style they met on Monday, became engaged on Friday and were married three months after that. Almost thirty years and three children later, they are still in love. (Susan does not advise her children to return home one day with a similar story, as she may not take the news with the same fortitude as her own mother!)

Susan had written several non-fiction books when fate took a hand. At a charity costume ball there was an after-dinner auction. One of the lots, 'Spend a Day with an Author', had been donated by Mills & Boon® author Penny Jordan. Susan's husband bought this lot, and Penny was to become not just a great friend but a wonderful mentor, who encouraged Susan to write romance.

Susan loves her family, her pets, her friends and her writing. She enjoys entertaining, travel and going to the theatre. She reads, cooks and plays the piano to relax, and can occasionally be found throwing herself off mountains on a pair of skis or galloping through the countryside. Visit Susan's website: www.susanstephens.net—she loves to hear from her readers all around the world!

PROLOGUE

'DARKER than night and twice as dangerous' was how the magazine he'd snaffled from his secretary's desk referred to the al Maktabi brothers. Razi al Maktabi replaced it with a wink at the only woman who knew how he took his coffee.

Razi's lips were still curving when he shut his office door. The media was struggling for dirt on him, apparently. Coming to a halt in front of a wall of windows, he placed his first call. While he waited for it to connect he studied a gunmetal slice of the Thames, where the never-ending action soothed him. Across the river, in what felt like touching distance from his penthouse, stood the Houses of Parliament, while behind him was the sleek cocoon of the CEO of Maktabi Communications, a company he had driven to international prominence. Ahead of him lay the Phoenix throne of the Isla de Sinnebar, but before he assumed the duties of his desert kingdom he was calling one last reunion.

The magazine article had got some things right, Razi reflected as the telephone droned in Lord Thomas Spencer-Dayly's Gloucestershire mansion. Razi's elder brother, Sheikh Ra'id al Maktabi, was every bit as hard as the journalist supposed and with good reason. Their father had sown enough wild oats to seed the whole of the American Midwest and there were numerous pretenders to Ra'id's Sapphire throne.

This went some way to explaining why Ra'id ruled mainland Sinnebar with a rod of iron, earning him the sobriquet 'The Sword of Vengeance' by those who liked a lick of Hollywood with their sheikh. The journalist had left one thing out. Razi would die for the brother who had made his childhood bearable, and who had fought for him to share the same rights Ra'id enjoyed as their father's legitimate son…

Razi's face lit as the voice of his closest friend came on the line.

'What's up, bad boy?' Tom growled, sounding as if he had just climbed out of bed.

Razi outlined his proposal.

'The press turning up the heat?' Tom suggested with amusement.

'They don't bother me. I'm more interested in us taking one last break before I assume control.'

The air between London and Gloucestershire stilled. Both men knew the seriousness of the task awaiting Razi. The moment he was hailed ruling Sheikh of the Isla de Sinnebar, Razi would immerse himself in caring for his people. 'It's a task I relish, Tom.'

'I know…I know.'

Tom had his serious side too, but today was all about lifting his best friend's mood. 'I can't pick up a newspaper without seeing your ugly face staring back at me,' he complained. 'I've got the morning press right here.'

Razi's lips tugged with amusement. Brought to Tom's suite of rooms having been ironed first by his butler, no doubt.

'Here's just one example...'

Furious rustling ensued as Tom attempted to tame the broadsheets. 'Can the playboy prince work the same magic on the Isla de Sinnebar as he has on Maktabi Communications.'

'I've heard it, Tom,' Razi interrupted good-naturedly.

'They say you're a danger to women everywhere.'

'Business is my passion,' Razi cut across Tom flatly. And now he would turn those skills to the management of a country.

'And the women?' Tom pressed, not ready yet to let him off the hook.

'I have a vacancy.' And could be as dangerous as any woman wanted him to be.

Tom laughed. 'That shouldn't take long to fill. This journalist describes you and Ra'id as educated muscle.'

'Yes, I rather liked that,' Razi admitted, succumbing to Tom's good mood with a grin. 'Doesn't it go on to say we've proved ourselves to be fighters and lovers of unparalleled vigour?'

'Was the woman talking from personal experience?'

'Hang on while I rack my brain for memorable encounters with someone audacious enough to take notes while I made love to her.'

Tom laughed and read on. 'It's Razi al Maktabi's unforgiving gaze and striking physique, clothed in misleadingly sedate Savile Row, that gives him the edge, in the opinion of this writer.'

Razi's looks were the result of a union between the Middle East and middle England, but even he would admit they were unusual. Emerald eyes contrasted sharply with the jet-black hair and deep bronze complexion of his

Bedouin ancestors, and it was said he had the eyes and lips of the courtesan who had bewitched his father.

The same courtesan who had dumped him in the arms of whichever child-care professional court officials had seen fit to appoint. But that was another story. He'd moved on. He wasn't interested in looking back, breaking hearts or taking revenge. On the contrary, he adored women. His love for them had remained undiminished throughout numerous attempts to trap him into marriage. As had his determination never to be tied down.

'Enough,' Razi exclaimed as Tom started reading another article about him. 'Are you coming skiing with me or not?'

As he might have predicted Tom embraced his suggestion with enthusiasm. The ski company was a small part of Razi's business empire and he kept it for pleasure rather than gain, moving to a different chalet each year, both to test them for his guests and to keep the press guessing. Was there any better way of celebrating life, loyalty and friendship before the duties and responsibilities of ruling a country ruled him than this one last trip into the mountains?

Tom gave a short, masculine laugh. 'Though we'll have to put a bag over your head if we're to get any peace from the ladies.'

'With you and the rest of the boys around I'll blend into the crowd.'

'Really?' Tom murmured dryly.

'This is a boys-only trip. There won't be a woman in sight.'

'With you involved I find that hard to believe,' Tom argued in the upper-class drawl that always made Razi smile. 'How do you intend keeping them away?'

'That's your job, Tom.' He was lapping up this return to

the easy humour they'd shared as boys at school and then later in the special forces. 'You always were my first choice of wing man. Just watch my back.'

'And if it's a frontal attack?'

Razi's lips settled in a smile of happy anticipation at the thought of all the beautiful women in the world waiting to be adored. 'In that case, Tom, wait for my signal.'

CHAPTER ONE

SHE had the list of this week's guests clutched so tightly in her hand her knuckles had turned white.

'Hey, Luce, what's the problem?' demanded Fiona, another member of the elite chalet staff as she snuck out of the chalet Fiona's usual good half-hour early. 'You look like you got some troublesome guests coming to stay.'

'No particular problem,' Lucy Tennant replied distractedly over Fiona's hearty laugh, glancing deep into the flames of the aromatic pine log fire Lucy had lit earlier. Was it only minutes before she had been feeling on top of the world? Shouldn't she still be feeling elated? She had just opened a letter explaining she had been voted top chalet girl both by her colleagues and by her employers and it was the first time she'd won anything, let alone an acknowledgement that meant so much to her. But along with that letter had come this list itemising the preferences of that week's guests, and for some reason, having read it, her confidence had shrunk to the size of a pea.

Tom Spencer-Dayly: no special requests.
Sheridan Dalgleath: Porridge made with salt, plenty

of single malt to drink and any beef served must be
Aberdeen Angus.
William Montefiori: Only fresh pasta, never dried,
please.
Theo Constantine: Good champagne—lots of it.
One other:

It was the world of white that yawned after the fateful
words *One other* that had got to her. For some reason it had
sent a shiver down her spine. There was also an addendum
to let Lucy know that two bodyguards would be travelling
with the party, one of whom, Omar Farouk, would be
housed on the top floor, while the second, Abu Bakr, would
take the small bedroom opposite the ski room.

The clients must be people with serious connections,
Lucy reasoned, hence the unusual level of security and her
apprehension. She had to remind herself that she'd seen it
all before. Each week head office sent her the same standard form detailing the needs and expectations of the new
arrivals and she always felt a little anxious, wanting not just
to meet expectations, but to exceed them.

But she had never felt as uneasy as this before, Lucy
realised, checking each line again. The list was quite
straightforward. Which should have been enough to stop
the shivers running up and down her spine, but wasn't.

To calm her nerves she reasoned things through. This
was one of the most expensive rental chalets in one of the
most expensive ski resorts in the world. She was hardly a
stranger to wealthy people, their needs, or the entourages
that travelled with them. In fact, compared to most, this
group appeared small and quite reasonable in their demands. Experience suggested a group of men would be

mad keen to be on the slopes every daylight hour so she'd hardly see them, other than at mealtimes. Their main requirement would be lots of good food, plenty of hot water and clean towels and a never-ending supply of liquid refreshment when they got back to the chalet. With brothers of her own, it wasn't long before she was starting to feel a lot more confident.

They would almost certainly be public-school educated, Lucy mused, studying the names again. So one man preferred to remain anonymous—there could be any number of reasons why that should be and none of them her business.

Stroking back a wisp of honey-coloured hair, she realised it was the note scrawled in ink on the bottom of the page that set alarm bells ringing: 'If anyone can cope with this group, Lucy, we know, you can—' Translated loosely, that said she was less likely to make a fuss if the clients were more demanding and difficult than usual, because Lucy Tennant was not only a highly qualified cordon bleu chef, but a quiet girl, a good girl, a girl who took pride in her job managing the company's most prestigious chalet, someone who worked diligently without complaint. Her line manager knew this. So why did she get the feeling there was something he wasn't telling her?

She shook herself round. Time was moving on. With Fiona's social life making heavy demands on Fiona's working hours, there was always plenty of work at the chalet for Lucy. But the crystal-clear alpine light was streaming in, tempting her outside…

Pushing back the quaint, carved chair, she went to draw the cherry-red gingham curtains a little way across the ecru lace to stare out wistfully. It seemed such a shame to close out the perfect mountain day, but if she didn't she'd never get to work.

Work had always been enough for her—and working here, where she could almost taste the freedom of the mountains, the silence, the space, the intoxicating air.

And the loneliness...

Working here was fantastic, Lucy thought fiercely, blotting out the rest. A pang of loneliness was inevitable in a chic French town where everyone seemed to be part of a couple. She'd always known she would be on the outside looking in. It was a small price to pay to be part of so much energy and fun. Shy, plump and plain was never going to be a recipe for non-stop action in a community where glamorous, confident people revelled in using their bodies to the full—and not just for skiing. But she could cook for them and she could make a chalet cosy and welcoming, which had always been reward enough.

And one day my prince will come, Lucy mused wryly, fingering the tiny silver shoe she wore for luck around her neck—though whether he'd notice her amongst so many beautiful, sleek, toned bodies seemed highly unlikely.

'See ya—'

The front door slammed and moments later she saw Fiona throwing her arms around the neck of her latest conquest.

Lucy pulled back from the window, knowing the snow scene and towering mountains with spears of brilliant light shooting through their jagged granite peaks were just a magical starting point. What she really valued was the good-natured camaraderie of her colleagues and the guests who gave her real purpose in life. Everything she lacked at home in the bosom of a relentlessly book-bound family living in the centre of a smoky, noisy city was here in this part-tamed wilderness of unimaginable icy splendour.

She loved books too, Lucy reflected, dipping down to look inside the fridge, but she liked to put what she read into practice, to experience things in reality. That was why she was here in a picturesque corner of an alpine village with a stream gurgling happily outside the pitched-roof wooden chalet, feeling reassured by the sight of the delicious local cheeses, along with the milk and cream she had sourced from the neighbouring farms. She still found it hard to believe that little Lucy, as her brothers still insisted on calling her, could negotiate the best of terms with local artisan producers, or that she held such a position of responsibility as a chalet chef for the ski season with the top company in Val d'Isere.

But she had paid her dues, Lucy remembered wryly, logging the items she would need to order for the week ahead before closing the door. She had come to France from a top restaurant in England where she had worked her way up from the bottom to the point where she received praise, as well as that all important reference, or *lettre de recommendation*, from Monsieur Roulet himself. Catering for demanding clients would never be easy, but she loved the challenge of the work as well as the opportunity it had given her to break free from her brothers' shadow.

Lucy's six brothers all excelled in areas her mother and father valued far more than cooking and it saddened Lucy to know she had never found a way to please her parents. Her self-respect had taken a real hit on the day her mother had alarmingly confided that they didn't know what to do with a girl—especially one who cooked. Her mother had said this as if a passion for cooking were somehow degrading for a woman, and when she had added in her airy, distracted way that it was better for Lucy to stay close to home and cook for her family where there was no chance of getting herself into trouble, Lucy had known it was time to leave.

Get herself into trouble? Some hope!

Lucy's wry smile returned. Her mother would no doubt applaud the irony that led men to treat Lucy as though she were their kid sister. At least she had escaped from other people's expectations of her, and thanks to her own endeavours, had the chance to discover who she was. She knew she wanted to make a difference in life and if that meant giving people pleasure with her cooking then she asked for nothing more.

Her breakout moment from home had been the first time in her life she'd done anything unexpected. She had been prepared to wash dishes for however long it took until she could persuade Monsieur Roulet to take her on, and had been amazed when the ferocious chef had granted her one of his sought-after training places, and even more surprised when her training had finished and he'd said she should see something of the world and that he would personally recommend her. Not wanting to disappoint the man who had launched her career, she had come up with an audacious plan to cater a dinner party for the director of one the world's most celebrated chalet companies. It was such a novel approach the woman had accepted and the rest was history. Lucy had returned home that night in triumph, and had sat patiently through the usual heated academic discussion taking place around a dinner table littered with dirty plates. Each time a break had come in the conversation she had tried to explain her exciting news, but her mother had hushed her and turned back to the boys, so Lucy's opportunity to share her happiness had never come. She still wasn't sure anyone had noticed her heaving her suitcase out of the house.

Enough reminiscing! She'd lose the job she loved if she didn't get moving! Fiona leaving early meant there were still beds to be made and floors to be swept and washed, but at least the food was ready. In fact, if it weren't for Mr One Other making her heart judder with apprehension she'd have a happy day ahead of her, doing all the things she liked best.

Razi scrunched the letter in his fist. It had been couriered to the helicopter taking him from Geneva to Val d'Isere and made him want to grab the old guard in Isla de Sinnebar by the collective throat and tell them, No way!

But that would mean cancelling this trip.

He barely noticed the sensational landscape of ice-capped peaks. Promised in marriage to a cousin he had never met? He realised his throne was the real prize—and not just the throne of Isla de Sinnebar. From his kingdom it was a short stride across the channel to the mainland and Ra'id's throne. But if anyone thought they could turn him against his brother—

His anger turned to cold fury as he ripped open the package that accompanied the letter. In his hand was a photograph. He studied the image of a beautiful young girl. She was his distant cousin Leila, apparently. Leila's long black hair was lush, but her eyes were sad. She was as beautiful as any girl he'd ever seen, but he felt nothing for her. It was like looking at a beautiful painting and registering the perfection of its composition without wanting to hang it on his wall.

'Poor Leila,' he murmured, feeling some sympathy for

a girl who clearly understood she was being used as a bargaining counter by her unscrupulous relatives.

Wrapping up the picture in its silken cover, he stuffed it into the net at the side of his seat. He would not be trapped into marriage by parent, child, or a council of elders. When he married, it would be to a girl of his choice; a girl so cool, so keenly intelligent and effortlessly sophisticated, she would make a Hollywood movie star look clumsy.

Disaster! She'd spilled everything! Canapés littered the floor. The floor was awash with champagne. One man was mopping his jeans, while Mr One Other stared at her, frowning.

Even her training under the strictest of chefs could never have prepared her for her first encounter with the mysterious One Other. Tall, bronzed and serious about working out, he was a formidable force in the room and in the space of a condemning glance had reduced her to a dithering wreck.

Everything ruined in the blink of an eye. She would be sacked for this. Lucy's eyes welled with tears at the thought. She had planned so carefully, getting up at four to prepare the chalet and start cooking for the new guests.

She had left nothing to chance. There was a log fire blazing in the hearth, and fresh flowers she had arranged herself to bring the delicate fragrance of the French countryside into a chalet so clean you could eat the cordon bleu feast she had created off the lovingly polished oak floors. The menu she had devised encompassed every delicacy she could think of to tempt the palates of sophisticated men. Those men were currently lounging on the sofa, their faces registering varying degrees of surprise at her ineptitude, while the man in the shadows, the man who had compelled her attention from the moment she left the kitchen, gave off an impression of biting reproof. Her lovingly prepared tray of canapés was upturned in a puddle of vintage champagne and she had not only knocked the tray off the table when her gaze had locked with his, but had sprayed the designer jeans of a man whom, apart from the striking good looks he shared with his companions, she had barely noticed at all. Her attention had been wholly focused on the stranger staring at her now, and in holding that stare she had caught the toe of her shoe beneath the rug and had blundered forward.

How could a man standing in shade give off so much light? How could green eyes burn so fiercely? How could a man framed by four astonishingly good-looking friends eclipse them completely?

Breaking eye contact with him, she determinedly shook herself back to the task in hand. She had worked hard for this job and had no intention of losing it in the space of one compelling stare. 'My apologies, gentlemen—if you will allow me to, I will quickly repair the damage—'

Then *He* stepped forward, blotting out the light. 'Don't you think we should complete the introductions first?'

There was no warmth in his voice. That was not a suggestion, but an order, she concluded, quickly trying to collect the crushed canapés from the floor. 'Yes, sorry—' She looked up, only to find her gaze level with a part of him that shocked her rigid. Jerking her head up past the heavy belt securing his jeans, and on over the tactile dark blue top he wore with the sleeves pushed back revealing muscular arms, she saw a face of impossible design, a face so strong and beautiful she could have stared at it for ever. He had wild, thick, blue-black hair that caressed his chiselled cheekbones and fell in heavy waves across his proud, smooth brow, while some of it had caught on sideburns that mingled with the night-dark stubble on his face.

Wow, she thought silently, standing up.

Wow again. *One Other* was a mountain of a man, a man with hard green eyes and an uncompromising mouth. She didn't need to be told that he was the lead guest, and not just the lead guest, but the leader of the pack. The man with the voice like bitter chocolate was the man she had to please or lose her job. No wonder he came with a not so subtle warning, she thought, remembering the scrawled note from her manager on that week's guest list.

She was still standing speechless when the kind man called Tom came to her assistance. 'And this is Lucy,' he announced smoothly.

Having introduced her, Tom stepped back.

CHAPTER TWO

RAZI took in the trail of collapsed canapés on the floor, and yet more crushed in the girl's hands. Being ever the gentleman, Tom was being careful to hide his thoughts, but it was clear to him that the blushing, flustered girl currently hopping from foot to foot in front of him wasn't up to the job. She had gone to pieces like her canapés, spilling expensive champagne all over the floor as well as over William Montefiori's jeans.

'It's nothing,' William murmured, with relaxed charm, easing away from the promise of more disaster. 'I'll go and change.'

Razi was not so forgiving. His thumb was already caressing the speed dial to his personal chef.

'Allow me,' his friend Theo cut in with a predictably wolfish smile. Removing the cloth from the girl's hands, Theo proceeded to hold her troubled stare as he dabbed ineffectually at the puddle of champagne.

'For goodness' sake—' Razi's whiplash tone prompted Tom to snatch the cloth from Theo and repair the damage as quickly as he could. Razi doubted either of them had ever held a cleaning cloth in their life and wouldn't be doing so now if they hadn't some intention of getting into the girl's knickers. As for the girl, she was too badly shaken up to do anything—shaken up by what, exactly, he'd find out later.

'Lucy,' Tom repeated discreetly in his ear. 'Lucy Tennant, our chef and chalet girl.'

'Lucy…' His friends faded into the background. The girl was visibly trembling. He saw how young she was then and flashed a reprimanding glance at Theo. The girl was not only unused to such an imbalance of female hormones and testosterone she was terrified of losing her job.

'Pleased to meet you, sir.'

In her favour, her voice was musical, her stare direct, but that was no excuse for ineptitude. He employed the best across his organisation; only the best.

'Lucy won the chalet girl of the year award,' Tom broke in helpfully.

'Thank you, Tom,' he murmured in a voice that clearly said, Not now. Tom's soft heart was one thing, but he was conscious of how slender a thread his leisure time hung on and how soon this last ski-break indulgence would end. When he looked at the girl he was working out how much incompetence he was prepared to put up with before he ordered in his own staff and they took over.

'And you are?' she asked tentatively, her cheeks pinking up as she made a last stab at maintaining the formalities.

He looked at Tom for inspiration.

'Mac?' Tom suggested with a shrug.

'Mac,' the girl repeated shyly.

Their gazes remained locked and her grip was warm and firm as they shook hands, though she removed her hand from his faster than he would have liked. The report he'd received about her said she was self-possessed, calm, intelligent, organised, multilingual and a cordon bleu chef. The last two he had no proof of yet—strike the rest.

Then she surprised him.

'Once again, I apologise,' she said, almost literally shaking herself round. 'I hope the accident won't spoil your enjoyment of the meal I have prepared.'

'Not at all,' Tom chipped in, falling silent when Razi shot him a warning stare.

But something did smell good. 'What's on the menu?' he demanded.

She brightened and immediately proved to be one of those people who could deliver a menu and make the palate sing with greedy anticipation.

'Freshly made French onion soup topped with a slice of Parmesan baguette, followed by crispy duck breast in a fruit reduction, with a chocolate torte and cinder-toffee ice cream to follow.'

'I say,' Tom exclaimed, while his other friends sighed happily, prepared to forgive her anything now. Even Razi was inclined to give her the benefit of the doubt. If Lucy could deliver what she'd promised she could stay with his blessing too.

'Tom,' he said, still staring deep into Lucy's complex turquoise gaze, 'would you kindly ring the chalet company?' In spite of Lucy's calm, sweet voice, tumultuous thoughts were still boiling behind her eyes. With his last words that tumult had turned to panic. She was certain he would not give her another chance, and she looked utterly devastated. It was then he came to a decision that surprised even him. 'Would you tell them we don't need any more staff hanging round? But we'd like Lucy to stay—Abu and Omar can handle anything else we require.'

She slumped with relief, but then another thought must have occurred to her because the panic was back.

'You'll be quite safe with us,' he promised dryly as she took a jerky step away from him. 'We're here to ski.' His lips tugged. 'You'll hardly see us.'

She swallowed deep. 'That's what I thought,' she said awkwardly, her cheeks blooming a deeper shade of scarlet.

You may go, he might have said at this point, had they been in the old palace on the Isla de Sinnebar, but this was both a different and more complex situation. Lucy worked for him and yet this situation demanded more of them both. The intimacy of a chalet was very different from life in a palace. She'd put her own stamp on the chalet, he noticed—personal touches. There were fresh flowers on the table, and fruit that looked as if it had been picked that morning. Cakes and biscuits, still warm from the oven, tempted with their delicious aroma, and there were books and a couple of decks of cards. He liked being spoiled—what man didn't? She had done every-thing she could think of to make them welcome. Cer-tainly, she could stay.

Seeing she was still uncomfortable after her bad start, he asked her discreetly, 'Would you like me to call Omar and Abu to help you?'

'Oh, no,' she exclaimed, her eyes widening with a genuine desire to please that turned up the heat from hot to scorching. While he was admiring pearl-white teeth he could so easily imagine nipping him in passion she was glancing across the large, open-plan sitting room to her much smaller kitchen area. 'I don't mean to be difficult,' she explained, 'but my cooking space is very small—'

'And you prefer to do things your way?' he suggested,

inhaling her wildflower scent. It was a surprise to be so attracted to such subtle charm, but then novelty was the most valuable currency of all to men who had everything.

'I love my work, and I'm not very good at having people interfere.'

'Really?' A smile creased his face. 'Than I shall be sure to keep everyone away from you.'

'You're teasing me,' she said uncertainly.

'Am I?'

She blushed deeply. 'I'm sorry for what happened just now—'

'Forget it—start again,' he encouraged, enjoying the sight of her blue eyes blazing as she assured him she would. 'You've got five hungry men to feed.'

Her eyes flickered as she glanced at his friends. Her expression said she had forgotten them.

He could hardly blame her for that, when so had he.

She started by preparing a fresh tray of canapés—something fast and delicious—and was stunned when Mac joined her at the stove. The space was small and he took up most of it. He was cool and she was hot. She picked up the tray and gripped it tightly so he couldn't see her hands were shaking.

'Don't bother warming them up.'

'It will only take a minute and I promise you they'll taste better.' Confident where her food was concerned, she only wished that confidence could stretch into her everyday life—if it had she might even have been able to hold the stare of a man to whom disagreement was clearly something new, and humour his constant companion. 'I'll just flash them under the grill,' she told him in her most professional voice. 'Excuse me, please.'

He stood back.

But he was too quick for her and stole one off the tray, biting into it with relish.

'These get better when they're warm?' he demanded with surprise.

'Yes, they do taste better warm,' she assured him, growing enough in confidence to block his route to the grill before he could eat the rest. The desire to please him was dangerously strong. The sight of his sweeping ebony brows rising in genuine appreciation for her food was like receiving an award ten times over. Plus she was relieved. She had a suspicion that if she failed to please Mac his authority over the other men would leave her with an empty chalet.

'So, tell me how you made them,' he demanded, aiming that disturbingly intense green gaze into her eyes.

'You want the recipe?'

His face creased in a devastating smile. 'I'll get one of my chefs to make them for me.'

Of course. She should have known that. Nothing in her life could have prepared her for this, Lucy realised. Mac was no ordinary guest and however friendly he might appear it was time to rein back and put everything on a professional footing. 'Tiny circles of toasted Bruschetta topped with goat's cheese,' she recited firmly, clinging to her one area of expertise, 'finished with a slice of fresh fig and a drizzle of honey. And I promise you they're even better when they're heated up,' she said, gaining in confidence.

'Aren't most things?' he murmured close to her ear before moving away.

She needed a moment. She couldn't play these games. In a few words Mac had succeeded in turning her body into liquid fire. He was a playboy and she was an unsophisticated cook—she had none of the know-how. She never flirted with guests, and that short bout with Mac had left her reeling. That he was a player, she had no doubt. That he was playing with her, she had no doubt either. Women were a game for men like Mac, and he was way out of her league. The only way she could survive the week with her self-respect intact was to stick religiously to what she knew—which was cooking.

He had only been here five minutes and he was already suffering from a painful bout of sexual frustration made worse by noticing small things about Lucy—such as she was very tidy, very precise and very contained; the latter was in itself a challenge.

He shouldn't be noticing her at all, he told himself sternly, trying to pay attention to a conversation between his friends about stocks and bonds that would normally have held him riveted. For some reason, watching Lucy loading a clean china platter with perfectly warmed canapés prior to handing them round was far more interesting—possibly because her hands were small-boned and pale, and yet her fingers were flexible and strong, and the thought of those hands touching him was…intriguing.

He liked her. He snapped a response when one of his friends tried to draw him into their conversation, and then she caught him looking at her and coloured up. He liked that too.

It was a relief when Lucy redeemed herself with an excellent meal. Her lush curves pleased him and he didn't want to replace her with some fashionably thin creature whose only goal was to get a trophy lover in her bed. Where was the challenge in that?

Then Lucy mentioned cheese and everyone groaned.

She flushed with embarrassment and both the desire to defend her and the pressure in his groin increased.

'My apologies for feeding you too much—'

'Too well,' he corrected her.

Her swift intake of breath brought on another surge of interest from parts of him that were now refusing to be ignored.

Her face brightened. 'Then shall we eat French-style tomorrow?' she suggested, full of innocent delight to think her menu had gone down so well. 'I mean, cheese before pudding,' she said, visibly paling as he stared at her. 'If that's all right with you…?'

His lips quirked, but he kept a commendably straight face. 'We're in your hands,' he assured her, matching her stare for stare.

Her cheeks were flaming. What was happening? Her life had been straightforward up to tonight. She worked in the background cooking and never connected with a guest. Not that she was connecting with Mac—she didn't flatter herself to that extent. But it was impossible to ignore him—impossible to forget what she'd seen when she'd been on her knees in front of him at eye level with his crotch. Now he was suggesting he was in her hands… How was her imagination supposed to deal with that?

It was no use wishing that she were better looking, or more sophisticated, or that the right words might sometimes come smoothly to her lips. But just because she was quiet and good and plain, didn't mean she lacked outrageous thoughts. Those thoughts ranged a lot further than serving Mac cheese.

She refocused as Tom left the table. 'You're an excellent chef, Lucy.'

'Thank you. Whatever you prepare for us, and in whichever order you choose to serve it.' Tom went on, 'I, for one, shall certainly relish every mouthful—'

'As shall we all,' Mac cut across him sharply in a tone that startled her. He stepped in front of her, shielding her from the other men. 'There will be three types of canapés tomorrow,' she promised hectically, desperate to return to safer ground. 'And none of them broken.'

The men laughed, and to Lucy's relief Mac relaxed too. She laughed along with them, but her laughter sounded strained. Mac was still close by and her body insisted on reacting violently to him. Her nipples were erect, and another, far more intimate part of her was swelling so insistently a man like Mac, so sexual and knowing, must surely know…

She was so wrapped up in these thoughts she barely noticed the other men thanking her, and one by one, leaving her alone with Mac.

'Three types of canapés, and some really good cheese? That sounds good to me,' Mac commented approvingly.

His voice pierced her trance. Now the meal was over her confidence was stripped away. 'It's not a problem,' she said, hoping Mac would leave her to it as she glanced at the deserted dinner table. 'Just let me know what else you'd like and I'm sure I can handle it.' She was thinking of recipes—he was clearly not.

'I'm sure you can,' he agreed, resting back against the wall.

CHAPTER THREE

DID Mac have to be so attractive when he smiled that lazy smile with his green eyes glinting? She was the last person on earth who knew how to deal with a man like that, Lucy told herself sensibly as she served the men lunch the next day. It wasn't just Mac's fierce looks, which set him apart in a world of bland, but the sexual energy he exuded. If she got too close to that she'd get scorched. She only had to glance in the mirror to know he wouldn't be attracted to her.

'Do you want me to help you clear the table?'

'No,' she exclaimed, feeling awakward. Mac's smile was confident and sexy as he leaned back against the wall.

She was in a hurry to finish cleaning up. She had a date tonight. The honour of the chalet company was at stake. Her colleagues swore this was something only she could do for them.

'Do you have some special routine you follow?' Mac said, breaking into these thoughts. 'Lucy?'

'Rinse and stack?' she said hopefully, glancing at the dishwasher. She could do with some help.

Mac's lips pressed down in wry approval. 'Don't let me stop you.'

She was still open-mouthed when one of his friends poked his head round the door.

There was a moment of complete stillness as he took in the scene and then spoke to Mac. 'We thought we might take a walk into town.'

Lucy breathed a sigh of relief.

'Fine,' Mac said, without breaking eye contact with her for a moment. 'You go right ahead.'

He was staying with her?

He wanted to stay with Lucy. He wanted to know why she was in such a hurry, and why, when she had just served another fantastic meal, she was still lacking in confidence. Lucy wasn't good at her job, she was outstanding—so why the angst?

'Don't you want to go into town?' she hinted.

'I'm in no hurry.'

He didn't have to give Lucy a reason for staying in a chalet he owned. If he had he might have said he didn't want her bolting while he was gone. The last thing he wanted was to have to replace her with some sex-starved Seasonnaire. But that was only part of the truth. The novelty of a quiet, self-effacing girl attracted him. She tried so hard, and had overcome the problems quickly and efficiently. He wanted her to grow in self-belief. He wanted to hear this quiet girl scream with pleasure when she lost control in bed.

She'd never had this much scrutiny from anyone, but with her calm head on she could understand that Mac would want to be sure she could hold things together for the week—though he could ring head office and have her replaced at once if he wasn't satisfied with her work. Would that be too easy for him? He didn't look like a man who embraced easy.

Dragging her thoughts from Mac, Lucy turned with relief to rinsing plates. But he was still there in her head. Mac with his glossy black hair and fabulous emerald eyes—Mac steeped in pure, potent power—Mac who unnerved her—deliciously. *Unnerved her?* She was completely out of sync.

'Lucy?'

'Yes?' Her guilty gaze flew to Mac's face.

'You seem…distracted?' he probed.

'Distracted?' She gave a nervous laugh. 'No… I was just planning tonight's meal.'

'Do you like the uniform?' Mac enquired as she fiddled with it.

'Yes, I do.' She met his gaze, determined not to be put off her stroke. She didn't wear the uniform with the same flair as, say, Fiona, but at least it made her feel anonymous and safe. 'I feel…like I belong,' she added as an afterthought, undoing her apron now they'd finished clearing up.

She had turned away to hang her apron on the peg behind the door and so she didn't see Mac frown.

Then Tom came back to have another go at persuading Mac to go with him into town.

'I'll leave Omar here should you need anything.'

'No, take him too,' Lucy told Mac, thinking the invisible presence of a bodyguard she might stumble across at any moment almost as alarming as having Omar's boss scrutinise her every move. 'There are people on call at the chalet company if I need anything.'

'In that case, see you later, Lucy.'

'My pleasure,' she added to an already empty room. If she had needed a reality check on how vital she was to Mac's existence, she just got it.

As the front door shut behind the men she sank down on the nearest chair. She was trembling. She felt as if she'd run a marathon. She had. She had just completed the most important race of her life—to keep her job, though she wasn't foolish enough to think that couldn't change at any moment if Mac changed his mind.

She had to get back to work. Dreaming didn't clean floors—plus she had some eggs to beat for tonight's meal before covering them and leaving them in the fridge…

Staring round the gleaming kitchen as she cracked eggs in a bowl on autopilot, Lucy mulled over what she had learned about her guests. Aside from an overload of testosterone in the chalet, there were a lot of heavy gold rings in evidence engraved with family crests. Theo didn't wear one, but Tom's crest, along with Sheridan's and William's, marked them out as members of the British aristocracy. That was simple enough to work out, but what was she supposed to make of the fierce lion and the scimitar engraved on Mac's ring?

The vision of an awe-inspiring desert landscape came to mind. But where had the green eyes come from? And such eyes…eyes that spoke of billowing Bedouin tents and the pearly light of dawn on the oasis as lovers woke and stretched their pliant limbs before making love again and again and again…

It took remarkably little imagination to take the hunk in jeans and place him in flowing robes. Hmm. Whisk suspended. As the picture drew clearer the whisk picked up pace again. The silk sheets on their Bedouin cushions would cling tenaciously to Mac's powerful limbs, hinting at the brute strength underneath. But the sheets were covering him.

So she'd throw them off.

'Are you going to beat that egg to death?'

She nearly hit the ceiling as Mac stopped her hand. She hadn't realised he'd come back.

'What has that poor egg done to you?' He held her gaze in the most disturbing fashion.

'I was just surprised when you came back.'

'Is there a curfew in operation?'

'Sorry.' Her brain was addled. Mac in cool black performance gear, ready for the snow, was even more alarming than Mac in jeans. And he was still holding on to her hand.

'Don't look so worried,' he said, releasing her. 'I'm not checking up on you.'

Then why was he here? Lucy nursed her hand. Mac's touch was warm, firm and commanding—and he'd let go of her far too fast for her daydreams and not nearly fast enough for here and now.

'So, what are you up to?' he said, staring into her eyes.

She gazed around, desperate for an answer. 'Something for tonight…cake.'

'Cake?' Mac prompted, staring pointedly at the array of cakes already laid out on the table.

'Isn't Tom waiting for you?' Lucy said hopefully.

'And if he is?'

'Could you pass me the cake tin, please?'

He held it out. She took hold of it, but he didn't let go, so now she was joined to Mac by an inflexible ring of tin.

'Lucy?'

She blinked and returned to her customary kitchen-confident self. 'If you'd like a piece of the cake I've already made, just sit down, and I'll—'

'Serve me?' Mac suggested wickedly, releasing the tin.

'I'll cut the cake,' Lucy said primly, reaching for a knife.

'I've changed my mind,' Mac told her, and with one last mocking stare, he left the room.

Mac might have left the room, but he hadn't left her thoughts. He was very much part of them and doing things to her that were almost certainly forbidden by law in several countries. How not to long for that? Running through a list of ingredients for the next meal didn't come close.

CHAPTER FOUR

LUCY spent the next hour in her small attic room, pacing up and down. If only plain girls could be born with a lust bypass, she reflected, pausing by the mirror to view her unchanged reflection, it would make life and rejection so much easier for her. Of course, she knew her relationship with Mac was purely professional, and she'd only known him five minutes, but it would have been nice if, only for a few moments of that time, the frisson she felt could have been a two-way connection. The best thing now was to have a long soak and try to forget him. But she couldn't, because she had somewhere to be and there were jobs to do first—beds to turn down, bathrooms to clean, towels to check, fires to bank up…

She was running late by the time she finished all her remaining tasks and she still had to get ready—number one on the list was a quick bath, and then she'd have to run all the way to the club where her friends would be waiting for her.

Interest laced with concern for Lucy had developed into hot, shameless lust. Razi had to have her. She was beautiful, unaffected and available—and as soon as he had given her a chance to clear up the chalet and set up for the morning he was going to have her.

His impatience was easy to explain—apart from the ache in his groin the clock was ticking. He had never felt the weight of duty more. He embraced the responsibilities coming his way with enthusiasm, but was under no illusion as to the effect they would have on his lifestyle. A traditional marriage—even if not to his cousin Leila—was on the cards. He owed it to his country. But before then…

'Preoccupied, Razi?' Tom asked him discreetly.

'You know,' he said offhandedly. They were sitting in a noisy bar and he was already itching to move on. The drinks weren't cold enough and the nibbles tasted of cardboard after Lucy's delicacies.

Next time she could serve them on her naked body and he'd lick the champagne she spilled off her belly.

'We can move on if you like,' Tom suggested.

'Sorry, Tom. Didn't mean to ignore you—things on my mind.'

'Oh, no.' Tom sighed theatrically and passed a hand across his eyes. 'Let me guess.'

'Don't,' he said sharply. For some reason he couldn't stand the thought of anyone, even Tom, making sport of Lucy. 'Don't even go there, Tom. Let's just move on.'

Muffled up in a super-sized ski jacket, a long scarf, a woolly hat with a bobble on top and a thick pair of gloves, Lucy hurried along the empty streets towards the club. The streets were deserted because everyone was already cosy and warm inside one of the many restaurants and bars by this time of night. It was a world of muffled music and the occasional blast of noise and laughter as a door opened briefly.

She was feeling guilty as she scudded along, knowing her brothers would have loved an event like the one she was due to take part in, while she felt shy at the prospect of entering a crowded club where everyone would know each other. She only hoped she could find her colleagues straight away when she arrived—and that Mac and co didn't decide to go there too. She shivered at the thought of it and almost lost her nerve and turned around.

Her enthusiasm for the event shrank even more when a member of a rival chalet company barred her way at the entrance. 'Here's the runner up,' he announced to his friends, who all started laughing. She hurried past, but her confidence had taken a dive. It got worse when she saw all her colleagues waiting for her and looking so hopeful.

'Ready?' they chorused.

'As I'll ever be,' Lucy confirmed, wondering why she had agreed to sing in the first place. Being a good choir girl hardly qualified her for the annual karaoke competition between the rival chalet companies, and the moment she entered the makeshift dressing room, which doubled as the ladies' restroom, she knew she'd made a big mistake. She didn't have the personality for something like this.

'Make-up?' one of the girls prompted, waking her out of the terror stupor. They were stripping off her coat and scarf, and one of them plucked the hat from her head.

'I don't have any make-up.'

'You don't?' The girls looked at each other in alarm.

'I've never bought any.'

Alarm was replaced by incredulity.

'I'm not very good with it.'

'Not surprising if you never tried,' one girl said with an encouraging smile, stepping forward. 'No worries—we'll do it for you.'

'Oh, no, thank you—but if I wear make up, I'll look awful.' I look bad enough already, Lucy thought, gazing in despair at her reflection. Compared to the other girls she was a real plain Jane.

'You couldn't possibly look awful,' one of the other girls said kindly.

'I only took off my apron five minutes ago.'

'So imagine the transformation.'

They were all so eager to help. How could she let them down? She dragged her confidence cloak tightly round her. 'Okay, I suppose we'd better get on with it.'

Hasty words, Lucy realised as one of them produced a costume for her to wear with a flourish, carolling, 'Ta da!'

'No,' she said firmly. Singing was one thing, but she was going to wear her sensible off-duty clothes, which comprised jeans and a pale blue fleece.

The girls looked at each other and then, recognising the straw that might well break the camel's back, they gave in.

'Just tell me when I have to sing and I'll be fine.' Or she might be, if her upper lip didn't feel as if it were superglued to her teeth.

'Here, have a drink of water,' one of her colleagues said as Lucy licked to no effect with a bone-dry tongue.

Then they all went silent as the contestant from the opposing chalet company began to sing.

'He's got a great voice,' Lucy commented, swallowing hard.

'And he's hot,' one of the girls added.

Better to know she didn't stand a chance before she headed for the makeshift stage, Lucy reasoned. 'I'm going to give it everything I've got.' She smiled bravely as a pile of make-up bags hit the counter.

Then the girls took over, transforming her while she could only watch helplessly. One of them brushed out her hair and curled it with a heated wand, while another made up her face.

'Relax—I do this as a living when I'm not doing the ski season,' one girl assured Lucy as she applied a brown stripe beneath Lucy's cheekbones, a white one above and a blob of red on the apple of her cheek.

Now she looked like a painted doll with exaggerated colouring. She should never have let this happen.

Lucy closed her eyes, resigned to her fate, so it was a surprise when she opened them to find that once the stripes had been blended in she didn't look half bad. Her skin looked even, radiant, and her face sculpted. The make-up was like a mask, Lucy realised with relief—a mask to hide behind. Careful work on her eyes and lips had turned her into someone she hardly recognised and Mac would certainly never recognise her if he decided to come in for a drink. 'I had no idea,' she murmured, leaning forward.

'No time for that,' the girls insisted as she continued to stare into the mirror, amazed at her reflection. Taking hold of her on either side, they ushered her outside.

One last glance confirmed the surprising fact that, left loose, her hair didn't look half bad either. Thanks to the styling wand it hung in thick waves almost to her waist. She had never worn her hair like this before, because her mother said long hair was untidy, and, of course, in a professional kitchen her hair was always covered. Make-up? She pressed her rouged lips together anxiously—she'd never get used to it, but at least the girls looked pleased.

'You look amazing,' one of them assured her and they all agreed.

'Amazingly silly?'

'No!'

'Have some confidence,' one girl insisted. 'You won our award when you least expected it, and now you're going to win this.'

'If I could sing better.'

'It's karaoke, Lucy.' They all laughed. 'You're not supposed to sing—just get into the spirit of it and you'll be fine.'

'And if you're not, we'll hide and pretend not to know you,' another girl teased her.

They had left the bar and headed back to the chalet for their skis to satisfy Razi's whim to expend a small part of his energy skiing down the black slope with just the ultra-lights on their helmets to show them the way. With precipices on either side and at the speeds they travelled it was like playing Russian roulette with a loaded gun that had no bullets missing. It was both exhilarating and dangerous. Irresponsible, maybe, but it had left him on a high. The five of them had been doing this since school when they had first climbed out of a chalet window at midnight, leaving the school masters on the trip snoring. These days Razi pleased himself. He owned the chalet and could leave by the front door, but the thrill had not diminished.

They were all down safely, but with adrenalin surging through his veins he still had energy to burn.

'Champagne?' Theo suggested.

'Lead me to it,' Razi agreed, snapping off his skis in anticipation of a short stroll to his favourite bar.

'Do you think we could drop by the chalet? Let Lucy

know what we're up to? Invite her along?' Tom questioned with a knowing wink.

As Razi might have anticipated, this drew comment from the other men. They were experienced men of the world, but they had all seen something in Lucy—just as he had. His hackles rose. 'Lay off her, boys,' he warned, lifting off his helmet. 'You could all see Lucy was overwhelmed when we rocked up.'

This drew a second chorus of knowing smirks, which he ignored. 'The least we can do is give her a chance to get used to us.'

'To you, don't you mean?'

He refused to dignify Theo's comment with a reply.

Tom drew alongside him to observe discreetly, 'That's extremely thoughtful of you…'

'It's nothing.' Razi dismissed the comment with an impatient gesture. 'Lucy was fine when we left and she's probably asleep by now. She also left food on the table at the chalet, so if we need anything to eat later we can rustle up something for ourselves.'

'Just like the old days,' Theo agreed, coming up on his other side.

Not at all like the old days, Razi's exchange of glances with Tom confirmed. This trip was not the same as the trips they had enjoyed in their carefree teenage years, but the briefest of stops before the weight of responsibility tied each one of them in their different ways. But for all their machismo they were up to the task, Razi concluded, taking a look around his friends. 'Last one to the bar buys the drinks.'

Impossible to imagine their fortunes could be counted in billions as the four friends jostled and wrestled their way across the piste.

* * *

Okay, so this was it. But she needed an urgent trip to the ladies' room first…

'No looking back,' the girls warned Lucy as they accompanied her to the stage.

'I feel sick.'

'There's a fire bucket in the wings,' one of the girls pointed out helpfully.

'I can't remember the words.'

'You don't have to remember the words,' the girls reminded her in chorus. 'This is karaoke, Luce.'

'What if I can't see the screen?'

'We'll sing along with you.'

'What if I can't hear you?'

'You'll hear us,' they promised.

The compére was already on stage, waiting for the crowd to quieten so he could introduce Lucy. Would they ever quieten enough to hear her? It seemed unlikely, thank goodness. Freeing herself from her supporters, Lucy stepped reluctantly up to the red curtain someone had hastily drawn across the makeshift stage and peered through. She couldn't see anything; the light was so bright—much better backstage in the dark where no one could see her. 'Couldn't I sing from back here?'

'That's a no, then,' Lucy muttered as her friends exclaimed in protest.

She wished the spotlights weren't quite so bright, or so well aimed. She felt nervous, hot and scared—and desperate not to let the side down.

'There is one positive.'

'A positive?' the girls encouraged as she fought for breath.

'Yes, I can't make out any faces in the crowd—I took

out my contact lenses,' she managed on a gasp, breathing deeply into lungs that seemed suddenly on fire.

All she could hear now were whistles, shouts and catcalls. The compére had succeeded in whipping the crowd up to fever pitch just in time for her appearance. Great. The position of the fire bucket had never held such colossal significance.

'You'll be all right once you get on stage,' the girls assured her, hands poised on Lucy's shoulders in readiness to push her on.

She didn't have time to think about it. Blundering through the curtain, she was instantly deafened by the booming bass on the backing track and blinded by the lights. She put up her arm to shield her eyes and in doing so missed the introduction. The crowd was silent like a fierce beast preparing to pounce and rip her into shreds, while she stood curled in a protective huddle in the middle of the stage, spotlights illuminating her humiliation, while her backing track moved inexorably on.

Somewhere in the distance she heard the girls shouting her name…

It was no good. She couldn't do it—not even for them. Blinking like a mole, she realised with horror that she couldn't see or hear anything, let alone sing…

Clenching her fists with determination, she forced herself to make a tremulous start, and no one was more surprised than Lucy when her voice gradually gained in confidence and strengthened as the beauty of the melody overpowered her fears. She had insisted on singing a love song when everyone had begged her to sing an upbeat number, and, what with the poignancy of the words and the beauty of the music, she only had to imagine Mac and she was away.

She would never have believed she could enjoy herself so much on stage—even the crowd had silenced in appreciation. They'd gathered round her and many of them were arm in arm as they stared up at her, listening. Discovering she could lose herself in music was a magical experience... Thinking about Mac made it perfect.

CHAPTER FIVE

WHAT the hell?

As they entered the bar Razi's gaze was immediately drawn to the stage where Lucy was singing.

Lucy was singing?

He couldn't believe his eyes, though he'd have known her anywhere. But this was a very different Lucy. Her hair was a shimmering curtain of gold, hanging to her waist, and she was wearing make-up that enhanced her features without being too heavy. Her top was something blue and soft that framed her face and set off the lustre of her hair, but it was her singing voice that really captivated him—as it had every other man in the room.

His expression darkened as he took in all the other male onlookers lusting after Lucy. Her singing and the sincerity of her interpretation had them gripped. Her voice was richly seductive and as beautiful as if it came from her very soul. It was also the husky tone he had imagined hearing in bed...

There was a solid mass of bodies at front of the stage between him and Lucy, but it parted for him like the Red Sea. He didn't even have to elbow his way through. His motors were running and everyone knew it. No one cared to get in his way. She had finished her song and the audience was demanding an encore. Men were cheering and wolf-whistling as he reached the front, by which time she was singing again. The fact that that they found her pleasing was irrelevant to him—or maybe even made it worse. His warrior ancestry pressed down on him. The fact that he adored women demanded action. For however short a time Lucy Tennant was his to protect and defend—

And make love to, he added silently as she stared at him in alarm.

Her voice faltered. The audience fell silent. The tension mounted. He sensed a tipping moment when the crowd would either cheer her to the rafters or boo her off the stage. Her eyes locked with his in silent appeal.

For one fire-burst moment she was so high on adrenalin she exulted in the fact that Mac was staring at her. She had been persuaded to sing an encore, but she wanted to sing for Mac—so he could see who she could be and hear what she could never hope to express in words. This was Lucy Tennant flying high and wide, allowing the music to speak for her. Singing made anything possible…

Or would have done, had not Mac's eyes been narrowed. With disapproval? It was hard to tell. He was looking at her—the audience was looking at him—and then at her. And back to Mac. Their little drama was proving far more interesting than the karaoke competition and she could hardly ignore him. Slowly but surely all her confidence-inspiring adrenalin seeped away, and then everything spiralled in. What was she doing singing on a stage—other than looking ridiculous?

But then the incredible happened. Mac's face changed, relaxed. His eyes darkened as he stared at her and his mouth slowly curved in a sexy smile. Was that a nod of approval? Was it? Mac wanted her to sing for him and that was what she was going to do.

The moment she started singing again everyone began to cheer. They were on their feet applauding her—a noisy frame to the stillness that had developed between her and Mac. By the time she had finished the song, she was oblivious to the cheers. She was trembling all over, her brain in a whirl of confusion. How amazing that moment of connection between them had felt! Mac's power... His reaction to her singing... Her reaction to him... Arousal... Frustration... Overwhelming relief...

Mostly relief, Lucy realised now she was coming back down to earth. A few more seconds on stage without Mac willing her on and she might have turned into her usual bashful self—and for a crowd fuelled up on drink and excitement that wouldn't have worked.

Now she'd won. Incredibly, she'd won. She laughed, shaking her head in disbelief as her friends crowded to the front of the stage. Mac stood at the side at the foot of the steps, quietly waiting for her. That was perhaps the sexiest, the most telling moment of all. They had to call her name twice she was so distracted by him, and on the second time of calling her Mac looked up, his face creasing in the familiar bad-boy smile as he slowly began to applaud without ever once losing eye contact with her. 'Go on,' he mouthed. 'You won...'

Still shaking her head, she walked forward to accept her prize.

'I don't know why you find it so surprising,' Mac said, offering her his hand to help her down the steps at the side of the stage. 'You have a great voice, Lucy—and a great way of putting a song across.' He shrugged, muscles easing across the wide spread of his shoulders as he stared down at her with humour in his eyes.

'You're still here,' she said foolishly, all her shyness returning in a rush. Being on stage was one thing—being here in front of Mac with no spotlights between them was something else.

'Of course I'm still here,' he said as if she'd said something very puzzling indeed. 'Why would I go?'

Breathing was hard suddenly. She could think of a million reasons why he would go, but she wasn't going to give him any hints. Instead she forced a laugh, knowing he had to be joking. Mac was a guest and she was a chalet girl. He didn't want her—not in that way.

'Drink?' he suggested. 'Or back to the chalet?'

She blinked, refocusing in a rush. There was no mistaking his meaning. Even she wasn't naïve enough for that. It was all there in his eyes and in Mac's body language. It didn't come much more direct. His eyes spoke of sensual promise. There could be no misunderstanding. And, of course, she should rebuff, rebel, refuse—and to hell with the fact that Mac was a guest and she mustn't offend him—

But there was a small problem with that. She wanted him. She was violently aroused.

Mac's compelling gaze didn't waver from her face for a single moment, and suddenly the thought that he might want her back at the chalet to clear out the cinders or coddle him an egg seemed far more ridiculous than the realisation that he wanted her in bed. Mac, in casual clothes that moulded his powerful frame with formidable attention to detail, wanted her.

Mac, who looked as fresh and ready for action as if he

hadn't been thrashing the slopes for the past few hours, wanted her?

He looked lush. Mac was the quintessential forbidden fruit. She would miss out on her taste if she didn't find the courage to seize the moment—and when better than now? She would never get another chance like this one. 'I'd better get my coat.'

'You better had,' he said.

He felt a surge of heat and triumph—not that the final outcome had ever been in any doubt. Lucy had needs and he had urges. It was a match made in…Val d'Isere. It was a match that would last for precisely one night. He'd leave her happy, but he'd leave. His playboy life was over. Duty beckoned and he was ready to serve.

He smiled as she came shyly towards him, all buttoned up and ready to be undressed. He'd serve Lucy Tennant and then he'd serve Isla de Sinnebar with the same focus and energy—though for a lifetime rather than a single night.

By the time they reached the chalet he had extended Lucy's time with him to one night and one day to accommodate all his plans. He enjoyed her company. He loved her voice. She didn't have the slightest idea how beautiful she was. Granted, the outfit she was wearing now was dull, but that only whetted his appetite for unpeeling her. She'd be like a ripe, delicious fruit emerging from layers of tasteless pith, and from what he'd seen of Lucy on stage there was enough sensitivity and passion to keep his interest way beyond a single night. It was just a shame life didn't work that way. However he felt about her and whatever happened between them, duty would always come first for him, but that was no reason not to make the most of the time they had.

The chalet was empty when they got back. Taking off her boots slowly, she could feel herself blushing scarlet, second-guessing his plans. When it came to sex she knew she could only disappoint. What she knew about sex could be written on a pin head and to date Mac had only seen her camouflaged in layers of clothing, but when that came off—

'Are you cold? Shall I run a bath for you?'

She stared at him incredulously. Mac run a bath for her? Shouldn't it be the other way around?

His smile widened. 'Better still, let's use the hot tub together. Don't pretend it hasn't occurred to you.'

Now his arm was round her shoulder and he was leading her up the quaint wooden stairs, past the cosy living room, and on up the next flight of stairs to the main bedrooms, and then up another flight to the master suite on the top floor, which was entirely his.

She was trembling so hard she hardly registered what was happening as he closed the door behind them. Unzipping his jacket, he tugged it off and tossed it aside. 'Your turn,' he said, flashing a glance down the length of her safely bundled-up body.

He wanted to play striptease? 'I want to thank you for not sacking me,' she said primly, clinging with everything she'd got to the one thing that made some sense.

'I don't talk business after six o'clock—it's a rule I have,' he murmured, toying with the toggle on her jacket. 'And I'm still waiting. For you to take it off?' he prompted, angling his chin to direct his amused stare into her eyes.

She supposed that was okay. Unzipping her jacket self-consciously, she hung it neatly on a chair.

Mac flipped the braces off his ski pants and tugged off his top.

She gasped and looked away.

'I'm waiting, Lucy.'

Match that impossibly hard-muscled torso with something he'd find desirable? Match Mac's confidence? She couldn't— She really couldn't—

Mac gave her no chance to nurse her concerns. One minute he was leaning against the wall, looking relaxed, and the next she was in his arms.

'Shy?' he murmured. 'I like that. Though I would never have guessed you were shy after seeing you on stage tonight.' His mouth curved in a wicked grin, only millimetres from her mouth.

'That was a one-off,' she admitted, staring into his eyes.

This was all happening so fast she felt dizzy. But in a good way, Lucy decided. The sensation of being pressed into hard, unyielding muscle was amazing—and would have been even more so without quite so many layers in between. Mac toyed with the zipper on her fleece, sliding it down slowly. All she could think of was his erection, pressing insistently huge and hard against her. To say she was melting with desire was something of an understatement.

'Say something,' he murmured.

'I can't…'

Cupping her buttocks possessively, he smiled. 'You're right—why waste time talking?'

His hands tightened and released until every pleasurable sensation she had ever known in her life was exceeded by infinity. She couldn't stifle a moan or breathe steadily or pretend a moment longer. Every nerve ending in her body was primed and ready—every resolution she had ever made to remain at least pure-ish until The One came along meant nothing. There was no past, no future, there was only this, longing for Mac to make love to her.

As if sensing this change, he took her hand, linking their fingers in a gesture that was both deeply intimate and reassuring. He led her past the king-sized bed she had dressed herself with crisp white sheets, and on towards the doorway leading into the impossibly luxurious bathroom and from there to the deck and the hot tub. She cleaned the area twice a day and knew it well. She had even stood here dreaming, but she had never imagined in her wildest dreams that one day she might use it, let alone make love in it. It was as if she was seeing it all again through new eyes—the exquisite apricot-veined marble that complemented the azure skies and shimmering snow-capped mountains in daylight, now framed in black velvet shimmering with diamond stars. There was an uninterrupted wall of glass overlooking the moonlit mountains, and, as far as she was concerned, it was the most romantic place on earth…

'Second thoughts?' Mac murmured, misunderstanding her silence as she stood gazing out.

'None,' she assured him.

'Do you want to get undressed in the bedroom?' Lifting her hand to his lips, he held her gaze.

She looked so vulnerable she touched some long-forgotten part of him. He had learned to switch his feelings on and off like a light bulb as a boy when it had been the only way to cope with the disappointment of promised visits from a mother who never came to see him. Now he understood his mother had had too much to lose. The ruling sheikh, his father, wouldn't tolerate his mistress having another love interest—even if that love interest was their son. His mother had had to forget him, just as he had learned to forget all the other women who had passed through his life. But Lucy was different—at least, she was for tonight.

The hot tub was bubbling temptingly and steam was rising into the night sky by the time she returned from the bedroom. There was a mountain range of foam waiting for her to step into. He was gazing east towards the Isla de Sinnebar when she pushed the door open and came out to meet him. His heart juddered when he saw her. He was still half naked and his feet were bare, while Lucy was wearing an abundance of duvet in stark white—and still managing to look indescribably lovely to him.

'You won't need the duvet in the hot tub.' He grinned as he held out his hand to take it from her.

She stood her ground, clutching it tightly.

'Have you changed your mind?' He would never force her. 'Do you want me to leave you to it?'

'No need,' she whispered. And taking a deep breath, she dropped the duvet and walked towards him.

Two more paces and she was in his arms.

'Are you going to bathe with your clothes on, Mac?'

He smiled into her eyes. She was so trusting and so beautiful, and just for tonight they were going to live the dream.

She glanced at the glittering foam. 'Shall I undress you?' she suggested shyly. Her voice was shaking.

He smiled down at her. 'Or you could enjoy the hot tub all by yourself.'

She held his gaze with her honest eyes. 'I don't trust myself in all that water without something to hold on to…'

His lips tugged in a grin. 'You have all the answers, don't you?'

'It's work in progress,' she admitted with the truthfulness he loved about her, and then her face grew serious as she no doubt contemplated what was about to happen.

His mood changed too. Pushing the last of his doubts aside, he laced his fingers through her hair and, cupping her head, drew her close to kiss her. Her lips were plump and yielded softly beneath his mouth. Kissing Lucy filled him with feelings he couldn't name—feelings it was better not to name. Sex was what they both wanted and needed, and sex, like skiing, was a sport at which he excelled.

CHAPTER SIX

SHE ran her palms across the wide spread of Mac's shoulders and then down his arms, over muscles that bulged and flexed. His chest was shaded with just the right amount of dark hair that dipped in a V towards the buckle on his belt, below which she knew better than to look. But she couldn't help herself—she should feel, had to feel, for the fastening on his jeans.

'Need some help?'

Yes, she did, but she wasn't about to admit it. Mac's challenging smile, his strong white teeth, his lips, his tongue, promising far too much pleasure—the humour in his eyes, the pressure from his hands—she wanted everything he had to give her. 'No, thank you.' Her heart was pounding. She had to pretend she was up to this when she could hardly breathe. She rested her fingertips lightly on the top of his belt buckle and swallowed deep.

His kiss was still warm on her lips as he backed her towards the hot tub. She was in a daze as she felt the steps behind her heels. 'Aren't you overdressed?' she gasped as Mac nuzzled her neck, oh, so lightly as a prelude to feathering his hands down her naked arms.

'So? If I am undress me.'

Her eyes widened. She had imagined many things in the lonely wilderness of her bed, but never anything as erotic as the heat and humour radiating from Mac. But when he turned serious and started murmuring to her in a language she didn't understand she was a little nervous— Or at least she might have been, but her body spoke in tongues— Mac was telling her what he'd like to do to her and in what order. 'Oh, yes, please…'

She melted into him with a sharp exclamation of excitement. As he brushed a kiss across her neck she felt the promise of so much more, but Mac was in no hurry.

Telling herself she was relieved—that she needed time to handle the sensation of warm hard flesh on naked flesh—she allowed herself to relax against him. Tentatively lifting her arms, she laced her fingers in his hair and felt it spring thick and vital against her palms. This was wonderful. It was all she had ever dreamed of and more. Resting her face against his chest, she inhaled his clean, spicy scent, wanting to use all her senses to print the moment on her mind for ever. *For ever—*

She heard his jeans hit the floor, and shivered to think of him completely naked, but Mac was smiling against her lips, reassuring her. 'Why are you trembling?' he demanded huskily. 'I'm just a man like any other.'

Now who was dreaming?

As he swung her into his arms she basked in his strength and in his care of her. When he lowered her carefully into the hot tub she was ready for him to join her. He stepped in and moved behind her so she could lean against him, and when he wrapped his arms around her, nuzzling her neck as if they were lovers of long standing, she felt complete.

* * *

The combination of red-hot Lucy and warm, silky water was more aphrodisiac than required. He wrapped his legs around her, enjoying her trust as she rested against him, registering the fact that she made him feel warm and centred. More than that, she made him feel at home in a foreign land. That was Lucy's strength, her talent, he decided—the ability to create a haven, a sanctuary, a home. It seemed wrong that when, for the first time in his life, he wanted to progress a relationship, there was no chance with duty hammering on the door. But until then he would continue to drop kisses on her neck and shoulders and murmur words in his own language for the sheer pleasure of hearing her sigh. Kissing Lucy was equal to drowning in pleasure, and it was taking every bit of his control to hold back.

But then he noticed the silver necklace she was wearing and a worm of suspicion twisted in his gut. Was it a gift? If so, from whom?

It was none of his business—

He made it his business. Looping the dainty chain over his finger, he allowed the tiny silver slipper to dangle free. 'Who gave you this?' he murmured in between kissing her.

'I did,' she admitted.

'You gave yourself a Cinderella slipper?'

She shifted in his arms. 'It's not that,' she protested—a little too strongly, he thought. 'It's a reminder that one day I'll wear something other than snow boots.'

He laughed softly, not believing her for a minute as he rasped his stubble lightly across the tender spot at the base of her neck. She laughed too—in between begging him for mercy, but he was touched by what she'd told him. 'Some day your prince will come,' he promised as he dropped more kisses on her neck and shoulders.

What if he'd already come—and she couldn't have him? Lucy thought, starting nervously as Mac cupped her breasts. He had just reminded her that she was inexperienced—far more inexperienced than he had obviously imagined. Mac thought because her breasts were full and silky, along the lines magazines suggested were made to be admired, fondled and adored, she was used to this. If only he knew…

She cried out softly as he abraded the tips of her nipples very lightly with his thumbnails, wondering how she was supposed to remain silent and composed while he was working this sort of magic on her. Her nipples had never been so sensitive, her breasts so full. She was still getting used to the fact that such a level of arousal was even possible—or that such freedom to express how she was feeling inside was possible. She guessed it was because Mac had no inhibitions and he had made her strong—at least for tonight.

Some day her prince would come? He had. But, unfortunately, unlike her dream, he wouldn't stay—and she had to be content with that.

Content while longing was a new concept. Mac had moved from cupping her breasts to mapping the swell of her belly and now her thighs. The longing was rapidly turning into lust. She had grown warm and sleek in the perfumed water and braver than she could ever have imagined. Sinking lower in the water, she allowed her legs to part in idle invitation—so hungry for him she had no inhibitions left. Mac needed no encouragement—he was already there. Holding her in place with one firm hand, he slipped the other hand between her legs. 'What do you want, Lucy?' he murmured wickedly.

'I want you to touch me,' she whispered back.

She could feel him smiling against her shoulder as he interpreted that request with such an advanced skill and understanding of her needs it outstripped anything she had imagined possible. She was aware of nothing outside the sensation building inside her. Her whole mind was focused on it, her whole being depended on it. 'Oh, yes,' she murmured, moving against his hand, feeling the muscles in his chest bunching against her back. 'Don't stop...don't ever stop.'

With a gasp of surprise she came apart in his arms while Mac held her close. She had never known such release, such a fire-burst of sensation. Mac had woken an unsuspected appetite. She arched her body so he had to clasp her breasts and groaned when he played with her nipples and felt them tighten beneath his touch.

Lucy sighed and sought his lips, breathing whimpers of satisfaction into his mouth as he went on caressing her. He loved the sounds that she made—he loved the taste of her—and the scent of Lucy was like a field of wildflowers salted with fresh alpine air and when that was mingled with sultry bath oil it produced something unique and seductive.

His hunger to please her was growing. His hands embraced her buttocks, which felt so soft and warm and yielding beneath the warm foam. He knew just how to tease her until she clung to him, sighing in need. She was perfection. She exceeded every expectation he'd ever had for a woman. He had never thought to find a partner so candid in her needs or so sensual—certainly not one as faultless and innocent as Lucy. As far as he was concerned, she was woman.

As she timidly edged one leg over his he touched her again. Crying his name eagerly, she grabbed hold of him, but he lifted his hand away. 'Wait…' he whispered in her ear, loving the way she quivered just from hearing the suggestions he made. 'You mustn't be so impatient. You'll get it all… Everything you want…' And he knew exactly what that was.

The water rose and fell around them to the rhythm of his hand. Lucy's lips parted to drag in air as she gazed at him in wonder. Her beautiful eyes had darkened almost to black, and this time he was going to hold that gaze and watch her pleasure unfold. She tried everything she knew to hold off, but soon gave way, bucking violently and crying out wildly in abandon as pleasure took her over. The motion of her body stirred the water and it cascaded to the floor, but neither of them realised until she quietened and they looked around—and when they saw the devastation they laughed like naughty children.

He wondered in that moment if he had ever felt closer to any woman. Having never felt close to any woman, this was quite a revelation to him. 'I hope you've got enough towels in store to cope with a flood?' he said, acting stern.

'How about I use your robe,' she suggested cheekily.

'Before you do that you'd better get out of the tub.' Water fell away from his naked body as he stood. Stepping out of the tub, he reached for a towel and beckoned to Lucy. It made him smile to see she was still a little shy to show him her beautiful ripe body, but he had her swathed in the warm towel before she had chance to be embarrassed. Swinging her into his arms, he carried her into the bedroom.

'What now?' she said, a new confidence in her eyes as she smiled up at him.

'Whatever you're thinking—double the amount of pleasure involved.'

His kisses in the bedroom were leading one place only, but even as his hands cupped her buttocks, tilting her, so that the very place she needed his attention was pressed up hard against his erection, he was raging against the fact that in spite of all the power he wielded there was one thing he couldn't change: this first time with Lucy would also be the last. He'd almost decided to stop when she pressed her tiny hands against his chest. 'I can hear your heart beating,' she said, and, falling silent, she rested her face where her hands had been.

He had meant to hold her away, but somehow his hand got tangled in her hair, and then the fever was on them both and their hands were everywhere, while her warm breath bathed his naked body. 'This isn't right,' he murmured, his thoughts on the Isla de Sinnebar and duty—

'Do we have to decide that now?' she whispered.

Cupping her face in his hands, he used his thumbs to keep her exactly where he wanted as he kissed her again, and this time deeply.

Mac was a lithe, dark prince of the night. She felt so strong when he ran his fingertips over her; he'd made her strong. She'd waited for this moment all her life, but had never expected it to come, Lucy realised as Mac protected them both. She stared at his arms, pinned like steel girders either side of her shoulders, and the hard-muscled torso decorated with a single tattoo that matched the emblem on his ring. 'I know you'd never hurt me.'

'You know me so well, already?' he demanded softly.

'No,' she said honestly, 'but I know I can trust you.'

'Then know this too—I would never hurt you.'

'I'm only frightened I'll disappoint you—I've not had much experience—'

'You could never disappoint me.' His lips tugged with amusement. 'Is that it?'

'You don't mind about the experience?'

'You don't need experience. You just leave it all to me.'

She risked a shy smile.

'And you're reassured?'

'I am.' She trusted Mac more than she had ever trusted anyone in her life—and for no reason she could pinpoint that made much sense to her; she just did.

She drew in several sharp breaths as he moved in a tantalising pattern that never quite achieved the desired result. 'Oh, please—I want you so much...'

'And I want you,' he husked, catching inside her at last. 'You have no idea how much.'

'As much as this?' Arcing her hips, she thrust towards him, claiming him.

He sank deep into moist, hot velvet. Knowing how much he was stretching her, he took it slowly, while she gasped, looking at him for confirmation that it would be all right. 'If I'm hurting you, I'll stop—'

'Don't you dare,' she managed, clinging tightly to his shoulders.

'How much would you like?' he demanded softly, teasing her with a kiss.

'All of you. I want all of you.' With a final thrust of her body she enveloped him to the hilt.

Moving inside her was way too much pleasure. He had to say the alphabet backwards and write an imaginary shopping list of all the things he'd like to buy for Lucy just to bolster his legendary self-control—and that was definitely a first. She didn't even attempt to make it easy for him, moving with an enthusiasm that belied her protestations of inexperience. She had a natural talent for sex. She matched his rhythm, adding her own particular twist to what looked destined to become an exhaustive practical examination of the Kama Sutra. Seeing her confidence had grown, he gave her what she wanted. Grasping her hips, he thrust deep and fast until he was forced to muffle her screams of pleasure with a kiss.

She watched him sleeping, wondering if there had ever been a moment of such contentment, or of such wonder and love. Mac didn't curl up on the bed in her protective ball, he sprawled on his back so that his long, muscular limbs took up most of the available space. He looked so beautiful and so peaceful.

She traced the line of his perfectly sculpted lips with her fingertip, pulling her hand away when he sighed and turned his head slightly. Now she could see where the sweep of his eyelashes cast a blue-black shadow on his face. His ebony brows were slightly upturned, like an exotic warrior of the Steppes…or the desert. Wherever he came from, Mac was a stunning-looking man.

As he moved his hand his ring glinted, drawing her

attention to the symbol on it—the same crest as the tattoo on the left side of his chest—over his heart… A shiver gripped her. She could find no reason for it. Everything was good—better than good. After tonight she'd face things differently. Mac had made her feel like a woman, bolder and more decisive. Maybe she couldn't have him in her life long-term, but she would have the legacy of knowing him. Something told her she would never feel like this about anyone again. She just had to accept that one night with Mac was worth a lifetime without him.

Settling back on the pillows, she turned her face to drink him in. 'I love you,' she whispered, wishing there were something more she could say to express what she felt inside. There didn't seem to be words for falling in love within a matter of hours. Love struck like a thunderbolt. 'I love you' was used so often she worried it had lost its currency—certainly in this instance it seemed woefully inadequate. 'I love you,' she whispered again, knowing it could never come close to expressing what she felt for Mac.

CHAPTER SEVEN

BREAKFAST passed in a whirl of activity. What might have flustered some people—everyone wanting something slightly different—eggs poached, fried, scrambled, boiled—wasn't even a blip on Lucy's horizon. The only blip on her horizon was wondering how Mac would react when he saw her outside the bedroom.

It was time to put personal considerations aside and forget the fact that she had fallen in love.

Forget?

Forget. Just for now, at least. Because now it was time to remember how much she loved the mad hustle of preparing good food for hungry skiers as fast as she could so they could get out onto the slopes without time-wasting. She made sure there was always enough hot coffee, enough tea, enough hot chocolate, enough juice, and an endless supply of crusty French bread—and today was one such morning. The chat round the table was boisterous and bright.

Then Mac entered the room. Conversation dropped. Her heart stopped. He'd just showered; his hair was still damp. He looked amazing. Her insides clenched, relaxed, yearned.

A look passed between them. It was nothing more than

that—a look—but it made her thrill. It made everything perfect. She had vowed to behave with reserve and professionalism, but the look they had exchanged changed everything—and they had the rest of the week together…

Her heart was pounding with excitement as she poured coffee. 'Can I get anything else for you?' she asked the men around the table.

'Lucy has to get away,' Mac informed the group. 'She has an important appointment on the slopes this morning.'

Her heart bounced as Mac looked at her. He was going to take her skiing!

'Abu and Omar will clear up,' he said, dictating events. 'You'd better hurry up, Lucy.' His eyes were glinting with humour that only she saw. 'See you later,' he said casually to her.

'Yes, see you later,' she replied, tugging off her apron. *See you later*. There was a world of promise contained in those three words and her spirits were soaring as she left the room. *See you later* cleared the mist on her immediate future another day with Mac.

He blazed into the restaurant. Customers halted with soup spoons halfway to their mouths to stare at the impossibly glamorous man who had just walked in in a storm of testosterone and muscle. Lucy knew the owner of the cosy mountain retreat and had been helping out by doing a little serving while she was waiting for Mac, but now she stopped as Mac, oblivious to everyone staring at him, headed straight for her. 'Ready?' he said, flashing a glance at the chef who poked his head round the door.

With arousal thundering through her she was already by his side, waving goodbye to the owner.

'Do you really need to moonlight?' Mac demanded, ushering her towards the pegs where her jacket was hanging and her ski boots were stacked. 'Doesn't the chalet company pay you enough?'

'It's not strictly moonlighting as I don't get paid for working here.'

'You do enough already,' he said, frowning as he held the door for her.

'The owner's a friend.'

'You let people take advantage of your good nature.'

'I'm fine with it, Mac. Honestly, I'm no pushover.'

The humour in his slanted glance made her blush.

They skied down from the restaurant to the first lift. Mac was every bit as good as she thought he'd be—far faster and more confident than she would ever be. She tried to keep up with him and then found it hard to stop. It was quite a collision, but Mac caught her in his arms and didn't even lose his balance slightly. 'Speed demon,' he commented wryly. 'I can see we're going to have some fun.'

Taking in his athletic form, dressed in the latest close-fitting performance gear, Lucy decided that was mainly what she was afraid of.

For the first time that season she managed to catch a tip and fall off the lift as she got off—or she would have done had Mac's awareness and reflexes not been lightning fast. Catching hold of her, he steadied her before she could suffer the ignominy of holding everyone up. 'It happens all the time,' he reassured her. 'Even Tom took a tumble yesterday.'

But there wasn't even a bump in the snow here and she could only blame Mac for distracting her—Mac who was so utterly gorgeous everyone was staring at him to the point where she couldn't understand why he wanted to be with her. Even though they'd slept together it wasn't exactly a holiday romance.

No, it was something more precious than that, she mused contentedly.

'Shall I lead, or would you like to?' he said, snapping her out of the daydream.

'You'd better lead and wait for me at the bottom—I can't ski as well as you.' She doubted few people could.

Mac stared at her, the customary amusement missing from his face. 'I wouldn't dream of leaving you—I'll ride shotgun. Off you go,' he prompted. As he spoke the clouds parted and the sun streamed down, illuminating his face almost as a Hollywood director would reserve the special lighting for the star, Lucy thought, dazzled for a moment.

'Come on, let's get moving. The sun might be shining, but it isn't the desert,' he pointed out.

She laughed too. They were as far away from the desert as she could imagine. But as she was about to start off Mac caught hold of her arm. 'I've got a better idea,' he said. 'Take off your skis.'

'What?' She looked at him in surprise. 'You are joking?'

'I'm perfectly serious. I'll put them in the rack and arrange for them to be collected.'

'And what do I do—slither down the slope on my backside?' It might be faster, Lucy conceded as several people turned to stare at her in amusement.

'Don't you trust me?' Mac murmured, holding her gaze until she blushed.

'You know I do.'

He was remembering how his brother, Ra'id, had done this for him once—though under very different circumstances. He'd been about ten years old, and on his first trip to a ski resort. Eager to show his big brother he could keep up with him, he'd watched Ra'id take the lift up the glacier and had followed him. Ra'id's instincts had saved his life. Sensing his foolish little brother was in trouble on the slope behind him, Ra'id had made a dangerous ascent of a perilous incline to rescue him. The weather had closed in, and it had taken Ra'id almost an hour in blizzard conditions to reach the snow bridge where Razi had been stranded. Even then Ra'id had been all patience, all control. He had checked for injuries, before taking him slowly down the slope to safety, as he would now take Lucy under much happier conditions. 'Take your skis off,' he prompted, seeing Lucy was still hesitating. Taking matters out of her hands, he snapped her bindings open so the skis fell away and she had no choice but to step out of them. He put her skis in the rack by the side of the slope and then beckoned to her. 'Stand on mine.'

'Now I know you're joking.'

His stare didn't waver. 'Come on, my skis are stronger than you know. Come in front of me and rest against me... Closer... Yes, that's right... Lean right into me.'

Was she really doing this?

'Relax, Lucy. Let me do all the work. I'm going to show you what living in the fast lane is like.'

'Please don't,' she said, suddenly anxious on a number of fronts. She'd broken so many of her own rules over the past few days—skiing fast might seem the least of them, but once again she was entirely in Mac's hands.

And that was something new?

Maybe she had invested so much in her feelings for him already she was frightened to invest more...

'I promise you—it's exciting.'

She was tempted. She stared round at him. Exciting? Had Mac got the slightest idea how exciting her life had become since they'd met? She guessed not.

He nuzzled his face close so now they were sharing the same sparkling champagne air. 'Don't be frightened,' he whispered.

She heard the smile in his voice and tried to relax.

'I'm going to take you places you've never been before, and show you what travelling at speed through the mountains should feel like.' With that he tipped her over the edge of the slope and they were off. She shrieked as her stomach flipped. 'Relax,' Mac yelled, tightening his grip on her. 'I won't let you fall.'

They started to build up speed and it gave him a buzz to know Lucy was gaining in confidence with every yard they travelled. Had Ra'id felt like this? That it wasn't so much an inconvenience taking someone he cared for down the slope, but a sacred trust? 'Feeling safer now?' he demanded as they cruised some flatter ground.

'Thanks to you.'

He tried to remember when he'd had so much fun outside the bedroom. Fun was in short supply when women had one eye on his throne and the other on his fortune, and anyway, he had no time to invest in relationships. He felt a hit of anger and frustration at the thought that this trip to the Alps would soon be over. He'd enjoyed keeping Lucy safe—perhaps more than he should have done.

Mac had asked her if she felt safe. She was safe. He kept her safe. With Mac's arms around her and his body moulded tightly to hers, she wasn't skiing, she was flying.

Mac's arms were firm around her waist and his warm

breath was on her neck as he steered her down the slope. She'd only felt closer to him when they'd been making love. As Mac took her into a wide, sweeping turn she even wondered if this was the most erotic experience of her life—out in daylight where everyone could see them moving as one, breathing as one—her body welded to his—feeling his muscles working and hers respond.

The steep descent to the village was over all too soon, and as Mac skied to a halt Lucy realised people were staring at them. Women were smiling; some of them enviously, but all of them a little dreamy-eyed at the most romantic sight they'd seen that day. She was sorry it had ended and wished they could start over when Mac nudged her off his skis.

'So—did I convince you?' he demanded, lifting off his helmet and ruffling his thick, wavy black hair. 'That skiing fast is great?' he prompted, dipping his head to stare at her.

Had it only been an adrenalin rush for Mac? With the sudden blinding force of understanding she knew the warm, pulsing effects of what had been a night of love for her had been sex for him. Mac was everything she wanted and more—and could never have. He was enjoying a brief affair—she had fallen in love.

'I'll take you back,' he said, shouldering his skis.

'Don't you want to meet up with your friends?' She wanted to give him an out and herself space and time to think.

Mac looked at her and frowned, his lips pressing down in his habitual amused expression. 'We're big boys now,' he said, catching hold of her with his free arm. 'Come on,' he insisted, linking arms with her. 'It's time for an early bath.'

And the rest...?

Lucy's heart bounced with joy as Mac put his arms around her and drew her close. She put her arm around him too, like any other couple in the resort, telling herself she worried too much. Maybe.

The rush of being in the mountains, the sheer glory of the scenery and the indescribable joy of being with Mac had left Lucy on the highest peak of the highest high.

'You feel the charge too—don't you?' Mac challenged, nuzzling her cheek as they strode along.

'Maybe,' she admitted playfully, trying and failing to keep the smile off her face.

'You do,' he said confidently.

There was a sense of urgency to their stride—they weren't running exactly, but it was purposeful and heading one place fast. The urge to be together, to be even closer than they'd been on the mountain, had infused both of them with unusual energy. Lucy felt like the most alive person on the planet—sight keener, hearing so acute her own heartbeat was hammering in her ears like a kettledrum, while the scent of Mac, deliciously spicy, clean and warm, filled every part of her with happy anticipation. It was as if every sense she possessed was keenly tuned to Mac's extraordinary energy levels. Surely everyone knew… They were attracting glances, as if the sexual bond that joined them was a palpable thing. She glanced up at Mac and saw the set of his jaw, the faint tug of his lips, and the look of absolute focus in his eyes. When Mac wanted something he radiated determination. No wonder people were staring at them. Knowing what he wanted—suspecting other people knew about it too—aroused her shamelessly. She wanted to feel like a sexual being, to be desired, to be…necessary.

'We're here,' she said a little self-consciously when they reached the chalet.

'What do you know,' Mac teased, opening the door. His eyes were wicked as he stood back to let her inside.

He shut the door behind them and suddenly all the energy that had spread in all directions was cooped up in one small space. The air crackled with electricity, though both of them suddenly took to acting as if it were a normal day. Tension simmered as they shed their boots, took off their jackets and hung them up. They walked upstairs almost at a leisurely pace, as if their feelings towards each other had been mastered. But it was an illusion, and without needing to say a word they both knew it. The sexual cord between them had never been stretched so far or so thin—the explosion had to come. Even the air they breathed seemed saturated with particles of lust that only added to Lucy's arousal.

'We're alone,' Mac murmured when they reached the landing.

'So we are,' she said, wondering if they had time to reach the bedroom.

Mac acted decisively. 'Kitchen,' he husked, backing her down the hall.

'What if someone comes?'

He grinned. 'Someone will.'

By the time he'd shut the door behind them her top was on the floor. One stroke of his hands and her briefs were round her ankles. He freed himself and lifted her, practically in the same moment.

'Oh, yes,' she gasped, clinging to him as he plunged deep.

Mac stretched her beyond anything she once would have thought possible. The feeling was so far beyond pleasure that to begin with she could only let him take her with firm, deep strokes, while she did nothing but enjoy, but then the urgent need for release overcame her, made her fierce, and she dug her fingers into his shoulders, shouting his name and rocking furiously while Mac pressed back against the door to support her weight. He was hers to please and enjoy. No one could get into the room while she had her legs locked around his waist, and she was beyond caring what anyone heard. They were both brutally aroused, and from here it was a short, fast ride to pleasure and oblivion.

CHAPTER EIGHT

HE LEFT Lucy to take her shower. He kissed her outside her room, brushing silky strands of hair away from her flushed face. For a moment when he released her her eyes were bright with hope, but then she understood. Pressing her lips together, she quietly left him.

He'd stood outside her closed door without moving before taking the stairs two at a time to his own apartment on the top floor. There was no point in wishing things could be different when he was chained to destiny.

Lucy had set the tradition for canapés and an aperitif before dinner. He settled for a coffee and a croissant in town. He chose an anonymous café none of his friends frequented. He needed space. He needed time to think, but whichever way he played it one thing was non-negotiable. He had to make a clean break from everything in his past in order to give his future to Isla de Sinnebar. He shouldn't be thinking about Lucy at all, let alone thinking about her in terms of taking her with him—

Forget it!

He pushed his chair back so violently the other customers turned to stare. He paid the bill and clattered outside in his ski boots to harness himself first to his skis and then to the challenge of the mountains where no troubling personal thoughts could intrude.

But they would.

Lucy already meant more to him than he, in fairness to her, could tell her. She always would. She had won his heart in no time flat, and when it came to things he had to give up to be the type of leader he intended to be, she was turning out to be the biggest sacrifice of all.

She was back in uniform, having showered, dressed and cooked dinner. Tom had asked her to hold everything for an hour as Mac had gone out again to ski. That news only added to everything Mac hadn't said to her outside her room. Fast sex was all part of his race to the finish. She could sense the fact that Mac would be leaving soon, though he was chatting to his friends now he was back as if an aperitif of hot, heavenly sex was an everyday occurrence for him.

Perhaps it was, Lucy reflected, handing round the canapés. Perhaps she was the one who needed a reality check to see those looks he kept flashing her way were just that— concerned looks. He didn't want her burning dinner, after all.

The meal was a triumph, the group of men told her, and now they were going out skiing on the floodlit slopes while she cleared up. 'Have a good time,' she called after them. 'Breakfast at seven?' she confirmed with Mac, acting bright and businesslike as if she weren't hoping for some words of reassurance long before then. He'd changed into jeans, boots and a hooded sweater after taking a shower and looked hot beyond belief, making the gulf between them unbridgeable and herself a fantasist for even imagining it could be any different.

'Are you sure you don't want me to stay and help you clear up?'

She did a double take, while his friends laughed good-naturedly as if this was the most hilarious suggestion Mac had ever made. 'Thank you, I'm good,' she said, smiling a casual smile as if there were nothing between them.

She thought Mac's look was almost one of disappointment, but then he flashed a glance at his watch and his expression firmed up. 'We'd better get going,' he announced to his friends. 'Time's running out.'

She shivered inwardly as Theo clapped a hand round Mac's shoulders as if he understood. They all understood—while, for all her intimacy with Mac, she knew nothing about his private life. 'Have a good night,' she said on autopilot, keeping her smile in place until Mac led the men out of the room.

But then her smile faded. She felt sick, weak, foolish and the rest. Someone should have warned her how much love hurt—she'd have been more careful to avoid it. But she could hardly blame Mac for wanting to ski with his friends when the slopes were floodlit for the torchlit procession down the mountain to the village. Skiing was what he was here for, after all. He was hardly going to stay behind on one of the best nights of the year to help her clean the chalet. Plucking a clean cloth from the drawer, she set to. However many knocks life threw at her she was going to bounce back and start over. The next stage would be to forget him.

Forget Mac? Impossible. She would never forget him. She wouldn't even keep him in her heart as a warning; she'd keep him in her heart because that was where he belonged. And if Mac couldn't see how she felt about him…

He was hardly going to see it now, Lucy reasoned sensibly, giving the table the polish of its life—it was proving harder to bring up a sheen while her tears were falling on it. She didn't need anyone to tell her that Mac would soon be gone, or that she only had herself to blame for falling in love with him, but it was one thing being a fool and quite another knowing it.

'Let me pick up the pieces for you,' Tom offered, ducking his head inside the helicopter.

Pieces? This was a car crash. 'No need, Tom. I've got it covered.' He'd been right thinking Lucy wasn't his usual type of woman, and right again, suspecting he was in too deep. So much for holding back on feelings. Lucy had drawn more feeling out of him than he'd realised he had. She'd given more than he'd ever expected anyone to give—and he had expected no more of Lucy than he expected of any woman.

'Do you want me to pass on any messages?' Tom shouted above the roar of the rotor blades starting up overhead.

It was better to make a clean break—better for Lucy. He'd known his destiny since Ra'id had explained it to him when he was just thirteen. He was going back to Isla de Sinnebar to put on the robes of duty and devote himself to the service of a country. In doing so he would lose his freedom. He did this gladly, but a pure, free spirit like Lucy Tennant deserved something better than a man who had to be so single-minded for the sake of his country.

'Razi?' Tom pressed him as the engine noise increased.

Guilt and longing swept over him. He felt so bad leaving Lucy. The first of many times he would experience such feelings, he suspected as the image of her open, trusting face remained steady in his mind. 'If she needs anything,

anything at all—a job, a reference…' Tom and he were almost as close as brothers and there was no need for explanation—they both knew he was talking about Lucy.

He felt diminished as he handed Tom his no-frills business card. He'd signed it so it carried his authority. 'See she gets this, will you, Tom?' Before Tom had chance to answer or he had chance to change his mind, he gave the signal and the helicopter lifted off.

What was this? She felt sick inside as she sank down on the bed. She had just switched on the bedside light and seen the money someone had left on the nightstand. Before this moment she hadn't even known there was such a thing as a five-hundred-euro note—and now there was a stack of them within touching distance.

Not that she wanted to touch them, even though they were crisp and new and looked as though they hadn't been touched, other than to have whatever paper bands had held them together removed.

There must have been tens of thousands of euros in the neat pile, Lucy realised, staring at them. And there was ice in the pit of her stomach, because she knew. She didn't need it spelling out to her—she didn't need to think about it. Mac hadn't come home with the other men and his bodyguards had gone too. Whoever he was—and she had shut the possibilities out of her mind just to live the fantasy—fabulously wealthy Mac had returned to whatever world he belonged to, leaving her with a small fortune in pinkish, purplish notes, as if sufficient money could paper over the cracks in her heart.

He thought money could do that?

She turned her face to the wall, biting down on the back

of her hand so she wouldn't cry out and the other men wouldn't hear her. Drawing a deep shuddering breath, she told herself she'd got what she'd deserved—a lot more than she'd deserved, in fact; there was enough money here to open her own restaurant…

And even that didn't begin to ward off the chill creeping through her veins. Her legs felt like lead as she dragged them up onto the bed. Tugging up the duvet to her chin, she lay unsleeping, fully clothed and shivering as she contemplated a world that was not just empty now, but irrevocably changed—by Mac's opinion of her, and by his pay-off.

Change was inevitable at the end of the ski season. Change was all-encompassing when a pregnancy test turned out to be positive.

Lucy rested against the wall of her bathroom with her eyes shut. When she opened them again the betraying blue line was still there. She'd been feeling sick every morning recently, and all-over funny—different—changed—as if she weren't alone in her body any longer. There was a very good reason for that, as she now knew for sure…

Stroking her hands down her still-flat stomach, she felt an incredible sense of wonder—instant love—instant fight-to-the-death protective instincts towards the little bud of life sheltering and growing inside her—someone to love—someone she hoped would love her—a family all of her own…

And Mac?

Why did he have to know?

Remembering the pile of money he'd left her and the way he'd left her—leaving Tom to pass on his business card of all things—he didn't deserve to know.

Grit her teeth against the pain as she might, she still

loved him. She would always love Mac. Though she hated what he'd done, she couldn't fight the flood of memories— so many good memories and so few bad—until that last bitter blow, when he'd left the resort without saying goodbye—without leaving a proper message, nothing but that wretched business card that Tom had put in an envelope and sealed. 'You never know when you might need something,' Tom had said in his kindly way, after explaining what the envelope contained.

'I'll never need anything from Mac,' she had assured him tightly, planting the unopened envelope deep in her apron pocket.

'A job, maybe?' Tom had said with a shrug as if he sensed her hurt and wanted to ease it.

'No, nothing,' she had insisted, shaking her head. When she'd returned to her room she had stuffed the envelope to the back of a drawer where it still lay to this day, untouched.

Well, it gave her a use for the stack of untouched bank-notes currently residing in a large padded envelope with her name on it in the company safe, Lucy reflected, throwing away the third pregnancy test she'd done that morning. There was so much to consider. She could hardly arrive at her parents' house with a baby. She would need a home for one—a home with a proper garden where a little girl could play. She was so sure it was a little girl. There was a business to think about. She'd get a job to start with to help with the fund and then she'd strike out on her own.

She was going to be a mother…

The thought had not only filled her with joy, but with renewed ambition. She had someone to fight for now— someone who would need a college fund and a prom dress and every advantage she could give her.

And Mac?

Unfortunately, she had to tell him. She had to relent. She didn't want anything from him, but he should know. Mac should be given the opportunity to know he was going to be a father. She had to give him that chance. She had no choice. Telling him was the right thing to do.

R. Maktabi. CEO Maktabi Communications. Having dived into her sock drawer in a frenzy of 'let's-get-this-over-with', she found that was all that was printed on the card. She almost laughed out loud to think Mac was in the wrong business—communicating was hardly his forte. But there were three telephone numbers: London, New York and somewhere in the Arabian Gulf called Isla de Sinnebar. So that explained Mac's exotic looks, Lucy mused, staring blindly out of the window. Mac had contacts in both east and west and now he had returned to… She shrugged and dialled the London number. Mac wasn't there, a frosty secretary told her. She could practically see the woman flinching over the phone when she'd asked for Mac. She realised now that Mac was an abbreviation of his surname, and guessed not many women used it—or, at least, not to the old battleaxe on the other end of the phone. 'Sorry to have troubled you—'

She drew a blank with New York too—but she'd saved the best 'til last. Closing her eyes, she allowed the vision of a desert encampment complete with billowing ivory silk tents to flow through her mind—and had to stop that thought dead when she discovered how many gorgeous women dressed in rainbow hues like so many lovely butterflies were queuing up to serve canapés to a recumbent Mac, who was reclining on silken cushions as they fed him dainty morsels. That wasn't such a great image.

'An appointment with the CEO of Maktabi Communications?' a very polite man enquired in the softest, creamiest voice Lucy had ever heard when she got through to Mac's office in the Arabian Gulf. 'I'm afraid that won't be possible.'

'But he is there?' She was clutching Mac's card so tightly, she had crumpled it, Lucy realised as she waited for an answer. 'And if he is, may I speak to him, please?' she persisted, remembering who had made her brave. 'It's of the utmost importance.'

'May I enquire what your business is?'

Mac was there. She knew it. She clutched the phone to her chest, her heart hammering so hard she was sure the man could hear it beating in Isla de Sinnebar. She put the phone to her ear again. 'I'm afraid it's personal. Perhaps I could meet with him?' She had no intention of telling some stranger her business—but if she could just get into the building, maybe she could find Mac.

'You cannot possibly make an appointment to see—'

Cannot possibly? She held the phone away from her ear. Was Mac contagious? Had he suddenly become so aloof, so untouchable, he wouldn't speak to people he knew? 'But I know him,' she protested, 'and I'm sure he'll want to speak to me.'

There was silence and then a rather offensive laugh. 'You cannot imagine how many people say the same thing,' the man derided.

How many women? Lucy wondered.

Her heart shrank to the size of a bitter, joyless nut. Suddenly she saw how it must sound—a young girl that no one had heard of rang up to demand an appointment with the head of a large multinational corporation...

'And in any case,' the man rapped dismissively, 'we have a public holiday coming up so there would be no one here to see you. Should you be so foolish enough to decide to come you'll find no one here—everywhere will be shut from—'

'From when?' Lucy demanded eagerly.

'From Thursday,' he said, sounding surprised that she hadn't folded yet.

In three days' time. 'Perfect. Can we arrange our meeting for Wednesday?'

'*Our* meeting?' There was silence as the man absorbed her sleight of hand. 'I don't think you heard me. There can be no meeting, Ms—'

'Miss Tennant—'

'Goodbye, Miss Tennant.'

Lucy stared at the silent receiver in disbelief. How rude. It was another dead end, but she couldn't leave it here. She was shaking and not feeling brave at all after such a humiliating put-down, but with the baby to consider nothing would stop her seeing Mac. Dialling the operator, she got ready to book her flight.

CHAPTER NINE

THE purser on board had just announced they would soon be landing in Isla de Sinnebar. Consumed with curiosity, Lucy stared out of her tiny window as the commercial jet swooped in low over an azure sea. Tiny dots of white marked the passage of sailing boats while a patchwork quilt of ivory, green, gold and tan land stretched away towards distant purple mountains. As the plane banked a city came into view. White spires half hidden in a heat haze. No wonder Mac had an office here. If the rest of Isla de Sinnebar was half as magical as it appeared from the air, he was a lucky man.

A lucky man in so many ways. He was about to become a father. If Mac felt only a fraction of the love she already felt for their baby, he would be the luckiest man alive. She fretted as she thought about it, knowing she could only hope he would love their baby, and only hope that he would make time in his busy working life to see something of their child. He would miss so much if he didn't—and she couldn't wish that on him.

Resolutely, Lucy cleared her mind. It was early morning, and she planned to travel straight to Mac's office from the airport and wait for as long as it took to see him. She had to be businesslike and determined. This wasn't a social call. Her baby's happiness, and, yes, Mac's happiness depended on a successful outcome to this visit. And time was tight. Until she got a new job her savings from the ski season had to be eked out, and, much as she would have liked to, she had allowed no time for sightseeing on the Isla de Sinnebar, and just thirty-six hours for discussions with Mac on the way forward. Her homeward flight was booked in two days' time, just before the public holiday closed everything down.

Dragging her gaze away from the window, Lucy tried to contain her emotions. Fear and apprehension at what lay ahead of her in a country she didn't know competed with her blind faith in what she believed would be Mac's instinctive love for their child. She had to believe he would be thrilled by her news, especially when she reassured him that she was going to take on full parenting responsibility, bringing up their baby as a single mother. But with so little settled it was hard to stop doubt setting in.

She had to concentrate on the positive, she told herself; even on such a short visit she could absorb so many things in a land of eternal sunshine where everything was new to her, but before she could do that she had to change her clothes before the seat belt sign lit up. She had worn a tracksuit for the twelve-hour flight, but had brought a light-weight business suit to wear when she met Mac. She was carrying such momentous news she had left nothing to chance. She must look professional and in control when she met him. She had even run a number of scenarios in her mind to work out how he might react when he heard the news. The only thing she was sure about was that it was important to keep her cool—and in every respect. Her time with Mac was done. She had to face that and get over it. She had a baby to think about now.

Everything ran like clockwork. The airport terminal was a haven of calm, clean efficiency, and the cabs were lined up outside the exit door. Lucy began to relax and to believe that in this sunlit, purposeful country things could only work out well for her.

Everything was so exotic she couldn't stop staring around and had to be reminded with a gentle nudge from a kindly woman standing behind her to move along in the queue. How hard was it to believe that she was here—surrounded by the swish of robes, the click of prayer beads, the faint scent of spice in the air, and the pad of sandalled feet? How could she not feel excited—by the sight of everything around her and the thought of seeing Mac again?

Well… She'd warned herself that he might not exactly welcome her with open arms. And that was before she told him her news. But for now with her heart thundering in her chest she would feast her eyes on his country and, though she might not have long here, she would make the most of every minute so she could tell her baby about it one day.

He had stamped his authority on the kingdom in the first few hours of ascending the Phoenix throne. He had been conducting from the wings as CEO of Maktabi Communications with an office in the capital of Isla de Sinnebar, but now he was firmly established centre stage. The learning curve had been steep for those of his courtiers who were used to the old, lax ways—and for men like his cousin Leila's father, who had imagined the playboy prince would be an easy target when he became King. They should have realised his success in business was founded on his overseeing everything, and that he might be expected to run a country to the benefit of its people in exactly the same way. There would be no sleaze, no corruption, no royal favourites; no exceptions. Even he would have to learn to live within the tight moral structure he had laid out in law. His personal life would be an arid desert until the day he took a wife—and even then he didn't expect love to enter the equation; mutual respect was the most he could expect.

All this activity, along with the eighteen-hour days that accompanied it, should have come as a relief, because it left no time to dream about a young woman who would have been a breath of fresh air amongst all the girls they tried to foist on him now he was the ruling Sheikh. His new powers had encouraged a steady parade of dunderheads with porcelain teeth and falsely inflated bosoms to pay court to him, along with those who had to be dusted down as they were removed from the shelf. When he compared any of them to a girl too honest for her own good and as natural as sunlight, he was tempted to swear off women for life. She might not know it, but Lucy Tennant was as rare a find as a flower in the desert. And like that flower he had carelessly trampled her underfoot.

For Lucy the drive to Maktabi Communications was an education in itself. There was clearly order in Isla de Sinnebar, and a respect for the history and tradition of the ancient land that went as far as a camel lane on the six-lane highway. There was a respect for the environment too. Lucy had yet to see a single piece of litter, or graffiti, and the wide, perfectly constructed roads were lined with vivid banks of flowers.

Flowers in the desert, Lucy mused, settling back in her seat as the cab she'd taken from the airport turned onto a slip road, heading for the city, and one rampant lion waiting somewhere close by. The thought that she was getting closer to Mac with every yard the cab travelled had an inevitability about it that made her quiver with excitement and doubt her own sanity all in the same instant. Instinctively cradling her stomach, she wished she could reassure her baby that this was for the best, and that whatever happened her mother would protect her.

The cab drew to a halt outside one of the buildings with gleaming white spires she'd seen from the air. It was even more magnificent from this perspective, and absolutely huge. Maktabi Communications was written over the entrance, and there was a flagpole outside with a large standard fluttering. Her stomach clenched as she identified the rampant lion and scimitar she had last seen on Mac's ring. How at home that emblem seemed here in this land of power and wealth and glittering exoticism. Now everything made sense about Mac's striking looks. And nothing made sense, Lucy thought, noting the guards on the door. Doormen, she might have expected—but soldiers?

Fortunately, she had changed from the shy, self-effacing girl who, having left the family home, had gained her first lesson in what she could achieve in Monsieur Roulet's kitchen, her main lesson in Val d'Isere and, with the gift of life inside her, had transformed utterly, to the point where she wasn't about to be put off by guards on the door.

'I have an appointment,' she told one of them pleasantly, quoting the name of the man who had so reluctantly spoken to her on the phone. Before the guard even had time to ring through and check she brought out the crumpled card. Mac's card. The card Mac had signed so carelessly before passing it on to Tom,

Thank goodness she'd kept it. It acted like a magic wand. The guard saluted and then reached for the door. He stood stiffly as she walked past him into the vast marble-floored entrance.

Power, Lucy thought, staring up in wonder at an atrium that must have qualified for one of the biggest in the world—if not the biggest. Power was her overriding feeling as she looked around. This whole fabulous white, steel and glass building that Mac called his office thrummed with power. There was a desk at the far end of the lobby manned by immaculately dressed men in white robes and flowing headdresses. Even in her smart suit she felt self-conscious as she click-clacked her way across the marble floor towards them. Everything about the building, including their work station, was low-key and high-tech, while she was too unstylish to be either. But with her baby at the forefront of her mind she was able to explain her business clearly, and after a little wrangle between the two men one of them, with the utmost courtesy, showed her to a low-backed sofa where she was to wait.

And wait.

She visited the restroom twice. She bathed her face in ice-cool water and gazed at her face in the mirror. Nothing had changed. There were dark circles under her eyes, and she looked haggard. She wished she could be one of those effortlessly glamorous people who could wait around and still look as fresh as a daisy, but even at this early stage of pregnancy her energy seemed to be sapped beyond anything she could have anticipated. Of course, it might have helped if she could have something to eat or drink, but she daren't leave her station in the lobby for longer than a few minutes in case she missed Mac.

Having checked at the desk to be sure there wasn't anyone she could see who might bring her one step closer to him, Lucy returned to her seat. There were magazines to read on a low glass table, but she would never have been able to concentrate long enough. The idea had always been to get into the building and then find Mac. She'd been prepared to wait for as long as it took, but could have had no idea she would wait quite so long.

So she'd take this opportunity to set her thoughts in order, Lucy told herself firmly. She wasn't going to give up now. When she'd first arrived and shown Mac's card, one of the men on Reception had seemed impressed and had even stood to greet her, but the other had given him a hard stare and so he had sat down again. She guessed the unhelpful man was the man she had spoken to on the phone. She also deduced that Mac was expected soon and that all she had to do was wait. That Mac was immensely rich had never been in any doubt, but that quite so many barriers would be raised when she tried to see him had been a surprise. Perhaps his company was working on something crucial to the government, Lucy reasoned, glancing at the soldiers outside. Her stomach growled insistently as she studied her surroundings. It was a reminder that she hadn't eaten properly since the previous day and that she had to be more responsible now she was eating for two.

She passed some more time marvelling at a national flag picked out in gold above the reception desk. As she studied the incredible workmanship in the scimitar and rampant lion a wave of quite irrational fear swept over her. It was a struggle to brush it aside, but her imagination was notoriously extreme, and pregnancy hormones were clearly adding to her jumpiness. She glanced at her watch and sighed to see another half an hour had passed. Getting to her feet, she approached the desk.

'My apologies,' the awkward man said insincerely with an elegant flourish of his hands.

'How much longer, do you think?' Lucy said anxiously, feeling a wave of dizziness sweep over her. She glanced back across her luggage sitting forlornly in the lobby. She still had to book into her hotel and didn't want to lose the room.

'That I cannot say,' the man told her with a shrug.

'Then may I wait outside Mac's office, please?'

This garnered a withering look. Lucy's shoulders slumped, but then she tensed, hearing the entrance doors behind her sweep open. There was a guttural cry in Sinnebalese and then a clatter of arms as the guards shot to attention.

Mac had arrived. She didn't need to turn around to know it was him when she could sense him in every fibre of her being.

As the pad of sandalled feet drew closer, and the scent of spice and sandalwood filled the air, her mind cleared, but her body let her down, and just as everything shot into clear focus, all of it making complete sense—the rampant lion—the scimitar—the royal standard—the fact that Mac was not easy-going, sexy Mac at all, but someone else completely—she sank into a faint on the floor at his feet.

CHAPTER TEN

SHE woke in a luxurious bedroom and took account of her surroundings carefully before moving a muscle. It was a large, airy, sumptuous room. A brocade quilt in shades of ivory and gold had been stripped away from the crisp white sheets and folded neatly before being placed on a seat at the end of the very large bed. Blinds had been drawn so that the room was in shade, and at the far end two men were conferring in muted voices. They were both dressed in Arabian robes, but even in the shadows the older man's robes were blindingly white, while the younger, taller, broader, much more imposing individual was wearing robes of royal blue. Of course, Lucy thought hazily, Mac probably had blue blood too.

As full consciousness returned to Lucy everything was instantly clear. Mac was a king. No wonder they wouldn't let her see him. Mac was a sheikh. Mac was the ruling Sheikh of the Isla de Sinnebar. The man she loved was a desert king.

She only had to stir for there to be a change in the room. Without a word being spoken the older man Lucy presumed must be a doctor left Mac's side and closed the door softly behind him, while Mac strode towards her across several acres of exquisitely patterned rugs.

Her world shrank around him. Her heart responded as it always had, with heat and with longing. He stopped a short distance from the bed, with his face in shade. Even though she couldn't see his features clearly she knew immediately that this was not the passionate, easy-going lover she had known in Val d'Isere, but a stranger far removed by rank and dignity from the pitiable aspirations of a kitchen girl.

'Lucy?'

The voice was the same. Mac was the same, and yet he was utterly changed. And not just by a costume, but by the fact he was a king. He had assumed his powers, and with them the weight of duty that had turned his face set and hard. He was looking at her, but she sensed his inner gaze was turned towards a future she could never share.

She had been shrinking back on the pillows, Lucy realised, pulling herself upright. She had to rally for the sake of her baby. She couldn't allow herself to be intimidated by anyone, not even the ruler of Isla de Sinnebar. She must have fainted for want of food and that was unforgivable. She had to be responsible now she was pregnant. She had to think clearly and act for a baby that couldn't act for itself.

The baby wasn't the only reason her body had let her down. When Mac had entered the building her soul had flown to him. That was one part of her that steadfastly refused to accept reality. And perhaps should take a look at him now, Lucy reasoned as Mac surveyed her coldly.

Beneath the lightest of quilts she cradled her belly protectively, glad that whoever had carried her to the bed had at least left her fully dressed, minus her jacket and her shoes. She could see them close by, the jacket hanging on a chair back and her shoes lined up neatly underneath. They were a reminder that she had come here dressed for business and a discussion that would change both their lives. 'Who *are* you?' she murmured. She knew the answer and it was a crazy question, but she had to have her suspicions confirmed.

The man she'd known as Mac shrugged and as he moved his robes swirled, filling the air with the mysterious aromas of Eastern spices. 'My name is Razi al Maktabi. Some of my friends know me as Mac.'

'Razi al Maktabi? Known to the world as His Imperial Majesty, Sheikh Razi al Maktabi of the Isla de Sinnebar?' The implications of this swamped her thinking and her heart raced in terror as the man she'd known as Mac swept into the gracious and traditional Arab acknowledgement.

'Why didn't you tell me?' She hated that her voice sounded so hurt and weak, but she had never been a good actress.

'It never came up.'

No, they'd been too busy making love, or having sex, as Razi al Maktabi must no doubt remember it. It was too late now to curse her blindness, or to remember that even when she'd studied Mac's business card her imagination had failed to extend further than thinking Mac some distant cousin of the ruling Sheikh—if she'd thought about it at all.

The chasm that had always existed between them had just widened to a gulf, Lucy realised, taking in the stern face beneath the flowing headdress. Razi al Maktabi wore the clothes of a king well. The exquisite workmanship of the gold *agal* holding his headdress in place only hinted at the power he wielded, but it was her love for the man that made her heart ache with longing. She had to remind herself she was here for her baby and couldn't be distracted, not even by Mac's fierce glamour.

'What do you want from me, Lucy?'

She sank back on the pillows, speechless. He was so cold towards her. Their time together had meant nothing to him. Mac had closed his mind to ever seeing her again, and yet here she was, stirring up unwanted memories of how easy she'd been, how plain, how infinitely replaceable. She couldn't blame him for thinking she would only be here if she wanted something from him.

She had to leave her feelings aside and concentrate on rescuing something for the sake of their child. Easing her legs over the side of the bed, she tried to stand, but only succeeded in swaying towards him as a second wave of dizziness swept over her. Mac's lightning reflexes prevented her from falling to the ground. But there was such a thing as pride. He had taught her that. Easing her arm from his grip, she felt for the side of the bed and shakily sank down. 'Could you give me a moment, please?'

To his credit, the man she must learn to call Razi stood back as she planted her fists on the mattress, willing herself to be as strong and businesslike as he was. If she was going to finish what she was here to do she had to find strength from somewhere.

'When did you last eat?' he demanded.

She stared up distractedly. 'I can't remember.'

'You can't—' He stopped. 'Fortunately, I ordered broth from the kitchen.' He pointed to a dish on a heated trolley. 'You'd better drink it before we talk.'

There was no warmth in his eyes as he crossed the room to put the dish on a tray. He brought it to the bed where she had intended to turn her head, but pregnancy intervened and she was consumed by ravening hunger.

'Drink,' Razi insisted, standing back. 'I'll wait. You'll feel stronger when you've eaten something.'

She drank the soup greedily, relieved to feel warmth and nourishment flooding her veins. When she looked up to thank him Razi's expression remained unchanged. He was telling her the easy relationship they had shared in Val d'Isere was over and must never be mentioned again, let alone rekindled.

She had barely laid down her spoon before he took the tray away. Having put it down, he turned to face her. 'Why are you here, Lucy?'

Yes, why was she here? Suddenly all the reasons that had seemed so sensible in England appeared ridiculous. She had no idea about the laws governing Isla de Sinnebar, except that the ruling Sheikh held all the power. So where did that leave her? She was the chalet girl Razi had got pregnant on his last holiday before taking the throne. Would he care?

She had to steel herself to see beyond that. There was a child to consider. 'I apologise for arriving uninvited,' she began politely, 'but I had to see you.'

'You had to?' Razi's dark gaze narrowed with suspicion.

He didn't need to tell her the short time they'd shared was over and he had no interest in revisiting any part of it or that they were two strangers who shared no intimacies now. Razi was the all-powerful ruler of a country with much weightier matters to consider than some dalliance with a cook. Would he even be interested in her rights as a mother, or when she told him would he insist on keeping the child and simply dismiss her as superfluous to requirements?

This last thought was so shocking she grasped her throat in anguish and, misreading her gesture, Razi poured her a glass of water. 'You look exhausted,' he said. 'Was it really worth putting yourself through this?'

Yes. A thousand times yes, Lucy thought fiercely, drinking the cooling fluid down. But not for the reasons Razi imagined. He thought she was on some pathetic mission to reawaken his interest in her, which was why he was at such pains to make it clear he didn't want her. Why would he want her when she could only be an embarrassment to him?

'I asked you a question,' he prompted coldly. 'Why are you here? What do you hope to gain from this visit?'

'Gain?' She couldn't think of a single thing other than the knowledge that she had done what she believed to be right by coming to Isla de Sinnebar to tell Razi he was about to become a father, but it was clear from Razi's expression that he took her weak voice for an admission of guilt. 'I don't want anything from you,' she insisted firmly.

'You don't? Really?' he mocked. 'It's a long way to come for nothing, Lucy.'

What could she say to convince him? Lucy wondered as Razi's sweeping brows rose in disbelief. He was a formidable all-powerful sheikh, while she was a rumpled mess, sitting up in bed half dressed, sipping from a glass of water in an attempt to act normally, as if she were strong, as if she were recovering.

He walked across the room to flick a switch and the curtains parted. She recognised the familiar skyline outside and deduced the bedroom was a penthouse suite on top of his office building. There would be staff on call and she had no doubt her time with Razi could be counted in seconds now. The fact that he was here at all was nothing more than a common courtesy he had granted to a member of staff who had passed out at his feet. He could hardly ignore her under those circumstances—he could hardly wait to get away, either. 'Razi—I really must talk to you before you go.'

'I don't believe we have anything to say to each other.'

His stark rebuff showed how misguided she'd been. She had imagined the man she had known as Mac would take a civilised view after a civilised conversation in the sterile confines of his office. Trying to impose her thoughts and wishes on a ruling Sheikh was a hopeless task. Asking him to recall some holiday flirtation with a chalet girl sounded ridiculous, even to her. How could she tell Mac her wonderful news when there was no Mac?

'Are we finished here?' he demanded.

She was hit by panic as he turned to go. 'I don't even know what to call you.'

'Razi or Mac—whatever you like.'

His dismissive gesture suggested it really didn't matter what she called him as she wouldn't be part of his life for very much longer. Mac had seemed appropriate for the sexy guest who, once you got over the shock of his blistering glamour, was at least human, but this man was a warrior king with all that that implied. The desert had always seemed such a romantic place to her, as had the image of a desert king, but the reality was so very different. The desert was a hostile environment and the desert king a stranger. 'Your Majesty,' she called after him.

He spun around to face her at the door. 'Call me Razi.'

With that one command Mac had shed his playboy skin and become Razi the King, a man who was so resolute and inflexible he was as removed from her as if they'd never met. Yet there was something between them. And she had to believe it was more than the memory of what an explosive combination they'd been in bed. There was a real connection between them that she felt more strongly than ever and she refused to believe he didn't feel it too.

'What do you want?' he said, picking up on these thoughts.

It took all her strength to hold his dark, brooding gaze and not show the love she felt for him, or blurt out the truth for why she'd come in the pointless hope that Razi would relent and soften towards her and that somehow they could cross the barriers dividing them and make this work.

'Do you want a job?'

The question was so unexpected she almost laughed. Not even as his cook—and certainly not as his mistress. Any woman waiting for Razi al Maktabi would truly wait in lonely isolation until and if he found time for her. She had made a huge mistake coming to Isla de Sinnebar, and a second mistake imagining she could reason with this man—but worst of all she had placed her baby in danger, because Razi would never let her go if he knew she was carrying the royal child. Going home must be her aim. The only safe way to tell Razi about their child was from the safety of a lawyer's office.

'Didn't I leave you enough money?'

Lucy sucked in a shocked breath, realising money had never occurred to her.

'How much do you want?' he said, easing away from the door.

Could a man change so much? Lucy wondered, seeing the suspicion in his eyes.

A king would be suspicious of everyone's motives, she

reasoned, but Razi needn't worry, because his money was ring-fenced for her daughter's future. She hadn't touched it. 'I'm not here for your money—though now you mention it—'

'Yes?' His face eased into a cynical smile as if he had been expecting this all along.

'You left me a ridiculous amount of money in Val d'Isere,' she began nervously.

'Have you never received a tip before? I find that hard to believe.'

A tip for good service? Lucy wondered, feeling mortified as Razi's sweeping brows lifted in mocking denial of everything they'd shared. 'A tip? Yes,' she said as her mind cleared. 'Of course.' She borrowed Razi's mannerism and shrugged, as if a guest leaving her a tip big enough to buy a house with was an everyday occurrence. 'I can't think why else you'd leave me so much money.'

'What aspect of money and payment would you like to discuss first?' he offered, so certain of moral victory he opened his arms in a gesture of encouragement.

To see Razi so cut off from human feeling broke her heart. It hadn't even occurred to him that she might be here to see him, or that what she felt for him was deep and ever-lasting love that asked for nothing in return. But this wasn't about Lucy Tennant or even Razi al Maktabi, it was about a small defenceless child. She were here in Isla de Sinnebar to tell a man who no longer existed that they were going to have a baby together. The fact that something in Razi's history meant he couldn't imagine a woman loving him as she loved him was irrelevant.

The man she knew had gone and in his place was the ruler of Isla de Sinnebar, a warrior sheikh, who probably knew more about mastering a fiery stallion at the head of his troops than love. And now she was desperate to buy time. She might be strong and determined in her mind, but, unlike Razi, she was human and exhausted. Pregnancy had drained her and the enormity of the task ahead of her had begun to tell. 'Would you mind if I freshened up before we talk? All I need is—'

'Five minutes of my time?' he interrupted.

'If you can spare it?'

'I can spare you five minutes—in my office. When you're ready to see me ring the bell and someone will come to escort you. Don't keep me waiting, Lucy.'

And with a swirl of robes he was gone.

He was a king with measureless powers, a king who had sworn to devote himself to a country and its people, but he was also a man and had thought that part of him locked away before Lucy's reappearance.

She was a brief, bright memory, and must remain so, he told himself firmly. He wasn't a ruler under sufferance. He wanted to be King so that he could change things for the better in Isla de Sinnebar.

He wanted the responsibility that came with rebuilding a backward country and would allow nothing to stand in the way of progress or the happiness of his people—and that included Lucy Tennant. If she wanted more money she could have it, but she could not stay. His first action would be to get her out of the building and away from public view. Her mere presence in a country that was still so backward-looking was all it might take for unsettling rumours to start up.

But she had fainted at his feet and he was concerned about her. She didn't appear to be her usual robust self.

There had always been something luminous about Lucy, but now there was a fragility he hadn't noticed before. Perhaps it was just lack of food—or dehydration, the climate change or jet lag—or perhaps the stress of coming to see him. Whatever—he could at least feed her.

His arrival in the kitchens caused quite a stir. He ordered a picnic to be packed immediately. However suspicious he was of Lucy's motives, hospitality was the way in Isla de Sinnebar and that particular tradition insisted he attended to all of her needs before he sent her on her way.

CHAPTER ELEVEN

SITTING by Razi's side in an unmarked army Jeep, Lucy was filled with apprehension. He had dismissed the driver. The vehicle had been waiting for them with its engine running, at the back door of the Maktabi office building with her luggage already loaded in the back. Razi was wearing jeans, desert boots and a plain black top, with the sleeves cut off to accommodate his biceps and a pair of aviators concealing the expression in his astute green eyes. To a casual observer he would pass for any particularly good-looking government agent with an uneasy suspect at his side. 'Are we going to the airport?' she asked, dry-mouthed.

'Soon.'

So, where were they going? Lucy wondered, her anxiety mounting as the Jeep swept away from the kerb. Her great idea lay in ashes. Telling Razi her wonderful news now would be akin to walking into the lion's den and asking if the lion would like relish with his meal. She couldn't do it. Her first priority had to be going home to England where she could consult a lawyer. 'Is there another flight to the UK today?'

'Not as far as I'm aware.'

She craned her neck to read a sign as Razi drove down a slip road onto the highway. 'Where did you say we were going?'

'I didn't.' As you very well know, his quick glance seemed to say. 'We're going into the desert.'

The desert? Her heart was thundering so violently she felt sick. Why couldn't they have talked at the office as Razi had suggested? Because he didn't want anyone to see him with her, Lucy concluded.

But he could have ordered someone to take her to the airport.

And had chosen not to.

Because he wouldn't want any loose ends, she told herself sensibly, trying to calm down. Razi would never ask anyone to do something he believed was his duty; he took care of his own problems.

The highway cut through the desert, and at one time exploring that would have excited her, but the thought of travelling into such dangerous terrain with a man who could only wish she had never existed was a terrifying prospect.

Razi's grim expression did nothing to allay Lucy's fears. They sat in silence while he drove the same way he made love, with focus and a frightening degree of skill. 'I thought you were joking about the desert,' she said nervously as he took a turning off the highway.

'I never joke,' he said grimly.

Not these days. And now there was only the shimmering heat haze in front of them and the wilderness beyond.

When they arrived at their destination he had barely put the brake on before Lucy tumbled out of the Jeep. She gazed around in fear at what he realised must appear nothing more than featureless desert and mountainous dunes to her. 'There's more to come,' he assured her, springing down to stand by her side.

She didn't answer and the tension in her shoulders filled him with the urge to comfort her. He had forgotten how natural and unaffected she was, or that he hadn't met anyone like her before or since. He made the effort to see things through her eyes and then he realised that what was familiar to him was strange and threatening to Lucy, and as she stumbled on the sand he leapt forward to steady her. 'You're trembling,' he said, taking tighter hold of her. 'You've no need to be frightened of me.' He stared into her anxious eyes. 'I come here all the time,' he explained. 'It's quite safe. I thought it would be better for our talk than a sterile office building.'

'It's certainly more discreet,' she observed shrewdly.

He had forgotten how perceptive she was too. 'As soon as we've had our talk,' he promised, 'I'll take you back.'

She looked at him as if to say she knew as well as he did that the time of her departure would depend on him just as her arrival had and that he held all the cards. 'Lead on,' she said, firming her jaw.

Something had changed. Lucy was stronger than when they'd first met…

Whatever it was he didn't have long to find out.

Razi was a master of surprise. He'd sprung the first surprise at the door of his office where he'd been dressed in casual clothes and ready to leave, and now this drive into the wild interior. At first she thought there was nothing to see other than sand, but as Razi led the way up the shallow side of a dune and she saw the panorama on the other side she realised her dreams of a desert kingdom had been insipid stabs at conjuring the reality.

'No comment?' Razi demanded.

She was too stunned to speak. 'It's very beautiful,' she said at last. This was a massive understatement. The brow of the dune was flat, allowing them to stand securely and look over the surrounding land. She was acutely aware of Razi at her side, sharing the moment as she gazed up into a metallic-blue sky streaked lemon and baby pink. There was a gash of neon-orange at the horizon and all the vivid colours of the dying sun were reflected on the surface of a glittering oasis, whose water was so clear she could see each tiny pebble on the sandy floor. Lush green palm trees provided a frame and there was even fruit hanging thickly amongst the fronds. But it was the pavilion on the bank of the oasis, with its ivory silk walls framed in indigo dusk, undulating lazily in the night-time breezes, that really held her attention. 'Is that a traditional structure?'

'It's mine,' he said, following her gaze.

'It's so romantic.' She regretted the words the moment they left her mouth.

Razi remained silent, staring out across his desert king-dom. He moved down the dune and she followed him. He strode to the pavilion where he held the curtain aside for her to enter. As she dipped her head and brushed past him she was aware of his exotic scent, and as she walked deeper into the shaded interior she felt the heat of his stare on her back.

As she looked around he explained, 'Everything you see here was produced in this country.'

It said something about a man who could take his pick from the world's riches, and yet had furnished his desert retreat only with those items that carried a particular significance to him. Razi's devotion to the Isla de Sinnebar couldn't have been more starkly illustrated and she realised his trip to the mountains when they'd met had been one last indulgence before Razi returned to rule—and that her part in that trip had been nothing more than an entertainment for him.

'What do you think?' he said, interrupting these thoughts.

She brushed away the sadness and concentrated on her surroundings. 'I think it's magical,' she said honestly. Everything was new and strange to her—she had everything to learn about his country. As she ran the palm of her hand over the fabric walls Razi explained that they were woven so fine to keep out the sand. So like the furniture they were functional as well as beautiful. It was like a treasure trove— Aladdin's cave, she thought as she turned around to examine everything. There were chests of burnished ebony inlaid with mother of pearl, pierced brass tables and fabulous rugs intricately woven in jewel colours. Plump silk cushions invited rest, while polished lamps cast a subdued and honeyed light. As if a veil had dropped from her eyes, Lucy saw the heritage she was denying her child. The interior of the pavilion was so lovely she yearned for the opportunity to ask Razi for the history of every piece so she could squirrel the information away to tell her baby when the time was right. But how could she do that when he didn't want idle conversation—and when the time would never be right? How could she ever have a normal conversation with him when she was concealing such a vital piece of news?

He offered her water, which she drank, and then she waited while he went back to the Jeep to collect the picnic he'd brought with them. This gave her an opportunity to look at things more closely, and now she noticed the platters of sweetmeats and the jugs of juice. 'You planned this,' she said when he returned.

'You gave me around five minutes, I seem to remember,' he said dryly, placing the basket of food on the ground.

And servants would rush to do his bidding, Lucy realised. Razi had everything in the material sense, and yet he seemed to have lost his joie de vivre, along with his capacity to love or even empathise with a fellow human being. How could that be good for his country? How could a fun-free life with a duty-bound father be good for her child?

'Many of these gifts were left by the Bedouin,' he explained, oblivious to her concerns. 'And my brother uses the place sometimes.'

Lucy shuddered at Razi's mention of the man known as The Sword of Vengeance. 'You two must be very close,' she ventured.

'We trust each other completely.'

What would Ra'id make of her? Lucy wondered. She had to remind herself the great Sheikh probably wouldn't think about staff at all.

Some of this must have shown on her face, she guessed as Razi dipped his head to stare at her. 'Are you unwell?' he demanded.

'I'm fine,' she lied, knowing pregnancy had taken hold of both her body and her turbulent thoughts.

'Here, drink this.' He poured another glass of water.

'I'm perfectly all right,' she insisted as he stared closely at her. But gullible was one thing Razi had never been.

He was instantly suspicious. There had been too much force behind Lucy's assurance that she was all right. So what was she hiding? He refused to consider the most obvious explanation. Lucy was too honest to hide something so vital from him. But her eyes were wary and she was very pale...

The desire to protect Lucy and to defend a country combined in a surge of longing. He couldn't have both and had been right to get her out of the city and away from prying eyes. He could have taken her to any number of places, but had chosen the sultry, seductive setting of the Maktabi Lagoon, a place so rich in ecological treasures he and his brother Ra'id only allowed the passing Bedouin to use it. Why here? Because the desert freed him. This place was his haven when he needed to recall how it had felt to be free. And he supposed that, whatever Lucy's motives for coming to Isla de Sinnebar, some part of him that still remembered the time they had shared in the ski resort had wanted her to see this special place.

And now he wanted her to stay.

Why shouldn't she stay?

He argued violently with himself, only to come up with the answer that rules might be made to be broken, but that was not the type of leader he intended to be. But for now he'd make her comfortable. 'I keep a selection of robes in that chest over there,' he said, viewing her city clothes with some degree of sympathy.

'For your visitors?'

There was the faintest edge to her voice that made him smile inwardly. This was the Lucy he remembered: fire beneath the ice. And jealous too? He let that pass. What else could he do when he had changed her? He had always wanted Lucy to have confidence and self-belief, and now she had. 'The Bedouin leave a selection of robes and other products when they use this trail through the desert,' he explained. 'That's our custom here. If we have more than we need we pass it on to our neighbour—so, please, feel free to choose a robe to wear.' She was hot and flustered in her workplace armour and would be more comfortable in a loose local robe, plus he'd like to see her wearing one—one last image for him to keep. 'There's no one but us around,' he pointed out. 'Why don't you take a dip in the oasis to freshen up and then choose a robe?'

Maybe if she reversed that? Lucy thought as Razi strolled over to the ebony chest. She was still on edge with her mind full of what she had come to tell him. She watched as he raised the lid of a chest and rifled inside before pulling out a shimmering robe. In the palest shade of sky blue, it was embroidered with tiny pearls and diamanté, and was perhaps the most beautiful item of clothing she had ever seen. But as he held it up and the light streamed through it she realised it was completely sheer. 'Don't you have anything a little less revealing?'

'This?' he suggested, pulling out what was clearly a man's robe.

'That's perfect.' She nodded, plucking the dark, home-spun robe out of his hands. It would go round her three times at a guess.

He was cooking over an open fire when Lucy returned from her swim. He'd had plenty of time to think while she'd been enjoying the lagoon, and every answer he'd come up with to explain her unexpected visit remained the same. He shrugged it off, refusing to believe she'd keep something like that from him.

'You're cooking,' she said with surprise.

'I still have to eat when I'm in the desert.' He almost smiled. He hadn't meant to relax, but the desert did that to him. He never felt more calm than when he was alone in this isolated splendour. He had always thought he was ready to see Lucy too—images already formed and complete in his head—but she never failed to surprise him. This time he sprang to his feet to save her embarrassment. The robe she had chosen to wear was trailing round her feet, and instead of winding the headdress, or *howlis*, as it was known in Isla de Sinnebar, around her head and face leaving only her eyes on view, she had draped it over her hair like a scarf. 'Here, let me,' he offered, risking danger just in touching her—and more of the same in being close. Not that he'd ever shrunk from danger, but when that danger came in the form of a woman he wanted to touch—a woman he had always believed to be pure and uncomplicated and now had his doubts about...

'I'm not wearing it right?' she said anxiously.

Taking hold of her water-cooled hands, he moved them away from her head to arrange the yards of fabric. He dragged greedily on her intoxicating wildflower scent while he was covering her face until only her concerned eyes were on view. 'You are now,' he said, relieved that her lips were covered. 'Now all I need is a camera.'

'You're laughing at me.'

'You used to have a sense of humour,' he reminded her, aiming this over his shoulder as he returned to the fire.

'And so did you,' she called after him.

There was a moment of complete stillness between them as if they both accepted this, and then she went inside the pavilion to sort out her clothes, leaving him to see to the food. When she returned he tipped the omelette he had prepared for her onto a palm frond.

'Eat,' he encouraged as she sat cross-legged on the rug in front of the fire. He was still trying to talk himself into believing Lucy's pallor was due to the long flight—or to dehydration—or to not eating for some time—to anything other than what made the most sense.

'This is delicious,' she said with surprise.

They were both off guard and almost exchanged a smile, but Lucy's gaze dropped too quickly. He knew without doubt then that she was hiding something big from him.

She tossed away the headdress and began devouring the omelette as if she hadn't eaten for days. He remembered her appetite for more than food. Here there was privacy afforded by mile upon mile of unseen sand. That she wanted him, he had no doubt. That he wanted Lucy had never been in doubt—and now more than ever. This was one last chance to taste what might have been and her absence from his life had only sharpened his appetite.

She glanced at him as if she could read his thoughts, but there was strain in her eyes—the strain of keeping that secret from him.

CHAPTER TWELVE

WHEN Lucy had finished eating she went to rinse her hands in the oasis. Razi braced himself for her return when he knew he would be hearing something monumental. But she surprised him once again.

'I'd like to talk to you about money,' she said, settling down on the opposite side of the fire.

He scratched his jaw. 'I admire your candour.'

She had to make this work. There was no point wishing she and Razi could thrill together at the news of their child, when Razi was the ruler of a country and she was a chef. The best she could hope for was that she could get a good job back in England and secure her baby's future. Meanwhile, she had to open a discussion that would allow her to go home. 'I realised there could only be one reason why you left me so much money—'

'You did?' Razi's green eyes glinted.

'You wanted me to open a restaurant.' She let this hang, daring him to disagree. If he did, it would turn their brief, though precious—at least to her—liaison into something sordid.

'That was my intention,' he confirmed.

This gave Lucy the courage to make her next sugges-

tion. It was bold, but it was a way of keeping in touch with
Razi, so that when she was ready to tell him about their
child they could discuss their baby's progress—though
only over a boardroom table; something she believed he
might agree to and she could handle. It was better than the
prospect of never seeing him again and infinitely better
than entrusting their child to strangers to pass between
them. 'I have identified a small site suitable for a restaurant and I've drawn up a business plan—'

'Do you have it with you?'

'Well, no…' The one—the only thing on her mind when
she had left England for Isla de Sinnebar had been the
future of her child. She pressed on. 'I'd like to use some
of your money to help me with the start-up.'

'And that's why you're here?'

It went against the grain to tell him even the smallest
white lie, but when the stakes were so high and he had just
given her a way out… 'If you're interested in taking a look
at my predictions I'll email a copy of my proposal to you
as soon as I return.'

'I don't believe you didn't think to bring a copy with
you,' he told her flatly.

'I didn't presume to—' She dried up. What? She didn't
presume to stand her ground in front of the desert king?
Razi knew her better than that. And while she hesitated it
only took the slightest adjustment in his gaze to call her a
liar. She couldn't appear strong in one area and then fall
back on the old, self-effacing Lucy when it suited her. 'At
first, all I wanted to do was return the money,' she
admitted, remembering how humiliated and angry she'd
felt when she first found the pile of banknotes on the
nightstand.

'And now your situation has changed?'

'I got an idea for a restaurant.' She couldn't hold his gaze and her cheeks were blazing.

Razi's expression darkened. 'So you want to open a restaurant and you've drawn up a plan?' Springing to his feet, he stood towering above her, his anger palpable. 'You didn't have to come to Isla de Sinnebar to tell me that, Lucy. You could have emailed me your proposals as you've just offered to do now. You're a hopeless liar,' he said grimly. 'Isn't it about time you told me the truth?'

The ease that had briefly existed between them had vanished and in its place tension snapped like an oncoming storm. She stood up to face him. 'You're right. I'm sorry I came—I should have realised—'

'Realised what, Lucy?'

There was something potent in Razi's stillness that made her body yearn and fear him all at the same time, but she should have remembered that he moved a lot faster than she did. She should have remembered what it felt like to have him hold her firmly in place in front of him so she was drowning in his potent heat.

'You should have realised what, Lucy?' Razi pressed fiercely. 'That I'm not going to be easily drawn in—or fobbed off? What should you have realised? Why are you here?'

'Let me go—'

'Not until you tell me the real reason for your surprise visit. After—what is it? Almost twelve weeks?'

'You make it sound so—'

'Suspicious?' Razi rapped, all semblance of civilised behaviour stripped from his face. 'How would you feel in my place? Suspicious would just be a start, I'm guessing—'

'Please let me go.'

'Not until you tell me the truth—'

'I can't…'

'Why not?'

Her voice might be broken, but from some primal depth the fire of being a new mother rushed out of her in a shout. 'I just can't! Okay?'

'Don't ask me to believe you've come halfway round the world on the off chance I'd be free to speak to you about some plan you have to open a restaurant. Even if you didn't email those plans through first, you'd make an appointment—'

'I tried to.'

Razi called every bluff she'd had and had never seemed more the desert King than he did in that moment. He was so darkly forbidding, she was shivering with fright, but that was no use to her here. She had to think of her baby and for the sake of that child she would fight. She wasn't ashamed of herself or her baby and Razi was right on all counts. If she had wanted to put a business proposition in front of him a face-to-face meeting would have been unnecessary at this stage. Only a child would bring her here to face him. And now that child's father was waiting for her to prove herself unworthy of being a mother. She had to tell him.

'Are you pregnant?' Razi demanded, stealing the initiative.

His instinct shocked her to the point where she couldn't speak for a moment. 'Yes, I'm pregnant.' She would never deny the existence of her child.

'You're pregnant?' Razi's voice had taken on a new and frightening tone as if he had hit her with the most extreme reason he could think of for her coming to Isla de Sinnebar and had only just realised it might be true.

Lucy's hands flew to protect her womb as Razi stared at her and for one glittering moment the prospect of having

Razi al Maktabi as her protector and the hands-on father of her child was a heady prospect, but then she accepted reality. He would never acknowledge a foreigner who was virtually a member of his kitchen staff as an equal and a royal child would never be allowed to leave the country. She had told him the truth and was damned. If she hadn't told him she would have been equally damned, for then she would never have been able to look her child in the eyes and tell that child the truth about her father.

'So that's why you fell into a faint at my feet—and why you looked so pale when we arrived in the desert.' Razi's expression darkened. 'Have you no sense of responsibility? No concern for anyone but yourself? Don't you care about your child? Or—'

'You?' Lucy interrupted. She had paled beneath Razi's onslaught, but rallied to defend the truth. 'I care about you more than you know.'

Even as he exclaimed with disbelief she saw a look in his eyes she'd never seen before. It spoke of a fierce pain— a pain from the past that still had the power to hurt him. 'I'm pregnant, Razi,' she said quietly, 'and that's a fact as well as a cause for rejoicing. I'm afraid you'll just have to get used to it—I have.'

Get used to it? He was already changing. A baby? He was ice. He was fire. He didn't dare to hope. 'A baby or *our* baby?' he demanded, fuelled by unbearable suspicion.

'*My* baby.'

'That doesn't answer my question, Lucy,' he told her coldly. But he could tell it was a baby she had loved from the first moment she had realised she was pregnant. He didn't question Lucy's maternal instinct. She would defend her child to her last breath. He envied her that depth of feeling. But all Lucy's thoughts were centred on the baby and on her duties as that baby's mother and this passionate new love had blinded her to reality and to the world outside her own cosmos. She could have no idea of the repercussions inside a country like Isla de Sinnebar if the news leaked out. 'How do you know it's our child?' he said, feeling calmer now his mind had cleared to make way for this most crucial of tests.

'Because there hasn't been anyone else,' she said, appearing more vulnerable than ever as she made this innocent admission.

He closed his heart to her. 'How do I know that? How do I know I can trust you?'

Her steady gaze shamed him, but still he drove on to seek the truth. 'How do I know that I'm not one of many guests you…entertained?'

He stopped the flat of her hand before it reached his face, holding her wrist in a non-negotiable grip.

'Let go of me!' she insisted, struggling to break free.

His answer was to bring her closer so he could stare into her wounded eyes. 'I'll release you when you calm down and tell me the truth—and I mean all of it.'

This wasn't the civilised man she had met in Val d'Isere, but a warrior king, who was burning up inside with pain and fury. 'Let go of me. Of course it's our baby. I've never been with anyone else. If you need proof we can have a DNA test once the baby is born.'

Razi held on to her, his gaze unwavering.

'Do you really think I would fly halfway round the world,' Lucy demanded, throwing Razi's taunt back at him, 'without knowing it was your baby? I don't lie.'

She stared down at his hands on her arms and he

released her. 'I also have a bank statement, showing that I set up an account exclusively for the money you left at the chalet, and that I never touched a penny of it.'

'So you put your plans for a restaurant first, your child second and telling me about our baby a very poor third?' He threw up his hands in disbelief.

'I'm not saying that.' This was all going horribly wrong. She had never meant to lie to him.

'When, Lucy? When did you intend to tell me?'

'When I returned to England,' she confessed steadily. 'I came here thinking you were Mac—a businessman—only to discover you were the ruling Sheikh—'

And a man who clearly mistrusted women, believing them incapable of love. Lucy only had to look into Razi's eyes to know that his inner scars went a lot deeper than she had previously supposed. Some long-held wound was festering inside him. She couldn't know the details, but she could feel the effect, and while part of her was filled with compassion for his pain, the part of her that was a mother—and that part was swiftly becoming all of her—was terrified at the thought that the ruling Sheikh of Isla de Sinnebar's only interest now was to secure custody of their child.

And what power did she have to stop him? Once Razi had done that she'd be his captive for life, for she would never abandon her child to the care of strangers. Razi lived on an island halfway across the world from where she lived. How would that work? When would she see her baby? How could she bear her child to live so far away from her? She couldn't. And Razi wouldn't want her here.

It was a problem to which there was no solution, and in this case the only form of attack was defence. 'Why did you bring me to the desert? To show me a valuable ecological site? I don't think so, Razi. You brought me here to get me away from the city and prying eyes. You brought me here because you're ashamed of me.'

'I'm not ashamed of you,' he insisted. 'Why did you come to the Isla de Sinnebar if not to trap me in some way?'

'What? That's absurd. How would I do that when you're an all-powerful king?'

'That's what I want to find out.' He raked his thick black hair with angry fingers. 'Has it occurred to you that a scandal like this could rock my country? No—I didn't think so. If I acknowledge this child it will be seen as my first act in power. How will that look to my people? And the mother of that child a foreigner in this, the most traditional of countries.'

He made her feel as if she had done something wrong— and there was no mention of a baby to love, just a country to be ruled with a rod of iron, heartlessly, like a company meeting targets to be approved by the ruling Sheikh. 'It seems to me you support all the antiquated beliefs you have sworn to eradicate. And as for me—I don't want anything from you.'

'Well, that's clearly untrue,' Razi informed her coldly, 'or you wouldn't be here.'

'I thought you should know, that's all. I'm not trying to trap you into anything. I'm quite capable of standing on my own feet without your help.'

'So you plan to have the child and I have no say in the matter?'

'That's not it at all—'

'It must be one or the other,' Razi insisted coldly. 'Which is it, Lucy? Blackmail? Or sob story?'

CHAPTER THIRTEEN

LUCY drew on her inner strength. 'The man I knew in Val d'Isere would never have said that. And let me tell you something else,' she added without giving Razi chance to speak. 'You say you care about a country. I don't believe you. How can you care about anything if you're incapable of love? And if you're incapable of love, I don't want you to have anything to do with my child—'

'Our child,' he reminded her fiercely. 'Or so you say—'

'Yes, I do say,' Lucy insisted, bracing for battle. Where her child was concerned she was fearless.

He had never felt such wild emotions. He wanted to hug Lucy and rejoice—yet also turn his back on her and never see her again. He rued the day he'd met her and yet longed for her to stay. She had to stay if she was having his child. The realisation that he was about to become a father had left him drowning in happiness, while the thought that anyone, even Lucy, might imagine she could keep him from that child was an abomination he refused to consider. The memory of a child living in lonely isolation, waiting for his brother's visits to break the monotony of being cared for by strangers, was still too raw for that. If she was having his child he would not be denied the joy of seeing that child grow up. The thought of anyone but him protecting the baby, loving it as he would, was unthinkable. He wouldn't stand on the sidelines for Lucy—for anyone.

'Will I embarrass your wife?'

'My wife?' The red mist of anger was still on him as he refocused dazedly.

'I presume there's got to be a wife soon,' she said, turning from shy supplicant to virago in a moment. 'Tell me,' she insisted. 'I have to know. I have to protect my child. I don't imagine you'd want me here in Isla de Sinnebar muddying the water when the time comes for you to choose a wife—'

'There is no wife,' he roared, stopping her, 'or ever likely to be a wife.' The face of his cousin Leila flashed into his mind. He had sent her back to university where she so dearly wanted to be and then had dispatched her greedy father with a flea in his ear and a cheque large enough to keep him off Leila's back.

'So, you're married to duty?' Lucy suggested, taking another tack.

'And what if I am?'

'That isn't what I want for my baby, Razi. And if you're closed off from love what good are you to a country?'

'Let me be the judge of that,' he snapped. 'I'm interested in cold, hard fact—like what do you want for your child, Lucy?' He was already calculating the amount.

Her wounded gaze said no child of hers could ever be bought. 'I want my baby to be loved,' she said quietly.

'Yet you think me incapable of love?'

She didn't answer. She didn't need to and as his own doubts kicked in he turned on the person least deserving of his anger. 'You should have told me the moment you knew you were pregnant. We could have arranged something.'

'Like what?' she exclaimed fearfully, lifting her arm almost as if she was shielding her face from so much pain. 'Don't say any more, Razi,' she begged him. 'Don't say things I know you don't mean.'

He took himself aside until he was calmer. 'I mean I would have supported you and the baby,' he said then.

'If I were discreet? If I bowed my head—hid my child?'

'Did you really think this was something you could keep from me?'

'It's why I'm here.'

'And you think I'd be happy to have no say in my child's life? How little you know me.'

How true, Lucy thought. They had shared the ultimate intimacy, but they were still two strangers facing up to one of life's major turning points together. They had everything to learn about each other—everything to learn about how they would go on from here. But they had to go on from here and she had to make Razi listen. 'I wasn't keeping anything from you. I waited for three months to be as sure as I could be that the pregnancy was safe.'

His reaction shocked her. Wheeling away, Razi put his head in his hands as if for once there was a problem he couldn't solve. She gave him space, sensing the renewed onslaught of his pain, though in some ways it was a relief to see such a passionate response from a man who had grown so cold.

Razi was a warrior, exotic, fierce and passionate— while she was a chef, neat and tidy—cautious, some might say; at least, she had been cautious up to meeting Razi. They both had so much to offer their child if only they could put their differences behind them. They must do that because only then could they start to build a future for their baby. But right now Razi was at his most untouchable, his most remote, with every sinew and muscle in his body stretched tight.

There had never been a moment when she had been frightened of Razi, but she was frightened now, yet this was the very moment when she must reach out to him, while the pull of duty was warring with his warmer, human side. For all her ignorance of such weighty problems, one thing she did know—a country run for the sake of duty would be a cold and barren place. She touched his arm, expecting him to send her away—or, worse, ignore her. She was used to being invisible, but that didn't mean she liked it. You never got used to that sort of thing. It always hurt. She stood quietly, feeling foolish as the silence dragged on, but then the miracle she'd hoped for happened. Razi turned to stare at her. He didn't speak, but the fact that he had responded at all was enough for now.

There was a world of questions in Lucy's eyes, any one of which he could pick and break her heart. 'I have decided that this is the way forward,' he said instead, planning his words carefully.

He had no reason to mistrust Lucy, not if he made himself remember her innocence at the chalet. So he was already considering the timing for acknowledging Lucy's baby in public. He would sell the concept of an unmarried ruling Sheikh who already had a child to the older tribesman as proof of his fertility, turning disapproval into approval at a stroke. Yes, he was a cynic; business had made him that way. Before accepting the Phoenix throne he had founded an empire largely on his wits. For sure there had been no help from his father, the ruling Sheikh. Plus, he had vowed to revise the antiquated laws of Isla de Sinnebar, bringing

them into line with the modern world—so this *would* be his
first act and he would turn it into a positive act.

He would stop at nothing to make a better job of parenting than his own absentee parents, but he wanted the throne
too—and not for selfish reasons, but because he knew he
could bring progress and benefits to his people. With good
management and careful husbandry of the land and indige-
nous species, Isla de Sinnebar would thrive. There would
be justice for all, a first-class healthcare system and the best
education his money could buy. This was both his goal and
his passion. He existed for no other purpose than to serve
Isla de Sinnebar. He had not bargained for the additional
blessing of a child, but as he outlined his plans for Lucy he
realised it wasn't a question of wanting to take the child
from her, but more a matter of security for both Lucy and
their baby. He expected her to fight him when she heard
his proposals. He expected her to feel disappointed that she
couldn't be anything more to him than the mother of his
child, but he was confident she could only be reassured
when he told her what he meant to do to secure her future.

Lucy listened as Razi spelled out her glittering new life.
The biggest surprise of all was his intention to acknowledge their child. She was so stunned she didn't hear everything he was saying and had to ask him to repeat things.

Her eyes widened with disbelief. She hadn't come to Isla
de Sinnebar for this. She was to have a wonderful home of
her own choosing in England—a country estate with stables,
if she liked. She would have an income appropriate for the
mother of a royal child, and a private jet at her disposal so
she could visit their child—within reason—whenever she
wanted to. There was no mention of joint parenting—joint
anything. It was a clean cut. It was a life according to the

old saying—beyond the dreams of avarice—but greed she had none, just a longing for the family life she had always dreamed of, where children would thrive and grow in the full knowledge that they were loved. 'You're very generous,' she said politely when Razi had finished laying out all the benefits that would accrue from being, not even a royal mistress, but a royal brood mare.

He made a casual gesture, as if paying a king's ransom to keep her out of sight was more than worth it.

She couldn't leave it here. She had to find a way to touch him. 'And you, Razi—what part do you intend to play in our baby's life?'

He looked at her as if she were mad. 'A full part, of course.'

'And you'll have time for that? You'll have time to be a full-time parent?'

He waved his hand dismissively. 'You don't understand the life I lead.'

'Clearly.'

'I have over a thousand staff working for me in Isla de Sinnebar alone.'

'Staff,' she said quietly. 'Is that how you were brought up, Razi? By staff?'

She could not have predicted the look in his eyes. She could never have guessed they would fill with pain. She knew immediately the cause of Razi's seething anger and her heart went out to him, but where her own child was concerned it did not soften her by one iota. Her baby was not going to suffer the same fate as its father—and if that meant there would have to be some big changes in her own life, so be it. 'I'm going to stay,' she said.

Razi could not have looked more shocked. 'You can't stay,' he argued.

'Of course I'll stay,' she insisted. 'And I don't need a big house—just somewhere safe where I can bring up my child happily. You can visit any time you like. I would never keep you from your baby, Razi, just as I would never expect you to deny me access to my child.'

He stared at her in silence. Was that because he couldn't believe what she was offering? Lucy guessed she was very different from Razi's mother. He might not have spelled out the details of his childhood—he didn't have to: it was all there on his face. His mother had been compliant, she guessed, and most probably petted and pampered for falling into line. But then the old Sheikh had tired of her and she had been ignored.

Well, Lucy Tennant was prepared to do none of this. She would make her own way in life. 'I'm offering to stay without condition or expectation,' she explained when Razi remained silent. 'With your permission, I imagine I'll be allowed to open a restaurant.'

'What?' he cut across her.

'A restaurant,' she said patiently. 'It seems the obvious thing.'

'To you, maybe, but I cannot allow you to work.'

Lucy frowned. At a stroke Razi had forbidden her to have a career.

She must be reasonable, she warned herself. She could see that maybe she'd made a blunder—fronting a restaurant would be too high profile. 'I could be a silent partner—I could run things from the kitchen without ever showing my face. We have to find a solution, Razi. We must. We have to make this work.'

As he stared at her he realised that before this moment he hadn't believed a woman capable of a selfless act, but

Lucy had proved him wrong. She had proved herself in so many ways even he didn't think it was fair she had to continue doing so. It seemed some people were always fighting with their backs against the wall, while others had it handed to them on a plate. With Ra'id's help he had fought his way up and there was nothing lacking in his life, while Lucy was completely at his mercy.

She stood facing him, expecting nothing, asking nothing. He touched her cheek almost reverently, growing increasingly aware of her sacred role. 'I'll make sure you're well taken care of.'

By whom? her steady gaze asked him.

'Surely you can see the sense in my proposals?' he demanded, tightening his grip on her arms.

He had not expected her eyes to fill with tears, but having all the strength and every advantage he let her go. 'Don't look so downcast. I'll buy you two homes—one here and one in England, but you can't work. It wouldn't be—'

'Appropriate?' she supplied softly. 'I haven't come here looking for handouts, Razi. I don't want anything from you in the material sense. All I ask is your promise never to part me from our child.'

'And to change centuries of tradition?'

'If women don't work here, don't you think you're wasting a valuable resource? If traditions have been in place for centuries, maybe they're due an update. Sorry,' she said, seeing his face tense. 'It's really none of my business.'

As he stared at her he found himself wishing that it were her business.

CHAPTER FOURTEEN

RAZI shook his head in despair. At Lucy's naivety at thinking he could change centuries of tradition? She only wished she could tell him everything in her heart: how she loved him, how she wanted him—and not for his power or for his wealth, or even his good looks, or for any of the other obvious advantages a man as deeply layered and endlessly fascinating as Razi possessed, but for the simple pleasure of being in his company. She couldn't conceive of a palace grand enough or jewels big enough to compete with a glance from him when that glance was full of warmth and connection between them.

'What if I promise never to part you from your child?' he said. 'Is that enough?'

'It's all I've ever wanted.'

'In that you are unique,' he admitted, his lips tugging with just the faintest show of the old humour.

It might be all she'd ever wanted, but it wasn't everything. She wanted Razi's love too, but that was a fantasy too far. She settled for, 'I promise I won't embarrass you, Razi. I'll live a quiet life out of the public eye. I'm not missing anything. I've always been a backroom girl with no idea about fashion or moving in society—'

He cut her off with a laugh that sounded achingly like Mac's.

'What's so funny?' She knew deep down inside. She would never be exposed to society, or have any need to learn about fashion; the life she had planned out—the future they had practically agreed on—included none of that. She would live somewhere in the country where he could visit discreetly.

She gasped as Razi cupped her chin and made her look at him. 'I'm laughing because you're funny,' he said, his glance slipping from her eyes to her lips. 'Your ideas are funny. Your notion of how I live and what's important to me is so far off the mark, it's funny.'

'I'm sorry.'

'Don't be.'

A world of possibilities opened up as Razi's thumb caressed her jaw. She could do this... She could do just about anything to be with him...

Razi's smile was slow, and confident enough to make her believe anything was possible. Her breath sounded ragged in the silence as she waited, suspended somewhere between hoping things were changing and knowing deep down they could never change enough to make all of her dreams come true.

She was right. The tension between them subsided and he let her go. His next words proved that while she had been desperate to believe in a fantasy Razi's quick mind had covered all the bases. Every conceivable facility would be made ready for the expectant mother of the royal child. Lucy and her baby would want for nothing. Name it, and she could have it. If she preferred a different consultant— a different nursing team—anything—everything—too much of everything—was hers for the asking, while the one thing she wanted and longed for so badly, which was a normal family life, could never be hers. But as her emotions welled, so did her longing for Razi—one more night of pretending they could be together and she could cope with anything. One night of love to last a lifetime didn't seem so greedy. One more night of knowing how it felt to be loved…

With his senses so keenly tuned to Lucy he knew almost before she did when she surrendered her ideas to his. He was still coming to terms with the miracle of new life and the fact that Lucy was carrying his child and felt a great sense of wonder. There was also the urge to stake his claim again.

'This is crazy,' she murmured, shivering with desire as his lips brushed her mouth.

'That's the weakest protest I ever heard,' he observed, slowly backing her towards the entrance to the pavilion.

'I must be crazy,' she protested, reaching up to rest her hands on his shoulders.

'A little crazy goes a long way with me,' he murmured, giving her waist a reassuring squeeze.

Razi lowered her onto cushions that supported her frame and yet moulded themselves to her body in the most comfortable way. The curtain over the entrance was still drawn back to allow streamers of moonlight to decorate their cushioned bed. The interior of the pavilion was shaded and lit by two brass oil lamps and an incense burner. She was surrounded in a haze of delicious scent and refreshing night-time breezes kept her cool, but even in Razi's arms she was restless. There was so much to be decided yet and maybe this was a mistake. 'This is wrong.'

'Wrong?' Razi murmured against her mouth. Removing

her ugly robe, he tossed it aside. 'There's nothing wrong with this,' he said, shooting a wicked glance down the length of her body.

Just one more night...

It was as if all the humour and worldliness that had once drawn her to him was back. There were no divisions between them now, just the gasping, pleading sounds she was making as Razi rubbed his thumb across her bottom lip. Taking her face in his hands, he kissed her slowly, deeply, until her anxiety subsided and all thoughts of tomorrow disappeared.

'I'm almost frightened to touch you now you're carrying my child,' he murmured, kissing the tender place on her neck and then her collarbone, before travelling down to tug and tease her painfully engorged nipples, before moving on to lave her belly with his tongue. 'Almost,' he added in a wry murmur when she groaned in complaint. He proved this by working his magic on her swollen lips with delicate raids of his tongue. 'You taste different—fuller, richer, sweeter...'

And she was almost frantic with desire. How she longed to be full of him, stretched by him...loved by him. Where she had hungered for sensation, Lucy realised, now what she hungered for was closeness, reassurance and love.

Springing to his feet, Razi kicked off his boots and unfastened his jeans and as he eased them over his lean hips she realised she had forgotten how beautiful he was—how magnificent. And when he tugged his top over his head, exposing his naked, hard-muscled torso with the rampant lion tattooed in black ink whorls on hard bronze flesh, she wondered if ever a man had been born who was quite so perfect...perfect for her.

She reached for him as he lay beside her, caressing his

face, loving the sharp black stubble that could bring her so much pleasure and so much pain, and dropping kisses on his mouth as his erection, huge and hard, pulsed impatiently against her thighs.

'Slowly, carefully,' he murmured, moving on top of her.

How to tell him that pregnancy had made her hungrier for him than ever and that thanks to the riot of hormones in her body every nerve ending seemed to have received a super-charge of sensation and appetite? Or that some basic need—the need to claim her mate, perhaps—had made her leave her inhibitions at the door? That, together with her need for reassurance, meant there wasn't a moment to lose—she didn't want him carefully and slowly; she wanted him fiercely and now.

She should have remembered Razi's self-control. She might want to remember Razi's resolve and self-control in all future dealings with him, was her last thought before he made all rational thought impossible.

He claimed her slowly and carefully, resisting Lucy's best efforts to urge him on. This was different—she was different, she felt different, just as she had tasted different. Her body was ripe, unique, welcoming, adding both to his desire and to his sense of privilege. He felt possessive too, and with so much sensation going on, his mind went into freefall. He reined back, wanting to please her. Pleasing Lucy was his only goal. She was carrying his child and this was his way of saying thank you.

She had never felt closer to another human being than she felt to Razi that night as they lay, limbs entwined, in the middle of the night. Would they ever get enough of each other? It seemed unlikely. So what was she saying? What was he saying? Would she stay on in Isla de Sinnebar as his mistress and the mother of his child? Could Razi accept her terms? Did she have any right to state them? Her wish to live simply and out of the public eye—was that even possible here? Knowing Razi's intention to run his country like a business beyond blame, would the world's media seize on the new ruler's peccadillo and flaunt their child, leading to endless problems for her baby in the future?

Leaning on her elbow, Lucy fretted as she watched Razi sleeping. If only this were a fantasy she could make every part of it right. He was sprawled on his back with his long, muscular limbs taking up every inch of available space. He looked so beautiful and so peaceful... She traced the line of his lips with her fingertip, pulling her hand away when he turned his head slightly. Now she could see the sweep of jet-black eyelashes casting a blue-black shadow on his sculpted cheeks, and eyebrows that swept upwards like a fiery tartar, or a pirate king...

Razi was a stunning-looking man, but she could never forget he was a king. She traced the tattoo, the symbol of his country, which he had chosen to have indelibly inscribed over his heart. Was there room left in that heart for anyone, woman or child? A shiver gripped her as she thought about it and all her contentment flew away. Razi wasn't just a man she had fallen deeply in love with, he was the ruler of a country. And she was a cook—shortly to become the mother of his child, and, though she might fight with everything in her for her child's right to live free from any taint of shame she could bring it, could any royal child be truly free? Privilege was a poor return for freedom, at least in Lucy's value structure.

Now there was no hope of sleeping. Settling back on the cushions, she turned one last time to drink him in. 'I love you.' How she wished there were more meaningful words to express her feelings for Razi. 'I adore you,' she whispered, and even that didn't come close.

He stirred in his sleep, and, realising her restlessness was disturbing him, Lucy gently disentangled herself and crept silently away.

He stirred and realised Lucy was gone. He was on his feet in an instant, instinct telling him she was swimming in the lagoon, and while swimming at dusk with him when there was light was one thing, swimming in the dead of night when a cloud might cover the moon and she could misjudge the depth—

The thought that anything could happen propelled him out of the pavilion with one thing on his mind: Lucy—to hold her safely in his arms; to make love to her.

The water was like iced silk on her burning skin, and it was sweet and clear. There was firm sand beneath her feet as she plunged deep, loving the sensation of cold against her heated body. She barely had chance to clear her head with a single, lazy lap before she realised she wasn't alone and that Razi was swimming powerfully towards her. Slicing through the water, it took him no time to secure her in his grasp.

The breath left her chest in a rush as he dragged her close. 'What do you think you're doing?' he demanded, his dark eyes flashing fire.

'I'm a strong swimmer, Razi.'

His grip tightened. 'In the pitch-black middle of the night? Alone?' His voice was fierce with concern.

'You said it was safe,' she protested.

'Not on your own. Not again. Not ever. Do you understand me?' He held her back to stare into her face, and then, without waiting for her answer, he secured her in an iron grip and swam for shore.

Or she imagined that was his purpose, but as soon as he was within his depth Razi stood, and in the same fluid movement he took her.

He sank deep, the size of him making her gasp with surprise. She would never become used to him. The darkly exotic light of passion smouldering in his eyes said he understood her need and that this was all for her. Her arousal was extreme. The heat of their bodies and their passion contrasted strongly with the cold of the water to make every sensation bigger, stronger and far more intense. Razi encouraged her to lie back on the cooling water where she could gaze up at a desert moon planted in a field of stars. Could heaven improve on this? she wondered. The majesty of the desert had unleashed the untamed spirit in her heart, Lucy realised, sobbing with pleasure as Razi moved steadily and with absolute intent. He understood her as no one ever had, not just sexually, but in every way. And in turn, she loved his exciting, exotic country, with its passionate people, and its wild, unknowable desert... She loved him.

'I hope I have your full attention?' he murmured, lifting her into his arms so he could add something wicked in his own language.

'Can you doubt it?'

His lips curved.

Her answer to that could only be a groan of deep satisfaction as he sank deep inside again. She hardly had to cling to him at all with the water supporting her and Razi's strong hands controlling her buttocks. He thrust into her just the way she liked while her limbs floated lazily. All the pleasure centred at her core, just as he had intended until finally she couldn't hold him off any longer and her cries of release mingled with those of the eagle owl as it swooped down from its roost to hunt.

'More…' Razi spoke for her, as she was still beyond speech. He kept up a steady beat, gently and persuasively, so that one starburst sensation had barely faded before it began to build into the next. He took her slowly and carefully, making sure she savoured every moment. How could she not? Making love beneath a lemon moon and a deep blue velvet sky filled with diamond pinpoints of light was almost too beautiful, too perfect.

So perfect it frightened her. If only she could capture this experience somehow and bring it out when she was alone to convince herself this had really happened…

'Lucy?' Razi murmured, teasing her with a pass of his roughened cheek against her neck.

'Yes,' she whispered, closing her mind to doubt as he settled her back on the rippling water. She held her breath, waiting for words of reassurance that never came, but Razi knew her body so well—too well, and she had nothing more to do now than rock gently on a pool turned silver beneath the moonlight as he pleasured her, while all the worrying thoughts about the future drifted away.

He watched Lucy come apart in his arms again and again, wondering if she would ever tire, for he was sure he wouldn't. Moonlight had transformed her into an exquisite water nymph, and one whose appetite for sex continued to amaze him. They shared a fierce passion, he reflected as he swung her into his arms to carry her back to the bank, but tonight there was no urgency. They had every hour before dawn to indulge themselves in pleasure before reality reared its ugly head and put a stop to it. Until then he would make this a night to remember for both of them.

When they got back inside the pavilion he swaddled her in towels and dried her tenderly, rejoicing in her beauty as well as in the fact that she would soon be the mother of their child. Lowering her gently onto the silken-cushioned bed, he murmured, 'Hussy,' as she reached for him.

'Your hussy,' she said, smiling while her hand insisted on creating its own sort of havoc.

He drew in a sharp breath as she moved down the bed and then she snatched his breath away, cupping him firmly, her lips brushing him, her tongue teasing him. At first she was a little tentative, as if this was a first for her. He found he was fiercely grateful for that, and had to ask himself just how deeply he was committed to a girl he had so recently thought of keeping out of the public eye before making sure she caught the next flight home. They were way past that, he concluded as Lucy grew bolder. As she laved him with her tongue and closed her lips around him to draw him deeper into her mouth he wondered if he could ever bear to let her go. 'Stop,' he managed huskily, realising how selfish he was being—on all counts.

'Why?' she said, resting her chin on his thigh. 'Are you frightened you might lose control?'

He laughed and lifted her into his arms. She made him laugh. She made him happy. He was wary of losing his heart for the first time in his life. He was frightened of hurting her. She had never put her female powers to the test in quite the same way before and, having done so, she was flying high. She looked triumphant, and more beautiful than ever. She was more flushed, more aroused—more womanly and yet more vulnerable in every way. The newfound confidence on Lucy's face was everything he'd ever wanted to see, and he didn't want anyone to change that—especially not him. 'You're full of surprises.'

'Did I do something wrong?' she demanded softly as he swung her beneath him.

'You did everything right,' he reassured her. 'So right I had to make you stop.'

Her eyes reflected her innocence and her desire to please—to please him. He would never abuse that. It brought out all his protective instincts. 'I won't do anything that puts your pleasure at risk.'

A shadow crossed her eyes and he knew what she was thinking. This was about more than pleasure and in the morning they would have to face that. Where would they go from here? What did the future hold for Lucy—for her baby—for their child? 'It will be all right,' he promised. The clock was already ticking, but he refused to hear it—not yet.

'How long do we have?' she whispered as if she knew everything he was thinking.

'Time enough.' Teasing her lips apart with lazy passes of his tongue, he nudged his way between her legs, thrusting deep, exulting as Lucy's eager body moved to claim him. Whatever the future held, one thing was sure; few people were lucky enough to ever know a night like this.

CHAPTER FIFTEEN

THEY enjoyed a feast in the middle of a balmy night—fresh fruit, which Razi had brought in the picnic hamper, along with hunks of delicious local bread and creamy cheese—before making love again. It was in the sleepy, contented aftermath, when Lucy was nestled safe in Razi's arms, that he surprised her by confiding something of his childhood. The thought that she had touched him enough for that, and that trust was slowly building between them, was like a tiny flame she wanted to shield with her hands to help it to grow. When he told her about his mother she felt fiercely moved that he would do so, as well as fiercely protective of Razi. She was not just protective of her baby now, but of the man she loved.

His mother's name was Helena, Razi said, naming her for the first time since her death. Helena had been very young and frightened, and had found herself fighting for position in a land where she didn't speak the language, or have any rights to speak of. She had no place to run to, and no one to support her cause, as everyone lived in fear of Razi's father, the ruling Sheikh. She had no money, no contacts to help her to return home, and her sole purpose in life had shrunk to remaining beautiful and available twenty four seven in case his father paid a visit. And for a time, that was enough...

Enough? How could it ever be enough? Lucy wondered, tears stinging her eyes as she thought of the little boy who had never known his mother, other than from cruel gossip amongst the palace servants. She cried too for fear that history might repeat itself.

'Hey,' Razi said, kissing tears from her cheeks, 'I can't keep up with the downpour—and anyway, I've talked enough. It's time for you to tell me your story.'

It was so like him to make light of his history. Razi came with a self-pity delete key. But if anyone had a right to be angry about their parents, it was him. They had never had a chance like this to get to know each other, Lucy realised, and maybe they never would again. Thanks to Razi confiding in her, she understood the father of her child a lot better now, but she was still eager to learn more. 'I'm only interested in you,' she protested.

'Nice try,' he said, 'but I'm still waiting.'

'Nothing I've experienced comes close to a child being shunned by its mother.'

'Let me be the judge of that.'

'Do I take that as an instruction?' She stared into his eyes.

'No.' Razi's smile was slow and sexy. 'That was a command.'

It was always the same, he realised. Lucy never wanted to talk about herself. She had no idea how much she gave away just by adopting that attitude. When she finally gave in enough to share a few anecdotes with him, she only confirmed what he already knew. Listening to her as she laughed and joked her way through her family history, he realised she had felt as much the cuckoo in the nest as he had, and that sharing what they had tonight had brought them closer than he would ever have believed possible. His focus now was on reassuring her. 'All that's in the past,' he said, 'and you have your future to look forward to.'

'Do I, Razi?'

He wished she wouldn't look so sad. He wanted to make her happy—especially when he thought of the lonely child she'd been and the self-doubting young woman she'd grown into. She hadn't told him that, of course—she didn't need to. Instead, she made every excuse for her family and none for herself. 'You did nothing wrong,' he protested when she insisted that she always managed to let her family down. 'Everyone wants to be loved. Everyone wants to be understood. Everyone wants to be heard, and you deserve all those things, Lucy.'

'My family does love me.' She made a wry face. 'They just don't get me.'

'I get you…' Touching her face, he kissed her again, thinking how lucky he was to have this time with her.

'It's not as if I was abandoned like you.'

'It's not as if you had a brother like Ra'id to look out for you.'

'My brothers would have looked out for me—if they'd stopped arguing long enough.'

'I'm sure they would,' he agreed, stifling the urge to take all of them on at once for letting her down. Their loss, he supposed, hiding his feelings from her.

'I'd like to meet your brother, Ra'id.'

'You will.'

There was silence as she took this in. Under what circumstances? He could feel her wondering. Would he smuggle her into the palace for a private audience? Would he employ her in the kitchens and have Ra'id inspect the staff? 'I'd be proud to introduce you to Ra'id.'

'You would?'

'How can you doubt it?'

Maybe because every idyll had to come to an end and theirs just had. She was already sensing Razi starting to distance himself. It was no coincidence he was moving away from her in every way he could, physically and mentally as light strengthened inside the pavilion. She clung to him as dawn broke and for a while he relented and they lay in silence, staring out at the pearly sky streaked with lavender and jasmine yellow, until they both, without saying a word, broke apart and moved away in separate directions.

'I'll get the coffee on,' he said as she thought about taking one last swim.

'It's light now,' she said when Razi frowned, 'and I promise I'll be careful.'

He stared at her for some time and then he let her go. It was more than an acknowledgement that she would take care in the water. When they looked at each other she was telling him she could do this on her own—all of it, and that he had to know that and accept it.

It was a brave stand, but with dawn came reality, and the reality was Razi was a king and she was no one. She could no more make a stand in his country than she could fly, but he stopped short of pointing this out and humiliating her. As she picked up her robe and slipped it on he drew her to him and kissed her briefly—it felt like one last time; one last kiss. 'That was quite a night,' he said dryly, releasing her.

'Yes, it was…'

The look they shared now spoke of more than sex. They

had confided in each other and grown closer just as now they must live apart. She shrugged, as if she could handle that too. 'Don't worry—I understand,' she said as if she were reassuring him. 'And I'll always treasure the confidences you shared with me.'

She turned and walked away proudly, deeply conscious of the child inside her, and of the love in her heart, both for that child and for the man who had fathered her baby. Razi had given her new confidence, and by opening up his heart to her last night he had changed her for good, because now she knew love—she knew how it felt to trust and to be trusted in return, and even if this wasn't going to end in the traditional happy-ever-after, she believed him when he said he would never part her from her child.

She had to believe.

He had always thought the desert changed him, freed him, but now he realised it was only the space it gave him to examine his thoughts that made the difference. As they drank their last coffee in front of the campfire he realised that with Lucy at his side exchanging solitude for companionship had proved even more productive and that *she* had freed something inside him. He'd let someone else in and he'd never done that before. He glanced at her sideways, admiring her composure. They knew where they stood now. He'd take care of her in every way he could, but they'd live their own lives. A night that had started in heat and passion had changed them both. He cared about her. He always would. Perhaps more than cared—perhaps even loved—but that didn't mean there could be a solution to this. She was carrying his child and that had made him instantly protective, but it wasn't love—it couldn't be; it was…something else. The nervous smiles Lucy was darting at him suggested her thoughts had turned to concern too. If only she could know how much he wanted this. If only he could tell her that a family was all he had ever longed for, but he'd always accepted there was a high price to pay for privilege and that for every night of pleasure the bank of duty would exact its revenge. He just hadn't known how much it would hurt. To block it out he turned to practicalities. 'When was your last scan?'

Lucy paused with the coffee cup halfway to her lips. She was sitting opposite Razi in front of the campfire he had rebuilt. Dressed in jeans and a jumper to fend off the early morning chill, she had been glad of the hot coffee to nurse after her swim. Now she put it down. Razi had brought out his phone, which seemed incongruous in the wilderness, but not half as incongruous as a sheikh taking care of her maternity concerns.

'You do have baby scans in England?' he pressed, shooting her one of his intense looks as he stabbed in some numbers.

'Of course we do.'

'Well? Have you had one yet?'

'I have my first appointment when I get back—on Friday.'

'And this scan is for how many weeks of pregnancy?'

'Twelve.' She blushed.

'Twelve—and do you know if everything is progressing well?'

'I presume it is.'

'You presume?'

Razi's tone was a dash of cold water in the face. She had seen the doctor to confirm her pregnancy and was following the protocol set up in her health authority area to the letter. There was only one reason she could think of for Razi putting pressure on her now. 'I won't know the sex of my baby for sure until around seventeen weeks.' When he found out it was a girl as she both knew and suspected in a crazy, mixed-up, newly pregnant way, would he quickly lose interest?

'I want to know you're both healthy,' Razi pointed out in a stinging response to that thought. 'Please allow me to speed up the process.'

'I know I'm having a baby girl.'

The astute sea-green gaze flicked up. 'Mother's instinct is wonderful, I'm sure, but if you don't mind I'd like a medical professional to check you're both okay.'

Reality was pouring in thick and fast now, and as Razi held her gaze all the history behind that remark was reflected in his eyes, and she realised no woman would ever convince him that anything she said was true until she proved herself—and that included Lucy Tennant.

And was there something wrong with employing a belt and braces approach where the health of her child was concerned? She settled for, 'Thank you.'

Razi raised his hand as the call connected and started talking rapidly in Sinnebalese. 'It's all arranged,' he said. 'We leave from here and go straight to the private clinic in the capital.'

'Our news won't be very private if you accompany me.'

'Of course I'll take you there. Who else is going to take you? You're my responsibility and it's my duty to make sure you have the best of care.'

His duty? She had been transformed by happiness up to that moment. She had seen so many emotions cross Razi's eyes while they had been sitting cross-legged round the fire. His expression had even warmed and softened briefly, but there was none of that now. She had been transformed during the course of a cup of coffee from night-time lover into daytime responsibility and it seemed that with every inch the sun crept above the horizon the distance between them was growing.

'If one of my employees needed medical attention,' he said, 'don't you think I would personally ensure they got it?'

She wanted to put her fingers in her ears and blot that out—that was what she thought. Other than that she didn't know what to think that didn't hurt like hell. And that was mean-minded of her, Lucy concluded as Razi stood up and started kicking sand over their fire. She had heard nothing but praise for staff relations at Maktabi Communications since taking a closer interest in a certain R. Maktabi's business card; she should be glad she was under the boss's protection.

But she wanted so much more than that…

Then it was about time she got used to the fact she wasn't going to get it.

It seemed only moments later that Razi brought the Jeep to a halt outside a gleaming white building. Life seemed that way because it took on a frenetic pace with Razi in it, Lucy concluded as a nurse in a starched uniform escorted them to the appropriate department. It was a relief to hear they were to be seen immediately—and less of a relief when there was no offer from Razi to wait outside the room where the scan would take place. By the time she had changed into a robe he had taken a seat in front of the screen. She climbed up on the examination couch and risked a faint smile as the radiographer squeezed cold jelly on her stomach and started the hunt for their tiny child.

'Well, I can tell you you're definitely pregnant.'

Lucy gasped with shock and excitement as a hectic heartbeat broke the anxious silence. Razi remained absolutely still and utterly intent.

'And expecting a healthy baby,' the radiographer confirmed to everyone's relief.

As the tense mood in the small room relaxed, Lucy thought the amplified heartbeat was the most wonderful sound she had ever heard. It was certainly the most thrilling and the most life-changing. 'I can't believe it,' she whispered, wondering if it was possible to explode with joy. 'I can't believe my little girl is growing safe inside me—she is safe, isn't she?' she anxiously confirmed. 'There's nothing wrong, is there?' The hair was standing up on the back of her neck. The radiographer had gone very quiet. She looked at Razi for reassurance as the radiographer continued his investigations.

'Just a minute, please,' the radiographer requested, focusing all of his attention on the screen. 'Can you hear that?'

Lucy strained her ears, and only then realised she was squeezing the life out of Razi's hand. 'What is it? Tell me?'

'You're not expecting one baby,' the radiographer announced in triumph. 'You're expecting twins.'

'What?' Lucy's mind blanked with shock. Then elation, disbelief, and Wow! No way! took its place, followed swiftly by acute alarm as she raced through some terrifying financial calculations in her head.

'Are you sure?' Razi demanded tensely.

'Absolutely sure,' the radiographer assured him. 'Here…you can see for yourself.' He pointed out first one tiny little child and then the other.

Razi exclaimed in Sinnebalese. He couldn't believe it. Everything suddenly seemed more real to him. He could safely say he was ecstatic. Having heard the babies' heart-beats on the monitor, suddenly he could picture them being a family.

Razi felt a swell of pride within him and he knew then that he had to protect Lucy. He never wanted the twins or their mother to feel ashamed of who they were.

'Lucy?' Razi prompted.

She was terrified. Totally overwhelmed. All her hard-won self-belief had just taken a serious knock. She had planned to raise her baby under her own strength even if that meant doing so here in Isla de Sinnebar, but now... How could she work or support herself and her babies? Where was her security? She would be at Razi's mercy.

'Twins usually come early,' the radiographer was con-tinuing, 'so you won't have so long to wait before you're holding them in your arms.'

She knew the man meant to be kind. She knew he was trying to reassure her, but the timescale she had been working on to support one baby had just flown out of the window.

'Aren't you pleased?' Razi demanded, touching her arm to reclaim her attention.

'I'm overwhelmed,' she said honestly.

Her mind was racing, leaving her numb from an over-load of excitement, emotion, love, as well as the sense of responsibility coming her way, and most of all her fear of failure. She could be stand-up, determined and as independ-ent-minded as she liked, but she wanted to have her inde-pendence and know that whatever happened with Razi, she could support her children. She had to try and build a stake before they were born, and then—

She found herself grabbing the arm of the radiographer and asking him to double-check.

'There is no doubt,' he said.

'Sorry,' she said, self-consciously letting go of his sleeve. 'It's just that I can't believe it.'

'Neither can I.' Razi felt a rush of jubilation speed through him. He gave her a kiss, while she, still in shock, remained stiffly unresponsive.

'I often see this reaction,' the radiographer informed them. 'Fathers are generally the ones on a high, while mothers count the cost in terms of coping and expense. But of course, in your case, that won't be a problem.'

Oh, wouldn't it? thought Lucy as the man bowed low to Razi. Why should she be any different from any other woman—especially when she had no intention of putting herself in Razi's debt? Her little family had got bigger and she couldn't support them on her own. Her fate was even more firmly in Razi's hands.

'So glad to be of service to you, Your Majesty,' the radiographer was adding. 'If there's anything else I can do for you—anything at all—please, just let me know.'

Helping Lucy down from the couch, Razi smiled the heart-stopping smile that under other circumstances would have filled her with love and confidence, but right now filled her with something much closer to apprehension.

CHAPTER SIXTEEN

OUTSIDE the hospital, Razi escorted Lucy to the Jeep, keeping a firm hold on her hand and on her shoulder.

'I'm taking you straight back to the palace,' he said, gunning the engine and roaring away. 'We'll have a brief chat there—' He held up one strong, tanned hand to silence her as his call connected. A few ecstatic phrases later he cut the line. Lucy didn't need to be fluent in Sinnebalese to get the gist. 'Aren't they shocked?' she asked as he stowed the phone.

'Shocked? Their ruling Sheikh is producing children two at a time? I should hope they're rejoicing. We're well on our way to founding a dynasty.

'Joke?' he said dryly when Lucy looked at him with concern. 'Let the world believe what it will.' He turned serious. 'The main thing for me is my children's health and happiness. Am I supposed to hide the fact that I'm delighted by the imminent arrival of twins?'

'No, of course not,' Lucy agreed faintly, except she didn't appear to be included in his plans. A new fire was burning in Razi's eyes. Since he'd discovered he was to be a father of two children his protective instincts were firing on all cylinders—and God help anyone who got in his way, including Lucy Tennant.

She couldn't have been more surprised or delighted at the immediacy with which Razi had acknowledged their babies, but on the reverse side of that coin was the fact that Razi was a king and leader of a country, and while acknowledging their children was more than she had expected it meant living life on his terms, which in turn meant yielding her freedom, especially as she was not expecting twins. And if that wasn't right for her, how could it be right for her babies?

'This is the late sheikh's palace,' Razi explained, slowing the Jeep in front of some towering golden gates. 'Until my new eco-palace is ready for occupation I'm afraid both I and my guest will have to put up with some unrestrained splendour.'

It was hard if not impossible to remain immune to Razi's upbeat mood. 'I'll do my best,' Lucy responded. But the joke was quickly over. They still had discussions ahead of them and the black-robed attendants with curving scimitars glinting at their sides didn't exactly reassure her.

'Welcome to the Palace of Bling unbridled,' Razi commented dryly as they passed beneath a golden arch. He drove on down a broad avenue that glittered as if it had been sprinkled with gold dust.

For all she knew, it had, Lucy realised, feeling another jolt to her confidence.

'Quartz crystals in the mix make the surface sparkle,' Razi explained.

There were glorious banks of flowers either side of this glittering highway, but what really claimed her attention was the massive structure rising in front of them like something out of the *Arabian Nights*. There were pink towers and white minarets standing like bookends either side of jewelled cupolas of beaten gold. If she'd been a tourist she would have been overwhelmed—she was still over-whelmed, but the last of her courage had just drained away and everything began to swim before her eyes. She felt faint and sick, knowing she didn't belong, that she could never belong and that the discussions ahead of her could only be disastrous.

'Modest, hmm?' Razi murmured dryly. 'But I call it home.

'Lucy?'

Grabbing hold of her, Razi pulled into the side. 'Drink,' he insisted passing her some water and turning the air-conditioning on full.

'Sorry, I just felt—'

'You don't have to apologise,' he insisted, still with his arm around her. 'I understand this must be overwhelming for you.' He waited until she had drunk the water and then pointed out of the window. 'I'm going to open it to the public. What do you think?'

Of walls studded with sparkling jewels—or formidable battlements decorated with pennants bearing his royal insignia? 'It's too much to take in,' she admitted, breath-ing a sigh of wonder.

'I'm going to use this palace to showcase our heritage. There will be a museum, as well as an art gallery—and we'll hold concerts,' he added with a grin that carved a place in her heart. 'You'll like that,' he teased. 'Karaoke?' he reminded her.

She bit back tears and smiled as if everything were won-derful, but Razi made her want so much—too much.

'Feeling better?' he confirmed. 'Ready to go on now?'

She nodded her head and sat up, tilting her chin to show her determination. She would have to get used to these bouts of weakness as well as the pangs of longing, Lucy concluded as Razi drove them the last hundred yards.

He parked up in front of a wide sweep of marble steps and then came round to help her out before the attendants even had chance to reach her door. He lifted her down and steadied her on her feet in front of him. 'Don't look so worried,' he murmured, touching her face, seemingly oblivious to the phalanx of soldiers lining up as a guard of honour. 'You've had quite a day.'

'And so have you,' she pointed out, starting to feel queasy again.

'Let me get you in the shade,' he said, ushering her forward.

Razi guided her down vaulted corridors packed with treasures. She couldn't even begin to take in such a wealth of gold and jewels and fabulous art. It would take a lifetime of visits, Lucy concluded. They came to a halt in front of an intricately decorated golden door. 'The harem,' Razi explained, holding the door for her. 'No, really,' he insisted when she looked at him in surprise. 'Though these days you're the only occupant—maybe I should do something about that…' His lips quirked. 'Triplets next time?'

There wouldn't be a next time. She understood he was only being kind. They'd discuss practicalities and then she'd go home. She didn't belong here. But at least it was cooler in the splendid golden room, though her cheeks quickly heated up when she noticed the erotic murals on the walls: beautiful women with sloe eyes and full, ruby lips, and handsome men with brooding faces. How could Razi settle for her? Not that he would. That had never been on the cards.

He led the way across a magnificent marble floor and

through an archway that led into an inner courtyard where cooling breezes and a shimmering fountain added to the relaxing ambience. He suggested she sit on a gilded bench beneath the shade of a glorious jacaranda tree frosted with frowsy pink blossom. She didn't need much persuading. The fat velvet cushions looked so inviting. But when she sat down and Razi joined her he took her hands in the type of grip a person used when they were about to tell you something you really didn't want to hear. 'Why do I think this is going to be bad?'

'At a guess? You've just had the most stunning news of your life, and your emotions are all over the place?'

But by keeping hold of her Razi wasn't helping her concerns. The fine stone fretwork blurred as she stared straight ahead, not wanting to hear anything he had to say. But she couldn't silence him.

'I want you to know everything, so you're protected from cruel gossip and innuendo. There was a marriage contract— Let me finish,' he insisted when she jerked away from him. 'It was nothing—'

'Nothing?' This was everything she'd feared. Her children would never know their father. What woman would want her husband's bastard children flaunted under her nose? At best they'd be hidden away in a remote part of the country. She couldn't stand the thought of it. She wanted to raise her children where they'd be free. 'I always knew there'd be someone,' she exclaimed, imagining a face similar to those beautiful young women she had seen depicted on the walls.

'There's no one, I promise you.' Razi took hold of her arms, bringing her in front of him. 'There's no one but you, the mother of my children.'

'But we can't always have what we want,' Lucy anticipated with eyes wide and wounded.

He didn't want to be so brutally frank with her, but
while his council had applauded the forthcoming proof of
his fruitfulness a foreign bride would rock the country to
its very foundation—even a foreign mistress flaunted in
front of the traditionalists would be a step too far. The cold
truth was, he would acknowledge their children and afford
them full rights and privileges, but Lucy had to go. He
couldn't have Lucy and the throne so he had no option but
to send her away. His life was pledged to a country—and
Lucy was right. He couldn't have what he wanted any
more than she could.

'You don't have to explain anything,' she said.

'Yes, I do,' he argued, touching her cheek so she had
nowhere to look but in his eyes. 'And for once, you have to
listen.' His duty was to defend a kingdom, to help it grow
and to provide heirs, but he would do everything he could
to protect Lucy from further hurt. It would take more than
a few days to build her confidence in him until it could never
be shaken and words wouldn't do it; he had to prove himself.

'I can't stand by and watch you with someone else,
Razi. I won't.' She was growing ever more heated. 'Not
when I know that no one can ever love you as I do.'

'You love me?' He was brought up short by this admission.

'You must know I love you,' she told him, frowning.

'How would I know that?'

Razi was right. She had never been brave enough to tell
him that she loved him. And after everything he had
confided in her she had never once told him that it could
be different, that a woman could love him and that his

loveless childhood was not the norm. She had been too wrapped up in the fact that a desert king with more power and wealth than she could imagine would never take up with a cook, and had never once considered that what Razi needed most was love, and that love was the one thing she could give him. She had thought him aloof, but when had she risked her feelings? She would walk through fire for him, but when had she told him that?

A cold hand gripped Lucy's throat at the thought that she had never told her parents how much she loved them either. But it was no use burying her face in her hands. She had to do something about it. She had Razi to thank for building her confidence to the point where she'd caught a glimpse of what she could be, and only herself to blame for losing her grip on that image. She was about to become a mother and that had changed her. She was a woman who was deeply in love with one man—a woman who mustn't allow the old insecurities to master her a second longer. 'Yes, I love you,' she said defiantly. 'Make what you will of that.'

He smiled inwardly at this return of the battler and he knew Lucy's words came straight from her wounded heart. He wouldn't hold her to them. He had never looked for love, let alone expected to find it. He had never guessed that Lucy felt anything more for him than passion and fascination for someone who came from a very different culture, a very different world. She had always seemed so business-like out of bed—all this talk of restaurants and shares in a business. However he felt about her was irrelevant. He'd learned to smother feelings like those years back.

He told her everything about the supposed marriage contract with his cousin and how it could never have been, and that it was a cheap trick dreamed up by Leila's father. 'He couldn't have known that as far as my own father was concerned I didn't exist. I never even met him,' he explained to an incredulous Lucy. 'My father, the ruling Sheikh of Isla de Sinnebar, never once acknowledged me during his lifetime as his son.'

'Oh, Razi—'

He shook off her tender concern. 'That's why I'm so proud to acknowledge my children—and why I'll always be there for them—' He stopped, seeing the fear in her eyes. This was about reassuring Lucy, not about him. 'As my father never mentioned me, why would he arrange a marriage for me? I knew at once that the document Leila's father presented was a forgery, but I had it scrutinised by experts, just to be sure. And now it's all been put to bed.'

'With a large pay-off?' she interrupted, still fearing the worst.

He could see where this was going. 'Lucy, this is nothing like your situation.'

She pulled her hands out of his grasp.

'Things are going to be very different for you,' he stressed. 'I only wish there was time now for me to lay out all the plans I've made for you.'

'You've made plans for me?' she said softly.

He glanced around. 'Can't you see one of your wonderful restaurants here in this courtyard once I open this palace to the public? A café in the courtyard—and perhaps another restaurant for gourmet eating in the gardens?'

He was all fired up with his plans for Lucy's future, but at the back of his mind was the knowledge that he must shower and change into formal attire before the council meeting…

The more he thought about the meeting, the more he

thought about what could be if life were shunted onto a different track. And he could do that. He could do anything he wanted to as long as it embraced his vow to Isla de Sinnebar...

Now a plan was forming in his mind. He felt quite cool and certain as he mulled it over. This was right. It was hard to understand why he hadn't seen it before. 'I have a meeting,' he explained to Lucy, 'and I can't be late.' He was becoming more eager to take the action that would irrevocably change his life.

'Razi, wait,' Lucy said, picking up on his sense of urgency.

Taking hold of her hands, he pressed his lips to the palm of each of them in turn, and then, cursing softly in Sinnebalese, he shook his head regretfully. 'There's never enough time.'

'No, I can see that,' she said quietly.

'I'll have a maid show you to your room. A bath has been run for you.' He was already striding away. 'Food and juices are waiting for you along with your luggage.' He turned at the door to shoot her a grin. 'You might want to change your clothes and relax while I'm gone. Take a swim. Ask for a guided tour of the palace. Do anything you want to do.' He felt exhilarated and sure, though acutely conscious of the clock ticking as he spread his arms wide to bow and back away. 'Take care, mother of my children. Relax in the knowledge that from this moment on your life is transformed. Oh, and I'll be back before you know it,' he added with a wicked grin.

This time when Razi's lips tugged in the familiar heart-stopping smile, Lucy couldn't return his smile. Her life had been transformed, both by pregnancy and today by the knowledge that two small lives depended on her. She was a woman of purpose now, not a mistress of idleness who needed her days filling with aimless meandering. Was Razi's offer of creating a restaurant here at the palace a sop to keep her happy? She didn't know what to believe any more.

As she watched him stride away it was easy to see that Razi's life was full of purpose, but if he imagined she was going to live to his prescription—wait until he could find time for her, as his mother had waited—or, worse still, that he would be hard-pressed to find space in his packed diary for their children, he had underestimated the woman he had helped to grow in confidence. She loved him and to Lucy love meant working together to build a future. If she could never be his wife, she could at least put her skills at the service of his country. Razi had mentioned an eco-palace in construction, hadn't he? And a palace would have kitchens...

As she picked up the internal phone to call for transport Lucy realised she was not going to go back to England and consult lawyers, she was going to stay here in Isla de Sinnebar. She would live in some remote part where she could cause Razi no embarrassment, but she would keep her children with her and she would work for the good of Razi's people. And if that meant being a pioneer, setting a new trend, fine, that was what she'd do. She'd work discreetly so as not to offend anyone, but she'd do it, Lucy concluded, jutting out her chin.

CHAPTER SEVENTEEN

HE NEVER failed to feel a sense of history when he entered the golden chamber—the vaulted roofs, the jewelled panelled walls, the silent air of majesty. As all the men currently seated around the council table rose to greet him he was conscious of their wise faces turned to him and the trust in so many pairs of eyes. He stood for a moment, feeling the weight of destiny in his hands. He indicated that everyone should sit down, while he remained standing at the head of the table. He was prepared to sacrifice everything for Lucy. He had known this from the moment he had realised that a life of lies and self-deception wasn't for him.

He greeted his brother sheikhs and then repeated the wonderful news about his twins. Then to absolute silence he explained his proposal before calling on his council to vote on his decision to cede the Phoenix throne in favour of working alongside the woman he loved as a common man for the good of Isla de Sinnebar and his people. He finished by saying, 'I want you all to know that the decision I have made has been mine and mine alone. This was a thing I had to judge entirely for myself.'

Now he could only wait for their verdict.

He didn't have to wait long. The oldest and most trusted

advisor spoke for the rest. They supported him whole-heartedly. They believed in his vision of the future. If that vision included a foreign bride, they supported him in that too. He would keep the throne and their trust. Then they raised their fists and hailed him until they were hoarse as their undisputed leader.

'Stop the cavalcade!'

He sprang out of the lead limousine before it had drawn to a halt. Full of concern for Lucy's safety, he thanked destiny for urging him to see his new eco-palace in construction before he went on to his next meeting. He was eager to see Lucy too and his plan had been to conclude his business as swiftly as he could before driving straight back to her with his news. It had never occurred to him that he would arrive at the site of his new palace to find a pregnant woman in jeans, sneakers and a high-visibility jacket with a hard hat on her head and clipboard in her hand, conferring with Asif, his site manager.

His first action was to order his security staff to stay with the cavalcade. His second was to stride over to Lucy.

'What do you think you're doing?'

'Working,' she said, giving him a look he hadn't seen before.

For once he rued the fact that official limousines had blacked-out windows, but he didn't need to see inside the vehicles to know that everyone in the official party would be riveted by this unexpected distraction. 'Do you have to do this? Can't you see how dangerous it is?'

'Dangerous?' She frowned. 'I'm in no danger. Are you sure it isn't the idea of a woman working that's getting to you, Razi?'

Asif faded into the background with a respectful bow.

'You're pregnant.'

'Yes—not ill.'

'You're putting yourself in danger on a building site.'

'Asif was with me and now you're here. I'm appropriately dressed and I won't take any risks.'

'You don't have to work.'

The scorching look she gave him said Lucy would never subscribe to the world's view of how a wealthy man's lover should behave, but would plough her own furrow. Did he like that? Could his vaunted ego take it?

He had the opportunity to start a new page in the history of Isla de Sinnebar, one where opportunity was open to all, and there were no gender divides where jobs were concerned. He could use his vast wealth to change lives and Lucy wanted to be part of that—he wanted her to be part of it. As she stared up at him and firmed her dainty jaw he wondered if he'd left it too late to convince her he wasn't the tyrant she thought him—too late to explain that she didn't have to go to extremes to escape his mother's fate?

'I thought you were different, but you're such a dinosaur, Razi.'

'Am I?' he said dryly as she turned away.

'Women shouldn't do men's work?' She tipped her chin as she stopped to confront him. 'You can probably set it down in law now you've got the country at your command.'

'I can definitely send you back to the palace.'

'Where I can write my report? Good,' she said, refusing to be dismayed. 'I'll have it ready for you on your return.'

She was standing in the harem by the console table she had turned into a desk when Razi entered. She didn't need to turn around to know he was there or that he was still dressed in robes. She could hear the swish of the fabric as he walked towards her and inhale its scented folds. She remained standing, with her back turned to him, staring out across the shaded courtyard dreaming of all the things she would like to change in Isla de Sinnebar, given the opportunity. Razi, for one.

'Lucy…'

The swish of his robes, the click of the prayer beads at his waist, the fine, clean scent…

She turned, her heart juddering at the sight of him. She would never, no matter how long she knew him, become accustomed to the sight of Razi. It was more than his astonishing good looks. When he was in western clothes Razi carried the scent of soap and toothpaste and warm clean man, but the robes of state added the spices of the East and the unmistakeable scent of power. He was a formidable sight, an untouchable sight, this man she loved.

'What do you have to say?' he said quietly.

She intended to be calm and rational, but in the event it all burst out of her. 'I want you to be proud of me—I want my children to have a mother who leads from the front—'

'And you have to work on a building site to do that?'

'Whatever it takes! I realise it wouldn't be right for everyone, but I want to work. I want to earn my keep. I don't want to be your mistress-in-waiting.' Her voice broke. She had every intention of making a stand, or reminding him of his mother's plight, but pregnancy had made her so emotional and all she could think about was Razi's mother waiting in this same room, looking out at the same view as she waited for a ruling Sheikh around whom Helena's world had revolved. 'I want to make a difference.'

'You can do that without working on a building site!'

'Don't roar at me.' She hugged herself. 'I'm pregnant.'

Now they both almost laughed.

'I didn't mean to embarrass you, Razi. I just thought if I could talk to Asif and the architects on site before they put the kitchen walls in place I could come up with a really good working plan...' Her voice tailed away. Razi's expression was inscrutable.

Seconds ticked by tensely and then his gaze flicked over the papers she had laid out on the table. 'And are these your notes?'

'Yes...'

He walked past her and stood, staring down, and then he picked up her clipboard. Having scanned her bullet-pointed notes and the scheme she had sketched out, he admitted, 'This is good.'

She had to tamp down the excitement inside her. If she was going to stay here she had to prove herself effective. 'I thought if the kitchens could cater for the largest event— or just a family meal—and you have sections that can be brought into play, or shut off—'

'Yes, I see,' Razi said thoughtfully. 'We'll sit down with the architects tomorrow and discuss this in detail.'

'We will?'

'Unless you don't want to be part of the discussions?'

'Of course I do.' Her head was immediately full of more ideas.

'Well? What did you think of the site I chose for the eco-palace?' he probed, acting nonchalant as if it didn't matter hugely to him.

Did love at first sight work with a building site? It just had, Lucy concluded. Yes, there were cranes and diggers

and portable buildings and containers, not to mention
squads of men in hard hats and high-visibility vests
swarming over the scaffolding, but the site itself, framed
by mountains and bordered by a sparkling river of the
same ice-cold water she had bathed in back at the oasis,
was nothing short of fabulous. She'd stood in silence,
breathing the warm, spicy air, knowing it was where she
wanted to be.

And could never be, because one day Razi must take a
wife.

'Well?' he demanded. 'First impressions?'

She refocused on Razi's project—his palace, his life—
and, with the utmost reluctance, her reality. 'You're very
lucky.' She remembered the wise old site manager, Asif,
wearing a bright yellow hard hat over his headdress waving
to her as she was driven away. She'd waved back, wondering if she'd ever see the building site again. 'It's absolutely
beautiful,' she confessed wistfully, 'and the possibilities are
endless.' Unfortunately, the possibilities open to her were not.

'You know I'd never keep you here against your will?'
Razi demanded softly, running a fingertip down her cheek.
'With your talents you have so much to offer the world.'

He pulled away to look around. 'Seeing you here in this
place that was almost a prison for my mother—' His mouth
clamped shut and she knew what he was feeling. 'The bird
in the gilded cage.' He laughed, but there was no humour
in his voice. 'There'll never be another,' he vowed, almost
as if speaking to himself.

He ran his fingers across her makeshift desk, which
Lucy suddenly realised was almost certainly made of solid
gold. 'All this excess brought my mother nothing but
misery.' Razi's angry gesture at something he couldn't

change ripped her heart out. 'All this extravagant glitter is tainted with sadness, which is why I could never live here.' His eyes were fierce with the need for her to understand. 'I just hope that when I turn it over to the public—'

'It will be a wonderful and happy place,' Lucy exclaimed, unable to keep quiet a moment longer. 'I can see it now—facilities for culture and education…and for fun, Razi.' She smiled with encouragement as ideas for the palace bombarded her. She couldn't have been happier that Razi intended preserving the old palace so people could see how previous generations had lived. Whatever the history behind it, the workmanship was astonishing— the mosaics, the gold work, the mirrors, framed with carved gilt figures and tumbling ribbons so finely worked. 'I promise you,' she exclaimed with passion, 'this is going to be a great attraction. I can see it now. This old palace will come alive for all sorts of people and will become a talking point in the worldwide tourist industry. I doubt anyone could come up with a better competitive differential, if they tried.'

'A competitive differential?' Razi interrupted.

Was that humour on his face?

'Are you intending to become a businesswoman now?'

'I do have dreams,' she admitted.

'Some people—and I am one of them—would call that vision. They would go on to say that certain people are blessed with the determination to make that vision concrete, and that those people make a real difference in the world.' Picking up the scheme she'd drawn, he added, 'It seems to me like you've taken the first step towards doing that with this plan of yours.'

She reached out to take the drawing from him, but he wouldn't let it go. 'First a cake tin,' he murmured dryly, his green eyes so warm with humour she thought her heart would burst with happiness, 'and now a kitchen design.' He smiled the slow, sexy smile she realised in that moment she had been desperately starved of.

'Perhaps it's time to inject a little romance into this relationship?' he suggested darkly.

'I thought we were going to sit down and talk?'

'I do have something to tell you,' he admitted, 'but it can wait.'

Somehow, Razi's hand had enclosed hers and the drawings he'd been holding were back on the table.

Am I dreaming? Lucy wondered as he drew her into his arms. Should she pinch herself? 'Razi…?' Her eyes searched his. 'Where do we go from here?'

'Speaking for myself,' he said dryly, 'I'm finding it hard to get past the sight of you in your hard hat—though I'd make a few changes,' he admitted, his expression growing serious.

'You would?' she said anxiously.

'Yes…' He touched her arms lightly, which was enough for her body to respond with indecent eagerness to nothing more than the brush of his fingertips. 'I'd cancel the jeans, and dress you in a pair of very short shorts. The heavy boots could stay—they set off your fabulous legs.' He shrugged. 'The clipboard and pen could stay too—though I'd add a pair of really heavy specs so you look incredibly stern and enormously severe.'

'Razi…I don't know what to say.'

'There's no need to talk at all—unless you have some suggestions of your own to make?'

CHAPTER EIGHTEEN

'SUGGESTIONS of my own?' Thoroughly caught up in Razi's mood, Lucy forced a frown as she pretended to think about it. 'I'm happy to leave it all up to you—but just remember one thing.'

'Which is?' Heat radiated from him as he eased onto one hip.

'You're mine. And I'll never let you go.'

His face creased in the familiar grin. 'It's about time we agreed on something.'

Passion scorched through her like a lava stream as he dragged her into his arms. 'Well?' she managed to fire back as he stared down at her. 'I need you.' She writhed against him with frustration to prove how much.

'You think I don't know that?' His laugh was low and husky and amused.

It was Mac's voice—Razi's voice—the voice she loved. It was the tone of voice she had missed and adored—the voice of the man she loved.

And the wall—with its lurid depictions of lovemaking in every form—was the best friend she'd ever had, Lucy registered wildly, consumed by savage heat as Razi stripped her naked before proving how fast a desert king could lose his robe.

He had her at the first thrust. He was everything she wanted, and if there was a way for them all to be together, she felt that now they stood a chance of finding it.

Throwing back her head, she urged him on, while Razi loved her with an insatiable hunger that matched her own. He was her man, her mate. She loved him and she would fight for him with everything she'd got. She wailed convulsively as the first climax hit her, but instead of releasing him she dug her fingers into his shoulders and wrapped her legs even more tightly around his waist, daring him to let her go.

'Let you go?' Razi's lips tugged with amusement as he briefly paused. 'I would sooner join a monastery than consider life without you.'

'Don't you dare lie to me,' she warned him, sinking her teeth into his shoulder, before gasping with surprise and pleasure when he pounded into her again. 'And don't you dare stop until I tell you to stop,' she added fiercely, shrieking with pleasure as he bounced her hips against the wall.

But when she felt the tidal wave of pleasure was close it was time to bring some plans of her own into play. 'Now slowly,' she ordered him, relishing every deep, lingering thrust. And when his guard was down in those few last moments before she too would lose control, she took him to the hilt, and, using her muscles, worked him in a way she knew he loved until it was Razi who broke first and she who soothed him down in triumph. 'You're mine,' she told him fiercely as his heartbeat steadied. 'Mine—and I won't share you with anyone.'

'Share me?' Razi demanded with amusement as he lowered her carefully to the ground. 'Do you really think there would be anything left by the time you've finished with me?'

Glancing down, she hummed. 'I don't know, there seems plenty…'

'Only because I'm with you.' Dipping his head, he stared into her eyes. 'That's why I don't need or want anyone else.'

'What about when you're married?'

'I'll want you twice as much.'

She looked at him aghast when he laughed. 'But your wife,' she choked out as all the old doubts reared up to taunt her. She was what Razi wanted in bed, but she had always known that when it came to choosing a bride it would have to be a diplomatic match for the good of the kingdom. What would that mean for her babies? She could be as determined as she liked, but she could never bear the pain of seeing another woman at Razi's side.

'I don't want anyone else,' Razi reassured her, staring into her eyes. 'Why should I?'

She wasn't listening. 'I thought I could handle anything to be with you, but I can't take my happiness at someone else's expense—I could never do any of the things required of a mistress.'

'Will you calm down?' Razi demanded gently. 'You're upsetting the babies.'

'You fight dirty,' Lucy protested, only quietening when Razi wrapped his arms around her.

'I never said I'd play fair.'

'So what happens next?'

'What happens next will be set down in law,' he soothed her. 'I will make you my wife so I can keep you working. Oh, yes, I'll make you work,' he said when she looked at him.

'Wait, wait, wait—wind back a bit. Did you say wife?'

'There's plenty to stretch your talents here in Isla de Sinnebar—and I wouldn't dream of wasting such a valuable resource.'

'Razi,' she cut in. 'Are you teasing me or are you serious?'

'Do I mean you're going to work? Absolutely. Do I mean you're going to be my wife? Yes—if you'll have me?'

'Oh, yes, yes, yes—I think I can safely assure you I'd be happy to accept both positions. But what about your people? They would never accept me—'

'They already have.'

'What? How can they? Please stop teasing me and explain.'

'There's no need to bore you with the detail—one day, maybe,' he said softly. 'Let's just say they truly welcome you as their Queen. Oh, and did I mention how hard you'll be working?'

'You did say something,' she agreed dryly, smiling into his eyes.

'Along with being my first, my best, my only wife, and the only woman I will ever love for the rest of my life, you're going to be in charge of all the royal catering facilities as well as the mother of two children. That should satisfy all your feminist inclinations and keep you out of mischief for the foreseeable future.'

She looked at him and for a long moment neither of them spoke. 'So you really are serious?' she said at last.

'Of course I'm serious.'

'We're to be married…'

'How could I let you go when I've watched you sleeping in my arms, when I've seen the dawn dust your skin with gold and watched your eyes light with love and happiness—'

'And you're a romantic?'

'Of course.' Razi's face creased in the familiar smile. 'How's this? Even your shadow throws light.'

'Hmm—not bad.'

'Or this—I won't let you go.'

Did he mean it?

'But what about Isla de Sinnebar?' she said, turning serious.

'All the more reason for me to do what is right. And this is right, Lucy.'

Razi spoke with such confidence that when he started whispering to her in his own language in a way that soothed and convinced and seduced all at the same time it took all she'd got to root out her last doubt. 'So I won't be locked away in some love nest?'

'That's a colourful picture,' he murmured, backing her slowly across the room. 'Locking you in the kitchen, I could understand...'

They shared a look that told Lucy the mistakes of the past would never be repeated, and then they embraced, fiercely and passionately until they sank to the floor where they stood. This time Razi's lovemaking was slow and tender. He used all his skill to draw out her pleasure, and all the while he told her how much he loved her. By the time he released her they had moved far beyond hurt and confusion to a new ease and confidence that bound them together in a way that words never could.

They showered together—which took quite a lot of time. Fortunately, they dressed much faster, and then Razi drove Lucy back to the building site that would soon be his new palace, and, incredibly, their family home. Knowing they would live together in such a beautiful place was almost more than Lucy could take in and she made Razi tell her it was so over and over again.

It was as if she was seeing the half-finished building through completely new eyes, she realised when he finally convinced her. Had she noticed how seamlessly the sandstone structure blended into the desert landscape? Or how the purple mountains surrounding it provided a majestic frame? The colours seemed more vivid than ever—the golden sand and turquoise ocean, the green of the parkland being carefully cultivated in front of the lagoon where one day soon their children would play. This truly was the place where reality and fantasy met.

'You have no idea how much I love you—or how amazing you look,' Razi observed with a grin as they linked fingers.

They had both chosen to wear traditional robes for this visit to their new home. Razi's robe was heavy blue silk with a matching flowing headpiece and a gold *agal*, while Lucy's robe was softer sky-blue chiffon trimmed with silver embroidery, and she had to admit she felt a lot cooler than she would have done in western clothes.

'Are you happy?' Razi demanded, bringing her round to face him.

'I can't begin to tell you.'

'Then I'll have to find a way,' he said as he drew her into the shadows where her pale skin wouldn't burn.

As he caressed her face she caught hold of his hand and brought it to her cheek. 'I love you,' she whispered, still finding it incredible that she could say that, and that this strong, dark prince of the desert had told her that he loved her in return.

'You're so much more than I deserve,' he said, and when

she looked at him in surprise he shook his head. 'Why can't you believe how special you are?'

'Because I'm nothing special?' Lucy announced in her usual blunt way.

'Nothing special?' Throwing back his head, Razi laughed. 'I think you're looking for compliments,' he accused as the desert wind whipped his hair into a tangle.

Before she had chance to deny this, he added, 'You're brave and determined and strong—not to mention capable and talented.'

'Go on—I can't get enough of this now. Though you are starting to make me sound a like a trick pony.'

Razi narrowed his eyes. 'I was about to add—and sexier than any woman has any right to be.'

'That's much better,' Lucy approved, sharing Razi's smile.

'I love you, Lucy Tennant,' he stated frankly. 'And I want to share my life with you.'

'No ifs, buts, or maybes?' she said wryly.

'No doubts ever. And if I have to spend the rest of my life convincing you, then I'll sign up now. You're the only woman I want. You're the only mother I could ever want for my children.'

'Why?'

'Because I know you'll fight with everything you've got for them, and for me, and for all the people of the Isla de Sinnebar when they call you their Queen.'

'Their Queen?' Lucy echoed incredulously.

'Why so surprised?' Razi demanded with a nonchalant shrug. 'Haven't you realised yet that I'll stop at nothing to keep a good chef?'

EPILOGUE

THE women came for her at dawn. Lucy had spent the night in the tented city amongst her people, guarded by the royal security troops. But she longed for Razi. She longed for the last of the barriers keeping them apart to be removed. And, yes, she longed to step beyond the silken veil. The women Razi had sent to prepare her for their Sheikh would help her do that. Clothed in colourful robes like so many jewelled butterflies, they clustered round her, kohl-lined eyes smiling with excitement.

Slipping off her sandals, Lucy padded wide-eyed into the bridal tent, her own private sanctuary of luxury and warmth. Light streamed from a thousand tiny brass lanterns, and there was incense burning. Soft carpets tickled her feet and plump cushions in shades of soft pink and burnished gold were arranged all around the perimeter of the uniquely feminine pavilion. There was fruit and jugs of juice, and honeyed pastries piled in tempting mountains on low pierced brass tables, but Lucy had only one thought in her mind, and that was Razi. Only he could satisfy the hunger she felt now.

They bathed her in warm, scented water, before drying her on the softest of towels. Every hair on her body, other than her waist-length, honey-coloured tresses, her eyebrows and eyelashes, was then painstakingly removed—with the emphasis on pain, Lucy registered, biting down hard on her bottom lip as she told herself it would all be worth it if she could just keep in mind the rewards that would definitely follow.

After this they brushed her body until it tingled, before massaging her with fragrant oils that added to her sensitivity. Then she stood with all the confidence in her naked body Razi had given her and raised her hands as they slipped a cobweb-fine shift over her head. Next they seated her on cushions where she had her hands and feet decorated with intricate swirls and dots of henna, and when that was done her clean, scented hair was first polished with silk and then braided loosely.

Only then did they bring out the wedding robe she had chosen. In the palest shade of pink silk chiffon, it twinkled with diamonds and platinum hand-embroidery. There were jewelled slippers for her feet, and she would carry in her hands the good wishes of her people represented by semi-precious stones and gold coins painstakingly threaded onto a great ribbon of glittering light that would dazzle as she walked. This traditional royal Sinnebalese wedding scarf would be wound around her hands and Razi's during the ceremony that followed, binding them together for all eternity.

'There's just one more thing,' one of the women told her as they arranged Lucy's veil. 'A gift from the Sheikh,' she said, laying the golden casket at Lucy's feet.

'We need what's inside to secure your veil,' the same woman confided as Lucy trailed her fingertips across the intricately worked golden box. Trust Razi to put a packet of kirby grips in a gold box the size of this one, she was thinking before she opened the lid.

She gasped in shock. It appeared Razi's economies had bypassed his wedding gift to her. Nestled snugly on a night blue velvet ground, a fabulous chain of pink and white diamonds flamed and glittered with all the colours of the rainbow. She touched them reverently and then pulled her hand away. 'I can't—I mean, I don't—'

'Don't worry, Sheikha,' one of the hand-maidens told her. 'We'll arrange them for you...'

'I'm going to wear them?' She sat stock-still as they draped her in diamonds that felt surprisingly cool and soothing against her brow. The large central diadem, which was the size of the pigeon's egg, counterbalanced the weight of the rest so it held her veil in place. Diamonds were far more effective than kirby grips, Lucy conceded dryly as one of the women held up a mirror so she could see her reflection.

'Now do you see why I love you?'

At the sound of Razi's voice, all the women got up in a rustle of skirts, bowing low to their Sheikh as they backed their way out of the bridal pavilion.

'Should you be here?' Lucy demanded, slanting kohl-enhanced eyes to drink him in.

'I do as I please.' He said this with all the old humour. 'And I'm pleased to see you have taken to your new role as if to the manner born.'

'Like you?' Lucy suggested wryly. They shared a look that said neither of them had been born to this, but they were both ready to devote themselves to the country and to their family, and to each other.

'The old days are over,' Razi said, bringing Lucy to her feet in front of him. 'We will walk to our wedding as equals.'

'Some of the old ways are worth preserving…'

'Do I take it that means you enjoyed your preparations?'

'Being prepared for the Sheikh?' She shrugged ruefully. 'Yes, I liked most of it—though some of it was painful.'

'They hurt you?'

'I shall expect a suitable reward.'

'Then I must ensure that you get it.'

She exclaimed with delight as Razi teased her with his lips and with his teeth and with his tongue. 'I'll hold you to that.'

'Just hold me,' he said, inhaling deeply as he dropped kisses on her neck. 'Amber, jasmine and lemon grass.'

'The scent you designed for me.'

'And which will be all you wear tonight, and for every night from now on.'

She shivered with delicious anticipation as Razi took her hand in his.

She barely noticed anything for the next hour, other than the man at her side in his warrior robes of unrelieved black. Razi was a magnificent sight. Beyond the heavy gold *agal* holding his headdress in place and the fearsome Khanjar at his waist, he needed no decoration, and when he placed the diamond band onto her wedding finger and pledged his love, she knew that sometimes fairy tales did come true. He was her warrior king, her dark prince of the desert, and she loved him more than life itself.

What would her rowdy brothers make of little Lucy now? she wondered as the marriage ceremony ended in fierce shouts of joy from the throats of thousands of tribesmen seated on horseback. Her whole family had fallen silent for the first time that she could remember at the news that she was expecting twins, and then the noisiest discussion she could remember had broken out on the subject of whether some men had unusual advantages in the fertility stakes—one discussion she really hadn't wanted to get into.

As soon as the marriage ceremony on the beach beneath the flower-strewn canopy was over Razi's first duty was to lead her towards the Phoenix throne and present her to his brother, Ra'id, who had been seated in Razi's place for this one day to show him honour. Lucy shivered, remembering Ra'id was known as The Sword of Vengeance. Her first sight of him had left a fearsome impression of a dark force of nature lit by molten rays of sunlight shimmering around the golden throne that seemed to frame him in a ring of fire. She tensed as Ra'id stood and his shadow fell across her. He was a stern, darkly handsome man, who, having dipped his head to acknowledge her, embraced his brother warmly.

'What do you think of Ra'id?' Razi murmured as they walked on.

She was still shaken by the meeting, but she opted for the truth. 'He looks lonely.'

'Lonely?' Razi demanded incredulously. 'The man known as The Sword of Vengeance, lonely?' He shook his head as if she had a lot to learn. 'My brother, Ra'id, is the most powerful man in the Middle East.'

'And even powerful men need someone to love and need to be loved in return,' she insisted.

Razi smiled at her. 'Then I can only hope my brother is as lucky in love as I have been.'

'As we have been...'

Razi squeezed her hand. 'As we have been,' he repeated softly.

Her family was struck dumb again and it was a shock to see her mother crying. 'I love you,' Lucy said, touching her mother's arm.

They shared a glance, and then to her surprise her mother grasped her hand and brought it to her lips. 'I love you too,' she said, almost with desperation in her voice.

'We'll see them later,' Razi told Lucy to reassure her as the bridal procession moved on. 'The wedding celebrations continue for a week.'

'A week?'

The concern in her voice made him smile. 'Sadly, we have a prior engagement that will keep us away for the first half day.'

'Oh, no.' Then seeing the stallion waiting for them, caparisoned in gold and traditionally woven fabrics, she understood. Springing up, Razi lifted her in front of him and in a flurry of hooves they galloped away.

'Another tradition,' he assured her, holding her close as he acknowledged the cheers of the tribesmen as they rode the length of the seashore. But instead of turning back to return to the wedding party, he rode on towards a beach over the dunes and out of sight.

'Razi, we can't do this,' Lucy exclaimed, glancing over her shoulder.

'If you think I'm going to waste a single moment when I know you've been prepared for the Sheikh…' Reining in the stallion, he sprang to the ground and, reaching up, brought her down beside him.

They fell into each other's arms, kissing tenderly, deeply, passionately, rejoicing in this, their first kiss as husband and wife. Then, ever the pragmatist, Razi eased

Lucy's wedding robe from her shoulders and let it drop to the ground.

'Wow, that was easy,' Lucy remarked. 'Let's hope this form of traditional dress never goes out of fashion.'

Razi's face creased in a smile as he viewed the scattered silk. 'No buttons—no zips?' He shrugged. 'Who's going to better that design?'

'I agree.' Raising her arms, Lucy laced her fingers through Razi's thick, strong hair. 'So? What do you think, Your Majesty?'

'What do I think?' He shrugged off his robe and tossed his headdress aside, before kneeling at her feet. 'I think there are quite a few old customs worth preserving.'

She moaned with pleasure as he tasted her and his stubble scraped her newly naked skin. 'Another tradition?' she managed breathlessly.

'It will be,' he assured her.

Some considerable time later, when they had emerged from the bath-warm ocean, Razi found something in the pocket of his robe.

'What is it?' Lucy said as he first teased her and then slowly unfurled his hand. She gasped when she saw the dainty replica of her wedding ring studded in diamonds.

'I had it made so you can add it to the tiny slipper you wear to remind you that your prince has come.'

'Again?'

Razi laughed as he added the ring to the fine chain around her neck, and when they'd stopped laughing Lucy turned serious. 'Razi, what can I possibly give you to compare with all your fabulous wedding gifts to me?'

'Two babies?' Razi suggested dryly. 'Quite a bonus, I'd say—when all I've ever wanted is your love.' He grinned.

'But I'm sure I'll think of something else, given enough time. And as we have all the time in the world ahead of us…'

'Amen to that,' Lucy said softly as Razi kissed her.

SURRENDER TO THE
PLAYBOY SHEIKH

KATE HARDY

Kate Hardy lives on the outskirts of Norwich with her husband, two small children, a dog—and too many books to count! She wrote her first book at age six, when her parents gave her a typewriter for her birthday. She had the first of a series of sexy romances published at twenty-five and swapped a job in marketing communications for freelance health journalism when her son was born, so she could spend more time with him. She's wanted to write for Mills & Boon since she was twelve—and when she was pregnant with her daughter, her husband pointed out that writing Medical Romances would be the perfect way to combine her interest in health issues with her love of good stories. Kate is always delighted to hear from readers—do drop in to her website at www. katehardy.com.

For Liz Fielding—whose friendship I appreciate
as much as her books (and her gorgeous
sheikhs!)—with love

CHAPTER ONE

'Thank you so much for your time, Your Highness.' The journalist was practically curtseying to him. Something Karim really, really hated.

But he managed to stay polite. 'No problem. Nice to meet you.' He was aware that he was wearing just as false a mask as the journalist was.

No doubt she thought she had some great quotes to use in a diary piece. This was the kind of party that always made the gossip columns—high-level people from the business world, politicians and hotshot brokers and a sprinkling of actors and pop stars.

And he knew exactly what the spin was going to be where he was concerned. That His Royal Highness Karim al-Hassan had been partying hard, with a champagne reception every day for the last week and languorous lunch engagements that started before midday and never finished before three.

Five years ago, they might've been right. He'd partied with the best of them. Burned the candle at both ends.

But now…it was old news. Though in some respects it suited him—people were nowhere near as guarded with him when they thought he was just out for fun, a charming and sophisticated dilettante.

What the newspapers all missed was that Karim's glass

usually held sparkling mineral water rather than gin and tonic. That he had a retentive memory and didn't need to make notes—he could recall every detail of a meeting and follow it up with letters or reports as necessary. And none of them had any idea that when he left a lunch meeting or a party, he'd be working on complicated figures or reading reports from focus groups until the early hours.

Since his father had entrusted him with such an important task—developing tourism and foreign investment in Harrat Salma—Karim had been more businessman than playboy. He'd done the research, met the right people, made the right contacts, written his business plans. And now he needed to make the most of it. He'd set up a series of meetings with people he knew would bring in investment that would help create more jobs, better infrastructures and the chance to develop sustainable energy sources in his country. All of which would help put Harrat Salma at the forefront.

Even as he chatted pleasantly among a group of people, smiling and making appropriate comments in the right places to show he'd been listening, Karim's mind was working on his business plan. Though something nagged at him to turn round. Like a whisper in his head that wouldn't go away.

Eventually, he gave in.

Turned round.

The woman across the other side of the room caught his attention immediately, despite the fact that she was clearly dressed to be invisible rather than to shine. Her hair was an ordinary brown, caught back at the nape. Her black shift dress was simple, elegant and very plain. Her shoes were low-heeled, rather than strappy high heels. She wore no jewellery, not even a watch. No make-up, unless she'd gone for the 'barely there' look that he knew from experience was incredibly high maintenance—though, given the rest of her appearance, he didn't think so.

Odd.

She was the complete opposite of the women he usually dated. Given that she'd dressed to be ignored, he shouldn't even have noticed her. Yet she was beautiful in her simplicity. And something about her drew him. As if there were some connection between them.

He'd never seen her before. He would've remembered her, he was sure. He had no idea who she was—but right at that moment he *really* wanted to know. And even though he was supposed to be networking, he could allow himself five minutes off. Just long enough to find out who she was and ask her out to dinner.

She was talking to Felicity Browne, the hostess. Karim quietly slipped away from the group and sauntered casually across the room towards the two women. When their conversation ended and she turned away, he quickened his pace slightly and intercepted her path. 'Hello.'

'Hello,' she said politely.

She had a faint South London accent, he noticed. And up close he could see that her eyes were a serious, quiet grey-blue.

Serious and quiet. *Definitely* not like the women he usually dated.

'You don't have a drink,' he said, shepherding her over towards a waiter bearing a tray of glasses.

'Because I'm not really here,' she said.

Although she was obviously aiming to sound cool and collected, Karim had trained himself to notice the little things—and he noticed that she was very slightly flustered.

Given that she'd been talking to Felicity, it was a fair bet that she was a member of Felicity's staff. So it followed that she was probably worried about getting into trouble for hanging around at a party she really wasn't dressed to attend—or invited to.

Well, he could fix that.

'Let's go somewhere quieter,' he said. 'I'll get you a drink first.'

'Thank you, but I don't drink.'

'Then have a mineral water.' He took two glasses from the waiter's tray and handed one to her. A quick check told him that the reporter had indeed left the party: good. Now he could relax. He tucked her free arm through his before heading for the French doors he knew led to a balcony.

Oh, help, Lily thought.

She'd only slipped into the room for a few moments—very quietly and discreetly—to check that Felicity was happy with everything. Then she'd intended to go straight back to the kitchen and sort out the puddings. She certainly hadn't intended to let herself be waylaid like this.

Even if he was the most stunning man Lily had ever seen.

He was dressed like the rest of the male guests, in a dinner suit teamed with a white, wing-collar pleated-front shirt. His black silk bow tie was hand-tied rather than ready-made. A swift glance at his highly polished black shoes told her that they were handmade, and the cut of the suit was definitely made-to-measure rather than off-the-peg. *Expensive* made-to-measure, judging by the feel of the cloth against her fingers. Everything about him screamed class.

Well, it would. Felicity Browne was posh with a capital P, and her guests were the same.

Lily had met a few of them before—cooked for them, even—but she'd never met him. She would've remembered. He had the same accent as most of the men in the room—one she recognised as public school followed by Oxbridge—and his almost black hair was cut slightly too long with a fringe that flopped over his eyes. Definitely an upper-class playboy.

Though his olive skin and amber-coloured eyes were just a touch too exotic for him to be English.

'I really shouldn't b—' she began again as he opened the French doors, guided her onto the balcony and closed the doors behind them.

'Don't worry. If Felicity says anything, I'll tell her I kidnapped you and it wasn't your fault,' he reassured her.

'But—'

'Shh.' He placed his forefinger against her lips, his touch gentle yet firm enough to tell her he meant it. No more protesting.

And then he held her gaze and traced the tip of his forefinger across her lower lip. The lightest, sheerest contact—and yet Lily couldn't move. Didn't want to move. There was something compelling about him, something that drew her to him. From the look in his eyes, she had a feeling it was exactly the same for him.

Instant attraction.

Spark to a flame.

A single touch would be enough to ignite it.

She should leave now. If she acted on her heart instead of her head, it would be a disaster. She couldn't afford the kind of gossip that would undoubtedly follow—gossip that would insidiously eat away at the foundations of the business she'd worked so hard to build, and bring it crashing down.

But, for the life of her, she couldn't walk away.

'What's your name?' he asked softly.

'Lily.'

'Karim,' he introduced himself.

Exotic—and yet he had that very English accent. Intriguing. And she wanted to know more.

'One question,' he said softly. 'Are you married, involved with anyone?'

She knew instinctively that if she said yes, he'd let her go. Then she could escape back to the kitchen. She actually considered lying to him; although dishonesty was something she usually despised, in this case she knew a white lie would be the most sensible course of action.

But her body wasn't listening to her head. She gave the tiniest, tiniest shake of her head, and saw relief bloom in his expression. Followed quickly by a hunger that made her body tighten in response.

He put his glass down on the table, then took hers from her hand and placed it next to his, all the while keeping his gaze fixed on hers. He captured her hand and raised it to his mouth; as he kissed each fingertip in turn she couldn't help her lips parting and her head tipping back slightly in offering.

He saw the invitation and took it, dipping his head so that his mouth just brushed her own. The lightest, sweetest, erotic whisper of skin against skin.

It wasn't enough.

She needed more.

Much more.

She slid her arms round his neck, drawing his head back down to hers. Even as she did it she knew it was crazy. They'd barely spoken a word to each other. Had only just exchanged first names. She didn't *do* things like this.

Yet here she was, kissing a complete stranger. A man she knew nothing about, except for his first name and the fact that he had the sexiest mouth she'd ever seen.

And then she stopped thinking as he deepened the kiss and her fingers tangled in his hair, urging him closer. His hair felt clean and springy under her fingers and she could smell the exotic scent of his aftershave, a sensual mixture of bergamot and citrus and amber. Simply gorgeous.

In turn, his arms were wrapped round her, one hand resting on the curve of her buttocks and the other flat against her back, drawing her closer against his body. So close that she could practically feel his heart beating, a deep and rapid throb that matched her own quickening pulse rate.

She'd heard people talking about seeing stars when they kissed and had always thought it an exaggeration. Now she knew exactly what they were talking about. This was like nothing else she'd ever experienced: as if fireworks were going off inside her head.

When he finally broke the kiss, she was shaking with need and desire. Every nerve ending in her body was sensitised— and the sensation ratcheted up another notch when he traced a path of kisses along her jawbone to her ear lobe, and then another along the sensitive cord at the site of her neck. She shivered and arched against him; in response, he pulled her closer, close enough for her to feel his erection pressing against her belly. His palm flattened against her hip and stroked upwards, moulding her curves; when he cupped one breast, his thumb rubbing the hard peak of her nipple through the material of her dress, her knees went weak.

All her senses were focused on him. The tang of his after-shave, the more personal scent of his skin, the taste of his mouth on hers, the warmth of his hands through her clothes— a thin barrier that was suddenly way, way too thick for her liking. Right at that moment she really needed to feel his skin against hers. Soft and warm and incredibly sexy.

Then he went absolutely still. Lily opened her eyes and pulled back slightly, about to ask what was wrong, when she heard it, too.

The sound of a door closing.

People talking.

The chink of glasses.

Oh, Lord.

They weren't alone on the balcony any more. And she'd been so lost in the way he was kissing her…No doubt she looked as dishevelled as he did, with mussed hair and a mouth that was slightly reddened and swollen with kisses, making it obvious what they'd just been doing.

This was a disaster.

But hopefully it was fixable.

At least they weren't immediately in full sight; somehow while he'd been kissing her he'd managed to manoeuvre them behind one of the large potted palms at the side of the balcony, screening them from view.

Frantically, she smoothed her dress, removed the band keeping her hair tied and yanked her hair back into tight order. It was just as well they'd been interrupted, or who knew what they might have done?

She'd just broken every single one of her personal rules. Even though she'd hand-picked her staff and she knew they were perfectly capable of holding the fort, she should still have been there to oversee things and sort out any last-minute hitches. She was supposed to be *working*. And instead she'd let a complete stranger whisk her off to the balcony to kiss her stupid. She'd followed her libido instead of her common sense.

Had she really learned nothing from the wreck of her marriage?

Karim, too, was restoring order to his clothes.

'I really have to go,' she whispered, keeping her voice low so she wouldn't be overheard by the others on the balcony.

'Not yet,' he said, his voice equally soft. He traced the fullness of her lower lip with his thumb. 'Or I think both of us will be embarrassed.'

'But we didn't…' Lily's voice faded as a picture slammed into her mind—a picture of what would have happened if they hadn't been interrupted. A picture of him drawing the hem of her dress up around her waist while she undid his bow tie and opened his shirt. A picture of him lifting her, balancing her against the wall, and then his body fitting against hers, easing in and then—

'Don't,' he warned huskily, and she saw his pupils dilate. No doubt her thoughts had shown in her eyes, and he was thinking something along exactly same lines.

All he had to do was dip his head slightly and he'd be kissing her again. Tasting her. Inciting her to taste him, touch him in return. And, Lord, she wanted to touch. Taste. Feel him filling her.

She swallowed hard.

Whatever was wrong with her? She never, but never, turned into a lust-crazed maniac. For the last four years she'd been single and perfectly happy with that situation. She had no intention of getting involved again. But this man had drawn an instant response from her. Made her feel the way nobody had before.

Which, as he was a total stranger, was insane.

This shouldn't be happening.

She only hoped the people who'd come out onto the balcony would go back into the main room again. The longer they had to stay behind the potted palm, the more embarrassing it would be when they finally emerged.

Again, his thoughts must have been in tandem with hers, because he said softly, 'The French doors are the only way out. Unless you're a gymnast in disguise and can launch yourself off the balcony onto a distant drainpipe, then shin down it.'

'Hardly. And I haven't been on a double-oh-seven training course,' she said ruefully, 'or I could've magicked a steel line from somewhere and clipped it onto the ironwork and we could both have abseiled down to the balcony beneath this one and escaped through the downstairs flat.'

'Great idea.' His eyes glittered with amusement. 'I wonder if my watch…?' He tapped it gently with his forefinger. 'Sadly, no. It's just a watch, I'm afraid. I didn't do the double-oh-seven training course, either.'

His teasing smile was the sexiest thing Lily had ever seen, and she almost—*almost*—found herself reaching up to pull his head back down to hers. But she managed to keep herself under control. Just.

'Looks like we'll have to wait it out, then,' she said quietly.

A wait that grew more and more awkward with every second; she didn't dare meet his eyes, not wanting him to guess how much she wanted him to kiss her again.

But then, at last, the hubbub of voices on the other side of the potted palms grew quiet and finally died away, followed by the distinct sound of the balcony doors closing.

Alone again.

And although the feeling of danger should've vanished with the people who'd left the balcony, Lily discovered that it had actually increased.

'Just for the record,' she said, 'I don't do this sort of thing.'

He gave her a rueful smile. 'I had intended just to introduce myself and ask you to have dinner with me.'

The 'but' hung in the air between them.

Instant attraction, that neither of them had been able to fight.

Oh, Lord.

What if there had been problems? What if someone had come looking for her in the space of time she'd been out here with Karim, failed to find her, panicked?

She couldn't *afford* to do this. For her business's sake.

'I really do have to go,' Lily said.

He took a pen and a business card from his pocket, and scribbled a number on the back of the card. 'Call me,' he said, handing the card to her.

It was more of a command than a question. Karim was clearly a man who was used to people doing what he told them to. Normally, the attitude would have annoyed her. But that connection between them, and the way he'd kissed her… This sort of thing didn't happen every day. She had a feeling it had shaken him just as much as it had shaken her. And even though her head told her that this was a seriously bad idea, that relationships just messed things up and were more hassle than they were worth, her mouth had other ideas. 'I'll call you,' she agreed softly.

He cupped her face briefly with one hand, the gesture cherishing. 'Go,' he said. 'I'll stay here for a few minutes. And if Felicity isn't happy, text me and I'll go and talk to her.'

And charm her out of a bad mood, no doubt, Lily thought wryly. Not that she was going to let him make excuses for her. If there was a problem, it was her responsibility and she'd deal with it. But she knew he'd meant well, so she smiled politely. 'Thanks.'

As if he couldn't help himself, he brushed his mouth over hers. 'Later.'

And the promise in his voice sent another kick of desire through her.

CHAPTER TWO

'LILY! Oh, thank God you're back.' Beatrice, her chief waitress, sounded heartfelt.

'What's…? Oh.' Lily cut off the question, seeing Hannah, her assistant, clearing up a soggy mess from the floor. The bite-sized pavlovas topped with a slice of strawberry and a kiss of cream that she'd assembled fifteen minutes or so ago had turned into Eton Mess, splattered across the floor. The whole lot would have to go straight in the bin.

And now they were one large platter short of puddings.

Just as well that, knowing how easily meringues could shatter, Lily had brought extra to cover any breakages.

'Can you whip me some cream, Hannah?' she asked. 'And, Bea, if you can wash up that platter, please?' Meanwhile, she checked what she had left in the way of fruit. There weren't enough strawberries to do a full platter of mini strawberry pavlovas, but she could add some lemon curd to half the cream and add a slice of kiwi fruit for contrasting colour.

'I'm so sorry, Lily,' Hannah said, looking tearful. 'I wasn't looking where I was going, I tripped, and I—'

'Hey, no use crying over spilt meringues,' Lily interrupted with a smile. 'It happens. I have spares. It's fixable.'

'But…'

'It's *OK*,' Lily said, firmly yet gently. She knew exactly why Hannah was distracted. Hannah's marriage was coming to a very messy end and the strain of trying to minimise the effects on her four-year-old daughter while trying to keep her life together was spilling over into her work. Not that Lily intended to read the Riot Act. Hannah, despite having a newborn, had been there for her when things had gone so badly wrong with Jeff. This was Lily's chance to do the same for her friend.

Jeff.

A harsh reminder of exactly why Lily shouldn't ring the number scribbled on the back of Karim's business card. Relationships spelled trouble. They distracted you from your goals and made life difficult. Particularly when your judgement in men was so lousy that you trusted them completely and they took advantage of your naivety. Took everything, the way Jeff had. Crushing her self-respect, her pride and her bank account. The sense of betrayal, hurt and loss had been crushing. And someone as gorgeous as Karim would have women dropping at his feet—just like Jeff. OK, she knew that not all men were unfaithful, lying louses…but Jeff had hurt Lily enough to make her extremely wary of relationships.

Pushing both her ex-husband and the gorgeous stranger out of her mind, Lily applied herself to assembling another plateful of pavlovas.

Working rapidly, she moved on to filling tiny choux buns with the coffee liqueur mousse she'd made earlier and sent Hannah out with a tray of miniature chocolate muffins and Bea out with melon-ball-sized scoops of rich vanilla ice cream covered in white chocolate and served on a cocktail stick.

The platters all came back with just a couple of canapés left on each. Good. She'd judged the quantities just right: enough to leave Felicity's guests replete but not enough to be wasteful. Years of having to struggle to pay off the overdraft Jeff had run up in her name—an overdraft he'd spent on his mistress—

meant that Lily absolutely loathed waste. Quietly pleased, she concentrated on clearing up.

She'd just finished when Felicity Browne came in. 'Lily, darling, that was stupendous.'

'Thank you.' Lily had learned not to protest that no, no, she was just average. There was no room for false modesty, in business. She wanted her clients to feel reassured that they'd made the right choice in using Amazing Tastes for their catering needs, and accepting their compliments helped to do that.

'Those little choux buns…' Felicity began wistfully.

Lily smiled, guessing exactly what Felicity wanted. 'I'll send you the recipe. And you don't have to make the choux pastry if that's a hassle for you. You can serve the mousse on its own, in little coffee cups—just garnish them with a couple of chocolate-covered coffee beans and maybe a sprig of mint for colour.'

Felicity laughed. 'That's exactly why I always ask you to do my parties. You're so good at those little extra touches.'

'Thank you.' Lily acknowledged the compliment with a smile.

She stayed just long enough to make the polite social chat she knew was expected of her, made one last check that she'd left Felicity's kitchen completely spotless, then dropped Hannah at her house on the way home. As she took her equipment out of the van and put it away Lily couldn't help thinking about Karim. And even though she knew it was crazy and it was way too late to call him, she fished inside her handbag for his business card.

Though it wasn't in the little pocket where she usually kept business cards. Odd. She'd developed a habit of filing things away neatly—they were easier to find, that way.

She checked the rest of her bag. It wasn't there, either.

Impossible. She was *sure* she'd put it in her bag.

And then she thought back. When she'd returned to the mini-crisis in the kitchen, she'd probably put the card on the worktop instead of her handbag, knowing that before she did anything else she needed to reassure her staff and stop them panicking.

Which meant that the card had probably been swept up with the refuse and thrown away.

Damn, damn, damn.

She could hardly phone Felicity and ask if she could rummage through the bin. And she definitely couldn't ask her for Karim's number or the guest list, because that would be completely unprofessional and Elizabeth Finch was never, but never, unprofessional.

Well, OK, *occasionally* she acted unprofessionally. As she had on a certain balcony, a couple of hours earlier that evening, when she'd kissed a tall, dark, handsome stranger. Really kissed him. And if they hadn't been interrupted, who knew what would have happened?

But it was over now.

Which she knew was for the best. Karim and his exotic amber eyes had tempted her to break all her personal rules. Losing his card had done her a favour—it had saved her from herself.

Karim was working through a set of figures when his phone rang. He answered it absently. 'Karim al-Hassan.'

'Your Highness, it's Felicity Browne. I wanted to thank you for these gorgeous roses.'

'My pleasure,' he said. He'd sent Rafiq, his assistant, to deliver a bouquet thanking her for her hospitality, along with a handwritten note of thanks. 'And please call me Karim.' He didn't insist on using his title in England, preferring people to be more relaxed with him.

'Karim,' she repeated obediently. 'Hardly anyone even

writes a note nowadays, let alone sends such a lovely gift, especially on a Sunday,' she continued. 'Anyway, I won't keep you—I'm sure you're busy. But I couldn't just take these flowers for granted.'

He smiled. 'I'm glad you liked them. Actually, I had planned to call you later today.' He'd discovered this morning that he had a problem, and he hoped that Felicity would be able to give him a quick solution. 'The food last night was fabulous.'

'Thank you. But I'm afraid I can't take the credit for anything other than choosing the menu, and even in that I think I was guided,' Felicity admitted with a little laugh.

'Your staff?' he asked.

'Sadly not—it's a catering firm, Amazing Tastes.'

A very accurate name, Karim thought.

'I've asked Elizabeth Finch—the owner—several times if she'd come and work for me, offered her stupendous amounts of money, but she won't let anyone tie her down. I was lucky she could fit me in, because she's usually booked up for months in advance,' Felicity confided.

So the cook was freelance. Good. That meant there wouldn't be a problem asking her to cater for his presentations. Even though Felicity would probably have allowed him to poach her personal cook for a few days, this avoided any awkward obligations.

'Actually, I'm looking for a good caterer for some business presentations.' He'd had a caterer lined up. But as her sister had had a baby that morning, two months early, Claire had phoned him in a panic, saying that she needed to drop everything and look after her niece while her sister spent all her time at the special care baby unit. Except Claire's sister lived in Cornwall, a good five hours away—and as Claire was her only family, there was nobody else to do it.

He knew what it was like when family needed you to drop everything. He'd done it himself. So, although it left him in a jam, he wasn't going to give Claire a hard time about it. He still had enough time to fix things. 'I wondered if I could trouble you for your caterer's contact details?' he asked.

'Of course, but, as I said, she's very in demand,' Felicity warned. 'Though if she can't fit you in she might be able to suggest someone. She's good like that.'

Better and better.

'Let me get my contact book.' There was a pause; then Felicity dictated Elizabeth Finch's phone number and address.

Karim scribbled it down as she spoke. 'Thank you, Felicity.'

'My pleasure. And thank you again for the flowers.'

When he replaced the receiver, he flicked onto the Internet and looked up the address. Islington. A nice part of it. So she'd have a price tag to match.

Though money wasn't an issue. He needed quality—and he'd tasted that for himself, the previous evening. He glanced at his watch. Right now, a busy freelance caterer would be smack in the middle of preparations for an evening event, so this wasn't the best time to discuss a booking. He'd call in tomorrow at nine; from experience, he knew that face-to-face meetings were more effective than phone calls.

He glanced at his watch. Two hours, and he'd need to shower and shave and change for a garden party. A party that Renée, one of his prettiest recent dates, would also be attending. Given that the weather was fine and the garden in question had some nice secluded spots, it could be an interesting afternoon. A pleasant interlude.

Though, strangely, it wasn't Renée's face in his thoughts as he imagined kissing her stupid in the middle of the maze. It was Lily's.

He shook himself. It was highly unlikely that Lily would be there. And besides, now he thought about it, dating her would be too complicated. There had been something serious about Lily, and he wasn't in a position to offer anything serious. In less than a year's time he'd be back in Harrat Salma and his parents would be expecting to arrange a marriage exactly like their own. These were his last few months of playing. Of dating women who knew the score and didn't expect him to change his mind.

And he had no intention of changing that.

The next morning, Lily was sitting in her kitchen, drinking coffee and planning menus for the following week's events, when her doorbell buzzed. Too early for the postman, she thought, and she wasn't expecting any deliveries that morning. She wasn't expecting any visitors, either.

She opened the front door and stared.

Karim was the last person she'd expected to see. She'd only told him her first name—and it was her nickname rather than her full name. How come…?

'Lily?' he asked, looking as surprised as she felt. 'Do you work for Elizabeth Finch?'

She shook her head. 'I *am* Elizabeth Finch.'

He frowned. 'You told me your name was Lily.'

'It is.'

He looked sceptical, as if he wasn't sure she was telling the truth.

She shrugged. 'I couldn't say Elizabeth when I was tiny— I called myself "Lily-ba". The name kind of stuck. Everyone calls me Lily. Though obviously I use my full name for work.'

'I see.' He inclined his head. 'I was impressed by the food on Saturday night. I asked Felicity Browne for her caterer's contact details.'

Then this was a business call, not a social visit. Good. Business made things easier. She could section off her emotions and deal with this. Even better: if he became her client, that would be yet another reason not to act on that attraction. She knew first-hand that relationships and business didn't mix.

Lord, did she know that first-hand. She'd been there already with Jeff and had her fingers well and truly burned. 'Come through.' She ushered him into the hall, closed the door behind him and led him through to the kitchen. 'Would you like some coffee?'

'Thank you. That would be nice.'

'Milk? Sugar?'

'Neither, thanks.'

'I'll put the kettle on. Do take a seat.'

At her gesture, Karim took a seat on one of the overstuffed sofas set in the open-plan conservatory area, while Lily busied herself making fresh coffee. Her kitchen was clearly a professional kitchen—very up to date appliances, sleek minimalist units in pale wood, a central island, and what looked like granite work surfaces and splashbacks. Everything was neat and tidy, including the shelf of cookery books and box files. He wasn't surprised that she was the meticulous type.

And yet the room was far from sterile. The walls were painted a pale terracotta, adding warmth to the room, and there were photographs and postcards pinned to the fridge with magnets. A simple blue glass vase full of daffodils sat on the window sill behind the sink. And he could smell something gorgeous; a quick scan of the room showed him a couple of cakes cooling on a wire rack. For a client? he wondered.

Lily herself was dressed casually in jeans and a camisole top, and looked incredibly touchable. He could remember the softness of her skin against his and the sweetness of her scent when'd he kissed her on the balcony the other night, and his body reacted instantly.

Not good.

This was meant to be business. He knew that mixing business and pleasure wasn't a good idea—he needed to get himself under control again. Right now. He really shouldn't be thinking about hooking a finger under the strap of her top, drawing it down, and kissing her bare shoulder.

'Nice kitchen,' he commented when she returned with two mugs of coffee.

'It suits me,' she said simply.

And she suited it, he thought.

'So what did you want to discuss?' she asked.

She'd made quite sure she was sitting on the other sofa rather than next to him, he noted. Fair enough. This was business. And sitting next to each other would've risked them accidentally touching each other. Given how they'd both gone up in flames the other night at the first touch, distance was a very good idea.

'As I said, I was impressed by the food at Felicity's party. I'm holding a series of business meetings and I need a caterer.'

'And you want m— You're asking me?' she corrected herself hastily.

A little slip that told him her mind was still running along the same track as his. 'Yes.' To both, he added silently.

'That depends when you have in mind. I'm booked up for the next three months.'

'They're set up for the end of the month.'

She shook her head. 'In that case, sorry, no can do.'

He backtracked to what she'd just said. 'You're working every single day for the next three months?' And people called *him* a workaholic.

'All my work days are booked.'

He picked up the subtext. 'So you don't work every single day.'

'Actually, I do,' she corrected. 'But I don't cook for other people every single day.'

'What do you do on the days you're not cooking for other people?'

'I develop recipes. I have a column in a Sunday newspaper twice a month, and a monthly column in a magazine.'

He couldn't resist. 'Are they work in development?' He gestured in the direction of the cakes.

'Is that a hint?'

He smiled. 'Yes.'

She rolled her eyes but, as he'd hoped, she smiled. 'OK. I'll cut you a slice. But be warned that it's a test, so it might not taste quite right.'

When she handed him a slice of chocolate cake on a plain white plate, he took a mouthful. Savoured the taste. 'Works for me.' Though such a vague compliment would sound like flattery—something he knew instinctively she'd scoff at. 'It smells good and it's got the right amount of chocolate. Enough to give it flavour but not so much that it's overpowering.'

She tried it, and shook her head. 'The texture's not quite right. It needs more flour. Excuse me a minute.' She scribbled something on a pad.

'Notes?' he asked.

'For the next trial,' she explained.

He nodded in acknowledgement. 'So, to return to our discussion. Basically you have how many free days a week?'

'I have three days when I don't cook but they are my development time. Not to mention testing the recipes three times and setting up my kitchen so the photographer can take shots of the different stages. And time to do my paperwork.'

'But they're days you could use—in theory,' he persisted.

'In theory. In practice, I don't. If I do it for one person, I'll have to do it for everyone, and I don't want to end up working eighteen-hour days to fit everything in. I need time to refill the well. Time to let myself be creative.'

He tried another tack. 'You have people working for you, don't you?'

'Part time, yes.'

'But you've worked with them for a long time.'

She looked surprised. 'How did you know?'

'Because everything was so polished at Felicity's party. That kind of teamwork only comes with experience, when you know each other and trust each other.'

She recognised the compliment and smiled.

'And your staff help with the cooking?'

'Some of it.' She frowned. 'Why?'

'I was thinking. Maybe you could delegate more to them. Then you could expand your business without encroaching on the days you don't cook for people.'

She shook her head. 'Absolutely not. My clients expect my personal attention, and that's exactly what they get. The only way I can expand is if I get a time machine or a clone—neither of which are physically possible. I'm at capacity, Karim. Sorry. The best I can do is put you in touch with some of the people I trained with who also run their own businesses—they're good, or I wouldn't recommend them.'

This was where he knew he should be sensible, thank her for the recommendations, and call each one in turn until he found someone who could fit him in.

The problem was, he didn't want just anyone. He wanted *her*.

And he was used to getting exactly what he wanted.

'Thank you,' he said, 'but no. I want Elizabeth Finch.' He paused. 'Would any of your clients consider rescheduling?'

'No. And don't suggest I throw a sickie on them, either,' she warned. 'I'd never cheat my clients.'

'Good,' he said. 'You have integrity. I respect that.' He paused. 'Whatever your usual rates are, I'm happy to double them.'

'No.'

'You want to negotiate?' He shrugged. 'Fine. Let's save us both some time. Name your price, Lily.'

She folded her arms. 'You honestly believe everything can be bought?'

'Everything has a price.'

She scoffed. 'You must have a seriously sad life.'

He laughed. 'On the contrary. But it's basic business sense. Someone sells, someone buys. The price is negotiable, depending on supply and demand.'

'You can't buy people, Karim.'

He rolled his eyes. 'I know that. I'm not asking to buy *you*.' He paused just long enough for the colour to flood her face completely. 'In business, I look for the best. That's why I'm asking you to do the catering for some meetings that are going to be pretty crucial to *my* business.'

'I'm flattered that you've sought me out,' she said, 'but, as I've told you plenty of times already, I'm afraid I'm already booked and there's nothing I can do about it.'

'Firstly,' he said, 'persistence is a business asset. And, secondly, there's always a way round things if you look.'

'Hasn't anyone ever said no to you?'

He didn't even need to think about it. 'I always get what I want in the end.'

'Not in this case, I'm afraid. Unless you're prepared to take my next open slot, in three months' time.'

'I can't wait that long. The meetings are already set up.'

'Then, as I said, I'm sorry.' She went over to her filing system, took a box down, and made notes on a pad. She tore off the sheet, then brought it over to him. 'Here. They all come with my recommendation—and I'm picky.'

'So,' he said, 'am I.' He drained his mug. 'Thank you for the coffee. And the cake.'

'Pleasure.'

She was being polite, and he knew it. He also knew that if he gave in to the impulse to pull her to her feet and kiss her stupid, he'd push her even further away—she'd respond, but she'd be angry with herself for acting unprofessionally. And he wanted her willingly in his bed.

'If you change your mind—' and he had every intention of making sure that she did '—call me. You have my card.'

'Actually, I mislaid it.'

Had she? Or had she ripped it up in a fit of temper? Because now he knew exactly what she'd been doing at Felicity Browne's party, he could guess at her reaction that night after she'd left the balcony—anger at herself for letting him distract her when she'd been there in a business capacity. And underneath that cool, quiet exterior lurked a passionate woman. A woman who'd responded to him so deeply that they'd both forgotten where they were.

He took a business card from a small silver holder, scribbled his personal number on the back, and handed it to her. 'To replace the one you…' he paused, his eyes challenging hers '…mislaid.'

She didn't flinch in the slightest; she merely inclined her head in acknowledgement, and went back over to her filing system. She glanced at the name on the card, then paper-clipped it into a book. Then she took a card from a box and handed it to him. 'In case you change your mind about the dates. But please remember that I have a three-month waiting list.'

'People plan parties that far in advance?'

'Weddings, christenings, anniversary dinners…' She spread her hands. 'I don't question my clients' social lives. I just talk to them about what kind of thing they want, and deliver it.'

'So you do dinner parties as well?'

'On Thursdays to Sundays,' she confirmed.

'And what if one of your regular clients needed you on a Monday, Tuesday or Wednesday?' he asked. 'Or they just decide to throw a party on the spur of the moment?'

'My clients know that I don't cook for people on Mondays, Tuesdays or Wednesdays. Apart from the fact that I have other commitments, everybody needs time off.'

'True.' That, together with her comment about a time machine, had just given him another idea. 'Well, it was good to see you again, Lily.'

'And you.'

For a moment, he thought about kissing her on the cheek—but he knew he wouldn't be able to leave it there. And he needed the business side of things sorted out before he addressed the issues between them. Before he took her to bed.

He knew that kissing her hand would be way too smarmy, so he settled for a firm handshake. 'Thanks for your time.'

Even something as impersonal as a handshake made his skin tingle where she touched him. And, judging by the look in her eyes—a look she masked quickly—it was the same for her.

This wasn't over.

Not by a long, long way.

CHAPTER THREE

'YOU, my friend, are just piqued. For the first time in your life, a woman has actually turned you down,' Luke said with a grin.

'I'm not piqued,' Karim said.

'You're distracted. Otherwise you'd have given me a better game tonight.'

Karim couldn't argue with that. Usually their Monday night squash matches were incredibly close, and tonight he'd lost badly. But he could argue with his best friend's earlier statement. 'Anyway, she didn't turn me down.'

Luke raised an eyebrow. 'I thought you just told me she was too busy to do the catering for your business meetings?'

'Kick a man when he's down, why don't you? Anyway, she'll change her mind.' Karim had every intention of changing it for her.

'Maybe I can help,' Luke suggested. Karim had explained the situation to him before the match. 'Cathy has some great ideas about revamping the café here—if you ask her nicely I'm sure she can come up with some menus for you and organise the catering. If it helps you out of a hole, she can use the kitchens here to sort out whatever you need done.'

'You'd let me poach your staff?' Karim asked. Luke had bought the health club three months ago and was in the process of making it reach its proper potential—a gym and spa bursting with vitality and an excellent café.

'Borrow. Temporarily. To help you out,' Luke corrected.

'But you'd want advertising or something in return.'

'I'm not *that* much of a shark. And I wouldn't make an offer like that to just anyone.' The corner of his mouth twitched. 'But I've just thrashed you at squash. And you're my best mate. So, as I'm feeling terribly sorry for you right now, you should take advantage of my good nature.'

Karim laughed. 'Ha. You wait until next Monday. I'll have my revenge.'

'In your dreams,' Luke teased back. 'Come on. We're both disgustingly sweaty and smelly—if we hang around here, bickering, we'll put off all my customers.'

'Whatever you say, boss.'

After a shower, they grabbed a cold beer in the bar.

'You're still brooding,' Luke said.

Karim made light of it. 'Just sulking about losing a match to you for the first time in a month. And by such a huge margin.'

'Are you, hell. You don't waste energy being competitive over something unimportant.' Luke paused. 'She must be really special.'

'Who?'

'The woman you're brooding about. Let me guess. Five feet eight, blonde, curvy and just lurrrves parties?'

Karim laughed dryly. 'That's your type, not mine.'

Luke grinned back. 'Don't kid yourself. I go for brunettes. Preferably ones without wedding bells in their eyes.'

And just in case they developed wedding bell-itis, as Luke had dubbed it, nobody ever made it to a fourth date.

'Actually, she's nothing like the type I usually date,' Karim said thoughtfully. 'Try five feet four, mid-brown hair and very hard-working.'

Luke blinked. 'You're kidding.'

'I wish I was. If she were a party girl, I'd know what made her tick. Lily…' Karim blew out a breath. 'She's different.' And maybe that was why he couldn't get her out of his head.

'And she's the caterer you want to work for you?' Luke queried.

'She cooks for the rich and famous. Hand-picked client list.' Karim leaned back against the leather club chair. 'She's the best. And I tasted her food at Felicity Browne's do, the other night, so I know what I'm talking about.'

He'd tasted her, too…and he wanted to do it again. And again. A lot more intimately.

Luke wrinkled his nose. 'I don't like the sound of this. Mixing business and pleasure—it never works, Karim. It'll end in tears. I've seen it happen too many times before.'

'Maybe.'

'*Definitely.*' Luke raised an eyebrow. 'So what's the plan?'

'I'm going to persuade her to change her mind.'

'You're going to charm her into working for you?'

Karim shrugged. 'I offered to pay her double. She just said that you couldn't buy people.'

'Too right. If you can buy them, they're not worth having around. They'll be unreliable.' Luke frowned. 'And if she drops clients in favour of you, what's to stop her dropping *you* if she gets a better offer?'

'I don't expect her to ditch long-standing arrangements in favour of me—and she told me up front she had no intention of dropping any of her clients for me. But I also happen to know there are three days a week when she doesn't have bookings. I want her on those three days.' Karim turned his glass of mineral water round in his hands. 'So it's a matter of getting to know her better. Finding out what's important to her. And then…negotiating terms.'

'It still sounds to me as if you're planning to mix business and pleasure. If you're going to be her boss, it's practically harassment,' Luke pointed out.

'She's her own boss. Technically, I'd be her client.'

'Same difference. Let it go,' Luke said. 'Sure, you're attracted to her. But there's a lot riding on these meetings. Screw it up for the sake of—what, half a dozen dates, before you get bored or she gets too serious and you back off?—and you'll never forgive yourself.'

'I'm not going to screw it up.'

'You will do, if you're thinking with another part of your anatomy instead of with your head,' Luke advised. He finished his drink. 'Think about what I said. If you want me to have a word with Cathy, let me know. It's not a problem.'

'Thanks. I appreciate the offer.'

There was a tinge of sympathy in Luke's eyes. 'It's tough, living up to a parent's expectations.'

Not as tough as having no family at all—though Karim didn't say so, knowing just how sensitive his best friend was about the issue. Particularly as Luke had been the one to walk away. 'I always knew I'd have to grow up and pull my weight in the family firm some time.' He just hadn't expected it to be this way. He'd seen himself in a supporting role, not the limelight.

But all that had changed five years ago when his brother had died. The whole world had turned upside down. So he'd done the only thing possible: given up his PhD studies and gone home to do his duty as the new heir to the throne.

A duty he still wasn't quite reconciled to. Not that he'd ever hurt his parents by telling them how he felt; and he would never, ever let them or his country down. But no matter how hard he worked or played, he still missed the studies he'd loved so much. Filling his time didn't fill the empty space inside him.

Karim finished his own drink. 'I've done quite enough loafing around for today. I'll see you later.'

'You're going home to work?'

Karim laughed as he stood up. 'Says the man who's going to do exactly the same thing.' Their backgrounds were miles apart, but Karim thought that he and Luke had a very similar outlook on life. They'd met on the first day of their MBA course, liked each other immediately, and the liking had merged into deep friendship over the years. Karim thought of Luke as the brother he no longer had, and Luke was the only person Karim would ever have talked to about Lily. And even though part of him knew that Luke was right, that mixing business and pleasure would lead to an unholy mess, he couldn't stop himself thinking about her.

By the time he'd walked home, he'd worked out what to do. There was something more important than money: time. And maybe that was the key to Lily. For the next couple of weeks, his work was flexible. He could fit in the hours whenever it suited him.

So maybe, just maybe, he had a way to convince her.

The following morning, he leaned on Lily's doorbell at nine o'clock sharp.

She opened the door and just stared at him for a moment.

And he was very, very aware that her gaze had gone straight to his mouth.

With difficulty, he forced his thoughts off her mouth and what he wanted to do with it. 'Good morning, Lily.'

'Good m—' she began, then frowned. 'What are you doing here?'

'I'm your new apprentice.'

She shook her head. 'Apart from the fact I already have all the staff I need, you can't be my apprentice—you don't have catering experience and you don't have a food hygiene certificate.'

'And how do you know that?' he challenged.

'I looked you up on the Internet.' She paused before adding, 'Your Highness.'

She'd looked him up. Just as he'd looked her up, the previous day. On her own website as well as the gossip pages. Nobody had been linked with Lily's name for the last four years—probably, he thought, because she'd been too busy setting up and then running her business to socialise. Which suited him fine.

He met her gaze. 'And that's a problem?'

'If you think I'm going to let my clients down in favour of you just because you've got a title, then I'm afraid you'll be disappointed, Your Highness.'

He smiled, pleased that she had principles and stuck to them. 'My title has nothing to do with it. To you, I'm Karim.'

'*Sheikh* Karim al-Hassan of Harrat Salma,' she pointed out. 'You're a prince. Your dad rules a country.'

'The title bothers you, doesn't it?'

'Not particularly.' She shrugged. 'I've met people with titles before.'

And worked for them. He already knew that. And he liked the fact that she was discreet enough not to mention any names. 'Then what bothers you, Lily?'

You do, she thought. *You do.* It wasn't his title; she was used to dealing with wealthy, famous people. It was the man. The way her body reacted to him. The way he sent her into a flat spin when he so much as smiled at her. 'Nothing,' she fibbed.

'So. As I said. I'm your new apprentice.'

'You're nothing of the sort. Without a food hygiene certificate, you can't work with food.'

'I can still run errands. Make you coffee. Wash up.' He smiled, showing perfect white teeth. Sexy teeth. Sexy mouth.

Oh, Lord. She was near to hyperventilating, remembering what that mouth had done to her. Thinking about what she wanted it to do to her.

'I could make you lunch,' he suggested.

She aimed for cool. Since when would a sheikh do his own cooking? 'You're telling me you can actually cook?' she drawled.

He laughed. 'Making a sandwich isn't exactly cooking. But if you want to know just how well I can cook, have dinner with me—and I'll cook for you.'

Lord, he was confident. Most people just wouldn't attempt to cook for a professional chef, worrying that their food wouldn't come up to standard.

But she had a feeling that Karim al-Hassan would be good at everything he chose to do.

He was definitely good at kissing.

Flustered, she tried to push the memories out of her head, the insidious thoughts about what Karim might do next after he kissed her again—because he wasn't going to kiss her again. She was absolutely resolved about that. 'It's very kind of you to offer, but I'm afraid I don't have time.'

'It's Tuesday. You're not cooking tonight,' he pointed out.

'I still have preparation work to do. And my column to write. And admin—catering is the same as any other business, with bills that need paying and books that need balancing and planning that needs to be done for future events.'

'All right. Next Monday night, then. I'll cook for you.'

This was sounding suspiciously like a date. Something she didn't do.

'Or we can make it lunch, if it'd make you feel safer,' he added.

'I'm not afraid of you.' Which was true. She was afraid of *herself.* Of her reaction to him. She'd never felt like this before. This overwhelming blend of desire and need and urgency. Not even with Jeff—and she'd lost her head over him.

She'd lost a hell of a lot more, too. Her business, her home, her self-respect, and her heart. She'd worked hard to get them all back, and she knew better than to repeat her mistakes.

'So you'll have lunch with me on Monday.' It was a statement, not a question.

The sensible side of her wanted to say no.

But the woman who'd been kissed wanted to know…This man would be a perfectionist. Would he cook as well as he kissed? Would he make love as well as he cooked?

But just as she was preparing a polite but firm refusal, her mouth seemed to work of its own accord. 'Lunch would be fine. Thank you.'

'Good. And in the meantime I'll be your apprentice. Starting now.'

'Thank you, but I really don't need an apprentice.'

'You don't have to pay me, if that's what you're worrying about. I'm giving my time freely.'

She felt her eyes narrow. 'If you're trying to get me to change my mind about catering for your business meetings…'

He spread his hands. 'I'm not trying to buy you, Lily. And time is more precious than money. If I give up my time to help you, then maybe you might reconsider giving up some of your time to help me.'

So he wanted a quid pro quo.

At least he'd been honest about it.

And he wasn't expecting to push his way into a queue. He wanted some of her non-catering days. He recognised that her time was important and he was offering her something that he valued more than money, too.

Even though she knew her head needed examining—the man was a definite danger to her peace of mind—she took a step back from the door. 'Come in.'

Karim smiled, and let her lead him to her kitchen. 'So, boss. First off, how do you take your coffee?'

'Milk, no sugar, please. And I'm not your boss.'

'I can take orders.'

He was teasing her. No way would this man take orders. Give them, yes.

She must have spoken aloud because he laughed. '*Habibti*, I can definitely take orders. Just tell me what you want me to do.'

She knew he wasn't talking about coffee or anything of the kind. There was a sensual gleam in those amber, wolfish eyes that suggested something completely different. That doing her bidding would be his pleasure—and most definitely hers.

'Coffee,' she said, before she did or said something to disgrace herself. Like telling him to carry her upstairs and rip all her clothes off and make love to her until she didn't know what day it was any more.

Coward, his eyes said. She knew he knew damn well what had just gone through her mind.

'Lots of milk or just a dash?' he asked.

'Somewhere in the middle.'

'OK. Carry on with whatever you were doing, and I'll make coffee.'

She sat at the little island in the centre of her kitchen, where she'd set up her laptop earlier that morning. So much for editing her article on summer food. How could she possibly concentrate with this man in the room? She was aware of every movement he made, even when she wasn't looking at him.

She typed and erased the same three words a dozen times.

This wasn't going to work. It was going to drive her crazy, him being in here. Invading her space. Looking in her cupboards for china—she bit back the words before she told him that she kept the mugs in the cupboard above the kettle, because she didn't want him knowing that she was watching him instead of working.

She forced herself to concentrate on the screen of her laptop.

A few moments later he brought a mug of coffee over to her—along with a plate, with a little gold box sitting on it.

Her heart missed a beat.

Then she shook herself mentally. *Stupid.* Even if he was a sheikh and impossibly wealthy, of course he wasn't going to lavish jewellery on her. They barely knew each other.

Besides, she recognised the embossing on the box: the name of a very exclusive and extremely expensive chocolatier.

'Is this what I think it is?' she asked.

'That rather depends on what you think it is.'

'Unless you've recycled the box, this is definitely chocolate.'

Again, his eyes glittered with amusement, as if he'd guessed the crazy idea she'd had a few seconds before. 'It's a new box,' he confirmed. 'I wasn't sure if you preferred white, milk or dark.'

She opened the box. He'd bought two of each sort. Enough to be a thoughtful gesture, but not so much that she felt too uncomfortable to accept his gift. From what she'd read about him online, he could've afforded to buy the contents of the shop with his spare change, and still had enough left over to buy the entire stock of the florist's next door—but he'd been restrained rather than over the top. He'd remembered what she'd said to him about not being bought.

And she liked that.

'As long as it's chocolate, I like it,' she said. 'But, as there are two of each, I think you should share them with me.'

'Thank you. I accept.' His tongue moistened his lower lip briefly. 'I have to confess to a weakness for chocolate. But I like mine dark. Rich. Spicy.'

How could the man make her think of sex when he was talking about chocolate? *Breathe*, Lily reminded herself.

He sat on the pale wooden bar stool next to hers—not close enough to crowd her, but near enough for her to be incredibly aware of his body. The first time she'd seen him, he'd worn a dinner jacket. The last time, he'd worn an expensively cut business suit. Today, he was in jeans, very soft denim that just screamed out to be touched, and a collarless white cotton shirt. It made him look younger. Approachable. And incredibly sexy.

No. Sexy was bad.

He was just…

She gave up trying to describe him, because her mind filled the gap with all sorts of descriptions that made her heart skip a beat. Hot. Touchable. Kissable.

This couldn't be happening. Shouldn't be happening. They moved in different worlds. No way could anything happen between them.

Except maybe a fling, her libido reminded her. A hot and very satisfying fling. Something temporary. No strings, no promises to be broken.

And the idea sent her temperature up another notch.

Lily reached out to take a chocolate from the box, to distract herself, and her fingers brushed against his. She found her lips parting automatically, inviting a kiss, and felt her cheeks flame when she realised that she was staring at his mouth. When she lifted her gaze she saw that he was staring at her mouth, too.

Remembering.

Wanting.

All she had to do was move towards him and she knew he'd touch her, his fingertips skating across her face and then sliding behind her neck to urge her closer. And then his mouth would touch hers. So lightly. Asking. Promising.

And this time they were on their own. There was no risk of being disturbed. No reason why he couldn't scoop her off the chair and carry her up the stairs to her bed.

She really, really had to get a grip.

She edged her chair slightly away from his. His expression told her that he'd noticed. And that he'd guessed why.

'So what are you doing?' he asked.

Trying to resist temptation, she thought. 'Editing my article about seasonal foods. Gooseberries, courgettes and broad beans.'

'It's spring now. You're talking about summer foods.'

'Magazines work three or four months in advance,' she explained. 'So although for my catering work I prefer to buy seasonal ingredients, produced as locally as possible, for this kind of work I can't.'

'So you do the pictures as well?'

'No, the magazine sends a photographer over. I've emailed them some rough shots so the designer has some idea of what the finished product looks like and can brief the photographer with the kind of angles she wants taken, and we'll be setting up the final shoot tomorrow.'

'So what are you cooking?'

'Broad beans with pancetta, gooseberry and elderflower fool, and courgette and chocolate cake.'

He looked surprised. '*Courgette* and chocolate cake? Are you sure?'

She smiled. 'Did you taste the courgettes in it yesterday?'

'That was courgette and chocolate cake?'

'Yup.'

He spread his hands. 'What can I say, other than that you're a culinary genius, Lily Finch?'

She gave him a tiny bow, acknowledging the compliment. 'We didn't tell the kids, either. Until they'd scoffed it.'

'Kids?' he queried.

Ah. She hadn't intended to tell him that. 'Never mind.'

'Talk to me, Lily,' he said softly. 'Kids?'

She flushed. 'My friend Hannah, who works with me—she takes my trials to her daughter's nursery school. Depending on what it is, they either use it for the children's break-time snacks or offer it to parents in return for a donation to nursery funds.'

'That's good of you.'

She shook her head. 'This might be a nice middle-class area now, but there are still quite a few kids around here who have nothing. Nursery's the only place where they get to play with toys and books. So this is my way of giving something back.' That, and offering a romantic dinner for two cooked by

Elizabeth Finch at the nursery's annual fund-raising raffle. Because she owed Hannah for supporting her through the mess of her divorce—and she never forgot her debts.

'It's still a nice thing to do.'

She wriggled on her seat, not comfortable talking about it; he clearly noticed, because he moved over to the window and changed the subject. 'Nice garden.'

'I like it,' Lily said. 'Though it's not just flowers. There's a raised bed at the bottom which I use for vegetables, and there are pots of herbs on the patio.' She joined him at the window. 'And there at the bottom is my Californian lilac. My favourite shrub—it's a mass of bright blue flowers in May, and it attracts all the butterflies.' She shook herself. 'But this isn't getting any work done.'

'Tell me what you want me to do, and I'll do it.'

'I can't think of anything.' Well, she could—but none of those things were on the agenda. At all. She raked a hand through her hair. 'I just need to finish editing my article, and make sure I have all the ingredients in so I can make at least four sets of everything tomorrow—one finished article, two showing the cooking process at different stages, and a spare in case there's a last-minute hitch.'

'Give me your recipes, and I'll check the ingredients for you,' he said.

'Thanks, but I'd rather do it myself.'

'You don't trust me?'

'I'd rather do it myself,' she repeated. 'I can see at a glance if I need anything. It's quicker than explaining.'

'You're not a team player, then.'

Not since Jeff's betrayal. She'd vowed that she'd never, ever have another business partner again. It had been devastating to lose the restaurant she'd worked so hard to build. Even though it meant that Amazing Tastes couldn't expand, it also meant that she couldn't lose the business she loved because of someone else's failings. Been there, done that, worn the T-shirt to shreds. 'I don't have a problem with my colleagues in the kitchen.'

'But you have a problem with me?'

She nodded. 'You're...distracting.'

'Which wasn't my intention.' He smiled. 'OK. Hint taken. I'll leave you in peace. Don't worry, I'll see myself out.'

'Thank you. And for the chocolates,' she added belatedly.

'Pleasure.' He gave her a warm, sweet smile that instantly made her feel all gooey inside, then left her kitchen—which suddenly felt cooler and more shadowy. Which was ridiculous and self-indulgent, she told herself crossly.

'I'll see you in the morning,' he called—and then closed the front door behind him before she could protest that, no, he couldn't possibly turn up tomorrow, because she was busy and...

'Argh!' Lily suddenly realised she'd pressed the wrong button and accidentally deleted her entire article. She said something very pithy, then stalked over to the kettle to make herself another cup of coffee and calm down before tackling her laptop's 'recycle bin' and making it give her article back.

Karim al-Hassan had a lot to answer for. He was distracting, irritating...and impossibly sexy. And even if she sent him away when he turned up on her doorstep tomorrow morning, she wouldn't be able to get him out of her head.

Where was her professionalism when she needed it?

'Just be sensible. You know what happened last time,' she told herself.

But Karim wasn't Jeff, an insidious voice said in her head. Karim was a man who believed in honour. The attraction was very much mutual. There was no reason why they couldn't act on that attraction. Keep it between themselves. Provided he wasn't actually seen out with her, the chances were that the paparazzi would leave them alone. And adding him to her client list would be the perfect cover...

Ha. There was an old saying that if something appeared too good to be true, it usually was.

And, as she had no intention of picking herself up, dusting herself down, starting all over again and struggling to get back to where she was right now, she'd have to think of a way to get Karim out of her head and out of her life.

thank she this she... pretty a soft lavender.

CHAPTER FOUR

LILY was pretty sure that she was ready to face Karim, the next morning. That all her arguments were marshalled neatly and they were completely persuasive.

Then she discovered that she wasn't ready at all.

Far from it.

Because when she opened the door to him, he disarmed her with the sweetest of smiles and a large terracotta pot full of violets.

'They're dog violets. Although they don't have a scent like sweet violets, apparently they attract butterflies.' His eyes crinkled at the corners. 'I would've liked to give you a proper bouquet—roses, lilies and what have you—but I don't want you thinking I'm trying to buy you.'

So instead he'd given her something much less showy, the kind of floral gift that appealed to her much more. Clearly he'd been listening to what she'd said, the previous day, about liking flowers that attracted butterflies. The dog violets would be perfect for her patio. 'Thank you. They're lovely.' So pretty: a soft lavender blue with a white throat. And he'd taken time out of his day to find these for her—she knew without having to ask that he hadn't just sent an assistant to pick up the first thing she saw in a florist's. 'Where did you find them?'

'In a little shop down the road from my place. They'll go well with your thyme, even though these are both cultivated.'

'Violets and thyme?' Thyme was pretty, but it was a savoury herb, and these weren't the sort of violets she'd crystallise and use to decorate a cake. What was he talking about?

Obviously her confusion showed, because he said softly, 'I know a bank whereon the wild thyme blows, Where oxlips and the nodding violet grows.'

'Poetry.' Though not something she recognised.

'Shakespeare. *A Midsummer Night's Dream.*'

Clearly he'd expected her to know the quote. 'Sorry.' She shrugged. 'I've never really been into the theatre.'

'You like films?'

'Yes, but I don't get the time to go to the cinema. I don't really watch TV, either,' she admitted.

'So what do you do for relaxation?'

She damped down the pictures in her head, of tangled white sheets and Karim's skin sliding against her own. 'I cook,' she said simply.

'It's more than just a job to you, isn't it? It's your passion.'

'It's my life,' she said. And she hoped he understood that she meant it.

He closed the door behind him; she thought at first he'd followed her to the kitchen, but then she realised he'd stopped before the watercolour in the hallway, her favourite, one of lavender fields in Provence.

'That's a beautiful painting.' He looked at the signature, then at her. 'Amy Finch. Is she any relation?'

'She's my mother.'

He joined her in the kitchen. 'Were you ever tempted to follow in her footsteps?'

'No. It was always cooking, for me. Though I suppose some of it's rubbed off, because presentation's an important part of cooking—you need to make it look nice when you plate it up.' Memories brought a lump to her throat and a wave of homesickness—which was crazy, because she was still in England. Amy was the one who'd moved abroad. 'On rainy days in school holidays or at weekends, Mum would get her huge old cookery book off the shelf, open it at random and then close her eyes and circle her finger over the pages—wherever her finger landed, we'd cook that recipe. Or we'd improvise if we didn't have all the ingredients in the cupboard.'

'You're close to your mum?'

'I don't see her as often as I'd like, but we speak a lot. She lives in France now—in Provence. That picture's the view from her house, the lavender fields.' She unlocked the conservatory doors and placed the pot on the patio, near to the terracotta pots full of lavender from the fields her mother had painted, then closed the doors again and washed her hands.

Karim glanced over at her oven. 'You're already cooking something?'

'That's the finished article,' she said. 'I'm cooking it now because it needs time to cool before Hayley does her stuff.'

'Hayley being the photographer?' he queried.

She nodded.

'So what time is she going to be here?'

'Midday.' Lily took a deep breath. Time to tackle him about this apprentice thing, make him see how crazy and unworkable it was. 'Look, Karim, I know you mean well, but—'

'I won't get in your way,' he interrupted softly. 'Humour me. I'll fetch and carry whatever you want. I'll even wash up for you without complaining.'

'Wash up?' She couldn't help smiling at the thought. 'You're telling me I'm going to have a prince washing up in my kitchen?'

'If you're being picky, it's sheikh rather than prince.'

'Same difference.'

He leaned against the worktop and looked at her. 'I'm a perfectly ordinary person, you know.'

There's nothing ordinary about you, Lily thought—and then really, really hoped she hadn't said that aloud.

'Besides,' he continued, 'if you're afraid of getting your hands dirty, you'll be no good as a leader. You need to see what has to be done and make sure it gets done. If you can't delegate a task because there simply isn't time, then you have to do it yourself.' He rolled his eyes. 'What, do you think I have an enormous staff or something?'

'Don't you?'

'No. I admit, I use a laundry service because life's much too short to iron shirts.'

'Agreed.' She used a laundry service for her chef's whites, but everything else went through her washing machine and then was hung to dry on hangers to minimise creasing and avoid ironing. 'And I bet you have a cleaner.'

He spread his hands. 'I admit, someone comes in a couple of hours a day.'

'And cooks for you, too?'

'No. I do that myself. And, before you start accusing me of being princely for having a cleaner, just about any other business-man living on his own would do the same thing. Time spent cleaning the house is time you can spend more profitably at work.'

'Bottom line,' Lily stated, 'you have staff.'

'They're not live-in.' He paused. 'Except my assistant—whose duties include security.'

She felt her eyes widen. 'You have a bodyguard?'

'Just one and, as I said, he's also my assistant. He's not scary. Provided you're not threatening me, that is,' Karim added meditatively. 'Then, I guess, he might be.'

'But…you're here on your own. You were on your own at Felicity's party.'

'Rafiq is discreet.'

Colour scorched into her cheeks. 'You mean, he was on the balcony that night?'

'No.'

'But he knew.'

'He knew that I was talking to you on the balcony, yes.'

She'd just bet that Karim's bodyguard had guessed exactly what his boss had really been doing. Some of the newspaper articles she'd seen had talked about the playboy desert prince. 'And he knows you're here now.'

Karim walked over to her and pressed his fingertip lightly against her mouth. Just as he had, that evening, before he'd kissed her. For one insane moment, Lily actually considered opening her mouth and taking his finger lightly between her teeth.

Bad, bad idea, she remonstrated with herself. Hayley would be here in a couple of hours—and a couple of hours wasn't nearly long enough to do what she wanted to do with Karim al-Hassan.

Which was completely crazy. She took a step backwards.

'You don't have to be afraid,' Karim said softly.

Oh, but she did. Not of him. Of *herself*.

'It's standard procedure.'

'In your world. Not mine.'

For a moment, his eyes were shadowed. And then he nodded. 'Rafiq's been with me for a long, long time. I trust him with my life—literally.'

'So where is he now?'

'Outside. Doing his job.'

'So, what, he's going to frisk Hayley at the door when she arrives?'

'That's a bit over-dramatic.' Karim frowned. 'I thought you said you didn't watch much television?'

'I don't, or I would've thought about this before. You're royalty, so of *course* you're going to have a bodyguard. And if he's stuck waiting outside while you're slumming it in here, the poor man's going to be bored out of his skull. Tell him to come in.' And apart from basic hospitality, it would mean that she and Karim weren't on their own. An added safety net.

'Firstly, I'm not slumming it, as you so delightfully put it. Secondly, he won't be frisking Hayley. And, thirdly, I could tell him to come in, but he'd refuse.'

Lily blinked. 'Is he *allowed* to refuse your requests?'

Karim laughed. 'You mean, I snap my fingers and everyone jumps to my orders?'

'Yes.'

He spread his hands. 'You haven't.'

'That's different. I'm not from your country and I'm not one of your staff.'

'Actually, I prefer people who work with me to think for themselves. They have a job and they know what needs to be done. I trust them to do it without having to give them step-by-step instructions. Rafiq does the job his way.'

'But—' The timer on the oven pinged, interrupting what she was going to say. She switched it off, checked that the cake was done, then put the tin to cool for a few minutes on a rack.

Karim watched her deal efficiently with the cake. Despite the fact that she was wearing a very unfeminine and traditional chef's outfit—a thick white cotton jacket teamed with baggy black-and-white chequered pants—she still managed to look all curves. Desirable. He wanted to mould his palm over the curve of her buttocks. And he wanted to do a lot more than that. He wanted to unbutton the jacket and slide it off her shoulders. What would she be wearing underneath? A camisole top? Or a lace-trimmed bra? Or—

He'd better stop thinking about that before he embarrassed them both. 'As you're in chef's clothing, I'd expect you to wear a hat.'

'You mean a traditional toque, with a pleat in it for every single way I can cook an egg?'

It was his turn to blink in surprise. 'A pleat for every single way you can cook an egg?'

'Uh-huh. Which in practical terms means up to a hundred. The more pleats, the better the chef.'

'There are a hundred ways of cooking eggs?'

She laughed. 'Trust me, there are. But, no, I don't wear a toque. They're not that comfortable, especially because it means I have to pin my hair up. My Buff deals with it much better because it encloses my hair.'

'Buff.' He knew the word in a different context. A much more pleasurable one.

'It's tubular so I can tuck my hair in it—and when I fasten it my hair stays fastened too,' she explained. 'It's microfibre cloth, so it's cool when the kitchen's boiling. Much more practical than the old-fashioned chef's hat. Which, by the way, very few people wear nowadays.' She shrugged. 'If I had short hair, I'd probably use a skull cap.' She glanced at the clock. 'Right. I need to start getting things ready.'

'I'll start with the washing up,' Karim said.

She shook her head. 'You'll start by making that poor man a drink. I assume you know how he takes his coffee? Or would he prefer tea?'

Karim smiled. 'We've been here for long enough for him to like English coffee.'

'Then you know what to do.'

So she was taking the same approach that he did—telling him what needed to be done and just letting him get on with it? Karim hid his amusement and made the coffee. He took a mug out to Rafiq—who, predictably, said that he was staying put—and then returned to find Lily working her way through a list, ticking things off. Although she wouldn't let him touch the food, citing his lack of a hygiene certificate, she let him get dishes out for her. And the more he watched her work, the more impressed he was. She seemed to do six things at once, but when he looked closely he realised that she was managing her time brilliantly, performing every task in the right order and switching from one to another at the most effective point. A critical path analyst could learn a lot from just watching her for a morning.

And, even more impressively, he discovered that she could do all that and hold a conversation at the same time.

'So are you permanently based in England?' she asked.

'I have been for the last five years, but I'll be going back to Harrat Salma in a few months' time,' he said. 'I might take on some of my father's duties, or I might take an ambassadorial role and travel a bit. That's still under discussion.'

'But on the whole your future's pretty much mapped out?'

'Pretty much,' he admitted. 'Eventually I'll take over from my father, and obviously then, although there will be some travelling involved, I'll be based in Harrat Salma.' And there was another duty he'd have to perform. Producing an heir to the throne. 'And I imagine my parents will start marriage negotiations once I'm back home permanently.'

'Marriage negotiations?' She blinked. 'You mean, you're not even going to be able to choose your own wife? That's outrageous!'

'Far from it. Look how many so-called marriages for love end in divorce.'

She flushed. 'It's not always like that.'

'The statistics aren't on the side of love. What is it, practically two in three marriages ending in divorce? People talk about love, but it's nothing of the kind. It's a relationship based on lust and infatuation. And when that dies, the marriage dies with it because there's nothing left to support it.'

'That's incredibly cynical.'

'It's incredibly accurate,' he corrected. 'The statistics bear it out.'

She shook her head.

He shrugged. 'It worked for my parents. They respect each other and there's a deep affection between them.'

'Isn't that the same thing as love—respect and affection?' Lily asked.

'Maybe. Maybe not. Affection is something that grows with time.' He spread his hands. 'My parents didn't lose their heads and rush into an unbreakable contract with someone unsuitable. That's not what marriage is all about.'

'So what is it about?'

'It's about having similar expectations, working together towards the same end. It's about trust and respect and honour.'

'I can't believe you're actually going to marry someone you don't know.'

He rolled his eyes. 'It's not as if I'll only meet her on the morning of the wedding.'

'And what about physical attraction? Or are you going to have a harem to deal with—?' She stopped abruptly, looking embarrassed.

'Having sex?' he finished, guessing exactly what had been on her mind. The same as his. Going to bed with each other. 'Now you're talking fairy tales. We practise monogamy. And I would always be faithful to my wife. I'd never insult her by taking a mistress.'

'I'm not maligning your honour.' She blew out a breath. 'I just can't believe that you're talking so dispassionately about this—as if marriage is a business arrangement. Especially when the papers say you date a different woman every week.'

'Firstly,' he said, 'marriage is a business arrangement. And secondly, I date a lot, but it doesn't necessarily mean I sleep with all my girlfriends. And besides, they know the score—that I'm out for mutual enjoyment but I'm not able to promise them anything permanent. It's my duty to marry and produce an heir to my country, and I trust my parents to choose someone who will suit me and suit Harrat Salma. Yes, I will have some say in it, but I have to put my country first.'

'That's so cold-blooded.'

'It's sensible,' he corrected. 'Divorce is out of the question. I have a duty to my country. So I need to marry the right person—someone who will support me, someone I can trust and respect. The affection will grow between us afterwards.'

'But what if you fall in love with someone?'

'That's not going to happen.' He smiled wryly. 'I'm twenty-eight, *habibti*. If I were going to fall in love with someone un-suitable, I would've done it already.'

She still couldn't quite get her head round this. How he could be so cool and calm and discuss his future marriage as if it were a business arrangement.

Then again, she'd married for love. She'd been head over heels when she'd walked down the aisle to Jeff. And look what a disaster that had been.

She busied herself with ingredients, chopping and mixing and making sure he couldn't see her face. Couldn't see her struggling with the temptation to break all her rules—a temptation that was growing second by second.

Knowing that he would have to go through an arranged marriage, Karim wasn't free to have a permanent relationship with someone. And he was going back to his country in a few months' time. Which meant that having a fling with him would be safe—she could act on that incredible attraction between them. By definition, their relationship would have limits; it would have to end as soon as he left England. And because she knew that right from the start, her heart wouldn't get involved.

And maybe, just maybe, after the last four years of working hard and the months of utter misery before that, she deserved some fun.

A fling.

Mutual pleasure.

At half past eleven, Lily stopped. 'Is Rafiq a vegetarian?' she asked.

'No,' Karim said.

'Is there anything he can't eat on religious or health grounds?'

'No.'

'Good.' She busied herself chopping salad; then she slit a couple of pitta breads open and deftly filled them with sliced chicken and salad. 'Take him some lunch—and when the shoot's over he's very welcome to pudding.'

He was impressed that she'd thought of it. 'Thanks.'

'And it's up to you if you want to have lunch now, or eat what I make, after the shoot. The broad beans and pancetta work just as well cold as a salad as they do hot as an accompaniment.'

'Whatever's easiest,' Karim said. 'You're not going to eat until afterwards, are you?'

'No.'

'I'll join you, then.'

Just after he'd returned from sending lunch to Rafiq, the photographer arrived. Lily seemed completely at ease with the older woman, so he guessed they'd worked together quite a few times before.

'Hayley, Karim—Karim, Hayley.' Lily introduced them with the minimum of fuss.

For a moment, he wondered if Hayley would recognise his face. Though if she worked for the lifestyle magazines rather than the glossy gossip pages, she probably wouldn't.

'So how do you know our Lily?' Hayley asked.

'Through a mutual friend.'

'Ah.' There was a wealth of supposition in that tiny syllable. Clearly Lily didn't normally have 'friends' in her kitchen during the monthly photo-shoots—which set him apart from other people.

She looked at him with a professional eye, then walked over to the window. 'Hmm. You'd look good in one of these shots. On Lily's patio, eating that gooseberry fool.' She grinned. 'You'd have all the women sighing over you.'

Karim shook his head. 'Thanks, but no.'

Hayley nodded knowingly. 'I see. Pity.'

'What's a pity?' Lily asked.

'That all the best-looking men are gay,' Hayley said ruefully.

She definitely didn't recognise him, then. And Karim was highly amused that Hayley had misread him so badly. He was unable to resist asking, 'And what makes you think I'm not Lily's lover?'

Hayley burst out laughing. 'No offence, love, but our Lily isn't known for dating. She's married to her kitchen.'

Interesting. *Very* interesting.

'So if you're here,' she continued, 'you really are just a friend. And, looking the way you do, with nice manners and being dressed so beautifully…'

'I see,' Karim said, mirroring her earlier tone.

His eyes said something different to Lily—that he wasn't her lover…*yet*.

'All right. I'll do the shoot.'

'You don't have to,' Lily said, sounding almost panicky.

'Relax, *habibti*. It's fine.' He winked at her. 'Just let me know where and how you want me to sit, Hayley,' he said.

'Excellent. We'll do the inside shots first,' she said.

Hayley might be blunt—and completely wrong about the situation between him and Lily—but she was a good photographer, Karim thought. Her directions were clear and concise. She brought out the best in Lily as well as in the food. And watching Lily as she cooked…it was beautiful. Almost as if her movements were choreographed.

When Hayley was satisfied with the indoor shots and Lily had poured the gooseberry fool into a dozen pretty glass bowls, Hayley set up her tripod outside. She directed Karim where to sit and adjusted his pose several times.

It was Lily's turn to watch the photography session. And Hayley was absolutely right, Lily thought. Dressed in another of those collarless white shirts and stone-coloured chinos, Karim looked the epitome of summer. He was perfect for the shot.

And the way he licked the gooseberry fool off the spoon, under Hayley's direction, would make any woman seeing the magazine feel hot and bothered. He was making Lily feel distinctly hot and bothered.

He gave her a sultry look, and she felt her nipples tighten in response.

Oh, Lord.

She was just glad that her chef's jacket was so thick that it hid her body's reaction from him. And she really, really hoped that her thoughts didn't show in her face.

When Hayley had gone—taking a large chunk of the chocolate cake wrapped in greaseproof paper with her—Lily sent Karim out to Rafiq with the gooseberry fool, hoping that she'd be able to get her libido under control before he came back.

Fat chance.

She needed half an hour under a cold shower for that to happen.

When he walked back into the kitchen, even though her back was turned she knew the second he set foot in the room. Her libido sat up and started begging.

'Hey. This is my job. You've done all the hard work.' He took the dishcloth from her, and nudged her aside from the sink with his hip.

Even though the contact between their bodies was casual, and there were several layers of clothes separating them, it was all too easy to imagine his skin sliding against hers. His body pushing into hers. Her body closing round his.

'Lily? Are you all right?'

'Uh.' She swallowed hard, trying to drag her mind back out of the gutter. 'Thanks for your help today.'

'My pleasure.'

'And, look—Hayley pretty much pushed you into those shots. If you'd rather not have a photo of you in the magazine I'll have a word with my editor, explain the situation and ask her not to include it.'

'It's not a problem, Lily.'

'But you're…' She grimaced. 'Isn't it kind of like giving royal approval to my recipes?'

'Fine by me.' He shrugged. 'I approve of that gooseberry fool. Very much.'

That wasn't what she'd meant, and she knew he was deliberately avoiding the issue. 'Won't it cause a problem for you back in Harrat Salma?'

'No. Hayley merely took a shot of your friend sitting on your patio, enjoying a summery pudding.' He continued washing up. 'Who I am has nothing to do with it.'

'But people are going to recognise you.'

'So what if they do?'

'I…' Defeated, she gave up. If it didn't bother him, why should it bother her?

He smiled at her. 'I enjoyed it, actually. It was a lot of fun.'

'Hayley said she thought you were used to having your photograph taken.'

He shrugged. 'I am.'

'But she thought it was because you were a model or something.' She felt her skin heat. 'And she was convinced you were gay.'

His grin broadened. 'If only she knew that the whole time I was licking that spoon, I was imagining tasting *you*.'

Oh, damn. The picture that put in her head. 'Karim.' She breathed his name.

The teasing light disappeared from his eyes, replaced with something much more intense. 'It's going to happen, Lily,' he said softly. 'Sooner or later, it's going to happen. Between you and me.'

Even though she'd been thinking about it earlier, that had been the fantasy. This was the reality. And suddenly she panicked. 'I don't…'

'Date? So Hayley said.' He moistened his lower lip. 'Sometimes rules are made to be broken.'

The last time she'd broken a rule, she'd ended up with a broken heart. Not to mention a broken business. And enormous debts. Even though she knew the situation with Karim was different, the old fears swamped her into silence. She wanted him. Really wanted him. And despite her earlier thoughts about not letting herself get involved, she was scared that she might end up being in too deep.

As if he guessed how much she was panicking, he dried his hands, then took her right hand. Drew it to his lips. 'It'll be OK,' he said softly. 'More than OK. You just need to trust me.'

Trust.

Now, there was a sticking point.

She wasn't sure she was capable of trust any more. 'I…' Frustrated that she couldn't find the right words to explain it—not without telling him just how naïve and foolishly trusting she'd once been—she shook her head.

'Lily, I'm not going to hurt you.' He was still holding her hand; he turned it over, dropped a kiss into the centre of her palm and folded her fingers over it. 'I think right now you need a breathing space, so I'm going to leave now. But you know where I am if you want me.'

If she wanted him?

Of course she wanted him.

But this was all way too complicated.

'Later, *habibti*,' he said softly. 'Later.'

CHAPTER FIVE

LILY slept badly that night. Every time she closed her eyes, she could see that intense look in Karim's eyes. Could hear him saying, 'The whole time I was licking that spoon, I was imagining tasting *you*.' Could feel the warmth of his mouth against her skin...and it drove her crazy, making her ache with wanting.

When the alarm finally dragged her out of a fitful sleep, her head felt like lead and there was a dull ache across her brow. A cup of coffee, two paracetamol and washing her hair in a cool shower made the headache go away, but they did nothing to stop the unnatural heat in her veins. Nothing to stop the anticipatory kick in her stomach at the thought of seeing Karim.

For a moment, she considered going out to buy her supplies before Karim arrived, so she wouldn't be there to answer the door to him—but that would be the coward's way out. And Elizabeth Finch wasn't a coward.

'Good morning,' Karim said when she opened the door to him dead on nine o'clock.

'Good morning. You know where the kettle is, so feel free to make yourself a coffee.'

He glanced at her feet. 'You're wearing shoes.'

'I need to go to the market this morning. The earlier, the better.'

'Which market?'

'The street market round the corner,' she explained. 'There are a couple of organic veg stalls. If I go now I'll get the best choice for my client.'

'Of course. You're catering tonight.'

She nodded. 'I need to go to the butcher's, too.'

'Fine. But, first…' He handed her a bag. 'Better to leave this here than take up space in your basket. Plus it's a bit fragile, even with the bubble-wrap around it.'

'What is it?' she asked.

'You'll see when we get back. Do you have your bag? Your list? Your keys?'

She blinked. 'We're going to the market right now?'

'That's what you said you wanted to do,' he reminded her. 'So let's go.'

'You're going with me?'

He raised an eyebrow. 'As your assistant…yes. I'll carry your shopping for you. Though I'm flattered that you trust me enough to leave me alone in your house.'

So he was still playing that game. She sighed. 'Karim, it'd be easier if you didn't go with me. For goodness' sake, you're His Royal Highness Prince Karim al-Hassan of Harrat Salma.'

'A title doesn't stop me carrying your shopping.'

'What if the paparazzi find out and follow us?'

'Actually, they don't tend to bother with me much, except at parties,' he said with a smile, 'because I'm incredibly boring.'

Boring? Karim? Ha. As if she were going to fall for that one.

'Don't worry. You're not going to find your picture splashed all over the tabloids, along with a few paragraphs of speculation about how long you've been sleeping with me.'

She felt her face heat. 'You haven't slept with me.'

'So I haven't.' And even though he didn't say it, she could see the word in those amazing amber eyes again: *yet*.

She knew it was a promise.

Desire rippled down her spine, and she looked away, not wanting him to see just how tempted she was. It would be, oh, so easy to reach out, pull his head down to hers, and kiss him the same way he'd kissed her on Felicity Browne's balcony. She could still remember how it had felt when he'd kissed her palm yesterday, the warm, erotic pressure of his mouth against her skin, how much she'd wanted him to follow that through—touching his lips to the pulse-point in her wrist and then tracing a path up to the inner curve of her elbow, her shoulder, the sensitive spot at the side of her throat, her collarbones.

To her relief, he misconstrued the reason why she'd turned away and put the bag on her hallway table. 'You won't have photographers camped outside your door or anything like that,' he reassured her. 'You're safe with me. And it'll be nice not to have to carry everything home yourself, will it not?'

Carry. She wished he hadn't said that word. Because she could imagine him carrying her. Upstairs. To her bed.

She made a non-committal noise, not daring to speak in case the wrong words burst out. She was going to get these crazy feelings back under control. She *was*.

'Lily?'

Against her better judgement, she said, 'OK. If you really want to, you can come to the market with me. But you can't play at being my apprentice today. I'm cooking, and there are such things as health and safety regulations. I don't breach them. Ever,' she added, just so he was clear that she always played by the rules in business.

'I would expect nothing less of you,' he said softly. 'How about tasting?'

Finally, she nodded. 'Provided you use clean cutlery, and you use it only once, tasting's fine.'

'Tasting's fine? Good. I'm glad you said that. Because I really need to...' To her shock, he dipped his head and brushed his mouth against hers in a kiss that was completely chaste and yet incredibly sensual at the same time. It was over almost as soon as it had begun—and left Lily wanting so much more, her hands were actually shaking as she grabbed her handbag and shopping basket, then locked the front door behind them.

Karim didn't say a word as they walked together down the street. But every so often, the back of his hand brushed against hers. Casually. Accidentally.

On purpose?

But his expression was inscrutable. She had no idea if he was doing it deliberately or not. But every touch sensitised her skin; her nipples tightened and excitement coiled low in her belly.

No wonder he had a reputation as a playboy.

She'd never met anyone as sensual as Karim al-Hassan. And she'd certainly never thought that a simple visit to the market would bring her to fever pitch. She managed to force herself to concentrate, make sure she didn't miss anything off her list, but by the time they got back to her house she was a wreck. And even though she tried pretending she was cool, calm and sophisticated, she wasn't in the slightest. He knew it, too, because she fumbled her keys and dropped them.

'Allow me, *habibti*.' He retrieved them and unlocked the door, holding it open for her before scooping up the basket and following her indoors.

Lord, she needed a cold shower. Ice cold, so the temperature shocked her brain back to where it should be instead of being lost in erotic fantasies about Karim al-Hassan.

But a shower wouldn't be practical right now.

Particularly as she didn't trust herself not to invite him to join her.

She needed caffeine. 'Coffee,' she mumbled.

'I'll make it.'

Funny how he was already at home in her kitchen. Knew

where everything was, moved around without having to search for things or ask her. And he looked right there, too.

Don't start getting any crazy ideas, she warned herself. There couldn't be any future between them. Apart from the fact that she had no intention of letting a relationship derail her life again, he'd already told her that he would return to his desert kingdom, marry someone chosen by his family, and raise the next generation of heirs. If—*when*—something happened between them, it would only be a fling. It couldn't be more than that.

Get a grip, she told herself mentally, and busied herself putting things away. By the time she'd finished, Karim had made coffee for them and taken a mug out to Rafiq. And when he returned, he brought the paper bag she'd left on her hallway table.

'For you, *habibti*,' he said.

She took out the bubble-wrapped parcel, carefully unwrapped it, and stared in surprise. It looked like an intricate carving in the shape of a rose. 'Thank you. It's beautiful. Is it a carving from Harrat Salma?'

'It's not a carving—it's a desert rose,' he explained. 'Gypsum, with sand inclusions; in arid, sandy conditions the mineral crystallises in a rosette formation. Hence "desert rose".'

'It's lovely, but I can't accept something this valuable.'

He smiled. 'It's a mineral, *habibti*, not a diamond. You simply dig these up in the desert.'

'You dug it up yourself?' Then, before he could answer, she held up a hand to stop him. 'Of course you did. You said yesterday, a good leader's not afraid to get his hands dirty.'

'Precisely.'

There was a wistful look in his eyes, but it was there for such a short space of time that she wondered if she'd imagined it; within moments he was back to being his usual urbane, charming self, asking her about the finer points of planning a menu for a balance of texture, colour and taste. And she knew he wasn't questioning her judgement: he was trying to understand what she did, how she worked.

He spent the rest of the morning with her, and then he reached out to take her hand. 'I'm distracting you, *habibti*. This apprentice thing isn't going to work, is it?'

'No,' she admitted.

'Pity.' He rubbed the pad of his thumb over the back of her hand. 'You're distracting me, too, you know. You should see the pile of paperwork in my office.'

She bit her lip. 'So what are you suggesting? That we call it a day?'

'Not quite. Because, *habibti*, the last few days have shown me how good you are at time management. I think you have capacity to expand a little.'

'In other words, you still think I can manage to fit in the catering for your presentations.'

'Exactly. So I'm going to give you some space to think about it. Decide what you want to do.'

Lord, he was persistent, but at least he was giving her a choice. Perhaps she could give up some time on her freer days, fit in the flexible elements of her work where she could, and do what he wanted. It meant she'd be crazily busy for those weeks. She'd lose all her thinking time.

But with Karim around, she'd lost her thinking time anyway. She'd found herself being distracted by his presence all week, by fantasies of what she wanted him to do with her.

'Tell me your answer on Monday,' he said.

'Monday?'

'When you're having lunch with me,' he reminded her. 'I'll send a car.'

'I'm perfectly capable of get—' she began.

'I know you're perfectly capable of organising your own

transport,' he cut in. 'Just humour me, this once. Rafiq will collect you at half past eleven on Monday.'

'Half past eleven,' she repeated.

'Good.' He was still holding her hand; he raised it towards his mouth, but instead of giving her a polite kiss on the back of his hand he turned her wrist over. Touched his mouth to the point where her pulse was beating madly.

Her knees went weak.

He couldn't stop there.

Please, don't let him stop there.

All thoughts of him being off limits went completely out of her mind. The only thing she was aware of was Karim. The sound of his breathing. The exotic scent of his aftershave. The way her skin had heated up under his mouth.

And she wanted him to continue. Desperately wanted him to continue.

As if he could read her mind, he pushed up the three-quarter-length sleeve of her T-shirt and teased her inner elbow with tiny, nibbling kisses that made her practically hyperventilate. 'Karim.'

'I know,' he said quietly, straightening up and looking her in the eye. His pupils had expanded, leaving a tiny rim of bright golden iris around them. 'It's the same for me. My head's telling me not to do this while my body's saying something completely different. And watching you cook, the way you move…It's been driving me insane.'

'I can't stop thinking about the balcony. About when you kissed me. And I want…' She shivered.

'Ah, Lily.' He dropped her hand and cupped her face in both hands. His mouth brushed against hers, so very lightly—and yet it felt as if she'd been scorched.

The next thing she knew, her hands were fisted in his hair and his arms were wrapped tightly round her, and his mouth was jammed over hers. Somehow he'd moved so that he was sitting on one of the bar stools; he'd pulled her onto his lap so that she was straddling him.

Two layers of soft denim between them.

Too many layers of denim between them.

His erection pressed against her and she couldn't help rocking slightly, shifting closer.

He tore his mouth away from hers. 'Lily, you blow me away.'

It was very much mutual. She couldn't see straight, couldn't think straight. And she wanted his mouth back on hers, right now. She caught his lower lip between her teeth, nipping just hard enough to make him open his mouth—and then she kissed him the way he'd kissed her. Sliding her tongue into his mouth, exploring and tasting and inciting him, the way he'd incited her. Hot and wet and wanting.

The pressure against her clitoris intensified as he moved slightly, rocked against her. She moaned into his mouth, wanting more.

And then, just as suddenly as he'd started, he stopped.

'My self-control's hanging by the tiniest, thinnest thread,' he said. 'Part of me wants to say to hell with health and safety—I want to rip off your clothes and mine, and take you right here, right now, on this granite worktop.' He paused. 'But.'

She shivered. Such a tiny word, yet it felt so huge. 'But?'

He dragged in a breath. 'But I don't have a condom. And I'm pretty sure you don't, either.'

'No,' she admitted. 'I…' Her voice tailed off. How stupid and unsophisticated he must think her. She couldn't even remember the last time she'd dated anyone, let alone the last time she'd made love.

'It's OK.' This time, his kiss wasn't consuming. It was gentle, soothing, telling her that everything was fine. 'This isn't exactly normal for me, either.'

'No?' She didn't believe a word of it. Karim was six feet two of pure masculinity, exotic good looks combined with those intense amber eyes. Even without the added inducements of his title and his wealth, women would fall at his feet if he clicked his fingers. And hadn't the newspapers called him the playboy prince?

'No. I date, sure.' He drew the pad of his thumb along her lower lip. 'But I don't get distracted. I don't skip work with the flimsiest of excuses, just to spend time with someone.'

'You skipped work for me?'

'I rearranged my schedule,' he said. 'Worked late to make up for it.'

He'd rearranged his schedule to spend time with her. The thought warmed her. 'So what are we going to do…about this?'

'I know what I want to do,' he said huskily. 'But I'm not going to be selfish about this. You have a business to run. And although we both know I could make you forget all about it— just as you could make me forget what I'm doing—that wouldn't be fair. To either of us. So I'm going to do the noble thing.'

'Which is?'

Gently, he shifted her off his lap. 'I'm going to leave you in peace. Give you time to think about it—to think about what you want to do.' He stole another kiss. 'To think about what you want me to do.'

Just as well she was holding onto the worktop. Because the thoughts that put in her mind made her knees weak.

'And we'll talk on Monday.'

Monday.

Four whole days away.

Four days to get her sanity back: or four days to drive her demented and utterly desperate for him. Right at that moment, she had no idea which way it was going to go.

'Monday,' she said.

'Later, *habibti*,' he said. He brushed his mouth against hers just once—light, teasing, enough to make her mouth tingle and her body beg for more.

And then he was gone.

CHAPTER SIX

Four days of breathing space.

And every single second of it dragged.

Lily found herself missing Karim. Really missing him. And, although she made sure she gave her clients the service they were used to from her, she knew her heart wasn't completely in her work. She'd always been so excited by cooking, loved what she did. But now…everything felt faded, dull, in comparison with him.

'Want to talk about it?' Hannah asked on the Saturday night.

'About what?'

'Whatever's been distracting you for the last few days.'

More like whoever, Lily thought. 'I'm fine,' she fibbed.

'Hmm. I worry about you, Lily.' Hannah hugged her swiftly. 'You work too hard and, since Jeff, you've never…' She shook her head. 'Sorry. That wasn't tactful. And considering my marriage ended up in a mess, too, I don't blame you for not wanting to get involved with anyone. But it's been four years for you, Lily. I think it'd do you good to go and have some fun.'

'Have a fling, you mean?'

The words were out before she could stop them.

And Hannah's look of surprise turned quickly into interest. 'You've met someone?'

'Yes. No. It's complicated.' Lily wrinkled her nose. 'Well. It's sort of complicated. There couldn't be any future in it.'

'I would ask if he's married,' Hannah said, 'but I know you'd never do that.'

Lily appreciated her friend's belief in her. 'No, he's not married. But he's...' How could she explain without telling Hannah the full details? 'He's not going to be around for long.'

'So it'd be like a holiday romance?' Hannah spread her hands. 'That sounds perfect to me. No ties, no involvements, so you don't have to worry that he's going to let you down. You can just have fun, enjoy it while it lasts and move on afterwards.'

Put like that, it sounded like the perfect solution. 'Is it really that simple?'

'Of course it is.' Hannah smiled at her. 'Go for it. It'll do you good.'

They were too busy for the rest of the evening to discuss it further, but even though Lily was rushed off her feet she still found herself clock-watching. It grew even worse when she was at home during the day. The minutes seemed to stretch into hours. Several times, she picked up the phone and started to dial Karim's number before cutting the connection. It wouldn't be fair to distract him; he had work to catch up on, too. Besides, he was the one who'd suggested four days of breathing space.

Four days to decide what to do.

Cook for him? Or sleep with him?

Could she be greedy and do both?

Was it possible to have it all?

Cooking for Karim would be a challenge. She had a feeling that he wouldn't want sandwiches and savouries for his business meetings, and this could be a chance to explore a completely different cuisine. Broaden her repertoire. And although it would mean that her schedule was crazy and she'd be shattered by the end of it, it would only be temporary. She could move the more flexible side of her work around, lose some of her free time.

Besides, she liked what she'd seen of Karim. She wanted to help him.

And if she was going to break one of her rules, she might as well break all of them.

Temporarily.

By Monday morning, she was convinced that all her blood had turned to adrenalin. She couldn't settle to anything. And she was shocked to realise that she was more flustered by a simple invitation to lunch than she had been by any important rush-job at work.

For a start, she had no idea what to wear.

This was lunch, not an actual date, so she could keep it casual. Jeans and a T-shirt. Then again, it was going to be a business discussion. Maybe the black dress she wore to clients' houses…But no. Last time she'd worn that outfit, Karim had kissed her stupid and she'd wanted him to remove every scrap of her clothing.

She still wanted him to do that.

But she needed to get the business side of it sorted first.

In the end, she chose tailored black trousers, a slate-blue camisole top, and a black lacy shrug. With high heels, she looked businesslike rather than casual. Particularly because she took care over her make up. And she pinned her hair up in a chignon rather than pulling it back at the nape of her neck, the way she usually did at work, or leaving it loose.

She had enough time to spend an hour at her laptop—pretending to plan her column for the next month and trying very hard not to think about the fact she was going to break all her rules and make love with Karim this afternoon.

Then Rafiq arrived to collect her.

'Miss Finch? This way, please.'

'Thank you, Rafiq.'

It felt odd, sitting in the back of the enormous black car. She was more used to driving herself, in the small van she used for work, or taking the Tube. Rafiq was polite but not particularly chatty, and when she tried to ask him about Karim he clammed up even more. Karim could definitely rely on his assistant-cum-bodyguard's discretion.

And then at last Rafiq pulled into a parking place. He came round to open Lily's door for her, then escorted her to the foyer of an expensive-looking block of modern flats.

'You're not coming with me?' she queried.

He spread his hands. 'Karim gave me the afternoon off. Though he knows where I am, should he need me.'

Rafiq was close enough to his employer to use his given name rather than something more formal, Lily thought; he'd certainly been formal with her. Though it hadn't been a disapproving sort of formality. He'd actually smiled as he'd thanked her for her kindness in sending out lunch and coffee for him on the mornings when Karim had been playing at being her apprentice.

'Well, have a nice afternoon, Rafiq.'

He regarded her with almost a smile. 'And you, Miss Finch.' He gave a small bow. 'You need to press the top buzzer,' he said, gesturing to the intercom.

So Karim had the penthouse flat, did he? That didn't surprise her. She pressured the buzzer.

After a short pause, Karim answered. 'Good afternoon, Lily.'

'Good afternoon.'

'I'm on the third floor. Take the lift.'

She did so, relieved that the lift wasn't the kind with mirrored walls. She didn't want to see whether she looked as nervous as she felt.

There were two doors in the corridor. One was obviously a fire door, which led to the stairs; the other was Karim's front door. And in between was what seemed like acres of deep-pile carpet. She took a deep breath, walked steadily over to his front door, and knocked.

A few moments later, he opened the door. Smiled at her. And the look in his eyes made a pulse throb between her legs. 'Hello, Lily. Come in.' He ushered her into the flat.

The carpet there, too, was deep enough for her to sink into it. She slipped off her shoes, not wanting to ruin his carpet, and the soft wool caressed her insteps as she followed him into his living room. The room was enormous, light and airy, with what looked like a balcony or a terrace outside the floor-to-ceiling window. The walls were painted a deep sand colour, and rich silk hangings in jewelled tones were placed to catch the light. The sofas were low and overstuffed, upholstered with what looked like expensively soft leather—the sort you could sink into and never want to get up from. There was a sculpture on a low table, and photograph frames on the marble mantel-piece that looked as if they were enamelled but she suspected were works of art in themselves, studded with gems.

Even though she was used to being in the homes of the rich and famous, his flat was something else. Understated, tasteful—and very, very expensive. A completely different world from her own. Yet another reminder of the gulf between them.

But those sexy amber eyes were regarding her in a way that made her nipples tighten and her temperature rise a notch. And she'd spent the weekend arguing with herself: this was going to be safe. A fling with limits. She wasn't going to get hurt. Everything was going to be just fine.

'What would you like to drink?' he asked.

'Something soft, please.'

'Sure. Come through.'

His kitchen was almost as large as hers, incredibly tidy and full of the kind of equipment she'd been tempted by but that had been outside her budget. Instead of an island, there was a granite-topped table in the middle.

The words echoed in her head. *I want to rip off your clothes and mine, and take you right here, right now, on this granite...*

Oh, Lord.

Faced with this incredible kitchen, she didn't know whether she wanted to explore, start cooking, or just rip off Karim's clothes and straddle him on the kitchen floor.

'Lily?'

She shook herself. 'Sorry. Staring. Lusting.' To her horror, the last word slid out before she could stop it.

He laughed. 'Over my kitchen? Or—' his voice dropped an octave, grew husky with promise '—over me?'

Over him. Definitely over him.

Flustered, she took a box from her handbag and gave it to him. 'I meant to give you these. To say thank you for lunch.' The same kind of expensive chocolates that he'd bought her, the previous week. And she'd remembered what he'd told her: he liked his chocolate rich and dark and spicy.

He looked at the box and smiled his approval. 'I love these. Thank you. They'll go well with the *gahwa saada*—traditional Arabic coffee—at the end of our meal,' he said.

Something smelled gorgeous: she recognised the scent of spices and garlic and tomatoes. And he'd talked about Arabic coffee. 'You've made me a traditional meal from your homeland?' she guessed.

'You questioned whether I could cook. So I thought I'd show you rather than tell you. I put most of it together last night, so the flavours had time to infuse and mature.'

'But...as a prince, don't you have servants?'

'In Harrat Salma, yes. Here, no. Anyway, we've had this conversation. I cook for myself. I enjoy it—it relaxes me. Gives me time to think.' He shrugged. 'Arabic cooking involves time. Patience.' His eyes held hers. 'A virtue that's always rewarded.'

She had a feeling she knew exactly what kind of reward he had in mind.

The same one that she did.

This was impossible.

But he'd said something else, something that had surprised her. About letting flavours infuse. 'You think like I do about food.' She frowned. 'So why do you need me to cook for you? Why can't you just do it yourself?'

'Because, *habibti*, although I'm perfectly capable of multi-tasking, I can't cook in my kitchen and hold a business meeting in a different room at the same time. Nice idea but, as you pointed out to me last week, the laws of physics rather get in the way.' He took a jug from the fridge and filled two heavy-based plain crystal tumblers. 'Anyway. *Ya hala.* Welcome to my home.'

'Thank you.' She took a sip. 'This is very refreshing.'

'It's traditional orange *sharbat*. And what's in it?' he tested.

'Freshly squeezed orange juice and sparkling water—and you've clearly steeped mint in it for a while.'

'Not bad. But there's one ingredient left.'

She shook her head. 'Tell me.'

'Orange-blossom water.' He took a bottle from the fridge and handed it to her.

She couldn't resist taking a sniff. 'This'd be lovely in a sorbet, and to flavour some crisp biscuits to accompany it.'

'Nice idea. I'll remember that.' He looked at her. 'So. Are you ready for lunch, *habibti*?'

'Thank you. Is there anything I can do to help?'

'It's all done. Come and sit down.' He led her through to the dining room. The dining table was huge, more like a board-room table, and in one corner of the room there was a glass-topped desk where she guessed he worked, but all the office equipment was hidden away behind frosted glass.

The table stood in front of the huge floor-to-ceiling

windows with a view over the park; a blue damask runner was centred on the pale wood, set with granite placemats, silver cutlery, white porcelain and more of the plain crystal glasses. Again, there were rich abstract hangings on the walls, though this time they were in marine shades, toning with the dark blue curtains and pale blue walls.

'It's a beautiful setting,' she said.

'What were you expecting—a low table, silk cushions and a tented ceiling?' he teased.

'Maybe not the tented ceiling, exactly—but, given the scent in the kitchen…yes, I was expecting the rest,' she admitted.

He spread his hands. 'It can be arranged. As the saying goes, all I need to do is snap my fingers.'

'Very funny. Next you'll be telling me that you have a genie.'

'Djinn,' he corrected. 'No.' He glanced meditatively upwards. 'A tented ceiling wouldn't be right here, because I couldn't go outside and see the desert stars.'

'You can't see any stars in London,' she said, understanding exactly what he meant. 'It's one of the things I love about going to see Mum and Yves in France—I can sit outside and watch the stars.'

'Your mother and brother, they don't live in a city?'

'My mother and stepfather.' Of sorts, but it was too complicated to explain. 'They live in Provence. In the middle of nowhere. Well, they're about thirty minutes from the airport in Marseille, and there's a town about ten miles away, so they're not completely cut off from civilisation—but it's far enough away that there's practically no traffic around the vineyard or the village. Life's slow, and you can just relax and unwind in the sun.'

'Like in the desert,' he mused. 'But I'd bet serious money that the stars in Harrat Salma are like nothing you've ever seen.'

'You miss it, don't you?'

'Yes and no. I've been based in England for over half my life,' he said.

'So you went to school here?' she asked.

'When I was thirteen,' he said.

'It must have been hard, leaving your family.'

'I wasn't completely on my own. My b—' He stopped abruptly and his face grew shuttered. 'Anyway. Time for lunch. Sit down, *habibti*.'

What had he been about to say? His brother? And yet she couldn't remember seeing any reference to a younger or older brother in the news stories she'd glanced through. Just stunning models and actresses, with lots of blonde hair and incredibly long legs.

He brought in several platters, then took a seat opposite her.

'You've gone to a lot of trouble. Thank you.'

He shrugged. 'As I said, I enjoy cooking. It helps me think. Now, may I help you?' He talked her through the dishes; circassian chicken, tabbouleh and felafel she knew, but not the *hashweh*, courgettes and aubergines stuffed with a mixture of lamb, rice and spices, and the *shakshouka*, peppers stewed with garlic, tomatoes and coriander.

'Fabulous,' she said when she'd tasted each in turn. 'You know, you're really brave, cooking for me. Most people panic at the thought of cooking for a trained chef.'

'I don't panic easily.' He spread his hands. 'And I'd rather hear your professional opinion rather than your polite guest's opinion.'

She looked at him. 'There's a good balance of tastes and textures. You've got bread to mop up the juices, which is good—couscous or rice wouldn't work, as you already have grains in the tabbouleh. The only thing I'd ask is, I assume it's meant to be served warm rather than hot?'

He inclined his head. 'We're doing this the traditional way. Though I suppose in a way it's like Mediterranean food—the Greeks, too, serve their food warm rather than hot.'

'If you ever decide you don't want to be a sheikh any more,' she said with a smile, 'just go on a course and get yourself a food hygiene certificate.'

'And be your apprentice again?' he asked.

'No. Cooking as well as this, you'd make partner in a week,' she said.

'Partner.' His eyes glittered. 'I'll bear that in mind, *habibti*.'

She knew he was talking about a different type of partner. Not a business partner—a lover.

And she also knew that she was going to accept his offer. Maybe even instigate it.

Her mouth went dry, and her hand was trembling very slightly as she lifted the glass of orange juice to her mouth.

Pudding was a rosewater-scented sorbet, sprinkled with pomegranate seeds.

'Now that's a good combination,' Lily said. 'Taste, texture and colour.' She pressed one of the pomegranate seeds to the roof of her mouth, feeling the flavour burst over her tongue. 'Oh-h-h. Luscious.'

'Pomegranates represent forbidden desire,' Karim said.

'Persephone.' A story she remembered her mother telling her, a story connected with a painting at an exhibition Amy had taken her to see as a special treat.

'Some cultures believe that Eve was tempted with the pomegranate rather than an apple,' Karim said.

Temptation.

A word she could definitely associate with Karim.

She could imagine Karim feeding her a pomegranate, seed by seed, as she lay with her head on his lap, and the thought made her temperature go up a notch. Because the picture in her head grew clearer, sharper. Of Karim bending down to lick a stray trickle of juice from her lips. Of his mouth against hers, hot and demanding. Of...

'*Habibti*?' he asked. 'Are you all right?'

No. She wanted him. Here. Now.

It was an effort to get herself back under control. 'I'm fine,' she fibbed.

He allowed her to help him clear the table, but refused to let her wash up. 'And now I'm going to make you coffee.'

He gestured to one of the bar stools; she sat down and watched as he took a pot with a long handle, measured water in a tiny handle-less cup and poured it into the pot, then added two teaspoons of coffee.

'So you make Arabic coffee like Turkish coffee,' she said, fascinated.

'Sort of, but we add other things—some people add saffron and some add orange blossom water, but I tend to do it the traditional way. One teaspoon of coffee per cup and half a teaspoon of spice.'

She watched as he added a teaspoonful of crushed cardamom, heated the coffee, then removed the pot from the heat until the foam started to subside. He poured a small amount of coffee into two small handle-less cups made of white china, with a wide band at the top in an intricate silver pattern.

'Welcome to my house, Lily. To your health.' He handed the cup to her.

'Thank you. And to yours,' she responded. She tasted the coffee as he watched.

'Do you like it?' he asked.

'I think it's an acquired taste,' she said diplomatically.

He gave her a mischievous smile. 'You're meant to drink three cups, to be polite. It's very rude to refuse.'

'Three whole cups?' She could maybe manage one. But three?

'Not full cups. That's why we only put a little in, each time. Three little sips,' he said. 'The first is for health, the second is for love, and the third is for future generations.' He poured her a second mouthful. 'You wobble your cup very slightly from side to side when you've had enough. Like this.' He demonstrated.

'But it's rude to refuse.'

He inclined his head. 'However, we're in your country, not mine. I'm hardly going to send you to the tower and have you clapped in chains for refusing any more coffee.'

'I'm glad to hear it.' The first for health. The second for love...

She took another sip. 'Karim. The last four days have been—' She broke off, not wanting to admit just how much he affected her.

'I know,' he said softly. 'For me, too. I nearly cracked at three o'clock yesterday morning. Except I didn't think you'd appreciate a phone call right at that moment.'

'I was probably awake,' she admitted. Thinking of him.

'So you've had time to think about the situation.'

She nodded. 'This is driving me crazy. Driving us *both* crazy.'

'I know. I can't get you out of my head. Every time I close my eyes, you're there. And I never let myself get distracted like this.'

'It's the same for me,' she admitted wryly. 'It's a seriously bad idea. Completely against my better judgement.'

'Agreed.'

She could see that he was looking at her mouth. Just as she was looking at his. Wanting. Needing.

'Let's do this,' she said in a rush. 'Let's get it out of our systems.'

'Are you sure?'

She wasn't sure that it'd get him out of her system. But she was sure that if she didn't give in to her body's urging, she'd go insane.

He was clearly waiting for an answer. So Lily wobbled her

cup, the way he'd shown her. Put it down on the worktop. Then she walked over to him, slid her hands into his hair, and drew his mouth down to hers.

CHAPTER SEVEN

THE first touch of Lily's mouth on his broke Karim's self-control. And then he was kissing her back, his arms wrapped tightly round her. He could feel the softness of her breasts against his ribcage, the warmth of her skin through her thin camisole top and his shirt, and it wasn't enough. He wanted more. So much more.

That camisole top was driving him crazy. With the lacy shrug, her shoulders were covered, and the neckline wasn't plunging. She looked perfectly modest. And yet, at the same time, the material clung to her curves, as close to her skin as he wanted to be.

And she'd kissed him first.

He loved the fact that she'd been brave and honest enough to tell him what she wanted. Even more than that, he loved the fact they wanted the same thing. This was completely mutual. They'd both been holding back—and now they didn't have to, any more. They could give in to this crazy, whirling desire.

And he knew it was going to be amazing.

Still kissing her, he slipped the lace shrug from her shoulders and placed it behind him on the kitchen worktop. And then he broke the kiss so he could trace a path with his lips down her throat, across to her shoulder. He hooked one finger under the spaghetti strap of her top and the clear strap of her bra, drawing them both down to bare her shoulder. Taking his time, he kissed his way along the skin he'd just bared, breathing in her scent.

She tipped her head back, offering him her throat. He took full advantage, kissing the curve of her throat and lingering in the hollows of her collarbones before drawing the straps down to bare her other shoulder.

He nuzzled his way along her skin, breathing in her scent as he kissed her. 'You smell of…mmm…dulce de leche.'

'It's my shower gel.'

'It's gorgeous.' He dragged in a breath. 'Though I'm afraid it makes me want to taste you, Lily. Touch you. Make love with you.'

'Then do it,' she said, her voice husky and sexy as hell. And her pupils were enormous, so huge that her eyes looked almost black. It looked as though she wanted this—needed this—as much as he did.

'Sure?' he checked.

'Absolutely sure.'

'Good.' He slid one arm round her, then bent to scoop his other arm under her knees, lifting her up. She held onto his shoulders for balance, and he couldn't resist stealing another kiss before carrying her into the hall and up the stairs.

'Karim? I thought this was a flat?'

'It is. It's on two floors,' he said. 'Downstairs is the living quarters and my office. Upstairs is for sleep and bathing.' And, oh, he was looking forward to sharing a bath with her. Lathering her skin. Sluicing the foam off her again. And touching her until she was quivering and begging him to enter her.

He nudged his bedroom door open with his foot and carried her over to the bed before setting her on her feet again, letting her slide all the way down his body.

'If you're going to change your mind, Lily, do it now,' he

said. 'Because once we pass the point of no return...' It was a promise rather than a threat. Once they passed the point of no return, they were going to paradise. Both of them.

She looked him straight in the eye, proud and unafraid. 'I'm not going to change my mind.'

'Good.' He cupped her face in both hands. Dipped his head. Brushed his mouth so lightly against hers in the sweetest, gentlest kiss. Then he pulled back just far enough to look into her eyes. Serious grey-blue eyes. Eyes that told him just how much she wanted him.

'Hold that thought,' he whispered, and went over to the window to close the curtains. He left the blinds where they were, so enough of the bright spring sunshine filtered into the room to let him see her.

She was still standing where he'd set her down; he walked back over to her and took her hand again. Held her gaze. Kissed the tip of each finger, drawing it briefly into his mouth until he could see the flare of desire brighten in her eyes. And then he took the hem of her camisole top and drew it upwards. She lifted her arms, letting him pull off her top; although he'd intended to fold it neatly and put it over the back of the chair, his brain forgot to send the message to his fingers and he ended up simply dropping the garment on the floor. He traced along the lacy edges of her bra with one fingertip, enjoying the contrast between the stiffness of the black lace trim and the softness of her pale, pale skin. 'Lily. You're so beautiful,' he breathed.

'Thank you.' Her cheeks bloomed with colour.

He was charmed by her blush. She didn't take compliments for granted, and he liked that.

'This is, um, a tad uneven.' She gestured to her state of undress and then to the fact that he was fully clothed.

'Do something about it, then,' he invited.

She held his gaze for a long, long moment, and then she

began to unbutton his shirt. Precisely, carefully. She pushed the material off his shoulders; he had no idea where it landed and he didn't care, because then Lily was touching him. She stroked his arms, his shoulders, then let her hands trail down over his chest to his abdomen. 'Karim al-Hassan, you're beautiful, too.' Her fingers brushed against his abdomen again, and his body tightened. 'I take it you're a regular at the gym, to get a six-pack like this?'

'Not as much as I should do,' he admitted. 'Especially as my best friend owns several health clubs and nags me about the importance of exercise. But I play squash a couple of times a week, and I eat reasonably sensibly.'

She licked her lower lip; unable to help himself, he bent his head and caught her lip between his, sliding his hands down her sides and moulding them to her curves.

He wanted that chignon out of the way, too. He didn't want her smooth and sophisticated and businesslike. He wanted the passionate woman beneath, all tumbled hair and sexy pout. He searched for the pins in her hair, found them and gently removed them.

'Gorgeous. So soft,' he said softly as her hair fell over her shoulders. This was how he remembered her on the balcony, her mouth full from kissing and her hair mussed and her eyes full of desire.

He reached behind her back with one hand and unclipped her bra; then sucked in a breath as the garment fell and her breasts spilled into his hands. The perfect fit. Her nipples were all rosy and hard and just begging for him to touch them.

So he did. He dipped his head and took one nipple into his mouth, teasing it with the tip of his tongue and then sucking hard.

She dragged in a breath. 'Karim.'

He stopped immediately, hearing the quiver in her voice. 'Too much?'

She shook her head. 'No. I want more. A lot more. I want everything you can give me.'

'Greedy.' He nipped gently at her skin. 'Guess what?'

'What?'

'I'm greedy, too. I want everything you can give me, too, Lily. I want you so badly, it feels as if I'm burning up.'

She rested her hand briefly against his forehead. 'You are. Probably because you're still wearing too much and you need to strip off.'

'So what do you suggest we do about it, *habibti*?'

She gave him the wickedest smile he'd ever seen, then undid the button of his chinos and let her hand rest against the zip.

For a moment, he couldn't breathe, he wanted her so much. He wanted to feel her hand curled round his shaft. Wanted to feel her stroke him, tease him, wrap her legs round him. Wanted to fit himself to her entrance and slide into her hot, tight wetness.

Maybe he said the words aloud—he had no idea. He couldn't think straight any more. But then she slowly undid his zip. Pushed his chinos over his hips. Curled her fingers round his erection through the soft jersey of his jockey shorts, all the while keeping eye contact and giving him that wicked, wicked smile. And he found himself almost hyperventilating.

'Lily. Keep this up and I'll last all of five seconds,' he warned, when he was able to speak.

She trailed one finger along the length of his erection, still with that barrier of soft jersey between their skin. And now it was her turn to tease him, licking her lower lip and looking all the way down his body and all the way up again. 'So what do you suggest, Karim?'

Talking was off the agenda. Definitely off the agenda. He needed to act. Right now.

He undid the button of her trousers, slid the zip down, and gently pushed the soft material over her hips. And then she was standing before him in nothing but a tiny pair of black lace knickers and bright pink nail polish on her toes.

The ultimate temptation.

And right now she was all his—just as he was all hers.

Nothing else mattered.

He ripped off the rest of his clothes, shoved his duvet aside, scooped her up and laid her on the bed.

Lily couldn't remember desiring anyone so much—even Jeff, in the days before he'd hurt and disillusioned her. Karim was just perfect. He wasn't lean and skinny, but he wasn't fat either: just beautifully toned, with powerful shoulders and strong biceps and narrow hips and strong thighs. He really did look like a desert prince. And the contrast between his olive skin and her own very fair English complexion made her shiver with pleasure.

His hands were sure yet gentle as he tipped her back against the pillows, and when he kissed his way down her body, his face was soft and smooth against her skin. Obviously he'd shaved that morning.

And somehow he'd found erogenous zones she hadn't even known existed, making her wriggle beneath him, desperate for more. He circled her navel with his tongue, nuzzled her hip bones, and finally, finally removed her knickers and slid his hands between her thighs, parting them; but when they moved lower, caressing the backs of her knees, she almost whimpered.

She knew now exactly how he'd felt when she'd teased him through his underpants. Hot. Desperate. Wanting all the barriers gone so they could be skin to skin. So he'd be inside her.

'Karim. Stop teasing me. Please. I need…'

'I know, *habibti*. So do I,' he whispered, and kissed her swiftly before climbing off the bed.

Despite being completely naked, he was totally unselfconscious; Lily couldn't help watching him as he moved. He really was beautiful. Perfect musculature beneath that smooth olive skin. And she *wanted*.

He rummaged in his chinos, took out his wallet and removed a condom.

'My job, I think,' she said, taking it from him as he joined her on the bed again. She undid the foil packet, then slid the condom over his erect penis; and she was gratified when he gave a sharp intake of breath.

He knelt between her thighs, and she sank back against the pillows—purest, softest down. Karim stole another kiss, then whispered, 'Lily?'

She opened her eyes. 'Yes?'

'Now?'

'Now,' she confirmed.

Slowly, gently, he eased his body into hers. Slow, measured thrusts, going a little deeper each time, letting her body get used to his size and his weight.

And it was driving her crazy.

Lily had had sex before. Made love before. But nothing had prepared her for this. This strange feeling of…completion. That after a long, long journey, she'd finally come home.

This really shouldn't be happening.

She knew that she and Karim had no future together. How could they, when he was royal-born and would eventually go home to rule his desert kingdom with his family's chosen bride by his side?

And besides, she'd promised herself that this would be temporary. That her heart wouldn't get involved.

'This feels like paradise,' Karim said softly.

He slid his hands up her thighs, gently positioning her so that her legs were wrapped round his waist, and then he pushed deeper. Lily couldn't help giving a little 'oh' of pleasure. Karim smiled, but not as if he were smugly pleased with himself; more that he was pleased he was making her feel so good.

He kissed her throat—hot, wet, open-mouthed kisses that had her quivering and clutching at his shoulders, wanting him even closer, needing the ultimate contact. She was aware of the hardness of his chest against the softness of her breasts, and the friction of the hair against her sensitised nipples made her shiver—too much and not enough, all at the same time.

And then, as if Karim knew she was right near the edge, he slowed everything down. Slowly, so incredibly focused, he withdrew until he was almost out of her, then slid all the way back in again, putting pressure on just the right spot and making her feel as if she were floating. She should've guessed that he'd be as good at making love as he was at kissing—at cooking—at practically anything he put his mind to doing. But then he adjusted his rhythm to suit hers, stoking her desire higher and higher until she couldn't think about anything else except the way he made her feel.

When her climax hit, it was amazing: as if she were in a ballroom somewhere, dancing cheek to cheek with him, with the light of a thousand candles reflecting off a mirror ball in the centre of the room and whirling round her, making her dizzy.

'Now,' he whispered, and jammed his mouth against hers; she felt his body surge against hers, and knew that he too had just fallen over the edge.

It was a while before Lily floated back to earth. She found herself curled up against Karim, her head resting on his shoulder and her arm wrapped round his waist; his hand was resting on the curve of her hip. She felt warm and comfortable and safe, and it would be, oh, so easy to let herself drift into sleep—and let him wake her later with kisses and caresses.

Considering that it was a Monday afternoon, this was incredibly decadent. Lazing in bed together, as if they both didn't have other things to do.

'So what's the verdict?' she asked softly. 'Got it out of your system?'

Karim turned on his side and shimmied slightly down the bed so he was facing her, then brushed his mouth against hers. 'Not yet. How about you?'

'Not yet.' She smiled wryly. If anything, it had made the wanting worse. Because now she knew what it felt like to make love with Karim al-Hassan, she wanted to do it all over again. And again. 'So what happens now?'

He kissed the tip of her nose. 'You're all warm and soft and naked—and, best of all, in my arms. In my bed.' He nuzzled the curve of her neck. 'Mmm, and you still smell of dulce de leche. So my vote is I go and get those fabulous chocolates you bought and we stay right where we are. Unless you really, really have to be somewhere else this afternoon?'

'I don't mean now as in "right this second".' She shifted, looking awkward. 'Though it's the middle of the afternoon. We really ought to get up.'

'There's no ought,' he countered. 'But I take it you mean "now" as in "after this".' He brushed a strand of hair from her face. 'We *could* pretend this never happened.'

He might be able to, but she knew she'd find it a struggle.

'Or,' he said thoughtfully, 'we could carry on. But, Lily, I'm not going to lie to you. I can't offer you anything permanent.'

'I know that. And I'm not looking for a relationship anyway. I don't have room in my life.' She smiled wryly. 'Having sex with you—I just broke my personal rules. And I'm going to break the rest of them, too. I was going to tell you earlier, except...' She shivered. 'You distracted me.' And how. 'Anyway. I'll cook for you.'

'Business and pleasure don't mix.' He shook his head. 'Forget about the business meetings, Lily.'

'But they're important to you, aren't they?'

'I'll manage.'

He hadn't answered the question, so she knew the answer. They were important.

'You don't have to manage.' She laced her fingers through his. 'We're talking lunch and coffee, yes?'

'Yes. Morning and mid-afternoon coffee.'

'Then it's doable. Whatever days they are. If I get Hannah to do the shopping for me, I can cook for you in the mornings. And I have a couple of people I can call on when I need extra waiting staff—if you don't mind, they'll do the afternoon coffee, but I'll have cooked everything they serve.'

'I don't want to put pressure on you.'

She laughed wryly. 'Says the man who spent the best part of last week under my feet, distracting me.'

'Because I was being selfish and not looking at things from your point of view. As you said, everyone needs time off. If you fit in catering for my meetings on top of your current bookings, you'll be working stupid hours. You won't get any time to yourself.'

'Do you take time off?' she asked.

'No,' he admitted. 'There's always someone to see, a report to read, leads to follow up, plans to make.'

'Well, then. What's sauce for the goose, as they say. Yes, it'll be crazy, but it's a short term thing—a one-off.' As their affair would be. 'So I'll manage.' She paused. 'So what is it you actually do?'

He blinked. 'I thought you looked me up on the Internet?'

'I did. Just long enough to find out that you were Prince Karim al-Hassan of Harrat Salma.' She paused. 'And a serial party-goer with a taste for tall, glamorous, posh blondes.'

'Yes, to the first.' He rolled his eyes. 'The second is pretty much spin. For the record, I'm very attracted to a certain small, curvy woman with brown hair.' He twined the ends of her hair round his finger. 'Not that your hair's plain brown. It has gold and copper strands in the sunlight. Natural highlights.'

She couldn't resist it. 'Don't split hairs.'

'You have a very bad taste in puns, *habibti.*'

She laughed. 'So your life isn't a round of lunch appointments and cocktails and parties, then?'

He sighed. 'Yes and no. It looks like it is, I admit. But parties are the quickest way to network—to meet the people who can usefully do business with me. You can't promote something without some degree of partying.'

'So who are you really? Underneath the spin?'

Karim thought about it, not sure how to answer. Although it was something he didn't usually talk about, he felt compelled to be honest with Lily. To tell her the truth. He released her hair and lay back against the pillows. 'By training, I'm a vulcanologist.'

'A vulcanologist?' She blinked. 'You're telling me you have volcanoes in your country? But…' She shook her head. 'You're from Arabia. I thought…'

'Lawrence of Arabia, endless dunes and camels? No. We have deserts, but they're not all sand. That's why my country's called Harrat—that's the Arabic name for the lava fields around a volcano,' he explained.

'And they're active?'

He smiled. 'In Harrat Salma, not for thousands of years—though there were eruptions in Yemen, one in 2007 and others in the last century, and in the Red Sea in the century before that.'

'You've studied them?'

'In situ,' he said. 'My degree was in geology.' And half a doctorate in vulcanology. But she didn't need to know about that bit. About the fact he'd had to walk away from the studies he'd loved, without a backward glance. 'I loved every second of it. Especially the field trips, back in my country. I remember one incredible field trip when we spent the night sleeping in a volcano crater. We could see the minerals sparkle round us in the moonlight; it was like sleeping among the stars.' An experience he thought adventure travellers would enjoy, too. Those holiday expeditions were the one thing he'd promised himself that he would lead.

Not that he could, now that he was the heir instead of the spare.

'A vulcanologist,' she said in wonder. 'That's the last thing I would've guessed. I mean…there aren't even any volcanoes in Britain.'

'Actually, there are,' he corrected. 'Not active ones, but Edinburgh's built on an extinct volcano—Arthur's Seat.'

'So where's the nearest active volcano to here?'

'Italy or Iceland.' He shifted so that her head was on his shoulder and her arm was round his waist, while he cradled her against his body and curled the ends of her hair round his fingers again. It had been so, so long since he'd talked about this. But he had a feeling that Lily would understand. She had a passion for what she did, too. 'I loved Iceland. Seeing the midnight sun and the ice fields—so very different from home, and yet the land is the same in places. The lava fields.'

'Hot springs and ice hotels,' she said.

'They're pretty spectacular. And the Northern Lights. Even when you know how they're formed, they're still magical. Unearthly.' He dropped a kiss on the top of her head.

She cuddled into him. 'You're the same about volcanoes as I am about cooking.'

Yes. Once. But he couldn't afford to follow his heart now. His duty was more important. 'Was,' he corrected. 'I don't have time for it any more.'

She pulled back slightly to look him in the eye. 'And you miss it.'

Yeah, he missed it. Missed it so much that he blocked it out with work and constant partying, so he didn't have time to think about his previous life. 'I'm too busy to miss it,' he said. It was true—just not the whole truth.

'I really didn't expect this. A vulcanologist,' she said again in wonder.

'So what did you expect?'

'It's obvious there's more to you than being a serial partier. I assumed you did something with oil or money,' she said.

'We're not an oil-rich country.' He looked at her. 'Why money?'

'From the way you speak, I'd say you went to a public school over here. Then you studied at Oxford or Cambridge— I would have guessed a degree in economics or business studies, maybe followed by an MBA.'

He was surprised that she could tell so much just from his voice. 'I'm impressed. Apart from the subject of my degree, you're spot on. I went to Eton and then Cambridge. And I did my MBA in London.'

'Did you enjoy it?'

'I enjoyed the intellectual challenge,' he said, using his professional voice. The one he used with journalists. The one that gave nothing away.

'But it's not like your volcanoes. It didn't touch your heart, did it?'

Was it that obvious? He made a non-committal noise, not wanting to be disloyal to his family.

'At least your parents let you follow your heart for a while.'

'Yes.' The lump in his throat stopped him telling her why he'd stopped following his heart. His parents had been perfectly happy to let him study volcanoes while he was the second son. But when his brother Tariq had died, the whole world had turned upside down. And he'd known in his heart what he had to do.

His royal duty.

How could he put his parents through having to ask him to give up the career he loved and come back to step into Tariq's shoes? It would have made things so much harder for them. So, the moment he'd put the phone down, he'd left his volcanoes behind. Forgotten about becoming Dr Karim al-Hassan and gone straight to his parents. Grieved with them. And that day he'd told them that he was coming home to Harrat Salma. That he would try to live up to Tariq's abilities.

It had been his choice.

'Don't clam up on me,' she said softly. 'Tell me.'

He couldn't.

Not yet.

'I need a shower,' he said, wanting to avoid the subject. 'Come and join me.'

She pressed a kiss into his chest. 'Karim.'

He shook his head. 'I don't want to talk about it. I'm fine.'

'Bottling things up isn't good for you,' she said softly.

'I'm fine,' he repeated. 'Come on. I want to introduce you to my shower.' Something he knew would be spectacular enough to take her mind off what he'd told her—and stop her asking questions to fill in the rest of the gaps.

'That's a shower?' she asked when he led her into his bathroom.

'It's a wet room,' he said. There were oversized tiles on the walls with a narrow cobalt-blue border running across the room, and frameless glass panels around the shower area. A granite shelf jutted from the wall under a mirror, with a clear glass bowl basin balanced on top of it and most of the plumbing hidden away—just the taps showed, in polished chrome.

'That's stunning,' she said. 'I think you've just convinced me that my old-fashioned bathroom is—well, old-fashioned.'

'But it suits your house. An old-fashioned bathroom

wouldn't look right in this flat. It's modern. It's all about glass and light.' Which was the whole reason why he'd bought it.

'Don't you miss having a bath, though?'

He gave her a wicked grin. 'I have a bath, all right. I'll introduce you to it, later—it's in a different room. But this is my shower.' He took her hand and drew her within the glass panels. 'Would you like a waterfall or rain?'

She looked at him, clearly not understanding.

Oh, she was going to love this. Almost as much as he was going to love sharing this with her. 'We'll start with rain,' he said, savouring the moment, and switched on the water.

CHAPTER EIGHT

'Oh. My. God.' Lily had seen this kind of bathroom fitting in the 'dream house' kind of magazines Hannah loved—but this was the first time she'd been up close and personal to one.

The shower head was square, and the area of the spray was large enough to cover them both completely. And when the water flowed down, it really was like being in a rainstorm in the middle of summer. She closed her eyes and lifted her face up to the spray, loving the feel of it against her face.

Karim took the shower gel from an alcove in the wall and lathered her thoroughly. He paid attention to her shoulders and her back, working the knots out of her muscles, then slid his hands down to the curve of her waist, letting them drift lower, to her buttocks.

And then he turned her round to face him. 'Good?'

'Very good.' She was almost purring. If this was personal attention, she could take as much of it as he was willing to give.

He poured more shower gel over her breasts, teasing her nipples into tight points, then stroked lather over her ribcage, her belly. Lily quivered as he dropped to his knees in front of her. With his hair plastered back like that, he looked like a model for an expensive fragrance. Incredibly sexy. A gorgeous man with dark hair and a sensual mouth and olive skin and a regal air about him. The kind of man any woman would want to find in her shower.

He paid attention to her legs, next. Starting with the hollows of her ankles, he worked his way up her calves to the backs of her knees, then flattened his palms against her inner thighs, gently parting them. He looked up and gave her a look of pure desire, and her knees went weak; she had to hold onto his shoulders for balance. Karim lathered his hands again, then stroked between her legs, teasing her as he washed her. Every time his thumb brushed her clitoris, she quivered in anticipation. She knew he was doing it deliberately, increasing the pressure very slightly with each stroke; she tried to hold out, tried to be strong and not give in to the heavy, thudding pulse of desire.

But then Karim replaced his hand with his mouth, and Lily lost it completely, tipping her head back and climaxing hard as the water poured down on her. He held her close as her body tightened and relaxed, over and over again. And then, when the aftershocks had died away, he stood up again and stroked her hair back from her face.

'Sorry about that,' he said, looking not in the slightest bit repentant. 'I couldn't resist.'

'I…Karim.' She swallowed hard. 'That was amazing.'

'Good.'

She took a deep breath. 'My turn.'

'That's not the way it works. You don't have to return the favour. Not right now.' His eyes glittered. 'Though I think you've just put a picture in my head that's going to stop me sleeping tonight.'

Sleep. Right now she felt boneless. She wanted to curl up next to him in that huge bed, under the white sheets, and go to sleep.

'So you like my shower?' he asked.

'It's amazing.' Just as he was.

He flicked a switch to turn it to waterfall mode. 'It's half the reason I bought this place. Maybe it's coming from a desert land…but I just love water.'

'I never knew bathrooms could be sexy.'

'It's a shower room. A wet room,' he corrected. 'My bathroom's different.' He gave her a slow, sexy smile, full of promise. 'And I'll introduce you to that another time.'

Another time.

Lily wasn't sure if it thrilled her or scared her more. Because now she'd shared the ultimate intimacy with him, she was very afraid that she was starting to fall for him. Harder and faster than she'd ever thought possible.

Karim switched off the water, then stepped out from the screens and pulled a towel from the railing, tucking it round his waist. Then he took another towel and wrapped her in it—the biggest, softest, thickest towel she'd ever touched. It felt like being wrapped in a cloud, she thought idly, tucking a corner of the towel under the top edge to keep it in place.

He groaned. 'Not good. You look way too sexy like that. Like Cleopatra wrapped in a carpet.' His amber eyes glittered. 'It makes me want to unwrap you and carry you back to my bed.'

Sexy? When she'd just stepped out of the shower? She looked at him in surprise. 'My hair's in rats' tails and I've probably got panda eyes.'

'Your hair's fine and you're not wearing any make up.'

Probably his shower had got rid of it all, she thought. She squeezed water out of her hair. 'Do you have another towel, please?'

'Sure.' He passed her a hand towel; she wrapped her hair in it, turban-style.

'Lily.' He smiled. 'It's the wrong name for you—you're not a snooty hothouse flower. You're more like an English wild flower.'

'What, like a bluebell? Hmm. Bluebell Finch.' She laughed. 'Now there's a name. It sounds more like the sort of thing a farmer would call his favourite cow.' She grinned. 'Moo.'

He laughed back. 'You crazy woman. That's not what I meant at all.' He pulled her into his arms and spun her round so they were both facing the mirror; then he wrapped his arms round her waist and bent slightly so he could press his cheek to hers. 'What I meant is that you're natural and warm. There's no artifice with you. You look as good without make up as you do wearing it.'

'I'll have you know, I spent *ages* doing my make up this morning. Trying to make myself look professional.'

'You looked professional, all right. But I still wanted to take all your clothes off, the second I saw you.' He untucked the corner of her towel. 'Just as I do now.' He held her gaze in the mirror; the heat in his eyes made her knees feel weak.

'Do you really have nothing to do, this afternoon?'

'Are you telling me that you do?'

'It's rude to answer a question with a question.'

He laughed. 'Right now, I can't think of anything more important than taking you back to bed.'

She leaned back against him and placed her hand over his, stilling it. 'These business meetings of yours—how soon are they?'

'They start at the end of the month.'

'Which gives us two weeks,' she said thoughtfully. 'Then if you want me to cater for you, O esteemed client, we have work to do. Starting now.'

He blinked. 'What sort of work?'

'Planning.' Her fingers burrowed underneath his, retrieved the corner of the towel and tucked it back into place. 'So I suggest we get dressed.'

His lips quirked. 'You're bossing me about?'

'As you told me earlier, we're in my country, not yours. So I don't have to obey your royal orders.'

'What happened to the customer always being right?'

'The customer,' Lily retorted, 'often needs a bit of guidance to get what they really want instead of what they *think* they want.'

'That's profound.'

'Actually, it's true,' she said. 'Oh, and I'll need to borrow some paper and a pen.'

He blinked. 'You plan the old-fashioned way?'

'No, but I don't have my laptop with me. Unless,' she said thoughtfully, 'maybe you have one I can borrow, so I can work on it and email my notes to myself? That would save us both a bit of time.'

'No problem. I'll set it up for you.'

'Thank you.' She paused. 'Karim, I'm not going to be able to work if you're walking about half naked.'

'Are you saying I'll distract you?' he teased.

'You know perfectly well you will.' She eyed the reflection of the shower. 'And I'm going to need some coffee if I'm to have a hope in hell of concentrating, after what you did to me in there.'

A corner of his mouth quirked. 'You approve of my shower, then?'

'If we don't get out of this room right now,' she said, 'I could be very tempted to drag you back under there. And put it in waterfall mode. And I'd have you with your back flat against those tiles, seeing stars instead of water.'

'I do hope that's a promise.'

Desire coiled in her belly. 'It is.'

'May I point out that you're the one who tucked that towel back round you and said we had to work?' he said mildly.

'It's a woman's privilege to change her mind.' She closed her eyes. 'Uh. Take your hands off me, and go and get dressed, before you derail my mind completely.'

He laughed, releasing her. 'All right, *habibti*. I'll put some clothes on, and then I'll go and make us some coffee while you're dressing.'

'*English* coffee?' she asked hopefully.

'Yes, English coffee.'

Lord, he was gorgeous when he smiled like that. He had dimples. Cute, cute dimples. And it took all her will power to stop herself ripping off her towel and grabbing him.

'May I borrow a comb, please?'

'Sure.' He fished a comb out of a narrow drawer within the granite slab, and gestured to the built-in shelving at the side of the mirror above the basin. 'Help yourself to anything else you need.' He dipped his head and kissed the curve between her neck and her shoulder, his mouth warm and soft against her skin. 'And I'm going now, before I start letting you change my mind. Because once isn't enough, Lily. Not nearly enough.'

When Lily had finished dressing and came down to the kitchen, her hair damp but presentable, Karim was already there, having cleared up and made coffee. His clothes were crumpled; although he should've looked scruffy, he looked incredibly sexy.

'I'm probably going to regret asking this,' he said, 'but what are you thinking?'

'You. Rumpled,' she said economically.

He laughed. 'If you have a problem with that, I'll change.'

'Not a problem exactly.' She cleared her throat. 'You look as if you've just got out of bed.' And she wanted to take him back there again.

'Strictly speaking,' he said, 'it was the shower. I was too—um—distracted to tell you earlier, but the third door along the corridor is the guest suite. There are toiletries there, should you need them. Body lotion and what have you.'

She could imagine him smoothing body lotion into her skin, the way he'd lathered her in the shower. And he must have noticed her mouth parting, because colour slashed across his cheekbones. '*Habibti*, don't. You'll wreck my good intentions.'

'Coffee,' she said. 'We need coffee.' She dared not suggest a cold shower. Not after what he'd done to her under the spray.

'I'd rather take all your clothes off again.' He looked at the granite-topped table and then straight at her. 'I have a pome granate in the fridge.'

Her train of thought followed his, and she could imagine herself spread naked on the table, pomegranate seeds trailed down her body—and he'd eat them one by one, slowly, unti she was so hot and wet for him that…

'Coffee.' His voice had dropped an octave. 'And I think you'd better take your cup off the worktop yourself. Because if I touch you—even if it's just your fingers brushing agains mine as you take the cup from me—I don't think I can be held responsible for my actions.'

Lily dragged in a breath, fighting to get herself unde control. 'I don't do this sort of thing, Karim. I never behave like this. It isn't *me*.'

'I know. Hayley said you're married to your kitchen. You're focused on your career.' He took a swig of coffee, then swore softly in Arabic. 'This isn't helping. At all. For five years now I've played hard—but I've worked harder, and I've always managed to keep work and my social life entirely separate Right now I couldn't give a damn about business. I want to take you back to my bed.'

'You're the one who mentioned the pomegranate.'

'Go in the living room. Now. And don't sit anywhere nea me,' he warned, 'because I seem to have mislaid my self control temporarily.'

By the time they sat down in his living room—he'd moved a low table and set up his laptop on it for her—they were both back in control. Almost.

'So, these meetings—bearing in mind you're talking to m under client confidentiality now, can you give me any idea wha you're doing? Simply because I want to make the food work for you,' Lily said, 'and I'll have a better idea if I know wher it fits in.'

He leaned back against the sofa opposite her. 'Client confidentiality?'

'I can sign an agreement, if you'd rather. But I hope over the last few days you've got to know me well enough to believe that whatever you tell me stays with me. I need background information to help me plan the right sort of menu. I wouldn't serve the same kind of thing at a buffet for, say, financiers as I would for people who worked in the arts.'

'Why not?'

'Because financiers don't look at what they're eating, and people in the arts do—they notice colour and styling, so it has to be a bit more intricate to look at,' she explained.

'I see.'

'And I'm assuming that you want something special rather than the kind of sandwiches you could just ask the local deli to deliver.'

He was silent for so long that she was beginning to wonder if he'd changed his mind. And then he seemed to come to a decision. 'All right. My father's put me in charge of developing tourism and investment in Harrat Salma.'

'And that's why these people are coming? Because they'll invest or build hotels or what have you?'

'Yes. I've hand-picked them over the last few months—people whose work I like and whose beliefs fit with mine. People who believe in more than just a profit; people who'll put something back as well as taking it. I want them to use local people, local expertise—engineers and builders and the like—in the designs, and I want local people running the hotels, too.'

'So tell me about Harrat Salma,' she said. 'Work on the basis that I know absolutely nothing—apart from the fact it has deserts and volcanoes.'

He smiled. 'There's a lot more to my country than that. We're not one of the oil-rich states, but we do have a large

mining industry—zinc, copper and gemstones. My people
have a very long tradition of craftsmanship.'

She gestured to the wall hangings. 'Such as these?'

'And carpets, of course.' He raised an eyebrow. 'Not flying
ones—sadly, they're a myth—but beautiful hand-woven silk
ones.' He indicated the one in the centre of the room. 'Plus met-
alwork, jewellery, sculpture. We have ancient sites, we have
museums, we have marine heritage. We have the souks—the
spice market, the silk market, the fruit and vegetable market
where you haggle with the traders over mint tea; and we even
have ultra-modern malls for Western visitors who can't live
without their global stores. But I want our tourism to be as
carbon-neutral as possible.'

'So you're going for the Green bandwagon.'

'It's nothing to do with bandwagons.' His eyes narrowed
slightly. 'I want to look at harnessing geothermal energy. It's
not a bandwagon, Lily—it's just common sense and using our
gifts wisely. We have a very special landscape, and it deserves
conserving. And I will not permit dune-bashing. It's popular
in some of our neighbouring countries, but in Harrat Salma it's
absolutely out,' he asserted between clenched teeth.

She'd never heard him sound so haughty or so regal. For a
brief moment, anger blazed in his eyes, and then it was damped
down and he was back under control.

Part of her knew it was a dangerous question, given his
reaction. But she asked it anyway. 'What's dune-bashing?'

'Taking a four-wheel drive up to the top of a dune and going
straight down again—it's like white-water rafting on sand.'

The way he described it sounded as if it was something he'd
once done—and maybe enjoyed. 'Sounds like a white knuckle
ride in a natural theme park, to me. The kind of people who can
afford to do that would definitely bring money into the country.'

'Along with no respect whatsoever—for the land or for my
people. Not to mention the damage it can do.'

That sounded like the voice of bitter experience. Or someone so passionately committed to his country that he wanted to wrap it in cotton wool, at the same time as knowing that he needed to open it up to the world in order for his country to move forward.

'We don't need that kind of tourist.'

'So what kind of tourists do you want?'

'People who'll appreciate the traditional craftsmanship of our boats instead of demanding outboard motors. People who'll be content to dive and see the fish in their natural habitat rather than catch them for sport and throw them away. People who'll take the slow route to enjoy the landscape, on camels and on foot—a kind of desert safari—and listen to the stories of the guides.'

'People who'd want to spend a night sleeping outside in a volcano?' she asked with a smile.

He smiled wryly. 'Climbers and geologists, yes. I had thought to l—' He stopped abruptly.

'You'd thought to what?' she asked.

'Never mind. It's not important.'

His face had gone shuttered again, she noticed, so he wasn't being quite honest with her. It was important, all right: he just didn't want to talk about it. Like the dune-bashing thing; she was pretty sure there was more to it than simply conservation issues.

Though pushing him to talk about it when he was clearly unwilling really wasn't going to help her plan the menus. The best way she could help him, right now, was to do her job. And maybe he'd open up to her more when he'd relaxed again. 'So the people at your meetings are what, owners of tourist companies?'

'Specialist tourist companies,' he explained. 'I'm looking to do exclusive deals for the different areas—one for the diving and marine-based holidays, one for the desert safari trips, one for historical and educational tours, one for climbers. And another for those who'll invest in hotels.'

'Right.' She typed in some notes. 'Did you have anything in mind, food-wise? A sit down meal, a finger buffet, a fork buffet? And I assume you're looking to use traditional cuisine from your country rather than English food?'

'You're the expert, there,' he said, surprising her. 'What would you recommend?'

'I'd say do a fork buffet—and fusion food. Similar to the kind of food you cooked me, served a little warmer, and maybe with some slightly more English accompaniments. To give them a taste of the traditional, and yet at the same time show them your country has a modern outlook and welcomes those from other cultures,' she said.

'I like your take on that. Sounds good.'

'I'll also need to know if any of your guests have food allergies, and if any are vegetarian or vegan. Oh—and you'd better serve English coffee, not Arabic.'

He smiled wryly. 'I thought you might say that.'

'But you can offer a choice of your traditional mint tea as well as English tea. And the orange-and-mint concoction you made me—that'd go down really well.' She thought rapidly. 'At coffee break in the morning, I'll do you pastries to go with the coffee. Little ones that you can eat in one bite, including traditional pastries from Harrat Salma. Are Arabic pastries as sweet as Greek and Egyptian ones?'

'One of the most famous is *baklawa*,' he said. 'You may be more familiar with the Greek version of the pastry; in my country we add orange blossom water or rose water to the syrup.'

'But it'd still be very sweet,' she said thoughtfully. 'So I need to balance that with some not-so-sweet mouthfuls. OK. Give me a rundown of the kind of food people eat in your country.'

As he spoke she typed rapidly, occasionally stopping him to check spelling or ingredients. And finally she saved the file. 'Right. This will be a good basis for my research. I'll sort out some menus to run by you tomorrow, and I need to do a test run on the actual cuisine—not because I don't think I can do it, but because some of these dishes are new to me and I want to get the balance right before your meetings. Are you busy on Wednesday night?'

'Nothing I can't move.'

'Good. You're having a dinner party.'

'A dinner party?' he queried.

'Not the sort where you pay back social invitations, sit down and chat. I want you to invite your closest friends. People you trust. People who'll be willing to try a lot of different dishes, and give you an honest opinion on it.'

'Rafiq,' he suggested.

'Fine, but he's from your country. Can you invite someone English as well, so I can have a view from someone who doesn't know your culinary traditions?'

'How many are you looking for?'

'You, Rafiq and two more.'

'Luke. My best friend. *If* I can drag him away from work.' He paused. 'Did you want me to invite anyone female?'

'Women do own and run hotels and tourism companies,' she pointed out. 'Or aren't they allowed to do that in Harrat Salma?'

He smiled. 'Of course they are. It's not a backward country.'

'Sorry, I didn't mean to imply it was.' She gave him a rueful smile. 'But our cultures are different.'

'Yes. And I suppose you do have a point. Women are educated in my country and they can work if they choose to do so.' He paused. 'Except for the women in my family, of course.'

'Why "of course"?'

He frowned. 'Because it isn't appropriate for royal women to work for someone else.'

'I can see that, but couldn't they run their own business?'

'No.'

'Why not?'

'Because they have diplomatic duties. It's exactly the same for the men.' He shrugged. 'Maybe we can invite Cathy, then.'

'Cathy?'

'She's the head of the café in Luke's new health club. And he offered to lend me her services.'

'Did he, now,' she said dryly.

He raised an eyebrow. 'He knew I was in a jam—and you'd turned me down, at that point.'

'A jam?'

'Did you really think I'm that disorganised, *habibti*, that I'd set up meetings and not have all the details covered well beforehand? I had a caterer. But family circumstances meant that she had to let me down. Which is why it's all a last-minute rush now.'

'Didn't she organise a replacement before she left?'

Karim spread her hands. '*Habibti*, if your sister needed you badly, wouldn't you drop everything to help her?'

'I'm an only child.'

He inclined his head. 'Your mother, then.'

'Yes, of course I would. But I also wouldn't leave my clients in a mess.'

'What if it was an emergency, and you didn't have time to sort things out?'

'I'd *make* time.'

He gave her a sidelong look. 'You're hard on people.'

'I'm not. But I give my best. I expect others to do the same for me.'

'Noted,' he said dryly.

But it was still bugging her. 'So your friend Luke sorted

out your problem for you—but you've decided to drop this Cathy for me?'

'Nothing of the kind,' he said, lifting his chin. 'I haven't spoken to Cathy yet. I was planning to give you until Wednesday—and only if I hadn't persuaded you to cook for me by then did I intend to take up Luke's offer.'

'Well, I've agreed to cook for you now.' She moistened her lower lip. 'Though I don't mix business and pleasure.'

'Neither do I,' Karim said. 'But I'm breaking the rules as of now.' He moved to sit beside her, took her hand and kissed the pulse beating madly in her wrist. 'And so are you.'

'Temporarily. I'm your temporary cook, and your temporary…'

'Lover,' he said, and traced a path of kisses up her forearm.

He'd reduced her to a quivering pile of mush—almost. But there was one thing she needed to be sure about. 'Ground rules,' she said.

He nibbled the sensitive spot in her inner elbow. 'Rules?'

'Just one.' One that was really important to her. Even though she wasn't going to get involved with him. 'And it's a deal-breaker.'

That got his attention. He released her arm and looked straight at her. 'What's that?'

'While you're with me, no harem.'

He frowned. 'I've dated a lot, though it's always been one woman at a time. I'd never dishonour my girlfriends by doing otherwise.'

Now she'd offended him. Maybe she should explain…but she couldn't bring herself to tell him about Jeff. To let him know what a fool she'd been. 'Just checking,' she said. She took a deep breath. 'And I think you'd better go and sit back over there. Before you make me delete this lot accidentally. Like I did with my article, the other day.'

'I distract you?' he teased, but to her relief he did as she asked.

'You know damn well you do.'

'If it makes you feel any better,' he said, 'it's mutual. So. Ground rules. Number one, this is temporary. Number two, while we're seeing each other, neither of us will see anyone else. And number three, we keep our work together entirely separate from our private life.'

'Agreed,' she said, adding a private rule just for herself. Number four, no getting involved. This was going to be just for fun. Sex. Spectacular sex.

She flicked into his email program and emailed herself the notes she'd just made. 'Well, now it's time to work. I have research to do and menus to plan, and you have people to invite to dinner. Seven o'clock sharp on Wednesday.'

'Fine.'

'And I—' she glanced at the clock on the computer '—need to be gone.'

'I'll drive you back,' he said.

She shook her head. 'No need. I'll take the Tube. And don't argue, Karim. I'm perfectly capable of seeing myself home. I'm twenty-eight, not sixteen.'

'The offer's there if you change your mind.'

'I think,' she said softly, 'if you saw me home, I'd feel obliged to invite you in for coffee. And there's the small matter of you and me and, um, granite.'

His gaze went hot. 'Are there any pomegranates in your fridge?'

'No.' She sucked in a breath. 'Though there might be, tomorrow.'

'Then I'll see you tomorrow, *habibti*.' He dipped his head and kissed her lightly. 'Mid afternoon.'

'Business,' she reminded him.

He took her hand and rubbed the pad of his thumb over her palm. 'Business *first*,' he said softly. 'And then...pomegranates.'

CHAPTER NINE

'THAT'S two Mondays on the trot I've beaten you at squash now,' Luke said, 'and I've barely even broken a sweat tonight. This isn't good. It isn't good at all.' He spread his hands. 'But at least this week you're looking a bit happier. So are you going to fill me in on what's happened?'

'Lily agreed to cook for me,' Karim said.

Luke groaned. 'Please tell me you're not letting your libido rule your brain.'

'I'm not.' Much. 'Anyway. I need you on Wednesday night.'

'Need me for what?'

'Dinner. My place. And is there any chance you can bring Cathy?'

Luke frowned. 'I thought you just said Lily agreed to cook for you?'

'She has. But she wants to do a trial run of the food—and she wants some guinea pigs who'll give her an honest opinion. Which means you…and a professional one from Cathy would be good.'

'I'll see if Cathy's free, but I can't guarantee it,' Luke said. 'For all I know, she might have a jealous other half.'

'Then get her to bring him—or her—as well.' Karim paused. 'How come you don't know much about Cathy, if she's in charge of the club's kitchen?'

'It's not on her CV, and it's against the law to ask,' Luke said economically. 'Anyway, it doesn't matter whether she's single or attached. She's good at her job. That's all I need to know.'

'Aren't you supposed to show an interest in your staff?' Karim asked mildly.

'No. And, unlike some people around here, I'm not stupid enough to think about getting involved with someone I work with.'

'I'm not thinking about getting involved with Lily.' Strictly speaking, that was true. He wasn't thinking about it—he already *was* involved with her. On a temporary basis. With mutually agreed ground rules.

Luke gave him a sceptical look. 'OK. I'll sort Wednesday.'

'It's not interfering with work?'

'Not really.' Luke shrugged. 'I'd been invited to a party. But I'm getting bored with parties. Being a guinea pig sounds a lot more fun.' He raised an eyebrow. 'And it has the added bonus of me getting to meet this woman who's turned you into a gibbering idiot.'

'That's an exaggeration. I'm not a gibbering idiot.'

'Hmm. I reserve the right to comment until after I've met her.'

Karim laughed. 'I wouldn't expect anything less from a man who calls a spade a "bloody shovel". Come on. As I lost, I'll get the drinks. And you can tell me all about this new scheme of yours.'

The following afternoon, Lily opened the door to Karim, who had a veritable armful of deep blue irises and pink and white tulips.

'What's this, an entire florist's?' she asked.

'Hello to you, too.' He leaned forward and kissed her lightly on the lips.

'Karim! This is meant to be business.'

'Not until three o'clock.' He glanced at his watch. 'And right now it's ten minutes to. Which means,' he said, putting the flowers in her arms and closing the door behind them, 'I have ten minutes to kiss you stupid.'

He was gratified to see how swiftly she blushed. Her eyes looked huge and her mouth had parted, already inviting the said kisses. Then she shook herself. 'I...Karim, thank you for the flowers. They're lovely. But this isn't going to work.'

'Yes, it is.' He marched her into the kitchen, took the flowers from her, put them on the draining board, and fiddled with her oven.

'What are you doing?'

'Setting the timer. We have nine minutes before our business meeting.' He blew her a kiss, and placed a brown paper bag on the worktop.

'I'm going to regret asking, but what's that?' she asked.

'Pomegranate. In case you were out of stock. Stop talking, Lily, you're wasting time. Eight and a half minutes.' He pulled her into his arms and kissed her. Thoroughly. Until she was kissing him back and made no protest whatsoever when his hands burrowed under the hem of her camisole top to stroke her midriff and then unclip her bra.

He loved touching Lily. Kissing her. Loved the warmth of her response and the fact that she didn't hold back—she'd untucked his shirt and was teasing his skin with her fingertips, the same way he was teasing her, drawing lazy circles on the soft undercurves of her breasts.

Karim was just unzipping her jeans, ready to ease them down over her hips, when the oven timer pinged. For a moment, he considered ignoring it—but the sound was loud enough to break his concentration. Enough to remind him that he needed to prove to Lily that they could manage the fine line between business and pleasure.

He switched off the timer, then restored order to Lily's delightfully déshabillé clothes and tucked his own shirt back in place. 'Right. Menus.'

'Karim, I—' She sounded dazed.

He laughed. 'Your body's definitely out to lunch, *habibti*. And I think your mind might be, too. Where did my clever, competent cook go?'

'Let's just say you achieved your objective,' she said wryly. 'What?'

'You just kissed me stupid.' She laughed. 'Or maybe I should say, you just kissed me, stupid.'

'Playing punctuation games with me, are you, Miss Finch?' And he loved her fencing with him like this. 'I'm going to kiss you a lot more, later,' he promised. 'After our meeting. So where are we sitting?'

'You,' she said, 'are not sitting anywhere near me. I need a cold shower.'

'Mmm. *Shower*.' He looked speculatively at her. 'How would you rate your shower in comparison to mine?'

'One out of ten. Don't even think about it.' She tidied her hair, then went over to the kitchen sink and splashed her face with cold water before drying it on a towel. 'And don't do that again.'

'Do what?'

'Distract me when we're talking business.'

'We weren't talking business,' he reminded her. 'Our appointment was mid-afternoon—and I was early.'

'You're splitting hairs. So have you sorted out your guests for Wednesday?'

'Rafiq, Luke, probably Cathy, maybe Cathy's jealous boyfriend.'

'There's a jealous boyfriend involved?'

He shrugged. 'Luke has no idea. Could be a husband. Could be nobody.'

She groaned. 'This friend of yours sounds very like you.

Focused on work and nothing else penetrates your consciousness.'

Karim laughed. 'He's not a sheikh. He's a barrow boy.'

'I thought you said he owned a gym?'

'Several, actually. Oh, wait. I think he might have sold most of them. The new one's just because he was bored waiting for another project to get going.'

'He bought a gym because he was *bored*?' Lily blinked, as if unable to take it in. 'Why?'

'Because it was on its last legs, and he saw it as a challenge—to see how quickly he could turn it around.'

'You mean, he's an asset stripper? Buys things and sells them again almost immediately?'

'He buys failing businesses and turns them around and sells them as going concerns,' Karim corrected. 'And he's very, very good at what he does. He's loaded, although he started out with a single market stall. He also had the best brain on my MBA course.' He raised an eyebrow. 'Luke managed to talk his way onto the course with no qualifications whatsoever.'

She gave him a level stare. 'If you're talking about degrees, I didn't go to university, either. There's nothing wrong with that.'

'I didn't say there was—and, frankly, in your line of business, it's experience and flair that counts, not paper qualifications.'

She coughed. 'I didn't say I had no paper qualifications. Of course I do. I studied while I got practical work experience.'

'So when did you decide to go it alone?' he asked curiously.

Now there was a question and a half. 'I set up Amazing Tastes four years ago,' she answered carefully. Karim didn't need to know about before.

'Brave move.'

'I enjoy a challenge.'

He gestured towards the brown paper bag. 'There's you[r] challenge for today.'

'No,' she said firmly. 'Do you want a coffee while we're discussing menus?'

'Yes, please.'

'Then go and sit down.' She shooed him over to her conservatory, and put the flowers in water while she waited for the kettle to boil. She had just enough vases to contain them all, but it was a close-run thing. A completely over-the-top gesture, and one she should've disapproved of—but she loved the fact that he'd bought her so many beautiful spring flowers. Especially the irises, because he'd clearly remembered how much she loved blue flowers.

She took two mugs of coffee over to the conservatory and set them on the table, and made sure she sat opposite him— far enough away so they couldn't actually touch—before talking him through the menus she'd devised.

'Sounds good to me,' he said when she'd finished. 'So how does the catering work? Do you cook it here and bring it over, or do you have the ingredients delivered to my place and cook there?'

'I bring the ingredients to your place,' she said. 'Unless it's something that needs to be prepared well in advance, I prefer to cook everything fresh at my client's. And your kitchen's as good as mine.' She grinned. 'I'll bring my own knives and pans, though.'

'How do you know mine aren't good enough?'

'Apart from the fact I'm used to working with mine, they're the tools of my trade…and I'm fussy.'

'I'll remember that.' He paused. 'Actually, some of those dishes do need to be prepared well in advance. Preferably the day before, so they have time to marinade and let the flavours develop.'

She coughed. 'You once told me you believed in letting your staff get on with their job without interference.'

'I do. But you're not my staff.'

'You're paying me to do a job, which amounts to the same thing.'

'Not for tax purposes, it doesn't. You're not my employee.'

'Don't split hairs. You know what I mean. And you're interfering.'

'And whose country's cuisine are we talking about?' he fenced.

'Not yours *or* mine,' she said tartly. 'This is fusion food. It's designed to give people a taste of your country while also making them feel at home here.'

'Fine. What time do you need access to the kitchen?'

She looked at him. 'Oh. I assumed that you worked from your flat. Your dining room's a lot like a boardroom.'

'I do, and it is,' he said. 'Don't worry, I won't be under your feet while you're working.'

'Your kitchen will be completely out of bounds,' she warned. 'It'll be my work area. And I don't like being interrupted when I'm working.'

He grinned. 'So you're one of these temperamental chefs who swears a lot and hits people with a frying pan, are you?'

She laughed back. 'Hardly. But I'm serious, Karim. If you want me to do a good job, you need to give me the space to do it.'

'I'll be completely professional,' he said. 'So what's the plan for tomorrow?'

'I'll arrive at ten. I'll be bringing my van.'

'Fine. Park outside and call me—Rafiq will take your equipment up to the flat and park your van in the secure parking underneath the complex.' He smiled. 'Now that's all sorted...come and sit with me.'

'This is business.'

'We've finished business. This is you and me,' he corrected. 'So either you come here and sit on my lap…or I'll come over to you.'

'What, you're going to sit on *my* lap?' she teased.

'Now you're stretching my patience, woman. Enough.' He stood up, walked over to her, scooped her off the chair and sat down in her place, settling her on his lap.

'You're just a caveman at heart,' she accused.

'And your point is?'

Before she had the chance to answer, he kissed her. Thoroughly.

'So. Now we've agreed that,' he said, 'what are you doing for the rest of the day?'

'Writing my shopping list for tomorrow morning. I'm using as much organic stuff as possible, by the way,' she said.

'Fine.' He nibbled his way along her jawline. 'I'd love to take you out to dinner tonight.'

She could hear the 'but', and said it for him.

He sighed. 'I have a tedious meeting to attend.'

'You mean, you're going to a party,' she said dryly.

He nodded. 'Though I'll be leaving early.' He paused. 'Maybe I could come and see you on the way home.'

'That depends on your definition of early.'

'You're planning an early night?' He smiled. 'Good. I like the sound of that.'

Did he mean he was thinking of joining her? Was he inviting himself to stay overnight? This was moving way too fast for her. 'Karim, we can't do this.'

'Yes, we can. And don't argue. We both know all I have to do is kiss you.'

She scowled. 'That's arrogant.'

'Maybe, but it's also true.'

It was, and that made things worse.

'If it makes you feel any better,' he said softly, 'you put my head in a spin as well.'

Maybe, she thought, but not enough of a spin to ask me to go to the party with you. And even though she knew he looked on it as a business networking opportunity—which meant he'd be busy and she couldn't be there to distract him—it still rankled. So she ignored his comment. 'You'll need to prepare for your "tedious" party. And I need to prepare things for tomorrow.'

'You have a point. And I'm not going to encroach on your professional time. Though I reserve the right to encroach on your other time.' He kissed her lightly. 'Thank you, *habibti*.'

'What for?'

'Understanding that my job isn't just nine to five.'

She felt the colour rush into her face. She hadn't exactly been understanding. She'd been sulking and thinking like a jealous girlfriend—which she had no right to do, because she wasn't officially his girlfriend and they'd agreed that their relationship was temporary. Even crosser with herself, she slid off his lap. 'I'll see you tomorrow.'

He smiled. 'Bring the pomegranate with you.' He stood up, and she saw him out; though she found, once her shopping list was done, she couldn't really settle to anything.

This wasn't good. Wasn't good at all. She'd promised herself, after Jeff, that she'd never let anyone distract her from her business again. And what was she doing? Mooning around after a playboy who'd already made it clear to her that they had no future. So much for thinking that she could handle this.

Later that evening, her mobile phone beeped. She flicked into the text screen and realised the message was from Karim.

*Party **extremely** tedious, food nowhere near as good as yours.*

Good, she texted back.

Tomorrow's too far away. Can I call in on my way home?

Too, too tempting. *No. Am going to sleep now.*

Two seconds later, the phone rang. 'You're in bed?' Karim asked. 'What are you wearing?'

She sucked in a breath. 'Karim, you're in a public place You can't have this kind of conversation with me.'

'Yes, I can—I'm in the foyer outside and nobody can hear me. I excused myself to make a business call.'

'Even so—Karim, we're not having this conversation.'

He laughed softly. 'Chicken. Don't you want to have phone sex with me?'

Oh-h-h. Even the suggestion made her wet. 'I'm not a chicken,' she said primly. 'I'm being sensible.'

'How about I tell you what I'm wearing?' he suggested.

'No.'

'I could always tell you about my bath…' His voice was full of amusement, and she could imagine that sexy mouth smiling. That sexy mouth working against her skin, teasing her into arousal…

'*No,*' she said firmly. 'I'll see you tomorrow at ten.'

'Then goodnight, *habibti*. Pleasant dreams.'

'Goodnight,' she said, but she was smiling when she put the phone down again.

CHAPTER TEN

FIRST thing the next morning, Lily did the shopping, so her ingredients were the freshest they could possibly be. Then she drove over to Karim's flat, called him as arranged, and allowed Rafiq to carry her bags up to the flat and park her van in the car park beneath the complex.

'Good morning, *habibti*.' Karim opened the door. 'Now, are you Miss Finch or Lily today?'

She rolled her eyes. 'Lily, of course—but I'm here on business.'

He glanced at his watch. 'Actually, you're two minutes early. Which means you can kiss me hello.'

She'd barely uttered the first syllable of his name in protest before he kissed her. A warm, sweet and promising kiss that made her knees weak. And then he closed the door behind her. 'Right. Do you have everything you need?'

'I'm pretty sure I do.'

'Good. Rafiq is at your disposal, should you need anything. His number is on speed dial on the kitchen phone—dial hash then three.' He ushered her through to the kitchen. 'And I'll be next door, if you need any input from me.'

'Sure. Want me to bring you a coffee when I make myself one?'

He smiled at her. 'You are indeed a woman whose price is above rubies. Thanks. I'd appreciate that.'

She changed into her chef's whites and settled into the kitchen, spreading out her equipment and working through the first part of her list. When she'd sorted out everything that needed marinating and the first batch of bite-size Arabic short-bread was out of the oven, she made coffee and carried a mug and a plate through to Karim in the next room.

He was working on a spreadsheet on his laptop when she walked in. She'd never seen him at work before, and it was a revelation. He looked focused, brooding, intense—and sexy as hell. His face was all strong angles and planes, and with his hair raked back rather than flopping over his forehead he looked slightly forbidding rather than the teasing playboy she was used to.

He looked up and his eyes crinkled at the corners. 'Hello, *habibti*. How's it going?'

'Fine. You?'

'Fine.' His eyes widened as he spotted the shortbread. 'Is that for me?'

'It's still fairly warm and it's an early test. Client's privilege.' She smiled at him. 'I know I told you the kitchen was out of bounds, but with the rest of my clients I'm happy for them to come in and chat to me and taste things whenever they want.'

His eyes narrowed. 'So why can't I do the same?'

'Number one, you're busy. Number two, you'd distract me. So. The kitchen ban stays.'

He tried the shortbread and closed his eyes in seeming bliss for a moment. 'This is fabulous, Lily. If you ever decide you want to work in a warmer climate, you'd command premium prices as a pastry chef in my country.' He looked appreciatively at her. 'If the rest of the food's like this, you'll have done half my job for me.'

'It's really too early to say. Wait until you try the rest,' she said. 'But I'm glad you like it, so far.' On impulse, she leaned over and kissed the tip of his nose—and backed out of reach before he could react.

'You just broke the rules again, Miss Finch,' he said thoughtfully. 'Which means the kitchen is no longer out of bounds.'

'Oh, yes, it is.' She held both hands up in a 'stop' gesture. 'Stay!' she said, laughing, and fled back to the kitchen.

She was busy working on a rose-water cream filling, with everything else ticking over nicely, when Karim wandered into the kitchen. 'It's half past one. Do you want me to make you a sandwich or something?'

'It's sweet of you to offer, but no—and this room is supposed to be out of bounds,' she reminded him.

'*Habibti*, you've been on the go since you got here—surely you need to sit down and take a break?'

She shook her head. 'It's not like that in a kitchen. When I'm cooking, I work through.'

'Hmm. I don't want to be a slave driver.'

'You're not. I'm setting my own pace,' she reassured him. 'But if you're desperate to help, I'll let you set up the dining table later. I need all four of you on one side of that enormous table, and a big runner in the middle so I can set the dishes on it.'

'Of course. Do you mind if I make myself a sandwich?'

'I'll do it.'

He frowned. 'Lily, you're busy. I really don't expect you to wait on me as well as everything else.'

'It's fine. Don't fuss. Now, shoo,' she said with a smile. 'I'll bring you something through in a couple of minutes.'

She made Karim a sandwich and herself a mug of coffee, and carried on. The rest of the afternoon whizzed by; at five o'clock, she stopped for just long enough to take him a sample of the *baklawa* she'd made and a cup of very English tea.

'These are absolutely perfect,' he pronounced. He gave her a teasing sidelong glance. 'Dare I ask, given that the media has this thing about saving time at the moment…did you make the pastry yourself as well as the filling and the syrup?'

She gave him a speaking look. 'What do you think?'

'I think I've just insulted you. Of course you didn't cut corners. You're a consummate professional, Miss Finch.'

She inclined her head in acknowledgement. 'Thank you I'm nearly there.'

'Let me know when you want me to set up the room. I take it you're joining us?'

'Not to eat, no. With the amount of stuff I've tasted,' she explained, 'I'm too stuffed to face a meal.'

'You're the boss, *habibti*.'

At five to seven, Karim's guests arrived. 'Lily, this is Luke and Cathy—Rafiq you already know.'

'Good to meet you,' Lily said. 'And thanks for being guinea pigs tonight.'

'Pleasure,' Luke said.

Cathy just stared, open-mouthed. 'You're Elizabeth Finch I recognise you from your picture in *Modern Life* magazine.' She nudged her boss. 'Luke, why didn't you tell me *Elizabeth Finch* was cooking for us? Do you have any idea how much of a legend she is?'

'Karim told me Lily cooks for the rich and famous, not that she *is* famous. And as I don't exactly read the same kind of magazines you do…' Luke spread his hands. 'Sorry.'

'Enough of the celeb stuff. Call me Lily, and I'm just the cook,' Lily said. 'And you're all here to work.' She ushered them over to the dining table. 'I've put some sheets there for you all to fill in, but if you'd rather tell me than write it down that's fine. I want an honest opinion. Don't hold back. So if you like it, I want to know what you like about it, and if you don't, that's also fine: I need to know what the problem is whether it's the texture or it's too spicy or it's too bland. That'll help me do the final tweaks and get the right balance for the final recipe.' She smiled at them. 'You're getting a lot of different dishes, a lot of different tastes, so I'll bring you sorbet to cleanse your palate between dishes.'

To her relief, the savoury dishes went down well—her testers suggested a few adjustments, but in the main she'd kept on the fine line she'd intended to tread.

Then she brought in the pastries. 'OK. We have filo pastries filled with rose-water cream, some traditional date-and-nut pastries, *baklawa*—which is like the Greek pastry but flavoured with rose water—Arabic shortbread, and semolina cookies stuffed with date and walnuts,' she said.

'And the little muffins?' Luke asked.

She looked straight at Karim. 'White chocolate—and pomegranate.'

'You are *so* going to pay for that,' Karim mouthed at her.

She just laughed and made them try every single one, with a mouthful of sorbet in between each.

'I love these shortbread biscuits. Is that orange blossom water you added?' Cathy asked.

'And egg yolk,' Lily said.

'Can I beg the recipe, please? And for the pomegranate muffins? They'd go down really well with the breakfast crowd at the gym.'

'Sure.' Lily smiled at her. 'I was thinking about adding a little grated orange rind to the muffins. It's a fairly classic combination—and orange mixed with pomegranate juice, olive oil and a little ground coriander makes a fabulous salad dressing.' She caught Karim's eye, and gave him a wicked smile, guessing exactly what was going through his head. The words 'pomegranate' and 'dressing' had definitely sparked off an idea.

She finished the tasting session with mint tea.

'This and those little semolina and date cookies,' Rafiq said,
'are as good as my mother's.'

'Thank you.' She acknowledged the compliment with a dip
of her head, and gathered up the tasting notes, placing them in
a folder and then putting the folder in a briefcase. 'And thank
you all for being honest. I'll take your comments into account
when I tweak the recipes before Karim's meetings.'

'I can see why you held out for her to be your caterer,' Luke
said quietly to Karim at the doorway as he and Cathy left.
'She's very good at her job—the food was fabulous. And she's
incredibly focused. She even managed to concentrate on
talking to us and finding out what we really thought, when
every time she looked at you it was obvious that she just wanted
to rip all your clothes off and melt into your arms.'

'You don't have to do the "bloody shovel" bit,' Karim said,
feeling the colour flare in his face.

Luke simply grinned. 'I like the way there's no side to her,
no airs and graces—what you see is exactly what you get.'

'But?' Karim could see the word written all over his
friend's face.

'You're still an idiot. She's lovely, but it's going to end in
tears,' Luke warned. 'Mixing business and pleasure is a seriously bad idea.'

'We both know the score,' Karim said. 'She doesn't have
room in her life for a relationship. And she knows that I have to
go back to Harrat Salma. We have ground rules. It's not a
problem.'

'I thought you said you weren't thinking about getting
involved with her?'

'Technically, I wasn't thinking about it.'

Luke picked up exactly what he meant. 'You'd already done
it. *Idiot*.' He sighed. 'Just be careful. Because one or both of
you is going to get hurt.'

'No, we're not. We know what we're doing. Eyes wide open,' Karim insisted. 'It's going to be fine.'

His best friend didn't look convinced, but didn't press the point.

Rafiq, having offered to help clear up and been turned down by Lily, headed for his own quarters. Which left Karim alone with Lily.

He walked into the kitchen, where she was clearing up.

'You,' he said, 'did an amazing job.'

She shrugged. 'I try to live up to the name of my business.'

'You definitely did, tonight.' He took the pan from her hand.

'I need to finish clearing up, Karim.'

'No. *Enough*,' he said softly. 'You've been on your feet all day. I'll sort it out.'

'It's part of my job.'

'I don't care. *I'm* doing it. And remember that the client is always right,' he said. 'And I could pull rank and remind you that, actually, I own this kitchen.' Then, when her expression turned mutinous, he leaned forward to kiss the tip of her nose. 'Lily, you need a break. Even if you don't think you do. Come on.' He took her hand and drew her towards the stairs.

'Where are we...?' She stopped.

'You,' he said, 'are going to chill out a bit while I finish clearing up.' He led her up the stairs and stopped outside the door next to his room. 'I promised to introduce you to my bathroom. One second.' He flicked a couple of switches, then opened the door. 'Come with me.'

She stopped and just stared.

If anything, the room was even more gorgeous than his wet room. The tiles here were stone, textured and matte rather than smooth and glossy; a huge potted kentia palm stood in one corner. There was a freestanding bath finished in dark grey stone in the centre of the room, uplit with an aqua wash—and she could hear music playing softly. It wasn't something she knew, but it was incredibly moving.

'Like it?' he asked.

'Love it,' she breathed. 'What's the music?'

'Very English, actually,' he said with a smile. 'Something I heard performed when I was at Cambridge, and it blew me away. It's Vaughan Williams' "Fantasia on a Theme of Thomas Tallis". Perfect for chilling out. Though if you'd rather have something else, I can change it.'

'No. It's gorgeous.'

There were fluffy white bath sheets hanging on the towel rail, and the basin was a frosted glass bowl resting on a dark grey slab. Toiletries were lined up neatly on a glass shelf, and there was a mirror above the sink.

But she was drawn back to the bath. It was big enough for two people, with a shelf on one side; the kind of place where you could lie back in a pile of bubbles and read a magazine with a cup of tea beside you, Lily thought.

Utter, utter bliss.

Without another word, Karim leaned over the bath, flicked a switch so the plug sank down flush with the base of the bath, and ran the water.

The water flowing into the white interior of the bath was the same shade of aqua as the recessed lights under the bath.

'That's stunning. How did you...?' She gestured to the water.

'It's a tap light.'

When she drew closer, she realised that there was a beam of aqua-coloured light running through the water; the actual water in the bath was clear.

'Boys and their toys,' she said, rolling her eyes.

He grinned. 'You have to admit, it's seriously cool.'

'It's seriously cool,' she said. She glanced up at the ceiling.

'What?' he asked.

'I wondered if you had one of those glass roofs that turn clear so you can see the sky.'

He wrinkled his nose. 'There's no point, in London. You won't see anything other than an orange glow and the odd aeroplane. A hot tub under the desert sky, on the other hand…now, here it would be worth having a clear glass roof.'

She could just imagine it. And she could also imagine Karim in the bath with her, his wet hair slicked back from his face and his body easing into hers.

For a moment, she went dizzy and had to hold onto the side of the bath.

'Lily? Are you all right?'

'Just a bit tired,' she said, not wanting to admit how much he affected her.

'Hmm.' He tipped something from a small bottle into the water, and rich, lush bubbles began to form.

'Vanilla,' she said, sniffing the air, 'and…?'

He slanted her a look. 'Pomegranate.'

Ah-h-h.

She'd been teasing him about pomegranates all evening.

'Hmm. That word's a very effective way to shut you up,' Karim said thoughtfully. 'Though not half as much fun as this.' He spun her round and lowered his mouth to hers, then nibbled her lower lip until she opened her mouth and let him kiss her properly.

She shivered when he broke the kiss. 'Karim…'

'Humour me,' he said softly. 'You're tired. I want to give you a few minutes to relax.' He removed the Buff from her hair and ran his fingers through the thick tresses for a moment, letting it fall to her shoulders. Then he undid the buttons on her chef's jacket, so very slowly.

'Mmm. I wondered what you were wearing under this,' he said in approval as he saw her lacy white bra.

Her trousers were next. And by the time he'd finished undressing her, the bath was ready. He turned off the taps, tested the temperature of the water, then took off his watch and placed it on the granite surround by the glass bowl of the sink.

'What are you…?' she began.

He rolled up his sleeves and gently lifted her into the bath. 'Just lie back and relax. I'll bring you a drink in a minute.' He forestalled her protest with a kiss. 'No arguments. Your client demands it.'

Lily, realising just how tired she was, gave in.

This was bliss.

A deep, hot bath with lots of bubbles and the most gorgeous music… She lay back and closed her eyes.

She had no idea how much time passed before Karim returned, carrying an opened bottle of champagne and a champagne flute. In the bottom of the glass there was what looked like a hibiscus flower. As he poured the champagne into the glass the flower opened.

'Now that's showing off,' she said. 'But very pretty.'

He placed the bottle on the side of the bath, on the shelf she'd imagined with a cup of tea, and handed the glass to her.

She refused to accept it. 'That's a really lovely thought, but I can't—I have to drive home.'

'Actually, you don't have to,' he said. There was a long, long pause. 'You could—if you wished—stay here tonight. With me.'

Her heart missed a beat. 'Karim.'

'I know.' He smiled wryly. 'I can't believe I asked you, either. I've never invited anyone to stay here overnight before.'

'I…' She swallowed hard. She wanted to say yes. She really, really wanted to say yes. A whole night in Karim's arms.

But a practical voice in her head wouldn't let her do it. 'I don't have clean underwear with me,' she said, suddenly embarrassed.

'I have a washer-dryer. If I put your clothes in now, they'll be ready to wear in the morning.'

She blinked. 'I thought you said you used a laundry service?'

'I do. But I still have a washing machine.'

'But you're a pr—'

He touched his forefinger to her lips to silence the word. 'Forget about the wretched title, Lily. If I had to sit around until someone would come to dress me, like some Regency duke waiting for his valet, I'd get nothing done. I believe in taking responsibility for myself.' He let his hand drop. 'Stay with me tonight, Lily.'

Against her better judgement, she nodded.

He smiled. 'Good. And you can't change your mind any more—in about three minutes' time, all your clothes will be in my washing machine. Wet. And you'll have to wait at least until they're dry.' He scooped up her discarded clothing and disappeared.

She lay back and sipped the champagne. The bubbles burst against her tongue—a heady feeling, but nowhere near as heady as the feeling she got whenever Karim looked at her.

When he returned, he said nothing, but his gaze was very, very hot. He stripped efficiently, then took the glass from her hand and commanded softly, 'Move up.'

She shifted along the bath while he placed the glass on the shelf next to the bottle; he stepped in behind her, then scooped her onto his lap so that she lay back against him.

'That's better,' he murmured, wrapping one arm round her ribcage and kissing the curve of her neck. 'Much better.'

With his other hand, he retrieved the glass and took a sip, before holding it to her lips so that her mouth touched the place his had just left.

'I'm impressed by the hibiscus,' she said when he replaced the glass, tipping her head back so she could look up at him. 'Though I wondered if you were going to add pomegranate seeds.'

'Believe me, *habibti*, I thought about it,' he said. 'I'll save that for another time.'

'This is incredibly decadent. This huge bath, all these bubbles, and champagne, too.'

'Life,' he said, 'is for enjoying. Because it's way, way too short.'

Something in his tone told her that this was something that went deep. The key to Karim—who he really was, under the playboy mask. She took his free hand, brought it up to her lips and pressed a kiss into his palm, then curled her fingers over it.

'Careful, *habibti*,' he warned, his voice slightly cracked. 'I'm tempted to do something very, very rash.'

And, with his erection pressing against her, she could guess just what.

The really scary thing was that she could be very tempted, too.

He kissed the curve of her neck. 'I think we need to move out of here. While I'm still able to think straight.' He shifted her off his lap, climbed out of the bath and wrapped a towel around himself, then lifted her out and wrapped her in a towel before carrying her to his bed.

He flicked a switch, and uplighters set into the floor bathed the room in the softest of lights; then he closed the curtains, let his towel fall to the floor and walked slowly, slowly over to the bed. Lily's breath caught in her throat: Karim was gorgeous. All male. And she wanted him more than she'd ever wanted anyone in her life before.

'So, Lily. Just you and me,' he said huskily.

'Just you and me,' she agreed.

'And tonight you're going to sleep in my arms.'

How long had it last been since she'd spent the night in someone's arms? Years. She hadn't wanted to—not until now.

And she was absolutely sure she wasn't making the same

mistake she'd made with Jeff. The situation was different. And Karim at least was a man of honour.

His lovemaking was tender and sweet and brought tears to her eyes. And as his body curled round hers, making her feel warm and safe, Lily drifted off to sleep, feeling more content and fulfilled than she had in a long, long time.

CHAPTER ELEVEN

THE next week and a half went by in a blur of cooking and
planning and double-checking lists; Karim, too, was busy
planning and fine-tuning his presentations.

And then Karim's intense schedule of business meetings
began. Lily was at his flat early every morning to sort out the
food and brief the waiting staff, then on her usual catering days
she drove back via Hannah's in the afternoon, collecting the
shopping ready for the evening's work.

By the end of the fortnight, she was ready to drop. But she
still managed to celebrate with Karim on the Monday night,
when he told her just how well everything had gone. 'And the
food was a real talking point. It got them thinking about the
tastes of my country, the new combined with the familiar,' he
said. 'So, thanks to you, it's been a success.'

'It was just trappings,' Lily said. 'You're the one who came
up with the statistics and the forecasts. You're the one who's
worked out all the opportunities. And you're the one who sold
those opportunities.'

'Teamwork,' Karim said. 'Credit where it's due.'

After that his schedule went crazy. The networking lunches
and parties morphed into meetings with journalists eager to do
features on Harrat Salma, meetings with lawyers and accoun-

tants and financiers and surveyors—but Karim still managed to snatch time with Lily.

'I'm sorry, *habibti*,' he said one evening with a sigh, settling her on his lap. 'I would really like to take you out for dinner, but my life seems to have turned into wall-to-wall meetings.'

'It's OK.' She understood. It had been that way for her, when she'd first set up Amazing Tastes.

'No, it's not OK. And I don't want you thinking that I've used you to help with my business and now I'm just using you for sex, because it isn't like that.'

'No, because *I'm* using *you*,' she teased back, wanting to lighten his mood. 'Didn't you realise that you're officially my stud?'

He laughed, then stroked her face, suddenly tender. 'That's one of the things I love about you, Lily. Your sense of humour.'

He'd said it. The L-word. But he hadn't said it in the phrase that Lily secretly wanted to hear him say. A word she wasn't going to beg for. And she had no intention of being the first one to say it.

Oh, Lord.

She was in love with this man.

Really in love.

It hit her like a ton of bricks. What she'd felt for Jeff…that was nothing, compared with this.

She knew she had to mask her feelings. He was only hers temporarily; even if he felt the same, nothing could happen. Not with such a clash of cultures and lifestyles and expectations—and one day soon he'd have to go back to his duty, his destiny. Which meant it was doubly important that he didn't guess how she felt about him, didn't feel the pressure. Life would be hard enough for him, soon, with his time never his own and his whole world given over to duty.

So she simply smiled and kissed him and pretended everything was absolutely fine.

Without even discussing it, they fell into an arrangement: the evenings when she worked, they spent at her house, and the evenings when she didn't, they spent at his flat. And even though Lily tried to tell herself that this was casual and temporary, that she'd manage to protect her heart so it wouldn't turn to dust when it was all over, as the days passed she found herself falling more and more in love with Karim. Growing closer to him.

'So what do you see yourself doing in five years' time?' Karim asked one night, when they were curled up in her bed.

Picking our children up from school, was her first thought. And then she was horrified. Although she was fond of Hannah's little daughter Julie, Lily had never seen herself as broody. And she and Karim weren't in the position to think about having children anyway.

But now the idea was in her head, she could imagine her belly swelling with Karim's child. She could imagine his hands cradling her abdomen and feeling their baby kick. See the love and pride on his face as he held their newborn baby…

No, no, no.

It wasn't going to happen; there was no point in fantasising about it.

'I don't know,' she said, striving for a casual air. 'Probably the same as I do now. Wowing the rich and famous with my food, and writing articles to give others the confidence to cook something spectacular.'

'What about your articles? Have you ever thought about turning them into a book?' he asked.

'Maybe.'

'And you'd be great as a TV chef,' he said, warming to his theme. 'Watching you cook is amazing. I'm never sure whether you remind me more of a dancer or a magician.'

TV chef.

Even the words made her want to scream.

'Lily?' he asked.

'Nothing. Just a bit of a headache,' she fibbed.

He smoothed her hair back from her temples. 'I don't think so—from the look in your eyes just now, I touched a raw nerve. I apologise.'

'It's all right.'

'No, it's not.' He drew her closer. 'You once told me that it's not good to bottle things up. Talk to me, Lily.'

She sighed. 'It's not a pretty story. It's a while ago now, and I'm over it.'

'You were offered a slot, but you ended up with the producer from hell and it didn't work out?' he guessed.

Hardly. She could work with practically anyone. The truth was much, much more sordid. 'No. I was in partnership with someone.' She sighed. 'I might as well tell you the whole thing. And if you despise me for being a fool, so be it.'

'Elizabeth Finch, you're very far from being a fool.' He stroked her face. 'Tell me.'

'Jeff and I…we worked together in a kitchen, and we fell in love. Got married.' She bit her lip. 'Then Jeff suggested that we should set up our own restaurant. It was a challenge, and we worked stupid hours to get it off the ground, but we did it. We were doing well. I thought everything was fine.' How naïve and trusting she'd been. 'One of our regulars was a TV producer and thought he'd be a natural on TV. She was trying to set up a new kitchen series, and she said Jeff had the right touch to appeal to everyone. Her bosses liked the pilot, so she got the green light to do the new show. And it got to the stage where we didn't see that much of each other, because Jeff was at the studios all the time and I was busy running things at the restaurant.' She shrugged. 'I thought that was just the way business goes, and things would start to settle down a bit once production had finished and the show had started airing.'

'But it didn't?'

She blew out a breath. 'No. Because Jeff wasn't at the studios as much as I thought he was. At least, not for the programme.' Even now, the betrayal made her feel sick. 'He was having an affair with the producer.'

Karim held her closer. 'I'm sorry he treated you like that. You deserved a lot better.'

'Turns out I'm a really lousy judge of character,' she said. 'The affair might've blown over—I didn't have a clue about it, so maybe our marriage could've survived that. But I'd also trusted him enough to deal with the financial side of things.' She shook her head in frustration. 'He was my husband, my business partner. Of *course* I trusted him. I could've done the finances myself, but he knew I loved developing recipes and he said he'd take over the financial stuff to give me more time doing what I enjoyed most, especially as he wasn't pulling his full weight in the kitchen and leaving most of the work to me.' She lifted a shoulder. 'I thought he loved me, that he was working for *us*—just as I was.'

'What happened?'

'I got a phone call from the bank about a cheque I'd written to a supplier. It bounced. They said we were overdrawn, and I said we couldn't possibly be—I knew the kitchen was running at a profit.' She closed her eyes. 'It turned out Jeff had emptied our joint account, right up to the limit of the overdraft.'

He stroked her hair. 'Bastard. I hope you took him to court.'

'You can't sue your husband,' she said. 'We had joint liabilities—so that meant I was jointly responsible for the overdraft. And he'd also withdrawn nearly all the money from our savings account. There wasn't a thing I could do about it.' She swallowed hard. 'We sold the business, but obviously there was a mortgage and loans involved. By the time everything was paid off, there was nothing left. Except the overdraft.'

'There must have been some way to make him pay his share—and your half of the money he took.'

'No. He'd used the money as a deposit on a flat. It was in her name, so I couldn't touch it. Believe me, I took legal advice. Hannah found me in tears one morning, made me tell her the whole story and marched me straight to a lawyer.' She sighed. 'If I'd left the overdraft, the interest would've kept mounting up and I could've ended up with a county court judgment against my name. I didn't want that, because then I'd have had real problems getting another mortgage or business loan.'

He swore in Arabic. 'You still could have told a journalist—he was on television, so being a minor celebrity would be enough to make the media interested in what he did. You could have dragged him through the papers and shamed him into paying back what he owed you. Not to mention the fact that the papers would have paid you for your story.'

'And get into a public slanging match?' She shook her head. 'No. I didn't want my name dragged all over the papers, Karim. I didn't want people to remember me as the stupid bimbo whose husband cheated on her and took her to the cleaners—that kind of mud sticks and it isn't good for business.' She paused. 'But I sure as hell won't ever go into business with anyone again. And I'm never, ever, *ever* getting married again.'

'I'm sorry you had to go through such a horrible experience.' He cradled her close. 'It's kismet. What goes around, comes around. He'll get his comeuppance.'

'Right now,' she said, 'he's still doing perfectly fine as a TV chef. Even though he's split up from his producer. Apparently he couldn't stay faithful to her, either.'

'Kismet takes time,' Karim said thoughtfully. 'And he's a very stupid man. Didn't he realise what he had in you?'

'Obviously I wasn't enough for him.'

'More fool him,' Karim said. 'And I know he let you down badly but, *habibti*, believe me, not all men are complete bastards.'

'I know they're not. My dad wasn't. He would've been

turning in his grave if he'd known what a mess he left us in.' The words were out before she could stop them.

'Your dad?' Karim asked.

She'd started telling him. Might as well finish it. 'He died when I was four—it was one of those really unexpected, shocking things.'

'An accident?' Karim guessed.

'He just died, even though he was never ill,' Lily said matter-of-factly. 'Mum says the coroner thought it might have been an undiagnosed heart condition. And he really did love me and Mum. He was never too busy for me when I was little—I remember him doing finger-painting with me and drawing me lots of pictures. But Mum says he was pretty hopeless with money. He never got round to sorting out any life insurance.' She smiled ruefully. 'I suppose his head was too full of his art.'

'He was an artist, too?'

She nodded. 'That's how they met, at art school. They fell in love and got married when they were students, and Mum went into labour with me halfway through her last exam. I wasn't planned, but they loved me anyway and she said there was always going to be room in their life for me. Once they knew they were expecting me, they really wanted to be a family.' She sighed. 'She says Dad would've been a really great artist if he'd lived, but there just wasn't enough time. He never got his big breakthrough.' She looked away. 'We struggled a fair bit. Mum didn't even have enough money to cover the funeral costs.'

Which explained a lot, Karim thought. Lily had had to scrimp and save and make do when she was little—and then do it all over again to make up for the financial mess her ex-husband had left her in. 'Clearly you've worked your heart out for the last few years,' he said.

'Because of the house, you mean?' she asked, guessing instantly what he meant.

'Islington's a nice area. And your house isn't exactly small.'

'It's not actually my house—it's my stepfather's. Well, my sort of stepfather's,' she said awkwardly.

'Sort of?'

'Mum met Yves when I was a teenager. He fell in love with her, but she refused flatly to get involved with him. He bought every single one of her paintings from the gallery, one by one, so she had to talk to him each time; and finally she agreed to let him take her out to dinner. I was really pleased, because it was about time she did something for herself.' She smiled. 'And Yves is gorgeous. He's funny and clever and kind. I'll never forget my dad, but Yves has been there for me for the last twelve years. I think of him as my dad, and Mum really ought to make an honest man out of him.'

'But she's scared in case she loses him?' Karim asked.

Lily shook her head. 'The thing is, Yves owns a vineyard. And he's made a pretty good living out of it.' She bit her lip. 'She says she won't marry him until she's got as much money as he has. I can kind of see her point—she doesn't want people to think she's a gold digger.'

'Even though they've been together twelve years?'

'Even though,' Lily agreed. 'My mum has this independent streak. She refuses to rely on anyone.'

'And you're just like your mother,' Karim said. He'd recognised her refusal to rely on others from the moment he'd knocked on her door.

'Not quite, or I wouldn't be living in his house.' She sighed. 'The way Yves put it, it was an investment. Buying the house gives him a base in London—and in me he has a tenant he can trust to look after the house properly and tell him straight away if any work needs doing.' She wrinkled her nose. 'It was a cooked-up scheme between them to help put me back on my feet. I made them admit it, eventually. But they did it because they love me. And I suppose they do have a point—I needed a decent-sized kitchen for work and there was no way I could've afforded even a studio flat on my own, especially as I'd lost everything I'd worked for including all my savings. But I'm not some spoiled, brat of a daughter who takes it all for granted.' She lifted her chin. 'I pay Yves a fair rent. We had quite a big fight about it, but he accepts that I want to make my own way, not rely on others.'

'So you've been let down by two men you should've been able to expect to support you,' he said quietly.

'Dad didn't do it deliberately.'

He heard what she wasn't saying, and said it for her. 'But Jeff did.'

'He was ambitious. More ambitious than I am.'

'And that's why you don't want to be a TV chef—you don't want to put yourself in competition with him and have it all dragged up?'

'I never wanted to be a celebrity chef in any case. You're setting yourself up as an Aunt Sally—you can't put a foot wrong or make an off-the-cuff remark, or it'll haunt you for the rest of your life. And there's all the personal stuff, too—you get criticised for your wardrobe or your hair or your shape.'

'There's nothing wrong with your wardrobe. Or your hair.' He slid his palm across her curves. 'Or your shape. Especially not your shape.'

'That's not the point. Everyone thinks they have a right to comment about you, and I'm just not interested in being part of all that.'

'And yet you cook for celebs.'

'That's different.' She flapped a dismissive hand. 'I'm not in the limelight. And I happen to like doing what I do now. I know people actually use my recipes because they write in to the magazine, and I love it when they tell me they didn't think they'd ever be able to make something but they could follow my recipes.' She smiled. 'Someone once told me the best revenge is living well, so I'm doing exactly that. I'm working in a business I love, doing what I enjoy, and I can pick and choose my clients. If I'm not happy with the way a client acts towards me, the next time they ask for a booking I might fib about free slots and suggest they use someone else.'

He rubbed the tip of his nose against hers. 'Were you fibbing about free slots when I asked you?'

'No, I really am booked up three months in advance,' she told him.

'But you're not going to let your heart get involved again.'

'Absolutely not.' It was a lie. She already had.

Though she knew it couldn't go further between them. Couldn't be permanent. Wrong culture, wrong life, wrong everything. And even if Karim *could* ask her to be his wife, he'd told her that the women in his family didn't work. Marrying Karim would mean giving up her entire life. Relying on him. Losing her independence, everything she'd worked so hard for during the last four years.

It wasn't going to happen.

She changed the subject swiftly. 'So what about you, then? Where do you think you'll be in five years' time?'

'I already know that. Back in Harrat Salma.' His voice was toneless. 'Eventually my father's going to retire and I'll take his place.'

'And you really don't want to do it.'

'Yes and no,' he answered enigmatically. 'Does it show that much?'

'To me—yes.' She stroked his face. 'You're bottling it up, Karim. It's not good for you.'

Karim thought about it. She was right. And she'd told him a confidence. So maybe he could tell her the things he'd never told anyone else, even his best friend.

'Do you have a younger brother or sister who could take over and let you go back to doing the vulcanology stuff?' she asked.

He frowned. 'I thought you looked me up on the Internet?'

'I did, but I didn't snoop. I just learned who you were and that you spent a lot of time at parties,' she said lightly. 'Though I know now the serial party-boy bit isn't strictly true.'

'I have a younger sister,' he said, 'Farah. She's four years younger than I am.'

'And is she the sort who'd be happier running the country?'

'No.' He sucked in a breath. 'Even if she was, it isn't an option—because of the current laws of succession.'

Her eyes glittered.

'I know, you're Western-born, you have a different take on things,' he said, 'and I agree with you on this point. One of the things I will change is the succession laws. My father and grandfather have taken a modern approach in that women in Harrat Salma have the right to an education and the freedom to do any job they choose, but they don't have to do it if they don't want to. If they want to stay home and care for their family, then that is an option too. And I don't see why men can't take on that role too, should they choose.'

She smiled. 'Now that's forward thinking—few men do that, even here.' She paused. 'What would happen if you didn't rule?'

'The title would pass to a cousin. But that's a cop-out, Lily. It's my burden. I need to accept it and find a way of meshing my heart with my duty.'

She dropped a kiss on his chest, in the region of his heart. 'I'm sorry. But, as the oldest, you must have grown up knowing that this would happen?'

'No.' He looked away. 'Because I wasn't always the oldest.'

CHAPTER TWELVE

SHE stared at him, not quite understanding. 'You what?'

'I wasn't the always oldest,' Karim repeated. 'I was the middle child.'

So the fact he was the oldest now meant that tragedy had scarred his past. He'd lost his older brother.

Lily knew that if she asked questions now, pushed him to tell her about it, he'd clam up. Instead she shifted so that his head was pillowed on her breasts, wrapped her arms around him and waited for him to speak.

'I had a brother. Tariq. He's—he *was*,' he corrected himself sharply, 'four years older than I am. Very quiet and serious— everyone was always telling him he needed to have some fun before he took on running the country.'

Just as the media thought Karim was doing. The ultimate playboy, privileged and spoiled, frittering his time away while he waited to become ruler of his country. Expecting it all to be handed to him on a plate.

How little they knew.

'And eventually one of my cousins persuaded him to go dune-bashing. Except their buggy overturned. And they weren't experienced enough to get the car out of the dune before it sank into it. He suffocated in the sand.'

Her heart contracted. What a terrible way to die. And how

hard it must have been for those left behind, for those who'd told him to go and have fun—they must all have felt so guilty, as if they'd pushed him to his death.

No wonder Karim was so set against the idea of tourists going dune-bashing—the activity that had killed his brother.

'When did it happen?' she asked softly.

'Five years ago. It's strange to think I'm a year older now than he ever was.'

She didn't know what to say. Words weren't enough. So she simply held him.

'I couldn't believe it when my father called to tell me the news. Nobody could believe it.' He swallowed hard. 'I went straight home. And even as I walked in I was expecting to see Tariq sitting where he usually did, quietly reading. He wasn't there. Just an empty space.' He pressed a kiss against her skin. 'I still find it hard walking into the palace. And how much worse it must be for my parents and my sister, having to live with it every day.' He grimaced. 'Farah's name means "Joy". And she is a joy—I've loved her ever since the minute my mother first introduced me to my new baby sister. But since Tariq died, she's become so quiet and withdrawn. I worry about her.'

'And she probably worries about you. You're trying to cram every minute with work and partying, so you don't have time to think about your brother—except that all the partying's really a façade for work,' Lily said gently. 'Do you think that's what your parents really want for you?'

'There is no other choice. I have to step into Tariq's shoes.' He closed his eyes. 'That's why I gave up my PhD.'

He'd been studying for a doctorate? She'd realised he was clever. He could've reached the very top of his chosen profession. And yet he'd walked away from it to do his duty. He'd done the right thing by his family and his country, even though it was breaking his heart. She stroked his hair. 'For what it's worth, I think you'll make an excellent ruler. Because you listen.'

'I'll make a good ruler,' he said, 'because I would never dishonour my family or my brother's memory by doing otherwise.'

'That's the other reason you work so hard, isn't it?'

He frowned. 'What?'

'Not just to stop yourself missing your brother. To stop yourself missing your dreams.'

'Maybe.' He moved so that he was facing her. 'Nobody else knows about this, Lily.'

She cupped his cheek in one hand. 'I'm not going to betray your trust, Karim. I'm not going to tell anyone.'

'I know.' He turned his face and pressed a kiss into her palm. 'And thank you. For listening and not judging.'

'Isn't there any way you could compromise?'

'No. There is no middle way. And I made the choice freely.'

'Because you couldn't live with yourself if you turned your back on your family when they needed you most.'

'*Habibti*, you're scaring me now,' he said lightly. 'You're reading straight from my heart.'

She understood him. Just as she knew he understood her. And she really, really hoped that right now he couldn't read her heart. That he couldn't read the things she hadn't told him, for his sake. Because now she knew just how strongly he believed in doing his duty, she realised that she couldn't stand in his way.

But there was one way she could tell him. Without words.

She bent her head. Kissed her way along his collarbones and then drew a line of tiny, nibbling kisses along his throat.

Karim shivered and turned onto his back. She smiled against his skin and she worked her way downwards, along the line of his breastbone, down to his navel. She teased him with the tip of her tongue, drawing a complicated pattern on his skin.

He groaned. '*Habibti*, I think I'm about to lose my mind.'

She could guess what he was thinking. Wondering. And that was exactly what she had in mind. 'I've hardly started,' she said. She trailed the ends of his hair against his skin; he gasped and tilted his hips towards her. Smiling, she moved lower and breathed on his erection, and to her delight he actually quivered.

'Lily…you don't ha—' he began.

Oh, yes, she did. She opened her mouth, and closed it over his flesh.

'Oh-h-h,' he breathed, completely forgetting to finish his sentence. His hands slid into her hair, urging her on.

I love you, she said silently. I love you and I know I'm going to have to let you go, but I'm going to make memories with you. And right now I'm going to make you see the desert stars you miss so much.

Karim was muttering now in Arabic as she stroked him, teased him with her lips and her tongue and her fingers until he was completely lost to pleasure. She didn't have a clue what he was saying; she heard her name, and then something she couldn't decipher.

And then her mission was most definitely accomplished.

Telling each other their deepest, darkest secrets marked a turning point in their relationship. Lily was trying desperately to hold back, yet all the time she was falling more deeply in love with Karim. The man who put others first. The man who was strong enough to give up his dreams for his duty. The complete opposite of selfish, faithless Jeff.

And although neither of them spoke again about what they'd discussed, she noticed that Karim seemed to cherish her. As if he, too, knew that their time was limited and they were going to make memories. That every moment was precious. Little moments like an early Sunday morning drive to the beach in Karim's outrageously low-slung car before Lily had to be back to prepare for work, feeding the ducks on the lake at Finsbury Park, watching the sun rise from Karim's balcony.

Karim woke in the middle of the night, his body wrapped round Lily's. Her fingers had become laced with his during sleep; the only way they could've been closer was if his body had eased inside hers.

He pressed his face to her shoulder, breathing in her scent. Funny how it always seemed to calm him. Make him feel centred. Make him feel capable of running the entire world, let alone Harrat Salma.

And then it hit him.

He and Lily had argued about love and marriage. He believed that it was all about trust and respect and honour, and affection would grow. And she—despite the way her ex-husband had wrecked her life—believed in love. Which she'd defined as respect and affection and physical attraction.

That was everything he felt for her.

Respect for the way she ran her business, her independence and her drive. And he liked her as a person, enjoyed her company. Physical attraction—absolutely. She blew his mind, to the point where he actually slept with her as well as had sex with her. Something he'd never let himself do before. Something he'd never really wanted to do before.

And now he knew why.

Because now his heart was involved. He was in love with Lily. He was in love, for the first time in his life.

So much for the ground rules. He'd managed to stick to two of them: he'd been faithful to her and he'd kept work and their relationship separate.

The stumbling block was number one.

Temporary.

Because now Karim knew he didn't want their relationship to be temporary. He didn't want to leave Lily behind in England

and go back to Harrat Salma to marry someone of his parents' choice, the way he'd planned to do. No. Now, he knew he wanted to marry a woman of his *own* choice.

Specifically, he wanted to marry Lily. Because he loved her.

He wanted to spend the rest of his life with her. Help her bring their children up. Share his triumphs and his fears with her.

He wanted her. Needed her. And he was pretty sure she felt the same way, even though she hadn't said a word about it and they were both pretending that everything was just fine and dandy. If he asked her to marry him…would she be his?

Yet how could the heir to the sheikhdom marry a woman like Lily—a woman from a different culture, a woman who ran her own business, a woman who was divorced?

And that raised other issues. Lily had been hurt before. Lost everything. She'd built up her business from nothing, loved what she did. There was no way she could run Amazing Tastes in London from such a distance; and there was absolutely no way she could set up the same kind of business in Harrat Salma. The wife of the heir couldn't be a servant for someone else.

Would she be prepared to give it all up for him?

Karim spent three more days trying to talk sense into himself. Telling himself that giving her up would be the best thing for both of them.

He failed.

Dismally.

And he knew that the only thing he could do now was to face it. Bring everything into the open. And hope that somehow they'd find a way to secure their future. Together.

They'd managed to synchronise their schedules to snatch a morning together and were sitting on Lily's patio, holding hands and watching the butterflies settling on her ceanothus and the bees clustering round the hebe, when Karim's fingers tightened round hers. 'Lily?'

'Yes?'

'I've been thinking.' He paused. 'Our ground rules. I want to change them.'

She went very, very still. Was he telling her that it was over? 'How do you mean?' she asked carefully.

'Exclusive is fine. Keeping work and personal stuff apart is fine. But the first rule…that has to go.'

The first rule was 'temporary'. Her heart missed a beat. Surely he wasn't going to…? No, of course not. He *couldn't*.

'You asked me once what would happen if I fell in love with someone. I said it wasn't going to happen.' He shrugged. 'Seems I'm not always right. I learned something this week. That it could happen. That it *has* happened.' He slid from the chair and knelt on the patio in front of her. 'Lily, I want to marry you. Will you marry me?'

'I…' She couldn't believe he'd asked her that. The one thing she'd secretly wanted him to ask her. The one thing she knew she couldn't have. She so desperately wanted to say yes. But, for his sake, she had to do the right thing. 'I can't.'

'Why not? Your divorce from Jeff was finalised, wasn't it?'

'A long time ago.'

'So you're free. Why can't you marry me?'

'All kinds of reasons.' Did he really need her to spell it out for him? He knew just as well as she did why they couldn't do this. She dragged in a breath. 'Karim, you're royalty. I'm a commoner.'

'That's not an issue, as far as I'm concerned.'

'But it's not just *you* that you have to consider, is it? What about your parents? Your country? Karim, I'm everything you can't marry. I'm not Arabic, I'm not a princess, I work for a living, and I've been married before. I'm as unsuitable as you can get.'

'You suit me.' His eyes crinkled at the corners. 'I'm of sound mind. And I'm quite capable of choosing my own bride. Which is why I'm asking you to marry me—something, I might add, that I've never, ever asked anyone else.'

She shook her head. 'But you *can't*. You've already told me that your parents are arranging a marriage for you. You haven't even mentioned me to your family, have you?'

'No,' he admitted.

'You're the future ruler of Harrat Salma. You have so many things to consider. You can't do just as you like.'

'Actually, *habibti*, as the ruler of Harrat Salma, technically I can do exactly as I like. And I want to marry you.'

He wanted to marry her.

Which meant he felt the same way about her that she did about him.

He hadn't actually said the three little words—he'd skirted round it, saying that he'd fallen in love. But she knew what he meant. He loved her. Just as she loved him.

She ought to be doing cartwheels and whooping. Instead, all she felt was fear. Sickening, rushing fear that this was where everything was going to hit the skids. 'But...you'll be going back to Harrat Salma.'

'Eventually, yes. And there will be a lot of toing and froing between here and there in between,' Karim said.

'So that means you want me to go back with you.'

He rubbed his thumb against the backs of her fingers. 'That's the general idea of marriage, *habibti*—that two people live together and spend their free time together.'

'So I'll be leaving everything here.'

'Not exactly. Your family is in France,' he pointed out. 'And they're very welcome to visit whenever they like. Your friends, too.'

'And my business?'

He blew out a breath. '*Habibti*, I know how I feel about you and I think you feel the same way about me. I don't have a choice about my job, but you have a choice about yours. And some rules I can bend, but the work thing I can't.'

'So you're expecting me to give up my independence.' Everything she'd worked for. Everything she'd relied on, since Jeff.

'I know it's a lot to ask.'

Did he? He was used to everything falling onto a plate for him. 'Yes, it really is a lot to ask. Especially as you can't guarantee that your family or your people will accept me.'

'Rafiq likes you.'

'That's different. He's over here; he knows me as your cook and he probably guessed a long while ago that I'm sleeping with you. Accepting me as your wife would be a whole different kettle of fish.' She paused. 'OK. Let's put it the other way round. Would you give up everything for me, stay here with me?'

His eyes darkened. 'I don't have a choice in the matter. You do.'

'But if you had a choice,' she persisted.

'If I had a choice, yes,' he agreed. 'But I don't have the luxury of choice. You'd be asking me to choose between you and my family.'

'And you're asking me to give up everything I've built up over the years. For you.'

'Are you worried that I'm going to betray you, the way Jeff did—that I'm going to let you down?' Karim shook his head in seeming disbelief. 'Haven't you learned anything about me, these past few weeks? I've trusted you with things I've told nobody else. I've shared things with you that I've shared with nobody else. Doesn't that tell you anything?'

'Of course it does. But, Karim, you're not free to ask me to marry you, and you know it. You're living in a fantasy world.' One she so badly wanted to share. But it wasn't going to happen and they had to face facts.

He glared at her, clearly about to argue with her when the doorbell rang.

Coward that she was, she was glad that it stopped him saying something unforgivable. Stopped her saying something just as irrevocable. 'I'd better get that,' she said, and rushed from the garden before he could protest.

To her surprise, Rafiq was at the door, looking strained. 'Is Karim with you?' he asked.

'Yes.'

'*Al hamdu lillah*,' he said, sounding relieved.

'You'd better come in. What's happened?'

Karim, clearly having heard a snatch of the conversation, was already heading towards them. 'Rafiq? What is it?'

'I've been trying to get hold of you for the last hour. Your mobile phone was switched off.' Rafiq glanced at Lily. 'So was yours. And you didn't answer your landline.'

Now he'd said it, she looked at the phone and she could see the light flashing, telling her that she had a message. 'Sorry. We were sitting in the garden. We didn't hear the phone,' she apologised.

'I hoped that was the case. Because if you hadn't been here...'

'What's *happened*?' Karim asked again, and this time there was a regal note in his voice. A demand that his question should be answered.

'Your father. He's in hospital.'

'*What?*' Karim's face paled.

'He's had a heart attack. Your mother is with him, and she said to tell you that the worst is over. That he will recover.'

A muscle flickered in Karim's cheek. 'I need to be there.'

'Of course you do,' Lily said.

'I took the liberty of booking a plane ticket and bringing your passport,' Rafiq said. 'The car's outside. We can go straight to the airport.'

Karim looked at Lily, clearly torn.

'Go,' she said. 'We'll finish our discussion later. Go and see him for yourself.'

'Lily.' He held her close, resting his forehead against hers. 'Thank you for understanding.'

'I'd be the same if it was my mum. Go. Ring me when you can and let me know how things are.' Though she had a pretty good idea what this meant. That Karim would have to hand over the job he'd been doing to someone else, and stay in Harrat Salma to take over from his father. Maybe just until his father was better…but maybe for ever.

And she'd have to give him up.

With supreme effort, she kept her voice steady. Calm. Supportive. Even though she wanted to yell and cry and scream and tear her hair out. 'And if you need anything—anything at all—you call me, OK?'

He swallowed hard. 'Thank you, *habibti*.' He kissed her lightly—and then he was gone.

Karim sat on the plane, staring bleakly out of the window. This felt just like the last time, when he'd gone home to Harrat Salma from England after a frantic phone call. When he'd gone home to do his duty. When he'd gone home to find his beloved older brother dead.

This time…would it be the same? Would his father's condition have worsened while Karim flew halfway across the world? Would he make it back in time?

Eight hours. A lot could happen in eight hours. Plus the travelling time from Lily's to the airport, and from the airport to the hospital. He felt sick. Please, let his father hold on.

He wished he'd asked Lily to come with him. To be by his side. For her quiet strength to flow into him, bolster him while he faced his deepest, darkest fears.

But he knew it would have been unfair to ask her. She had

commitments. He couldn't expect her to drop everything for him—to let her clients down, break all her promises, lose her integrity. And besides, he needed to talk to his family about her, first. Though this really wasn't the right time.

The plane journey felt as if it took for ever. But there was an official car waiting at the airport, a silent and respectful driver who took him straight to the hospital. He sent Lily a text that he'd arrived safely at Harrat Salma, then switched off his phone as he walked into the hospital.

His mother and sister were there in his father's room. He hugged them both, letting them know his strength would be there to carry them, then sat beside his father's bedside and took his hand.

'My son. You came.' The older man made an effort to smile.

'Of course. The second I heard.' Karim squeezed his father's hand. 'How are you feeling?'

'I've felt better,' Faisal said dryly. 'But they say I'm on the mend.'

'He overdoes things,' Johara said, thinning her lips.

Karim smiled at his mother. 'Just as he's done for at least the last thirty-five years.' But his father's illness was a reminder to all of them that Faisal was getting old. That he was reaching the age where he should hand over the running of the kingdom to his son—or risk working himself to death. If he had another heart attack, he might not be so lucky next time.

'Forgive me,' Faisal said softly.

'There's nothing to forgive. But you need to rest, *Abuya*. And do what the doctor tells you.' Karim hugged his father. 'I'm just glad you don't look as bad as I expected.'

But his father still looked bad enough to worry him.

He was definitely going to have to come home for good. This was his burden, and he'd agreed to accept it five years ago.

He just hadn't expected it to be so heavy. Or to happen quite so soon.

And the idea of having to face all this without Lily...

For his family's sake, Karim kept his feelings to himself. He spent the rest of the evening at the hospital, and returned to the palace with his sister, Farah; his mother, as he'd half expected, refused to leave Faisal's side. He sat talking to Farah, reassuring her that everything was going to be just fine—even though it didn't feel it—and it was nearly three in the morning when he was finally on his own. He glanced at his watch. His country was only two hours ahead of Lily's...but she'd still be asleep by now. It wasn't fair to disturb her.

On the other hand, she'd told him to ring her when he could. She might be lying there, unable to sleep, worrying despite the text he'd sent her. And there was always the chance that the text hadn't arrived. The system wasn't infallible.

He picked up his mobile phone and called her.

She answered immediately. 'Karim? How is your father?'

'A bit sore and a bit subdued. I talked to the doctors, and they say he's on the mend. But I'm going to have to stay here for a while, *habibti*.'

'Of course you are. Your family comes first. Is there anything I can do for you, here?'

'No. But thank you for asking.' And trust her to put him first. He paused. 'It's good to hear your voice, Lily. I miss you.'

'Uh-huh.'

Non-committal. That wasn't good. She was already withdrawing from him. Trying to do what she thought was the right thing, perhaps?

He couldn't face that.

He wanted her. Needed her. *Loved* her. Life without her would be unthinkable. Unbearable. 'Lily?'

'Yes?'

'I might be miles away, but I need you to know one thing. Something I should've told you before I left. Something I meant to do but I made a mess of it—I suppose because I've never done it before. I love you, Lily,' he said softly.

There was a tiny noise at the other end of the line that sounded suspiciously like a sob.

'*Habibti*, are you crying?'

'No-o.'

That wasn't true, and he knew it.

'Karim, I…' This time, he heard her gulp back the tears. 'I love you, too.'

'Everything's going to be all right,' he told her. Though he knew it was an empty promise. Because without her beside him, nothing felt right.

'Sleep, now. I'll call you tomorrow. I love you.'

'I love you, too,' she whispered.

He cut the connection and looked up at the desert stars. The stars he'd missed so much in London. In a heartbeat, he would've traded the light pollution of London for this and never seen the stars again, if it meant that he had Lily.

'There has to be a way for this to work,' he told the stars. 'There *has* to be.'

And he'd go to the ends of the earth to find it, if need be.

CHAPTER THIRTEEN

BEING apart from Karim was hell, Lily found. Even though he called her every night, even though they sent each other texts and emails and tried to pretend everything was absolutely fine, absolutely normal—it was hell. He'd talked about there being an empty space in the palace, after his brother died. Now she knew exactly what he was talking about, because there was an empty space in her life, too. She missed Karim like crazy.

Her longing for him grew worse still on the day that Monica, her editor at *Modern Life*, sent her an early proof of the article—along with a note scribbled on the bottom of Karim's photograph, 'Who IS this gorgeous man?'

The love of my life, she thought. That's who he is. The man who loves me all the way back. And we can't have each other, because he has to go home and rule his country and take a fitting bride to be his sheikha, his queen.

Just as Hayley had promised, Karim looked fantastic, sitting there in her garden, licking gooseberry fool from a spoon. And Lily could remember every single second of that day. When he'd told her what he'd fantasised about during the photographic shoot. When he'd told her to trust him.

She trusted him.

But she couldn't see how they could make their relationship work. There was too much in the way.

With every day that passed, it got worse. And when her Sunday client croaked down the phone to her on the Saturday afternoon, saying that she'd picked up a viral throat infection and she was sorry but she had to cancel the dinner party, Lily knew exactly where she wanted to be.

Being with Karim wasn't an option—there was too much going on in his life right at that moment and he really didn't need the extra pressure of her being clingy—but there was someone she could talk to, someone who'd understand. She picked up the phone. 'Mum? Can I come and see you for a couple of days?'

'Of course, darling. When were you thinking of coming?'

'Tomorrow morning?' Lily suggested hopefully.

'Let me know when your plane's due in, and I'll meet you at the airport.'

Another phone call, along with her credit card, sorted out the ticket; and the fact she was escaping for a few days got her through the evening's work for a dinner party that went on much later than she'd expected.

Though it was good to be busy, because it meant she didn't have time to fret about Karim. His texts and emails and phone calls just weren't enough. And soon they would have to stop, too—when he realised that she was talking sense, that she couldn't marry him and he'd have to marry a suitable bride.

How was she going to face the rest of her life without him? *How?*

She packed the bare minimum of things that night in a flight bag—not wanting to be held up waiting for her luggage to be taken off the plane and knowing that, if necessary, she could borrow clothes from her mother—and caught the early morning flight from Gatwick to the airport at Marseille Provence. She'd texted her mother with her flight details, and to her relief the flight was on time. The second she was through Customs, she looked round for her mother; she could see Amy waving in the corner, and simply ran to her. It had been too, too long since she'd seen her mother.

Amy greeted her with a warm hug; and then, to Lily's horror, she found herself bursting into tears.

'Oh, darling. Whatever it is, it can't be that bad,' Amy soothed.

Oh, yes, it was.

'Come on. Let's go to the car—we'll be on our own and you can tell me everything.'

Lily cried all the way to the car. And for a good fifteen minutes before she could speak and finally tell her mother all about Karim. Everything. Including the marriage proposal that she'd refused.

'Why did you turn him down?' Amy asked, looking completely bemused.

'Not because I want to,' Lily explained. 'I have to. It's the right thing.'

'I still don't see it. Sweetheart, I know you had a horrible experience with Jeff, but it doesn't mean it'll be like that next time round.'

Lily shook her head. 'Karim's an honourable man. He's nothing like Jeff.'

'So why refuse him?'

'Because…' She dragged in a breath. 'Lots of reasons.'

'Such as?' Amy probed.

'Mum, it's hard enough without talking about it.'

'Actually,' Amy said, stroking Lily's hair back from her face, 'I think you'll find it's easier if you do talk. Because sometimes you need someone else's view to show you how things really are—and that they're not as bad as you fear.'

'They're bad, all right,' Lily said with a sigh. 'He's a sheikh, Mum. How can I possibly marry him? I'm not royal-born, I'm from a different culture, and I'm divorced. I'm not an acceptable wife.'

'And you know that for sure, do you? You've met his family and they've all threatened to disown him if he so much as speaks to you again?'

'Well—no,' Lily admitted. 'But I can't go to meet his family. His father's been taken ill and he's been called back to run the country. I don't know when he'll be back or when things will settle down.'

'Have you spoken to him?'

A tear trickled down her cheek. 'Every day. And it's so hard, Mum. I want to do the right thing, for his sake. I can't make him choose between me and his country.'

'Perhaps,' Amy said, 'you don't have to. If he loves you as much as you love him, then follow your heart and you won't go wrong.'

'It's not just his family and his country. Even if that works out and I'm allowed to marry him, I won't be able to work. I've spent four years building up Amazing Tastes. I don't want to throw all that away. I don't want to be dependent on him.'

Amy looked thoughtfully at her daughter. 'Like I was dependent on your father, you mean?'

Lily lifted her chin. 'Yes. And you refuse to be dependent on Yves.'

'Yves. Ah.'

Lily caught the hesitation in her mother's voice. 'Mum? Is everything all right?'

'Ye-es.'

'But?'

Amy simply held out her left hand. On her third finger, a single solitaire sparkled in the sunlight.

Lily simply stared. This was the last thing she'd expected. 'You're engaged? You're actually going to marry him?'

Amy nodded. 'I was going to call you today anyway, and tell you. I was going to ask if we could come over and stay for a couple of days and celebrate properly with you.'

'It's your house—you don't have to ask.'

'Only in name. We think of it as yours,' Amy said.

Lily, knowing this was an argument she couldn't win, simply evaded it. 'And of course I want to celebrate with you. I'm thrilled for you.'

'But?' Amy asked.

'But you've always been so adamant that you wouldn't get married again.'

Amy shrugged. 'Things are different, now.'

Lily frowned. 'Mum? What aren't you telling me?'

'You know I love you, don't you?' Amy's grey-blue eyes were serious.

'Of course I do. And I love you. You know that. But you're scaring me, Mum.' Ice slid down Lily's spine. 'What's happened?'

'Everything's fine now.' Amy took a deep breath. 'I had a bit of a health scare, the week before last. A lump.'

'A lump?' The world spun dizzily as Lily took in the implications. 'The week before last? But...' They phoned each other three or four times a week. Texted each other. Didn't let the distance between England and France get between mother and daughter. 'Why didn't you tell me?'

'Because you were busy, love.'

'*Busy?*' Lily shook her head vehemently. 'I'm never too busy for you, Mum. *Ever.*'

'I know. But I didn't want to worry you.'

'I'm worried now.'

'Darling, there was no point in telling you until I'd had the tests and knew what the diagnosis was—whether it was something to worry about or not.'

'Actually, Mum, there was *every* point. I would've been there with you. You know I would've dropped everything to support you.'

'I know you would.' Amy squeezed her hand. 'But I know

what your schedule's like and I didn't want to lean on you. Remember, I have Yves.' She blushed. 'Actually, he was the one who found the lump. And once we'd got over the initial shock, he told me that he was going to book me in with the best specialist, immediately—and he'd pay any costs for the treatment. The way he put it, I'm more important to him than money, and I'm far more important to him than my stubborn English pride.'

Lily could imagine the scene, and smiled through her worry. 'Sounds just like Yves. So, the results?'

'It was a cyst. Completely benign. And I had it removed the same day. It's healing nicely.' Amy smiled wryly. 'It did one thing, though. It made me reassess my priorities. So I proposed to him.'

'*You* proposed to *Yves*?' Lily stared at her mother in surprise—and then grinned. 'Did you go down on one knee?'

'Of course.'

'And what did he say?'

Amy wrinkled her nose. 'He roared at me. Told me I was a stupid, stubborn Englishwoman—that it was his job to propose, not mine, and he was going to ask me every three minutes for the rest of my life until I said yes.'

'Did he?'

'He timed it down to the second.'

'And you said yes.' Lily hugged her. 'Mum, I'm so happy for you. And should you be driving?'

'Yes, sweetheart, I'm perfectly fine. Stop fussing.' Amy rolled her eyes. 'You're as bad as Yves. And why do I have the nasty feeling you're going to gang up on me with him?'

Lily just smiled. And when Amy drove them back to the vineyard, she greeted Yves warmly. 'I'm so pleased my mother has finally seen sense.' She hugged him. 'To be honest, I've thought of you as my father for the last twelve years. But now I can officially call you *Papa*. And I'm so glad.'

'Oh, *chérie*.' Yves shook his head, clearly overcome with emotion.

'Careful,' Amy said, 'you'll have me crying, next.'

'Cry? We have a wedding to plan. And if I'm not doing the catering, there's going to be trouble.'

'You're not doing the catering,' Yves said, recovering himself, 'because you're going to be our bridesmaid. At least, I hope you are.'

'I wouldn't miss it for the world,' Lily said. 'But Amazing Tastes can still do the catering. Hannah and Bea will do it, under my direction.' She smiled. 'It'll be my wedding present to you. No arguments.'

'I think,' Amy said, 'we'd better give in.'

'As our daughter is a chip off the old block, yes,' Yves said, hugging them both. 'Thank you, *chérie*.'

And having a wedding to plan, Lily thought, was just what she needed—to keep her too busy to think about the wedding that wasn't going to happen.

Karim called Lily later that night; they'd agreed that it was easier for him to ring her. Just hearing her voice made him feel better. 'I miss you,' he said.

'Me too, *habibti*.'

He loved it that she'd tried to speak his language. Even though she'd got it wrong, she'd made the effort. For him. 'To me, you'd say *habibi*,' he said softly.

'*Habibi*,' she dutifully repeated. 'So I take it that *auhiboki* would be wrong, too?'

'Yes.' And not just in the way she thought. She couldn't love him. Not after today. 'To me, you'd say *auhiboka*.'

'*Auhiboka, habibi*.'

The words made him catch his breath. So simple.

Why couldn't life be simple? Why couldn't it have been how it was supposed to be—with Tariq as the heir and himself as a vulcanologist? Dr Karim al-Hassan could've married Elizabeth Finch without any problems and been happy. Deliriously happy. His Royal Highness Karim al-Hassan, on the other hand, wasn't free to make the decision. And it was ripping his heart into tiny, tiny shreds.

When he finally put the phone down, he couldn't bring himself to walk into the palace. His boyhood home, the place where he had so many good memories—and yet the place felt like a prison. Everything was topsy-turvy. So he stayed outside, looking up at the stars—stars that weren't even the same as Lily saw, because they weren't in the same hemisphere.

'Karim?' Johara came to sit beside her son. 'Your father's going to be fine, you know.'

'I know.' Karim reached out to take her hand. 'I love you, *Ommi*.'

'And I love you too.' She stroked his forehead tenderly. 'Are you going to tell me what's wrong?'

'I'm fine,' he lied, not wanting to put any pressure on her. His father's illness was hard enough for her, without having to worry about her son as well. Now wasn't the time to talk to her about Lily.

'*Habibi*, I'm your mother. I can tell there's something wrong,' Johara said gently. 'And it's more than the fact you're here and it's hard without Tariq. It's more than the fact that you're working too many hours to fill your time and stop yourself missing your volcanoes.'

'I'm…' He sighed. 'You're right. I'm not fine. But it's not fair to burden you.'

'Who else are you going to talk to, *habibi*? Your father?'

'Not when he's ill and needs to rest.'

'Then talk to me, *habibi*. Maybe I can help.'

He was silent for a long, long time. Finally, he sighed. 'I met someone in England. Lily. She's…' How could he even begin to describe her? 'She's strong and she's brave and she's quick and she's talented. When she's around, it feels as if the whole room's full of light.'

'You're in love with her.'

It was a statement rather than a question. He nodded.

'Does she feel the same about you?' Johara asked.

'Yes.'

'Ah.' She paused. 'Your father and I, we have been negotiating to find you a suitable bride. A woman of royal blood, an Arabic princess who can support you when you take over from your father.'

Karim dragged in a breath. 'I know. And I was prepared to follow our traditions—I wanted a marriage like you and my father have. A marriage with a partner I can trust and respect and grow to love.'

'But?'

He shook his head. 'I can't do that now. Not now I know what it's like to love Lily. I can't make those promises, knowing that I'm lying to my bride and I'm lying to my country and I'm lying to myself. It would feel…dishonourable. *Wrong*.'

Johara looked thoughtful. 'You've spent half your life in England. It's hardly surprising that the culture has rubbed off on you. And other rulers have married women from the West. Maybe the problem isn't so insurmountable.'

Karim closed his eyes briefly. So near, and yet so far.

'I haven't told you everything, *Ommi*. She's divorced. *Not* her fault,' he said. 'I won't break her confidence, but I'd quite like to break her ex's jaw.'

'Violence solves nothing,' Johara said softly.

'I know.' He looked at his mother. 'I'll lead Harrat Salma well.'

'Of course you will, *habibi*. You're a good man. A strong man. But you think you'll lead our country better if she's by your side.'

He bit his lip. 'I asked her to marry me. She refused.'

Johara arched one eyebrow. 'And yet you say she loves you?'

'Yes. And that's why she turned me down. She doesn't think she'll be accepted here as my wife. She's not royal-born, she's not Arabic, and she's divorced.' He sighed. 'I've argued with her about it. And she says I've already made too many sacrifices—she won't let me throw them all away on her.'

'You told her about your volcanoes?' Johara sounded surprised.

'She understands. It's the same with her cooking—she cooks,' he explained. 'She changed her schedule for me, worked stupid hours so she could help me with the business meetings. She made food like you would not believe.' He grimaced. 'Except obviously as my wife she couldn't continue to run her business—she'd be needed in a diplomatic role, by my side.'

'So you're asking her to give up everything,' Johara said thoughtfully. 'Her home, her family, her friends, her career. Her whole life. To live hundreds of miles away, in the public eye, in a place where she thinks the people will not accept her. It's a lot to ask of anyone, *habibi*.' She squeezed his hand.

Time to bite the bullet. Karim looked straight at his mother. 'You know I wouldn't willingly hurt my family. But I need to know…would you accept her?'

Johara said nothing, clearly weighing things up in her mind. And her next words surprised him. 'I guessed there was someone. I can always tell when you've just called her.'

He felt his eyes widen. 'How?'

'Because, just for a little while, there's a smile in your eyes.' She paused. 'As the ruler of our country, you will have many responsibilities. Many burdens. And the woman you've just described to me is not a suitable bride.'

He knew that his mother was speaking on behalf of his father, too. That they would be as one in their decision.

So help him, he'd have to learn to live with it. Live half a life, for the rest of his days. He wouldn't marry—if he couldn't have Lily, he didn't want to share his life with anyone—but he would be a good ruler. Bury himself in his duty. And he'd pray that Lily would find the happiness he so wanted to give her himself but knew he couldn't.

And then he realised that his mother was still speaking. '*Ommi*? I'm sorry. I was miles away.'

'I know.' She stroked the hair back from his forehead. 'I was saying, you need a wife who can support you, who will put a smile in your eyes when the days are hard. And if your Lily can do that for you then, regardless of her background, she is the kind of woman I will welcome as my new daughter.'

He couldn't quite believe what he was hearing. 'You'll accept her?'

Johara inclined her head. 'I'm not saying it will be easy. There will be talk, there will be mutterings. She'll need to compromise on a few things, learn some of our ways. But if we accept her, then our people will, too. They will learn to love her as you do.'

'One hurdle down,' Karim said softly.

'And yet so many more to go?' Johara asked perceptively.

He looked at her in surprise. 'It shows that much?'

'I know you,' she said. 'But if your Lily loves you, she'll see that your destiny involves more than one person's life. And she'll support you in that. She will be beside you all the way.'

'Like you've been to my father?'

'Exactly so,' Johara said. 'Would it help if I talked to her?'

'Probably not,' Karim said. 'Right now, I can't see a way forward.'

'I think,' Johara said, 'you need to go back to England. Talk to her. Show her what's really in your heart. And if it's your destiny to be together, you'll both know it.'

Karim squeezed her hand. 'It'll have to wait. You need me here.'

'We can manage without you for a couple of days. Follow your heart,' Johara advised him. 'And you have a good heart, my son. It won't lead you wrong.'

CHAPTER FOURTEEN

FOLLOW his heart.

The problem was, Karim thought, his heart was torn. Half of him wanted Lily. So desperately. Especially now he knew that his family wouldn't stand in his way.

Yet the sensible half of him knew that he was being unfair, that he couldn't expect Lily to give up her entire life for him.

He was going to have to do the right thing by her. He was going to have to say goodbye. But he didn't want to do it over the phone. He wanted to tell her, face to face—that he loved her more than anything, and that was why he was giving her her freedom.

So he called her. '*Habibti*? I'm on my way back to England.'

'When?'

'My flight gets in this evening.'

'Then I'll meet you at the airport.'

He knew he should refuse politely. But, so help him, he needed to see her. Needed to breathe her scent. Missing her was a physical ache in his gut. So he told her the flight time.

'But don't meet me in your van. I'll call Rafiq and tell him to sort out the insurance for my car.'

'You'd let me drive your car?'

He laughed. 'It's just a box on wheels, *habibti*.'

'It's a top-marque roadster, Karim,' she corrected.

'Whatever,' he drawled.

'But supposing I end up denting it when I park?'

'It's a lump of metal, *habibti*. It'll mend.' He couldn't care less about a scratch on his car, as long as she was all right. 'And anyway, you won't dent it. You're used to parking in tight spaces. You do it all the time.'

'In my van. Not in a high-performance car.'

'Which happens to be a little more comfortable than your van.' Though when it came to discomfort, he knew he'd walk barefoot over burning desert sands to be with her again.

'I love you, Lily,' he whispered. And he knew he'd never stop loving her. 'And I'll be with you soon.'

Soon?

His flight alone would take eight hours.

And every second would feel as if it were wading through treacle.

Lily kept an eye on the arrivals board in the airport lounge. Please don't let the flight be delayed. Please. It had been so long—she could hardly wait these last few minutes.

And then at last she saw Karim walking through Customs. Like her, he'd travelled with only hand luggage to avoid the wait at the other end of the flight. He was dressed casually, in a black, long-sleeved round-neck T-shirt with the sleeves rolled partway up his arms, black jeans and dark glasses. He clearly hadn't shaved since the previous day. And she'd never seen any man look so utterly edible.

She couldn't wait any longer. She just ran to him. And then his arms were round her, holding her tightly, and his mouth was jammed over hers, kissing her as if he'd been gone for a thousand years.

It had felt like a thousand years.

'Lily. I've missed you,' he murmured when he finally broke the kiss. His fingers tangled with hers. 'I hope you've parked nearby. And I'll drive.'

'You've been travelling for what, eight hours? *I'll* drive,' she corrected.

He grinned. 'So you like driving my car, do you?'

'Who wouldn't? And, just so you know, I haven't scratched it.'

'I told you that you wouldn't, O ye of little faith.'

As they walked to the car Karim felt his tensions drop away. The ache of missing her vanished. Just being with Lily made him feel complete, rested. All the same, he indulged her. Let her play at being his driver. Because he knew the conversation they would have to have was going to hurt her, just as it was going to rip his heart into two.

'So where are we going?' she asked. 'Your place or mine?'

'Doesn't matter.'

'Mine, then,' she said decisively.

Probably for the best, he thought. Because at least then she'd be home safely. And he would be the one to walk—well, drive—away.

He wanted to touch her. So badly. He wanted to strip that pretty little camisole top off her, unsnap her jeans, rip off her underwear and lose himself in her soft, sweet body, hot and hard and urgent. He wanted to hear those little incoherent cries she made when she came. He wanted to see her eyes go unfocused. To see her mouth swollen with passion and his kisses.

Though he knew that wouldn't be fair to her. Not when they had this conversation to go through. He couldn't just use her and discard her. So he forced his libido to back down. While she was driving, it was easy: his common sense told him that he couldn't distract her attention from the road, and besides he had to text his mother and Rafiq to let them know he was back in London.

But he found it a lot more difficult when Lily parked the car in the space a few feet away from her gate and handed the car keys back to him. His fingers brushed against hers and his temperature went up several notches. Crazy how just a little, casual touch could get him so hot and bothered.

And it was even tougher when Lily dropped her front door keys, bent down to pick them up, and the curve of her buttocks brushed against his thigh.

Karim was shaking with the effort of not touching her when he finally closed her front door behind them.

'Have you eaten?' she asked.

'I'm not hungry.' All too true. The airline food had tasted like ashes and he'd left most of it. He knew that even one of Lily's fabulous concoctions would taste bad, right now: nothing could get rid of the vile taste in his mouth. The guilt. The misery.

'Lily, we need to talk.' He gestured towards her conservatory sofa.

Without a word, she went to sit down. He sat opposite her, knowing that if he touched her just once he wouldn't be able to go through with this. 'Lily.' He dragged in a breath. 'I've missed you like hell. And being away from you has made me realise how much I love you—no, let me finish,' he said, putting up a hand to ask her not to speak. 'This is hard enough to say.' There was a lump in his throat the size of Vesuvius. 'I talked to my mother about you.'

'I understand.' Lily folded her hands in her lap. 'I told you I wouldn't be an acceptable wife.'

'Actually, no. I told her about you. How I feel about you. She says it won't be easy, but she'd accept you and the rest of Harrat Salma would follow suit.' He bit his lip. 'But she also said something else. She made me realise how much I'm asking you to give up. Your home, your family, your career—your whole life. And I know from talking to Luke that when you build something up from nothing, it's a part of you and it's impossible to let go.' He dragged in a breath. 'I want you to be happy, Lily. I can't be that selfish, to ask you to give up everything for me. So tonight I want to say goodbye. To let you walk away with all my love, and my blessing for the future. And I hope you find someone who deserves you.' His voice cracked. 'Someone who'll love you as much as I do but doesn't have all the complications.'

She was silent for a long, long time.

Well, he could understand that. He didn't exactly feel like talking, himself.

'I'll go now, *habibti*,' he said softly.

'What if,' Lily asked as he stood up, 'I don't want to walk away?'

He stared at her, not quite understanding. 'What?'

'I said,' she repeated, 'what if I don't want to walk away?'

'You have to.'

'No.' She stood up, too. 'You're not the only one who talked to your mother.'

This wasn't sinking in. Maybe the pain of losing her had made him completely stupid. 'You talked to my mother? When?'

'Not yours. *Mine.*' Lily's eyes were very clear. 'And she told me to follow my heart.'

Just what his own mother had said to him.

His heart skipped a beat. Was she saying…?

'And my heart lies with you, Karim.' Then she added the two words he'd taught her from his own tongue, just in case he hadn't got the message. '*Auhiboka, habibi.*'

She loved him.

'Lily.' Her name was a whisper. And then he cracked. Was at her side in nanoseconds. Swept her into his arms and kissed her thoroughly, a deep, hot, powerful kiss right from the centre of his being.

He wasn't aware of carrying her up the stairs to her bed. He had no idea who took whose clothes off or when or where or how. All he was aware of was the feel of her skin against his, her sweet scent, the brush of her hair against his face, the taste of her mouth under his. And then finally his body was easing into her, making them one. The ultimate closeness he'd craved so badly since he'd gone back to Harrat Salma.

With every thrust, he was giving her all that he was. And he could see in her eyes that she understood. That she accepted. That she was giving him just as much back.

And when his climax hit him, it felt as if the desert stars were shimmering above them, with the constellations rearranged to spell her name.

Later—much later—Lily was lying in his arms, her head pillowed against his shoulder, and his fingers were tangled through her hair.

'I've been thinking,' he said.

'Provided it's not the sort of thinking that led you to that ridiculous conclusion about giving me up,' Lily said, her voice slightly tart.

He laughed. 'You admitted that you were thinking along the same lines. About being noble. That's why you held back.'

'Not any more.' She pressed a kiss into his chest. 'And I want at least three more orgasms tonight.'

He felt his penis stir. 'Is that an order?'

'What are you going to do about it?'

'Make you come,' he said, and stole a kiss. 'After we've talked. Anyway, as I said, I've been thinking. Being a princess is going to drive you crackers.'

'You're offering to give it up for me?' She shook her head. 'No, Karim. Because what you do with your life affects your people, your country. I can't deprive them of that.'

Just how his mother had said she would react. Pleased, Karim drew her closer. 'That's not what I had in mind. But I won't ask you to give up everything for me, either. You're used to running a business. Making decisions. And doing what I want for the country—developing it in the right way, bringing prosperity to my people and keeping their lives peaceful and happy—is more than a one-person job.'

She traced circles on his skin with her fingertips. 'So what are you suggesting?'

'That we take joint responsibilities,' he said. 'In things that interest you. Obviously you can't set up another company like Amazing Tastes, but maybe you can share the responsibility of developing tourism with me. Doing something with fusion cooking. Talking to journalists. You could still do your cookery articles. Maybe write a book. Teach the world about the cuisine of my country—*our* country.'

'I'd like that,' she said. 'Though I was also thinking about taking some time off.'

'Time off?'

'You once told me that women also had the right not to work. That if they chose, they could take on a very important role—that of parent.'

He sucked in a breath. 'You're saying that's a role you want?'

'As well as working beside you,' she said. 'That's when I realised I was in love with you.' She gave him a serious look. 'I knew I was in trouble when I actually imagined my belly growing big with your child. I'd never, ever fantasised about being pregnant before.'

'Mmm.' He splayed one hand across her abdomen. 'You've just put the most beautiful picture in my mind. You all warm and round and incredibly sexy.'

'And if we have a son,' she said, stroking his face, 'then we'll call him Tariq.'

'I'd like that.' His voice caught. 'Lily Finch. I love you to distraction. But we seem to have skipped a couple of steps.'

'Skipped?'

'Later, *habibti*. Right now, all I want to do is go to sleep, with you in my arms. Then, I'm going to make you come so hard you see stars.' He kissed her, hard, as a show of faith. 'We have a lot of abstinence to make up for.'

'That,' Lily said, 'sounds just about perfect.'

* * *

On Lily's next days off, they flew to Harrat Salma—via Provence, so Karim could meet his future in-laws and receive their approval. And although Lily's stomach was in knots when the plane landed, knots that tightened even further when the official car drove them to the palace and she followed Karim to be received by his parents, the smile on Johara's face told her that everything would be all right.

'Welcome, my daughter,' Johara said, completely ignoring convention and hugging Lily. 'Welcome to our house. And thank you for taking the shadows from my son's eyes.'

Faisal and Farah were equally welcoming, and all Lily's worries about not fitting in vanished completely. They accepted her for who she was, and she discovered that they loved her already because of Karim. And by the time she went to bed that night—on her own, so as not to shock everyone—she felt as if she'd always been part of Karim's family.

The following day, Karim took her for a stroll in the city, introducing her to the spice market and teaching her the names of everything in Arabic. And in the afternoon he took her on a flight to the far side of the country, and drove them himself in a four-wheel-drive car through a harsh terrain of lava fields, pointing out all the geological features.

Lily had a feeling that she knew exactly what he had in mind. A trip that a certain type of tourist—the type Karim wanted to attract most—would enjoy. But as his eyes were almost pure gold with joy, she didn't say a word; she simply let him show her the wonders of Harrat Salma.

Finally, he parked the car. Helped her up a gentle climb.

She knew exactly what she was looking at when she stared at the crater. 'And you're absolutely *sure* this is extinct?' she questioned.

'Yes, *habibti*. I would never put you in danger,' he reassured her.

When they were on a broad plateau within the crater, he took the contents from his backpack—food, water, and a thick sleeping bag big enough for both of them. They ate a simple cold meal and watched the sun setting. As the temperature dropped Karim wrapped a cloak round her and together they watched the stars emerge in the darkening sky.

'Karim, this is incredible,' she whispered, awed. 'Like nothing I've ever seen. Not even the skies over the lavender fields in Provence match this.'

'Wait,' he told her. 'The best is yet to come.'

And as the moon rose she saw what he meant; the minerals on the inside of the crater glittered in the moonlight. 'Sleeping among the stars, just like you said.'

'I didn't think I'd ever be able to bear coming here again,' he said. 'Knowing that I always intended to lead the tourist expeditions here and everything had changed so I couldn't any more. But tonight…this is for you and me. Something special I can share with you.'

'Something really special.' She was blown away that he'd wanted to share something so spectacular with her.

'You've brought the joy back into my life, Lily. Thank you.'

'You've brought the joy back into my life, too,' she said. 'You've made me realise there's more to life than work. Taught me all about love.'

'As you taught me.' He brushed his mouth against hers. 'Remember I said we'd skipped a couple of steps? I think it's time we rectified that.' He shifted so that he was on one knee before her, and pulled a velvet-covered box from his pocket to reveal a single diamond that flashed fire beneath the moonlight. 'Elizabeth Finch, you're the light of my eyes and the heart of my heart. Will you marry me?'

'Yes,' she said. 'Most definitely yes.'

EPILOGUE

THREE months later, Amazing Tastes held its last important function under Lily's management: catering for the wedding of Amy Finch and Yves Lefebure after the ceremony in the tiny Provençal church. A wedding where Lily was the bridesmaid, but she only had eyes for her escort—tall, dark and utterly gorgeous in a wing-collar shirt, cravat and morning coat—who held her hand tightly all through the ceremony, knowing that soon they'd be making those same vows to each other.

And the month after that saw a much larger wedding in Harrat Salma. One where the whole country celebrated. Particularly when His Royal Highness Karim al-Hassan's very English bride made her wedding vows...and added some words of her own in their tongue when she addressed Karim.

'*Auhiboka. Ya rohi. Ya hayaati. Elal abad.*' I love you. You are my soul. You are my life. Always.

HER DESERT DREAM

LIZ FIELDING

Liz Fielding was born with itchy feet. She made it to Zambia before her twenty-first birthday and, gathering her own special hero and a couple of children on the way, lived in Botswana, Kenya and Bahrain—with pauses for sightseeing pretty much everywhere in between. She finally came to a full stop in a tiny Welsh village cradled by misty hills and these days she mostly leaves her pen to do the travelling. When she's not sorting out the lives and loves of her characters, she potters in the garden, reads her favourite authors and spends a lot of time wondering 'What if...?' For news of upcoming books—and to sign up for her occasional newsletter—visit Liz's website at www.lizfielding.com.

CHAPTER ONE

LYDIA YOUNG was a fake from the tip of her shoes to the saucy froth of feathers on her hat but, as she held centre stage at a reception in a swanky London hotel, she had the satisfaction of knowing that she was the best there was.

Her suit, an interpretation of a designer original, had been run up at home by her mother, but her mother had once been a seamstress at a couturier house. And while her shoes, bag and wristwatch were knock-offs, they were the finest knock-offs that money could buy. The kind that only someone intimate with the real thing would clock without a very close look. But they were no more than the window dressing.

She'd once heard an actress describe how she built a character from the feet up and she had taken that lesson to heart.

Lydia had studied her character's walk, her gestures, a certain tilt of the head. She'd worked on the voice until it was her own and the world famous smile—a slightly toned down version of the mile-wide one that came as naturally as breathing—was, even if she said it herself, a work of art.

Her reward was that when she walked into a room full of people who knew that she was a lookalike, hired by the hour to lend glamour to the opening of a club or a restaurant or to appear at the launch of a new product, there was absolutely nothing in her appearance or manner to jar the fantasy and, as a result, she was treated with the same deference as the real thing.

She was smiling now as she mixed and mingled, posing for photographs with guests at a product launch being held at the kind of hotel that in her real life she would only glimpse from a passing bus.

Would the photographs be framed? she wondered. Placed on mantels, so that their neighbours, friends would believe that they'd actually met 'England's Sweetheart'?

Someone spoke to her and she offered her hand, the smile, asked all the right questions, chatting as naturally as if to the stately home born.

A dozen more handshakes, a few more photographs as the managing director of the company handed her a blush-pink rose that was as much a part of her character's image as the smile and then it was over. Time to go back to her real world. A hospital appointment for her mother, then an evening shift at the 24/7 supermarket where she might even be shelving the new brand of tea that was being launched today.

There was a certain irony in that, she thought as she approached the vast marble entrance lobby, heading for the cloak-room to transform herself back into plain Lydia Young for the bus ride home. Anticipating the head-turning ripple of awareness as she passed.

People had been turning to look, calling out 'Rose' to her in the street since she was a teen. The likeness had been striking, much more than the colour of her hair, the even features, vivid blue eyes that were eerily like those of the sixteen-year-old Lady Rose. And she had played up to it, copying her hairstyle, begging her mother to make her a copy of the little black velvet jacket Lady Rose had been wearing in the picture that had appeared on the front page of every newspaper the day after her sixteenth birthday. Copying her 'look', just as her mother's generation had slavishly followed another young princess.

Who wouldn't want to look like an icon?

A photograph taken by the local paper had brought her to the attention of the nation's biggest 'lookalike' agency and overnight being 'Lady Rose' had not only given her wheel-chair-bound mother a new focus in life as she'd studied the clothes, hunted down fabrics to reproduce them, but had provided extra money to pay the bills, pay for her driving lessons. She'd even saved up enough to start looking for a car so that she could take her mum further than the local shops.

Lost in the joy of that thought, Lydia was halfway across the marble entrance before she realised that no one was looking at her. That someone else was the centre of attention.

Her stride faltered as that 'someone' turned and she came face to face with herself. Or, more accurately, the self she was pretending to be.

Lady Roseanne Napier.

England's Sweetheart.

In person.

From the tip of her mouth-wateringly elegant hat, to the toes of her matching to-die-for shoes.

And Lydia, whose heart had joined her legs in refusing to move, could do nothing but pray for the floor to open up and swallow her.

The angel in charge of rescuing fools from moments of supreme embarrassment clearly had something more pressing to attend to. The marble remained solid and it was Lady Rose, the corner of her mouth lifting in a wry little smile, who saved the day.

'I know the face,' she said, extending her hand, 'but I'm afraid the name escapes me.'

'Lydia, madam, Lydia Young' she stuttered as she grasped it, more for support than to shake hands.

Should she curtsy? Women frequently forgot themselves sufficiently to curtsy to her but she wasn't sure her knees, once down, would ever make it back up again and the situation was quite bad enough without turning it into a farce.

Then, realising that she was still clutching the slender hand much too tightly, she let go, stammered out an apology.

'I'm s-so sorry. I promise this wasn't planned. I had no idea you'd be here.'

'Please, it's not a problem,' Lady Rose replied sympathetically, kindness itself as she paused long enough to exchange a few words, ask her what she was doing at the hotel, put her at her ease. Then, on the point of rejoining the man waiting for her at the door—the one the newspapers were saying Lady Rose would marry—she looked back. 'As a matter of interest Lydia, how much do you charge for being me? Just in case I ever decided to take a day off?'

'No charge for you, Lady Rose. Just give me a call. Any time.'

'I don't suppose you fancy three hours of Wagner this evening?' she asked, but before Lydia could reply, she shook her head. 'Just kidding. I wouldn't wish that on you.'

The smile was in place, the voice light with laughter, but for a moment her eyes betrayed her and Lydia saw beyond the fabulous clothes, the pearl choker at her throat. Lady Rose, she realised, was a woman in trouble and, taking a card from the small clutch bag she was holding, she offered it to her.

'I meant what I said. Call me,' Lydia urged. 'Any time.'

Three weeks later, when she answered her cellphone, a voice she knew as well as her own said, 'Did you mean it?'

Kalil al-Zaki stared down into the bare winter garden of his country's London Embassy, watching the Ambassador's children racing around in the care of their nanny.

He was only a couple of years younger than his cousin. By the time a man was in his thirties he should have a family, sons...

'I know how busy you are, but it's just for a week, Kal.'

'I don't understand the problem,' he said, clamping down on the bitterness, the anger that with every passing day came closer to spilling over, and turned from the children to their mother, his cousin's lovely wife, Princess Lucy al-Khatib. 'Nothing is going to happen to Lady Rose at Bab el Sama.'

As it was the personal holiday complex of the Rama

Hamrahn royal family, security would, he was certain, be state-of-the-art.

'Of course it isn't,' Lucy agreed, 'but her grandfather came to see me yesterday. Apparently there has been a threat against her.'

He frowned. 'A threat? What kind of threat?'

'He refused to go into specifics.'

'Well, that was helpful.' Then, 'So why did he come to you rather than Hanif?'

'I was the one who offered her the use of our Bab el Sama cottage whenever she needed to get away from it all.' She barely lifted her shoulders, but it was unmistakably a shrug. 'The Duke's line is that he doesn't want to alarm her.'

Line?

'He thought the simplest solution would be if I made some excuse and withdrew the invitation.'

The one thing that Kal could do was read women—with a mother, two stepmothers and more sisters than he could count, he'd had a lot of practise—and he recognised an *as if* shrug when he saw one.

'You believe he's making a fuss about nothing.'

'He lost his son and daughter-in-law in the most brutal manner and it's understandable that he's protective of his granddaughter. She wasn't even allowed to go to school...'

'Lucy!' he snapped. This all round the houses approach was unlike her. And why on earth she should think he'd want to babysit some spoiled celebrity 'princess', he couldn't imagine. But Lucy was not the enemy. On the contrary. 'I'm sorry.'

'I've no doubt there's been something,' she said, dismissing his apology with an elegant gesture. 'Everyone in the public eye gets their share of crank mail, but...' there it was, the *but* word '...I doubt it's more than some delusional creature getting hot under the collar over rumours that she's about to announce her engagement to Rupert Devenish.'

'You're suggesting that it's no more than a convenient excuse to apply pressure on you, keep her under the paternal

eye?' He didn't believe it. The woman wasn't a child; she had
to be in her mid-twenties.

'Maybe I'm being unjust.' She sighed. 'I might believe that
the man is obsessively controlling, but I have no doubt that
Rose is very precious to him.'

'And not just him.' He might suspect the public image of
purity and goodness was no more than a well-managed PR
exercise, but it was one the media were happy to buy into, at
least until they had something more salacious to print on their
front pages. 'You do realise that if anything were to happen to
Lady Roseanne Napier while she's in Ramal Hamrah, the
British press would be merciless?' And he would be the one
held to blame.

'Meanwhile, they'll happily invade her privacy on a daily
basis in the hope of getting intimate pictures of her for no
better reason than to boost the circulation of their grubby little
rags.'

'They can only take pictures of what she does,' he pointed
out.

'So she does nothing.'

'Nothing?' He frowned. 'Really? She really is as pure, as
angelic as the media would have us believe?'

'It's not something to be sneered at, Kalil.' Her turn to snap.
'She's been in the public eye since she was dubbed the
"people's angel" on her sixteenth birthday. She hasn't been able
to move a finger for the last ten years without someone taking
a photograph of her.'

'Then she has my sympathy.'

'She doesn't need your sympathy, Kal. What she's desperate for is some privacy. Time on her own to sort out where she's
going from here.'

'I thought you said she was getting married.'

'I said there were rumours to that effect, fuelled, I have no
doubt, by the Duke,' she added, this time making no attempt
to hide her disapproval. 'There comes a point at which a

virginal image stops being charming, special and instead becomes the butt of cruel humour. Marriage, babies will keep the story moving forward and His Grace has lined up an Earl in waiting to fill this bill.'

'An arranged marriage?' It was his turn to shrug. 'Is that so bad?' In his experience, it beat the ramshackle alternative of love hands down. 'What does Hanif say?'

'In his opinion, if there had been a genuine threat the Duke would have made a formal approach through the Foreign Office instead of attempting to bully me into withdrawing my invitation.'

With considerably more success, Kal thought.

'Even so,' he replied, 'it might be wiser to do everyone a favour and tell Lady Rose that the roof has fallen in at your holiday cottage.'

'In other words, knuckle under, make life easy for ourselves? What about Rose? They give her no peace, Kal.'

'She's never appeared to want it,' he pointed out. Barely a week went by without her appearance on the front pages of the newspapers or some gossip magazine.

'Would it make any difference if she did?' She shook her head, not expecting an answer. 'Will you go with her, Kal? While I don't believe Rose is in any actual danger, I daren't risk leaving her without someone to watch her back and if I have to ask your uncle to detail an Emiri guard, she'll simply be exchanging one prison for another.'

'Prison?'

'What would you call it?' She reached out, took his hand. 'I'm desperately worried about her. On the surface she's so serene, but underneath there's a desperation…' She shook her head. 'Distract her, Kal. Amuse her, make her laugh.'

'Do you want me to protect her or make love to her?' he asked, with just the slightest edge to his voice. He'd done his best to live down the playboy image that clung to the al-Zaki name, but he would always be the grandson of an exiled playboy prince, the son of a man whose pursuit of beautiful women had kept the gossip writers happily in business for forty years.

Building an international company from the floor up, supporting Princess Lucy's charities, didn't make the kind of stories that sold newspapers.

'Consider this as a diplomatic mission, Kal,' Lucy replied enigmatically, 'and a diplomat is a man who manages to give everyone what they want while serving the needs of his own country. You do want to serve your country?' she asked.

They both knew that he had no country, but clearly Lucy saw this as a way to promote his cause. The restoration of his family to their rightful place. His marriage to the precious daughter of one of the great Ramal Hamrahn families. And, most important of all, to take his dying grandfather home. For that, he would play nursemaid to an entire truckload of aristocratic virgins.

'Princess,' he responded with the slightest bow, 'rest assured that I will do everything in my power to ensure that Lady Roseanne Napier enjoys her visit to Ramal Hamrah.'

'Thank you, Kal. I can now assure the Duke that, since the Emir's nephew is to take personal care of her security, he can have no worries about her safety.'

Kal shook his head, smiling despite himself. 'You won't, I imagine, be telling him which nephew?'

'Of course I'll tell him,' she replied. 'How else will he be able to thank your uncle for the service you have rendered him?'

'You think he'll be grateful?'

'Honestly? I think he'll be chewing rocks, but he's not about to insult the Emir of Ramal Hamrah by casting doubt on the character of one of his family. Even one whose grandfather tried to start a revolution.'

'And how do you suppose His Highness will react?'

'He will have no choice but to ask his wife to pay a courtesy visit on their distinguished visitor,' she replied. 'The opportunity to meet your aunt is the best I can do for you, Kal. The rest is up to you.'

'Lucy…' He was for a moment lost for words. 'How can I…'

She simply raised a finger to her lips, then said, 'Just take care of Rose for me.'

'How on earth did you swing a week off just before Christmas, Lydie?'

'Pure charm,' she replied, easing her shoulder as she handed over her checkout at the end of her shift. That and a cross-her-heart promise to the manager that she'd use the time to think seriously about the management course he'd been nagging her to take for what seemed like forever. He'd been totally supportive of her lookalike career, allowing her to be flexible in her shifts, but he wanted her to start thinking about the future, a real career.

'Well, remember us poor souls chained to the checkout listening to *Jingle Bells* for the umpteenth time, while you're lying in the sun, won't you?'

'You've got to be kidding,' she replied, with the grin of a woman with a week in the sun ahead of her.

And it was true; this was going to be an unbelievable experience. Rose had offered her the chance of a dream holiday in the desert. An entire week of undiluted luxury in which she was going to be wearing designer clothes—not copies run up by her mother—and treated like a real princess. Not some fake dressed up to look like one.

The euphoria lasted until she reached her car.

She'd told her colleagues at work that she'd been invited to spend a week at a friend's holiday apartment, which was near enough to the truth, but she hadn't told a soul where she was really going, not even her mother, and that had been hard.

Widowed in the same accident that had left her confined to

a wheelchair, Lydia's 'Lady Rose' gigs were the highlight of her mother's life and normally they shared all the planning, all the fun, and her mother's friends all joined vicariously in the excitement.

But this was different. This wasn't a public gig. The slightest hint of what she was doing would ruin everything for Rose. She knew that her mother wouldn't be able to resist sharing such an incredible secret with her best friend who'd be staying with her while she was away. She might as well have posted a bulletin on the wall of her Facebook page.

Instead, she'd casually mentioned a woman at work who was looking for a fourth person to share a last-minute apartment deal in Cyprus—which was true—and left it to her mother to urge her to grab it.

Which of course she had.

'Why don't you go, love?' she'd said, right on cue. 'All the hours you work, you deserve a break. Jennie will stop with me while you're away.'

That the two of them would have a great time together, gossiping non-stop, did nothing to make Lydia feel better about the deception.

Kal had been given less than twenty-four hours to make arrangements for his absence, pack and visit the clinic where his grandfather was clinging to life to renew the promise he'd made that he should die in the place he still called home.

Now, as he stood at the steps of the jet bearing the Emir's personal insignia, he wondered what His Highness's reaction had been when he'd learned who would be aboard it today.

It wasn't his first trip to the country that his great-grandfather had once ruled. Like his grandfather and his father, Kalil was forbidden from using his title, using the name Khatib, but, unlike the old man, he was not an exile.

He'd bought a waterfront apartment in the capital, Rumaillah. His aircraft flew a regular freight service into Ramal Hamrah, despite the fact that they remained stubbornly empty. No one would dare offend the Emir by using Kalzak Air Services and he made no effort to break the embargo. He did not advertise his services locally, or compete for business. He kept his rates equal to, but not better than his competitors. Took the loss.

This was not about profit but establishing his right to be there.

He'd been prepared to be patient, sit it out, however long it took, while he'd quietly worked on the restoration of his family home at Umm al Sama. But he'd continued to remain invisible to the ruling family, his family, a stranger in his own country, and patience was no longer an option. Time was running out for his grandfather and nothing mattered but bringing him home to die.

He'd do anything. Even babysit a wimp of a woman who wasn't, apparently, allowed to cross the road without someone holding her hand.

He identified himself to Security, then to the cabin crew, who were putting the final touches to the kind of luxury few airline passengers would ever encounter.

His welcome was reserved, but no one reeled back in horror.

A steward took his bag, introduced him to Atiya Bishara, who would be taking care of Lady Rose during the flight, then gave him a full tour of the aircraft so that he could check for himself that everything was in order.

He was treated no differently from any anonymous security officer who'd been asked to escort Lady Rose on a flight that, historically, should have been his grandfather's to command. Which said pretty much everything he needed to know about how the rest of the week was likely to pan out.

His aunt might pay a courtesy visit to Lady Rose, but even if she acknowledged his presence it would be as a servant.

Lydia rapidly exchanged clothes with Rose in the private room that had been set aside for her as guest of honour at the Pink Ribbon Lunch.

Lady Rose had walked into the room; ten minutes later Lydia, heart pounding, mouth dry, had walked out in her place.

She held her breath as a dark-suited security man fell in behind her.

Would he really be fooled? Rose had assured her that he would be looking everywhere but at her, but even wearing Rose's crushed raspberry silk suit, a saucy matching hat with a wispy veil and the late Duchess of Oldfield's famous pearl choker, it seemed impossible that he wouldn't notice the difference.

But there was no challenge.

Smile, she reminded herself as she approached the hotel manager who was waiting to escort her to the door. It was just another job. And, holding that thought, she offered the man her hand, thanked him for doing such a good job for the Pink Ribbon Club, before stepping outside into the thin winter sunshine.

Rose had warned her what to expect but, since rumours of a wedding had started to circulate, media interest had spiralled out of control. Nothing could have prepared her for the noise, the flashes from dozens of cameras. And it wasn't just the paparazzi lined up on the footpath. There were dozens of ordinary people hoping for a glance of the 'people's angel', all of them taking pictures, video, with their cellphones. People who thought she was the real thing, deserved the real thing, and she had to remind herself not just to smile, but to breathe.

It was the photographers who saved her, calling out, 'Lady Rose! This way, Lady Rose! Love the hat, Lady Rose!'

The eye-catching little hat had been made specially for the occasion. Fashioned from a stiffened loop of the same material as the suit, it had a dark pink net veil scattered with tiny velvet ribbon loops that skimmed her face, breaking up the outline, blurring any slight differences that might be picked out by an eagle-eyed picture editor.

Breathe, smile…

'How was lunch, Lady Rose?' one of the photographers called out.

She swallowed down the nervous lump in her throat and said, 'It was a wonderful lunch for a great cause.' Then, when there was still no challenge, no one pointed a finger, shouted, *Fake!*, she added, 'The Pink Ribbon Club.' And, growing in confidence, she lifted her right hand so that the diamond and amethyst ring on her right hand flashed in the sunlight as she pointedly touched the little ribbon-shaped hat. 'Don't forget to mention it.'

'Are you looking forward to your holiday, Lady Rose?'

Growing in confidence—it was true, apparently, that people saw only what they expected to see—she picked out the photographer who'd asked the question and smiled directly at him.

'Very much,' she said.

'Will you be on your own?' he dared.

'Only if you all take the week off, too,' she replied, raising a laugh. Yes! She could do this! And, turning her back on the photographers, she walked down the steps and crossed to the real people, just as she had seen Lady Rose do a hundred times on news clips. Had done herself at promotional gigs.

She took the flowers they handed her, stopped to answer questions—she could have entered *Mastermind* with Lady Rose as her specialist subject—paused for photographs, over-whelmed by the genuine warmth with which people reached out to her. To Rose...

'Madam...' The security officer touched his watch, indicating that it was time to leave.

She gave the crowd a final wave and smile and turned back to the limousine, stepped inside. The door closed behind her and, within moments, she was gliding through London behind a liveried chauffeur.

At which point she bit back a giggle.

This wasn't like any other job. No way. At this point, if it had been an ordinary job, she'd be heading for the hotel cloak-room for a quick change before catching the bendy bus back to work. Instead, she was in a top-of-the-range Mercedes, heading for an airfield used by people for whom the private jet was the only way to travel. The final hurdle before she could relax and enjoy being Lady Rose without the risk of someone taking a second look and challenging her.

It was a thought to bring the giggle under control. Not the fear of being challenged. The thought of getting in a plane.

Kal paced the VIP lounge, certain that he was wasting his time.

Lucy was wrong. Playing nanny to a woman known to the world as 'England's Sweetheart', or 'angel' or even *'virgin'*, for heaven's sake, wasn't going to make him any friends in the Ramal Hamrahn court. Unless there really was an attempt on her life and he saved her. Maybe he should arrange one...

He stopped fantasising and checked the time.

Another minute and she'd be late. No more than he'd expected. She was probably still posing for photographs, being feted by her fans.

He'd seen her on the news—she was impossible to avoid—a pale, spun-sugar confection, all sweetness and light. He knew she was a friend of Lucy's but, really, could anyone be that perfect?

He was about to pick up a newspaper, settle down to wait, when a stir at the entrance alerted him to her arrival. That she had arrived exactly on schedule should have been a point in her favour. It only served to irritate him further.

Lydia could not believe the ease with which she moved through airport formalities but when you were an A-list VIP, related to the Queen, even if it was goodness knew how many times removed, it seemed that the ordinary rules did not apply. Forget the usual hassle with the luggage trolley. She hadn't even seen the bags that Rose had packed for this trip.

And no one was going to make her line up at a check-in desk. Clearly, people who flew in their own private jets did not expect to queue for *anything*.

She didn't have to take off her jacket and shoes, surrender

the handbag and briefcase she was carrying to be X-rayed. Instead, she was nodded through the formalities and escorted to the departure lounge by Lady Rose's security officer.

Rose had explained that he would see her to the aircraft and after that she'd be on her own, free from all risk of discovery. And once she was in Ramal Hamrah, ensconced in the luxury of Princess Lucy's holiday cottage at Bab el Sama, all she had to do was put in the occasional appearance in the garden or on the beach to ensure that the paparazzi were able to snatch pictures of her while she lived like a princess for a week.

It was like some dream-come-true fairy tale. Checkout girl to princess. Pure Cinderella.

All she needed was a pair of glass slippers and a fairy godmother to provide her with someone tall, dark and handsome to play Prince Charming.

She wouldn't even have to flee when the clock struck twelve. She had a whole week before she turned back into Lydia Young, whose job as supermarket checkout girl was occasionally enlivened by a lookalike gig.

She automatically reached for the door to the VIP departure lounge, but it opened as she approached; a 'Lady' with a capital L did not open doors for herself. She was so intent on covering her mistake by adjusting the veil on her hat that she missed the fact that her escort had stopped at the door.

'Mr al-Zaki will take care of you from here, madam.'

Who?

She thought the word, but never voiced it.

All sound seemed to fade away as she looked up. She was tall, but the knee-meltingly gorgeous man waiting to 'take care' of her was half a head taller and as his eyes, dark and intense, locked with hers, she felt the jolt of it to her knees. And yes, no doubt about it, her knees melted as he lowered his head briefly, said, 'Kalil al-Zaki, Lady Rose,' introducing himself with the utmost formality. 'Princess Lucy has asked me to ensure that your holiday is all that you wish.'

Graceful, beautiful, contained power rippling beneath exquisite tailoring, he was, she thought crazily, the embodiment of Bagheera, the bold, reckless panther from her childhood favourite, *The Jungle Book*. She'd made her father read over and over the description of his coat like watered silk, his voice as soft as wild honey dripping from a tree.

Her own, as she struggled for a suitable response, was nonexistent.

Kalil al-Zaki might favour well-cut British tailoring over a fancy Ruritanian uniform but he was as close to her own Prince Charming fantasy as she was ever likely to come and she had to resist the temptation to look around for the old lady with wings and a wand who'd been listening in on her thoughts.

CHAPTER TWO

'YOU'RE coming with me to Bab el Sama?' she managed finally, knowing that she should be horrified by this turn of events. The frisson of excitement rippling through her suggested that she was anything but.

'There and back,' he confirmed. 'My instructions are to keep you safe from harm. I have a letter of introduction from Princess Lucy, but the aircraft is waiting and the pilot will not wish to miss his slot. If you're ready to board?'

Lydia just about managed a nod and the noise flooded back like a shock wave as, his hand curling possessively around her elbow, he walked her to the door, across the tarmac towards the plane. Where she received shock number two.

When Rose had explained that she'd be flying in a private jet, Lydia had anticipated one of those small executive jobs. The reality was a full-sized passenger aircraft bearing the royal livery.

She'd fantasized about being treated like a princess, but this was the real deal; all that was missing was the red carpet and a guard of honour.

If they found out she was a fake they were not going to be amused and, as Kalil al-Zaki's touch sizzled through her sleeve, Lydia had to concentrate very hard on marshalling her knees and putting one foot in front of the other.

This was anything but a fairy tale and if she fell flat on her face there would be no fairy godmother to rescue her with the wave of a wand.

Concentrate, concentrate…

She'd already had an encounter with one of Rose's security guards. He hadn't looked at her the way that Kalil al-Zaki had looked and he certainly hadn't touched. The closest he'd been was when he'd opened the car door and his eyes had not been on her, but the crowd.

No matter what he said about 'keeping her safe', it was clear that this man was not your standard bodyguard, so who on earth was he?

Should she have recognised his name?

Think…

He'd mentioned Princess Lucy. So far, so clear. She was the friend who'd lent Rose her holiday 'cottage' for the week. The wife of the Emir's youngest son, who was the Ramal Hamrahn Ambassador to London.

Rose had filled her in on all the important background details, a little of their history, the names and ages of their children, so that she wouldn't make a mistake if any of the staff at Bab el Sama mentioned her or her children.

But that was it.

This was supposed to be no more than a walk-on role with only servants and the occasional telephoto lens for company.

A few minutes performing for a bunch of journalists, and getting away with it, had given her a terrific buzz, but playing the part convincingly under the eyes of someone like Kalil al-Zaki for an entire week was a whole different ball game.

Hopefully, the letter of introduction would fill in the details, she thought as his hand fell away at the top of the steps and she was greeted by the waiting stewardess.

'Welcome aboard the royal flight, Lady Rose. I am Atiya Bishara and I will be taking care of you today.' Then, looking at the flowers she was clutching like a lifeline, 'Shall I put those in water?'

Lydia, back on more or less familiar territory, began to breathe again. This was the basic lookalike stuff she'd been doing since she was fifteen years old and she managed to go through the standard 'How d'you do?' routine as she surrendered the flowers and the dark pink leather briefcase that exactly matched her hat. The one Rose had used to conceal the cash she'd needed for her week away and which now contained Lydia's own essentials, including her own passport in the event that anything went wrong.

'Your luggage has been taken to your suite, Lady Rose. I'll take you through as soon as we're in the air,' Atiya said as she led her to an armchair-sized seat.

A suite?

Not *that* familiar, she thought, taking out her cellphone and sending a one word message to Rose to let her know that she'd got through security without any hiccups. Apart from Kalil al-Zaki, that was, and Rose couldn't do anything about that.

That done, she turned off the phone and looked around.

From the outside, apart from the royal livery, the aircraft might look much like any other. On the inside, however, it bore no similarity to the crammed-tight budget airlines that were a necessary evil to be endured whenever she wanted a week or two in the sun.

'Would you like something to drink before we take off?' Atiya asked.

Uh-oh.

Take and *off*, used in tandem, were her two least favourite words in the English language. Until now her head had been too busy concentrating on the role she was playing, enjoying the luxury of a chauffeur-driven limousine, free-wheeling around the unexpected appearance of Kalil al-Zaki, to confront that particular problem.

'Juice? A glass of water?'

'Water, thank you,' she replied, forcing herself to concentrate, doing her best not to look at the man who'd taken the seat across the aisle.

And failing.

His suit lay across his broad shoulders as if moulded to him and his glossy black hair, brushed back off a high forehead curled over his collar, softening features that could have been chiselled from marble. Apart from his mouth.

Marble could never do justice to the sensuous droop of a lower lip that evoked such an immediate, such a disturbing response in parts of her anatomy that had been dormant for so long that she'd forgotten how it felt.

As if sensing her gaze, Kalil al-Zaki turned and she blushed at being caught staring.

Nothing in his face suggested he had noticed. Instead, as the plane began to taxi towards the runway, he took an envelope from the inside pocket of his jacket and offered it to her.

'My introduction from Princess Lucy, Lady Rose.'

She accepted the square cream envelope, warm from his body, and although she formed the words, *Thank you*, no sound emerged. Praying that the dark pink net of her veil would camouflage the heat that had flooded into her cheeks, she ducked her head. It was embarrassment, she told herself as she flipped open the envelope and took out the note it contained.

Dear Rose,
I didn't get a chance to call yesterday and explain that Han's cousin, Kalil al-Zaki, will be accompanying you to Bab el Sama.

I know that you are desperate to be on your own, but you will need someone to drive you, accompany you to the beach, be generally at your beck and call while you're in Bab el Sama and at least he won't report every move you make to your grandfather.

The alternative would be one of the Emir's guards, good men every one but, as you can imagine, not the most relaxing of companions.

Kal will not intrude if you decide to simply lie by the

*pool with a book, but you shouldn't miss out on a visit to
the souk—it's an absolute treasure of gold, silks, spices—
or a drive into the desert. The peace is indescribable.*

*Do give me a call if there is anything you need or you
just need someone to talk to but, most of all rest, relax,
recharge the batteries and don't, whatever you do, give
Rupert a single thought.*

All my love,
Lucy

Which crushed her last desperate hope that he was simply
escorting her on the flight. 'There and back', apparently, included the seven days in between.

And things had been going so well up until now, she thought
as the stewardess returned with her water and she gratefully
gulped down a mouthful.

Too well.

Rose's grandfather had apparently accepted that taking her
own security people with her would be seen as an insult to her
hosts. The entire Ramal Hamrahn ruling family had holiday
'cottages' at Bab el Sama and the Emir did not, she'd pointed
out, take the safety of his family or their guests lightly.

The paparazzi were going to have to work really hard to get
their photographs this week, although she'd do her best to
make it easy for them.

There had been speculation that Rupert would join Rose on
this pre-Christmas break and if she wasn't visible they might
just get suspicious, think they'd been given the slip. Raise a hue
and cry that would get everyone in a stew and blow her cover.

Her commission was to give them something to point their
lenses at so that the Duke was reassured that she was safe and
the world could see that she was where she was supposed to
be.

Neither of them had bargained on her friend complicating
matters.

Fortunately, Princess Lucy's note had made it clear that Rose hadn't met Kalil al-Zaki, which simplified things a little. The only question left was, faced with an unexpected—and unwanted—companion, what would Rose do now?

Actually, not something to unduly tax the mind. Rose would do what she always did. She'd smile, be charming, no matter what spanner had been thrown into her carefully arranged works.

Until now, protected by the aura of untouchability that seemed to encompass the Lady Rose image, Lydia had never had a problem doing the same.

But then spanners didn't usually come blessed with smooth olive skin moulded over bone structure that had been a gift from the gene fairies.

It should have made it easier to respond to his smile—if only with an idiotic, puppy-like grin. The reality was that she had to concentrate very hard to keep the drool in check, her hand from visibly trembling, her brain from turning to jelly. Speaking at the same time was asking rather a lot, but it certainly helped take her mind off the fact that the aircraft was taxiing slowly to the runway in preparation for the nasty business of launching her into thin air. She normally took something to calm her nerves before holiday flights but hadn't dared risk it today.

Fortunately, ten years of 'being' Lady Rose came to her rescue. The moves were so ingrained that they had become automatic and instinct kicked in and overrode the urge to leap into his lap and lick his face.

'It would seem that you've drawn the short straw, Mr al-Zaki,' she said, kicking the 'puppy' into touch and belatedly extending her hand across the aisle.

'The short straw?' he asked, taking it in his own firm grip with just the smallest hint of a frown.

'I imagine you have a dozen better things to do than…' she raised the letter an inch or two '…show me the sights.'

'On the contrary, madam,' he replied formally, 'I can assure you that I had to fight off the competition.'

He was so serious that for a moment he had her fooled. Unbelievable!

The man was flirting with her, or, rather, flirting with Lady Rose. What a nerve!

'It must have been a very gentlemanly affair,' she replied, matching his gravity, his formality.

One of his dark brows lifted the merest fraction and an entire squadron of butterflies took flight in her stomach. He was good. Really good. But any girl who'd worked for as long as she had on a supermarket checkout had not only heard it all, but had an arsenal of responses to put even the smoothest of operators in their place.

'No black eyes?' she prompted. 'No broken limbs?'

He wasn't quite quick enough to kill the surprise at the swiftness of her comeback and for a moment she thought she'd gone too far. He was the Ambassador's cousin, after all. One of the ruling class in a society where women were supposed to be neither seen nor heard.

Like that was going to happen...

But then the creases deepened in his cheeks, his mouth widened in a smile and something happened to the darkest, most intense eyes she'd ever seen. Almost, she thought, as if someone had lit a fire in their depths.

'I was the winner, madam,' he reminded her.

'I'm delighted you think so,' she replied, hanging on to her cool by the merest thread, despite the conflagration that threatened to ignite somewhere below her midriff.

There had never been anyone remotely like this standing at her supermarket checkout. She was going to have to be very, very careful.

Kal just about managed to bite back a laugh.

Lucy—with Hanif's unspoken blessing, he had no doubt—was placing him in front of the Emir, forcing his uncle to take note of his existence, acknowledge that he was doing something for his country. Offering him a chance to show himself to be someone worthy of trust, a credit to the name he was forbidden from using. And already he was flirting with the woman who had been entrusted to his care.

But then she wasn't the least bit what he'd expected.

He had seen a hundred photographs of Lady Rose on magazine covers and nothing in those images had enticed him to use her friendship with Princess Lucy to attempt a closer acquaintance.

The iconic blue eyes set in an oval face, yards of palest blonde hair, the slender figure were, no doubt, perfect. If you liked that kind of look, colouring, but she'd lacked the dark fire, a suggestion of dangerous passion, of mystery that he looked for in a woman.

The reality, he discovered, was something else.

As she'd walked into the VIP lounge it had seemed to come to life; as if, on a dull day, the sun had emerged from behind a cloud.

What he'd thought of as pallor was, in fact, light. A golden glow.

She was a lot more than a colourless clothes horse.

The famous eyes, secreted behind the wisp of veil that covered the upper half of her face, sparkled with an excitement, a vitality that didn't come through in any photograph he'd seen. But it was the impact of her unexpectedly full and enticingly kissable mouth, dark, sweet and luscious as the heart of a ripe fig, that grabbed and held his complete attention and had every red blood cell in his body bounding forward to take a closer look.

For the briefest moment her poise had wavered and she'd appeared as nonplussed as he was, but for a very different reason. It was obvious that Lucy hadn't managed to warn her that she was going to have company on this trip. She'd swiftly gathered herself, however, and he discovered that, along with all her other assets, she had a dry sense of humour.

Unexpected, it had slipped beneath his guard, and all his good intentions—to keep his distance, retain the necessary formality—had flown right out of the window.

And her cool response, 'I'm delighted you think so,' had

been so ambiguous that he hadn't the least idea whether she was amused by his familiarity or annoyed.

His life had involved one long succession of his father's wives and mistresses, a galaxy of sisters who ranged from nearly his own age to little girls. Without exception they were all, by turn, tempestuous, sphinxlike, teasing. He'd seen them in all their moods and it had been a very long time since he hadn't known exactly what a woman was thinking.

Now, while the only thought in his own head should be *danger, out of bounds,* what he really wanted was for her to lift that seductive little veil and, with that lovely mouth, invite him to be really bad…

Realising that he was still holding her hand, he made a determined effort to get a grip. 'You are as astute as you are lovely, madam,' he replied, matching her own cool formality, as he released it. 'I will be more circumspect in future.'

Her smile was a private thing. Not a muscle moved, only something in her eyes altered so subtly that he could not have described what happened. He'd felt rather than seen a change and yet he knew, deep down, that she was amused.

'Rose,' she said.

'I beg your pardon, madam?'

'According to her letter, Lucy thought you would make a more relaxing companion than one of the Emiri guard.'

'You have my word that I won't leap to attention whenever you speak to me,' he assured her.

'That is a relief, Mr al-Zaki.'

Lydia had to work a lot harder than usual to maintain the necessary regal poise.

She had no way of knowing on what scale Princess Lucy measured 'relaxing' but she must lead a very exciting life if spending time with Kalil al-Zaki fell into that category.

With his hot eyes turning her bones to putty, heating her skin from the inside out, *relaxed* was the last word she'd use to describe the way she was feeling right now.

'However, I don't find the prospect of an entire week being "madamed" much fun either. My name is…' she began confidently enough, but suddenly faltered. It was one thing acting out a role, it was quite another to look this man in the eye, meet his dark gaze and utter the lie. She didn't want to lie to him, to pretend… 'I would rather you called me Rose.'

'Rose,' he repeated softly. Wild honey…

'Can you manage your seat belt, Lady Rose?' the stewardess asked as she retrieved the glass. 'We're about to take off.'

'Oh…' Those words again. 'Yes, of course.'

She finally managed to tear her gaze away from her companion—wild honey was a dangerous temptation that could not be tasted without getting stung—and cast about her for the straps.

'Can I assist you, Rose?' he asked as her shaking hands fumbled with the buckle.

'No!' She shook her head as she finally managed to clip it into place. 'Thank you, Mr…'

'Kal,' he prompted. 'Most people call me Kal.' The lines bracketing his mouth deepened into a slow, sexy smile. 'When they're being relaxed,' he added.

She just about managed to stifle a hysterical giggle. She hadn't hesitated because she'd forgotten his name. He'd made an indelible impression…

No.

She'd been so busy worrying about whether he knew Rose personally, countering the effect of that seductive voice, that she'd overlooked the really important part of Princess Lucy's letter. The bit where she'd mentioned that Kalil al-Zaki was her husband's cousin. As she'd said the word 'Mr' it had suddenly occurred to her who he really was. Not just some minor diplomat who'd been given the task of ensuring a tricky visitor didn't get into trouble while she was at Bab el Sama.

Oh, dear me, no.

That wouldn't do for Lady Rose. Cousin of the Queen,

patron of dozens of charities as well as figurehead of the one founded by her parents, she was an international figure and she was being given the full red-carpet treatment. Right down to her watchdog.

Kalil al-Zaki, the man who'd been roped in to guard their precious guest, was the cousin of the Ambassador, Sheikh Hanif al-Khatib. Which made him a nephew of the Emir himself.

'Kal,' she squeaked, slamming her eyes closed and gripping the arms of the chair as the plane rocketed down the runway and the acceleration forced her back into the chair, for once in her life grateful that she had her fear of take-off to distract her.

She was fine once she was in the air, flying straight and level above the clouds with no horizon to remind her that she was thirty thousand feet above the ground. Not that much different from travelling on a bus, apart from the fact that you didn't have to keep stopping so that people could get on and off.

Until now, what with one thing and another, she'd been doing a better than average job of not thinking about this moment, but not even the sudden realisation that Kalil al-Zaki wasn't plain old *mister* anyone, but *Sheikh* Kalil al-Zaki, a genuine, bona fide prince, could override her terror.

She'd have plenty of time to worry about how 'charming' he'd prove to be if he discovered that she was a fake when they were safely airborne.

But just when she'd reached the point where she forgot how to breathe, long fingers closed reassuringly over hers and, surprised into sucking in air, she gasped and opened her eyes.

'I'm sorry,' Kal said as she turned to stare at him, 'but I've never liked that bit much.'

What?

His expression was so grave that, for just a moment, she wasn't sure whether or not he was serious. Then she swallowed.

Idiot.

Of course he wasn't serious. He was just being kind and, for once in her life, she wished she really was Lady Rose. Because then he'd be looking at her like that…

'You'll be all right now?' she managed, still breathless when, minutes later, the seat belt light pinged out. Doing her best to respond in kind, despite the fact that it was his steadying hand wrapped around hers. That she was the one who'd experienced a severe case of collywobbles. Wobbles that were still rippling through her, despite the fact that they had left the earth far beneath them.

'I believe so,' he replied gravely, but in no rush to break contact.

It was perhaps just as well that Atiya reappeared at that moment or they might have flown all the way to Ramal Hamrah with their hands intertwined.

Not that there would have been anything wrong with that…

'Shall I show you to your suite so that you can change before I serve afternoon tea, Lady Rose?'

'Thank you,' she said, using her traitorous hand to pull free the seat belt fastening so that she could follow Atiya. Straighten out her head.

Not easy when she discovered that the sumptuously fitted suite contained not only a bed, but its own bathroom with a shower that lent a whole new meaning to the words 'freshen up'.

'Would you like help changing?' Atiya offered, but Lydia assured her that she could manage and, once on her own, leaned back against the door, rubbing her palm over the hand Kal al-Zaki had held. Breathing slowly until her heart rate returned to normal. Or as near to normal as it was likely to be for the next week.

Kal watched Rose walk away from him.

His grandfather, a man who'd lost a throne, lost his country—but not the fortune that his father had hoped would compensate him for choosing his younger brother to succeed him—was a man without any purpose but to enjoy himself.

He'd become part of the jetset, a connoisseur of all things beautiful, including women.

Kalil's father had, as soon as he was old enough, taken the same path and Kalil too had come dangerously close to following in their footsteps.

His boyhood winters had been spent on the ski slopes of Gstaad and Aspen, his summers shared between an Italian palazzo and a villa in the South of France. He'd gone to school in England, university in Paris and Oxford, post-grad in America.

He had been brought up in an atmosphere of wealth and privilege, where nothing had been denied him. The female body held no mystery for him and hers, by his exacting standards, was too thin for true beauty.

So why did he find her finely boned ankles so enticing? What was it about the gentle sway of her hips that made his hand itch to reach out and trace the elegant curve from waist to knee? To undress her, slowly expose each inch of that almost translucent peaches and cream skin and then possess it.

Possess her.

'Can I fetch you anything, sir?' the stewardess asked as she returned.

Iced water. A cold shower...

He left it at the water but she returned empty-handed. 'Captain Jacobs sends his compliments and asked if you'd like to visit the flight deck, sir. I'll serve your water there,' she added, taking his acceptance for granted.

It was the very last thing he wanted to do, but it was a courtesy he could not refuse. And common sense told him that putting a little distance between himself and Rose while he cooled off would be wise.

He'd reached out instinctively when he'd seen her stiffen in fear as the plane had accelerated down the runway. It had been a mistake. Sitting beside her had been a mistake. His brief was to ensure her security and, despite Lucy's appeal to amuse her, distract her, make her laugh, that was it.

Holding her hand to distract her when she was rigid with fear didn't count, he told himself, but sitting here, waiting to see if he'd imagined his gut-deep reaction to her was not a good idea.

Especially when he already knew the answer.

Then the name registered. 'Jacobs? Would that be Mike Jacobs?'

'You are in so much trouble, Lydia Young.'

She hadn't underestimated the enormity of what she'd undertaken to do for Rose and they'd gone through every possible scenario, using a chat room to brainstorm any and all likely problems.

And every step of the way Rose had given her the opportunity to change her mind. Back out. Unfortunately, she was long past the *stop the plane, I want to get off* moment.

It had been too late from the moment she'd stepped out of that hotel room wearing Lady Rose's designer suit, her Jimmy Choos, the toes stuffed with tissue to stop them slipping.

Not that she would if she could, she realised.

She'd had ten years in which being 'Lady Rose' had provided all the little extras that helped make her mother's life easier. She *owed* Rose this. Was totally committed to seeing it through, but falling in lust at first sight with a man who had flirtation down to an art was, for sure, not going to make it any easier to ignore what Kalil al-Zaki's eyes, mouth, touch was doing to her.

'Come on, Lydie,' she said, giving herself a mental shake. 'You don't do this. You're immune, remember?'

Not since she'd got her fingers, and very nearly everything else, burnt by a stunningly good-looking actor who'd been paid to woo her into bed. She swallowed. She'd thought he was her Prince Charming, too.

It had been five years, but she still felt a cold shiver whenever she thought about it.

Pictures of the virginal 'Lady Rose' in bed with a man would have made millions for the people who'd set her up. Everyone would have run the pictures, whether they'd believed them or not. Covering themselves by the simple addition of a question mark to the 'Lady Rose in Sex Romp?' headline. The mere suggestion would have been enough to have people stampeding to the newsagents.

She, on the other hand, would have been ruined. No one would have believed she was an innocent dupe. If it had been anyone else, she wouldn't have believed it either.

She looked at the bed with longing, sorely tempted to just crawl beneath the covers and sleep away the next eight hours. No one would disturb her, expect anything from her.

But, since sleeping away the entire seven days was out of the question, she needed to snap out of it.

She'd been knocked off her feet by the heightened tension, that was all. Unsurprising under the circumstances. Anyone would be unsettled. Kal al-Zaki's presence had been unexpected, that was all. And she turned to the toilet case and overnight bag that had been placed on a stand.

The first was packed with everything a woman could ever need. The finest hairbrush that money could buy, the best skin care products, cosmetics, a selection of sumptuous scents; a perfect distraction for out of control hormones.

She opened one, sighed as she breathed in a subtle blend of sweet summer scents, then, as she sprayed it on her wrist, she caught an underlying note of something darker that tugged at forbidden desires. That echoed the heat in Kal al-Zaki's eyes.

Dropping it as if burned, she turned to the overnight bag. On the top, in suede drawstring bags, were the cases for the jewellery she was wearing, along with a selection of simpler pieces that Lady Rose wore while 'off duty'.

There was also a change of clothes for the long flight. A fine silk shirt the colour of champagne, wide-cut trousers in dark brown linen, a cashmere cardigan and a pair of butter-soft

leather loafers in the right size. Supremely elegant but all won-
derfully comfortable.

Rose had also packed a selection of the latest hardback best-
sellers to while away the long flight. But then she hadn't
expected that her stand-in would be provided with company.

Or not. According to Princess Lucy, it was up to her.

While she'd urged Rose to allow him to show her the sights,
she'd made it clear that if she preferred to be alone then Kal
would not intrude.

Not intrude?

What had the woman been *thinking?*

Hadn't she looked at him?

Anyone with half a brain could see that he wouldn't have
to do a damn thing. One smile, one touch of his hand and he
was already indelibly imprinted on her brain. In her head for
ever more.

Intrusion squared.

In fact, if she didn't know better, she might be tempted to
think that the Princess had planned a holiday romance as a little
treat for her friend.

The idea was, of course, patently absurd.

Not that she didn't deserve a romance. A dark-eyed prince
with a killer smile who'd sweep her off her feet.

No one deserved a little fun more than Rose, but anyone who
knew her would understand just how impossible a casual, throw-
away romance would be for her. And that was the essence of a
holiday romance. Casual. Something out of time that had nothing
to do with real life. That you left behind when you went home.

Anyone who truly cared for her would understand that.

Wouldn't they?

About to remove the pin that fastened the tiny hat to her
chignon, she paused, sank onto the edge of the bed as a phrase
in Lucy's letter came back to her.

Don't give Rupert a single thought...

She and Lucy were in total agreement on that one. Rose's

grandfather, the newspapers, even the masses out there who thought they knew her, might be clamouring for an engagement, but she'd seen the two of them together. There was absolutely no chemistry, no connection.

Rose had made a joke about it, but Lydia hadn't been fooled for a second. She'd seen the desperation in her face and anyone who truly cared for her would want to save her from sleepwalking into such a marriage simply because it suited so many people.

Could Princess Lucy have hoped that if she put Rose and Kalil together the sparks would fly of their own accord without any need to stoke the fire? No doubt about it, a week being flirted with by Kal al-Zaki would have been just the thing to bring the colour back into Rose's cheeks.

Or was it all less complicated than that?

Was Lucy simply relying on the ever-attendant paparazzi, seeing two young people alone in a perfect setting, to put one and one together and make it into a front page story that would make them a fortune?

Who cared whether it was true?

Excellent plan, Lucy, she thought, warming to the woman despite the problems she'd caused.

There was only one thing wrong with it. Lady Rose had taken matters into her own hands and was, even now—in borrowed clothes, a borrowed car—embarking on an adventure of her own, safe in the knowledge that no one realised she'd escaped. That she could do what she liked while the world watched her lookalike.

Of course there was nothing to stop her from making it happen, she thought as she finally removed the hat and jewellery she was wearing. Kicked off her shoes and slipped out of the suit.

All it would take would be a look. A touch. He wasn't averse to touching.

She began to pull pins from her hair, absently divesting herself of the Lady Rose persona, just as she did at the end of every gig.

And she wouldn't be the victim this time. She would be the one in control, watching as the biter was, for once, bit.

Then, as her hair tumbled down, bringing her out of a reverie in which Kal touched her hand, then her face, her neck, his lips following a trail blazed by his fingers she let slip a word that Rose had probably never heard, let alone used.

It had taken an age to put her hair up like that and, unlike Rose, she didn't have a maid to help.

Just what she deserved for letting her fantasy run away with her. There was no way she was going to do anything that would embarrass Rose. Her part was written and she'd stick to it.

She began to gather the pins, but then realised that just because Rose never appeared in photographs other than with her hair up, it didn't mean that when she shut the door on the world at the end of the day—or embarked on an eight-hour flight—she'd wouldn't wear it loose.

She was, after all, supposed to be on holiday. And who, after all, knew what she did, said, wore, when she was behind closed doors?

Not Kalil al-Zaki, that was for sure.

And that was the answer to the 'keeping up appearances' problem, she realised.

Instead of trying to remember that she was Lady Rose for the next seven days, she would just be herself. She'd already made a pretty good start with the kind of lippy responses that regulars on her checkout at the supermarket would recognise.

And being herself would help with the 'lust' problem, too.

For as long as she could remember, she'd been fending off the advances of first boys, then men who, when they looked at her, had seen only the 'virgin' princess and wanted to either worship or ravish her.

It had taken her a little while to work that one out but, once she had, she'd had no trouble keeping them at arm's length, apart from the near miss with the actor, but then he'd been paid to be convincing. And patient. It was a pity he'd only, in the end, had an audience of one because he'd put in an Oscar-winning performance.

Kal, despite the way he looked, was just another man flirting with Lady Rose. That was all she had to remember, she told herself as she shook out her hair, brushed it, before she freshened up and put on the clothes Rose had chosen for her.

So which would he be? Worshipper or ravisher?

Good question, she thought as she added a simple gold chain and stud earrings before checking her reflection in a full length mirror.

It wasn't quite her—she tended to favour jeans and funky tops. It wasn't quite Lady Rose either, but it was close enough for someone who'd never met either of them, she decided as she chose a book, faced the door and took a slow, calming breath before returning to the main cabin.

In her absence the seats had been turned around, the cabin reconfigured so that it now resembled a comfortable sitting room.

An empty sitting room.

CHAPTER THREE

HAVING screwed herself up to be 'relaxed', the empty cabin was something of a let-down, but a table had been laid with a lace cloth and, no sooner than she'd settled herself and opened her book, Atiya arrived to serve afternoon tea.

Finger sandwiches, warm scones, clotted cream, tiny cakes and tea served from a heavy silver pot.

'Is all this just for me?' she asked when she poured only one cup and Kal had still not reappeared.

She hadn't wanted his company, but now he'd disappeared she felt affronted on Lady Rose's behalf. He was supposed to be here, keeping her safe from harm.

'Captain Jacobs invited Mr al-Zaki to visit the crew on the flight deck,' Atiya said. 'Apparently they did their basic training together.'

'Training?' It took her a moment. 'He's a *pilot*?'

Okay. She hadn't for a minute believed that he was bothered by the take-off, but she hadn't seen *that* coming. A suitable career for a nephew of an Emir wasn't a subject that had ever crossed her mind, but working as a commercial airline pilot wouldn't have been on her list even if she had. Maybe it had been military training.

A stint in one of the military academies favoured by royals would fit.

'Shall I ask him to rejoin you?' Atiya asked.

'No,' she said quickly. She had wanted him to keep his distance and her fairy godmother was, apparently, still on the case. 'I won't spoil his fun.'

Besides, if he returned she'd have to share this scrumptious spread.

Too nervous to eat lunch, and with the terrifying take-off well behind her, she was suddenly ravenous and the temptation to scoff the lot was almost overwhelming. Instead, since overindulgence would involve sweating it all off later, she managed to restrain herself, act like the lady she was supposed to be and simply tasted a little of everything to show her appreciation, concentrating on each stunning mouthful so that it felt as if she was eating far more, before settling down with her book.

Kal paused at the door to the saloon.

Rose, her hair a pale gold shimmer that she'd let down to hang over her shoulder, feet tucked up beneath her, absorbed in a book, was so far removed from her iconic image that she looked like a completely different woman.

Softer. The girl next door rather than a princess, because that was what she'd be if she'd been born into his culture.

Was the effect diminished?

Not one bit. It just came at him from a different direction. Now she looked not only luscious but available.

Double trouble.

As he settled in the chair opposite her she raised her eyes from her book, regarding him from beneath long lashes.

'Did you enjoy your visit to the cockpit?'

An almost imperceptible edge to her voice belied the softer look.

'It was most informative. Thank you,' he responded, equally cool. A little chill was just the thing to douse the heat generated by that mouth. Maybe.

'Did your old friend offer you the controls?' she added, as if reading his mind, and suddenly it all became clear. It wasn't the fact that he'd left her side without permission that bothered her.

The stewardess must have told her that he was a pilot and she thought he'd been laughing at her fear of flying.

'I hoped you wouldn't notice that little bump back there,' he said, offering her the chance to laugh right back at him.

There was a flicker of something deep in her eyes and the suspicion of an appreciative dimple appeared just above the left hand corner of her mouth.

'That was you? I thought it was turbulence.'

'Did you?' She was lying outrageously—the flight had been rock steady since they'd reached cruising altitude—but he was enjoying her teasing too much to be offended. 'It's been a while since I've flown anything this big. I'm a little rusty.'

She was struggling not to laugh now. 'It's not something you do seriously, then?'

'No one in my family does anything seriously.' It was the standard response, the one that journalists expected, and if it didn't apply to him, who actually cared? But, seeing a frown buckle the smooth, wide space between her eyes, the question that was forming, he cut her short with, 'My father bought himself a plane,' he said. 'I wanted to be able to fly it so I took lessons.'

'Oh.' The frown remained. 'But you said "this big",' she said, with a gesture that indicated the aircraft around them.

'You start small,' he confirmed. 'It's addictive, though. You keep wanting more.'

'But you've managed to break the habit.'

'Not entirely. Maybe you'd like a tour of the flight deck?' he asked. She clearly had no idea who he was and that suited him. If she discovered that he was the CEO of a major corporation she'd want to know what he was doing playing bodyguard. 'It sometimes helps ease the fear if you understand exactly what's happening. How things work.'

She shook her head. 'Thanks, but I'll pass.' Then, perhaps thinking she'd been less than gracious, she said, 'I do understand that my fear is totally irrational. If I didn't, I'd never get on one of these things.' Her smile was self-deprecating. 'But while, for the convenience of air travel, I can steel myself to suffer thirty seconds or so of blind panic, I also know that taking a pilot's eye view, seeing for myself exactly how much nothing there is out there, will only make things worse.'

'It's really just the take-off that bothers you?' he asked.

'So far,' she warned. 'But any attempt to analyse my fear is likely to give me ideas. And, before you say it, I know that flying is safer than crossing the road. That I've more chance of being hurt going to work—' She caught herself, for a fraction of second floundered. 'So I've heard,' she added quickly, as if he might dispute that what she did involved effort.

While opening the new wing of a hospital, attending charity lunches, appearing at the occasional gala might seem like a fairy tale existence to the outsider, he'd seen the effort Lucy put into her own charity and knew the appearance of effortless grace was all illusion.

But there was something about the way she'd stopped herself from saying more that suggested… He didn't know what it suggested.

'You've done your research.'

'No need. People will insist on telling you these things,' she said pointedly.

Signalling that the exchange was, as far as she was concerned, at an end, she returned to her book.

'There's just one more thing…'

She lifted her head, waited.

'I'm sure that Lucy explained that once we arrive in Ramal Hamrah we'll be travelling on to Bab el Sama by helicopter but—'

'Helicopter?'

The word came out as little more than a squeak.

'—but if it's going to be a problem, I could organise alternative transport,' he finished.

Lydia had been doing a pretty good job of keeping her cool, all things considered. She'd kept her head down, her nose firmly in her book even when Kal had settled himself opposite her. Stretched out those long, long legs. Crossed his ankles.

He'd removed his jacket, loosened his tie, undone the top button of his shirt.

What was it about a man's throat that was so enticing? she wondered. Invited touch…

She swallowed.

This was so not like her. She could flirt with the best, but that was no more than a verbal game that she could control. It was easy when only the brain was engaged…

Concentrate!

Stick to the plan. Speak when spoken to, keep the answers brief, don't let slip giveaways like 'going to work', for heaven's sake!

She'd managed to cover it but, unless she kept a firm rein on her tongue, sooner or later she'd say something that couldn't be explained away.

Lady Rose was charming but reserved, she reminded herself. *Reserved.*

She made a mental note of the word, underlined it for emphasis.

It was too late to recall the 'helicopter' squeak, however, and she experienced a hollow feeling that had nothing to do with hunger as Kal, suddenly thoughtful, said, 'You've never flown in one?'

She had never been in a helicopter, but it was perfectly possible that Lady Rose hopped about all over the place in one in order to fulfil her many engagements. Quite possibly with her good friend Princess Lucy.

She hadn't thought to ask. Why would she?

After what seemed like an eternity, when she was sure Kal was going to ask her what she'd done with the real Lady Rose, he said, 'So?'

'So?' she repeated hoarsely.

'Which is it to be?'

'Oh.' He was simply waiting for her to choose between an air-conditioned ride in leather-upholstered comfort, or a flight in a noisy machine that didn't even have proper wings. Her well-honed instinct for self-preservation was demanding she go for the four-wheeled comfort option.

Her mouth, taking no notice, said, 'I can live with the helicopter.'

And was rewarded with another of those smiles that bracketed his mouth, fanned around his eyes, as if he knew just how much it had cost her.

'It's certainly simpler,' he said, 'but if I get scared you will hold my hand, won't you?'

Lydia, jolted out of her determined reserve by his charm, laughed out loud. Then, when he didn't join in, she had the weirdest feeling that their entire conversation had been leading up to that question and it was her breath that momentarily caught in her throat.

'I don't believe you're scared of anything,' she said.

'Everyone is scared of something, Rose,' he said enigmatically as he stood up. 'I'll leave you to enjoy your book. If you need me for anything I'll be in the office.'

Showers, bedrooms, now an office...

'Please, don't let me keep you from your work,' she said.

'Work?'

He said the word lightly, as if it was something he'd never thought of, but a shadow, so brief that she might have missed it had she not been so intent on reading his thoughts, crossed his face and she felt horribly guilty at her lack of gratitude. No matter how inconvenient, this man, purely as a favour, had given up his own time to ensure she had the perfect holiday.

Or was he recalling her earlier slip?

'For the next seven days you are my first concern,' he assured her. 'I'm simply going to check the weather report.'

Whew...

His first concern.

Wow...

But then he thought that she was the real thing. And when he turned those midnight-dark eyes on her she so wanted to be real. Not pretending. Just for a week, she thought, as she watched him stride away across the cabin on long, long legs.

No, no, no!

This was no time to lose it over a gorgeous face and a buff body and, determined to put him out of her mind, she turned back to her book. She had to read the same paragraph four times before it made sense, but she persevered, scarcely wavering in her concentration even when Kal returned to his chair, this time armed with a book of his own.

She turned a page, taking the opportunity to raise her lashes just enough to see that it was a heavyweight political treatise. Not at all what she'd expect from a man with playboy looks who'd told her that he did nothing 'seriously'.

But then looks, as she knew better than most, could be deceptive.

Atiya appeared after a while with the dinner menu and to offer them a drink. They both stayed with water. Wasted no time in choosing something simple to eat.

But for the continuous drone of the aircraft engines, the cabin was quiet. Once she lifted her head, stretched her neck. Maybe the movement caught his eye because he looked up too, lifting a brow in silent query. She shook her head, leaned back against the thickly padded seat and looked down at a carpet of clouds silvered by moonlight.

Kal, watching her, saw the exact moment when her eyes closed, her body slackened and he caught her book as it began to slide from her hand. It was the autobiography of a woman who'd founded her own business empire. She'd personally inscribed this copy to Rose.

He closed it, put it on the table. Asked Atiya for a light

blanket, which he laid over her. Then, book forgotten, he sat and watched her sleep, wondering what dreams brought that tiny crease to her forehead.

'Sir,' Atiya said softly, 'I'll be serving dinner in ten minutes. Shall I wake Lady Rose?'

'I'll do it in a moment,' he said. Then, when she'd gone, he leaned forward. 'Rose,' he said softly. 'Rose…'

Lydia opened her eyes, for a moment not sure where she was. Then she saw Kal and it all came rushing back. It hadn't been a dream, then. She really was aboard a flying palace, one that wouldn't turn into a pumpkin at midnight. She had an entire week before she had to return to the checkout.

'What time is it?' she asked, sitting up, disentangling herself from the blanket that Atiya must have put over her.

'Seven minutes to eight in London, or to midnight in Ramal Hamrah if you want to set your watch to local time.'

She glanced at her wrist, touched the expensive watch, decided she'd rather do the maths than risk tampering with it.

'Atiya is ready to serve dinner.'

'Oh.' Her mouth was dry, a sure sign that she'd been sleeping with it open, which meant he'd been sitting there watching her drool.

Memo to self, she thought, wincing as she put her feet to the floor, searched with her toes for her shoes. Next time, use the bed.

'I apologise if I snored.'

His only response was a smile. She muffled a groan. She'd snored, drooled…

'Late night?' he asked, not helping.

'Very,' she admitted.

She'd had a late shift at the supermarket and, although her mother was determinedly independent, she always felt guilty about leaving her, even for a short time.

'I was double-checking to make sure that I hadn't left any loose ends trailing before taking off for a week,' she replied.

Everything clean and polished.

Fridge and freezer stocked so that Jennie wouldn't have to shop.

Enough of her mother's prescription meds to keep her going.

The list of contact numbers double-checked to make sure it was up to date.

While Rose wouldn't have been faced with that scenario, she'd doubtless had plenty of other stuff to keep her up late before she disappeared for a week.

And, like her, she would have been too wound up with nerves to sleep properly.

'I'd better go and freshen up,' she said but, before she could move, Kal was there to offer his hand, ease her effortlessly to her feet so that they were chest to chest, toe to toe, kissing close for a fraction of a second; long enough for her to breathe in the scent of freshly laundered linen, warm skin, some subtle scent that reminded her of a long ago walk in autumn woods. The crushed dry leaves and bracken underfoot.

Close enough to see the faint darkening of his chin and yearn to reach up, rub her hand over his jaw, feel the roughness against her palm.

She'd barely registered the thought before he released her hand, stepped back to let her move and she wasted no time putting some distance between them.

She looked a mess. Tousled, dishevelled, a red mark on her cheek where she'd slept with her head against the leather upholstery. She was going to have to duck her entire head under the cold tap to get it working properly, but she didn't have time for that. Instead, she splashed her face, repaired her lipstick, brushed the tangles out of her hair and then clasped it at the nape of her neck with a clip she found in the case that Rose had packed for her.

Then she ran through the pre-gig checklist in an attempt to jolt her brain back into the groove.

Smoothed a crease in the linen trousers.

Straightened the fine gold chain so that it lay in an orderly fashion about her neck.

Rehearsed her prompt list of appropriate questions so that there would never be a lull in the conversation.

Putting the situation in its proper context.

It was something she'd done hundreds of times, after all.

It was just another job!

Kal rose as she entered the main saloon and the *just another job* mantra went straight out of the window. Not that he *did* anything. Offer her his hand. Smile, even.

That was the problem. He didn't have to *do* anything, she thought as he stood aside so that she could lead the way to where Atiya was waiting beside a table that had been laid with white damask, heavy silver, crystal, then held a chair for her.

Like a force of nature, he just *was*.

Offered wine, she shook her head. Even if she'd been tempted, she needed to keep a clear head.

She took a fork, picked up a delicate morsel of fish and said, 'Lucy tells me that you're her husband's cousin. Are you a diplomat, too?'

Conventional, impersonal conversation. That was the ticket, she thought as she tasted the fish. Correction, ate the fish. She wasn't tasting a thing.

'No.' He shrugged. 'My branch of the family has been personae non gratae at the Ramal Hamrahn court for three generations.'

No, no, no!

That wasn't how it worked. She was supposed to ask a polite question. He was supposed to respond in kind. Like when you said, 'How are you?' and the only proper response was any variation on, 'Fine, thanks.'

'Personae non gratae at the Embassy, too,' he continued, 'until I became involved in one of Lucy's charitable missions.'

Better. Charity was Rose's life and, firmly quashing a desire to know more about the black sheep thing, what his family had done three generations ago that was so terrible—definitely off the polite questions list—Lydia concentrated on that.

'You help Lucy?'

'She hasn't mentioned what I do?' he countered.

'Maybe she thought I'd try and poach you.' Now that was *good*. 'What do you do for her?'

'Not much. She needed to ship aid to an earthquake zone. I offered her the use of an aircraft—we took it from there.'

Very impressively 'not much', she thought. She'd definitely mention him to Rose. Maybe they would hit it off.

She squashed down the little curl of something green that tried to escape her chest.

'That would be the one your father owns?' she asked. Again, she'd imagined a small executive jet. Clearly, where this family was concerned, she needed to start thinking bigger.

'Flying is like driving, Rose. When you get your licence, you don't want to borrow your father's old crate. You want a shiny new one of your own.'

'You do?'

A lot bigger, she thought. He came from a two-plane family. Something else occurred to her.

He'd said no one in his family did anything seriously, but that couldn't possibly be true. Not in his case, anyway. Obtaining a basic pilot's licence was not much different from getting a driving licence—apart from the cost—but stepping up to this level took more than money. It took brains, dedication, a great deal of hard work.

And, yes, a heck of a lot of money.

'You are such a fraud,' she said but, far from annoying her, it eased her qualms about her own pretence.

'Fraud?'

Kal paused with a fork halfway to his lips. It hadn't taken Lucy ten minutes to rumble him, demand to know what he expected from Hanif in return for his help, but she knew the family history and he hadn't expected his offer to be greeted with open arms.

He'd known the only response was to be absolutely honest with her. That had earned him first her sympathy and then, over the years, both her and Hanif's friendship.

Rose had acted as if she had never heard of him but, unless Lucy had told her, how did she—

'Not serious?' she prompted. 'Exactly how long did it take you to qualify to fly something like this?'

Oh, right. She was still talking about the flying. 'I do fun seriously,' he said.

'Fun?'

'Give me a chance and I'll show you,' he said. Teasing was, after all, a two-way street; the only difference between them was that she blushed. Then, realising how that might have sounded, he very nearly blushed himself. 'I didn't mean… Lucy suggested you might like to go fishing.'

'Fishing?' She pretended to consider. 'Let me see. Wet. Smelly. Maggots. That's your idea of fun?'

That was a challenge if ever he'd heard one. And one he was happy to accept. 'Wet, smelly and then you get to dry out, get warm while you barbecue the catch on the beach.'

'Wet, smelly, smoky and then we get sand in our food. Perfect,' she said, but a tiny twitch at the corner of her mouth suggested that she was hooked and, content, he let it lie.

Rose speared another forkful of fish.

'In her letter,' she said, 'Lucy suggested I'd enjoy a trip to the souk. Silk. Spices. Gold.'

'Heat, crowds, people with cellphones taking your photograph? I thought you wanted peace and privacy.'

'Even the paparazzi have children to feed and educate,' she said. 'And publicity oils the wheels of charity. The secret is not to give them something so sensational that they don't have to keep coming back for more.'

'That makes for a very dull life,' he replied gravely, playing along, despite the fact that it appeared to fly directly in the face of what Lucy had told him. 'But if you wore an *abbayah,* kept your eyes down, your hair covered, you might pass unnoticed.'

'A disguise?'

'More a cover-up. There's no reason to make it easy for them, although there's no hiding your height.'

'Don't worry about it.'

'It's what I'm here for.'

'Really?' And she was the one challenging him, as if she knew he had an agenda of his own. But she didn't wait for an answer. 'So what did you buy?' she asked.

He must have looked confused because she added, 'Car, not plane. I wouldn't know one plane from another. When you passed your test?' she prompted. 'A Ferrari? Porsche?'

'Far too obvious. I chose a Morgan.'

Her turn to look puzzled.

'It's a small sports car. A roadster,' he explained, surprised she didn't know that. 'The kind of thing that you see pilots driving in old World War Two movies? My father put my name on the waiting list on my twelfth birthday.'

'There's a waiting list?'

'A long one. They're hand-built,' he replied, smiling at her astonishment. 'I took delivery on my seventeenth birthday.'

'I'll add patient to serious,' she replied. 'What do you drive now?'

'I still have the Morgan.'

'The same one?'

'I'd have to wait a while for another one, so I've taken very good care of it.'

'I'm impressed.'

'Don't be. It stays in London while I'm constantly on the move, but for the record I drive a Renault in France, a Lancia in Italy and in New York…' he grinned '…I take a cab.'

'And in Ramal Hamrah?' she asked.

Suddenly the smile took real effort.

'There's an old Land Rover that does the job. What about you?' he asked, determined to shift the focus of their conversation to her. 'What do you drive for pleasure?'

She leaned forward, her lips parted on what he was sure would have been a protest that she wasn't finished with the question of Ramal Hamrah. Maybe something in his expression warned her that she was treading on dangerous ground and, after a moment, she sat back. Thought about it.

He assumed that was because her grandfather's garage offered so wide a choice. But then she said, 'It's...' she used her hands to describe a shape '...red.'

'Red?' Why was he surprised? 'Good choice.'

'I'm glad you approve.'

The exchange was, on the surface, perfectly serious and yet the air was suddenly bubbling with laughter.

'Do you really have homes in all those places?' she asked.

'Just a mews cottage in London. My mother, my father's first wife, was a French actress. She has a house in Nice and an apartment in Paris. His second wife, an English aristocrat, lives in Belgravia and Gloucestershire. His third was an American heiress. She has an apartment in the Dakota Building in New York and a house in the Hamptons.'

'An expensive hobby, getting married.' Then, when he made no comment, 'You stay with them? Even your ex-stepmothers?'

'Naturally. They're a big part of my life and I like to spend time with my brothers and sisters.'

'Oh, yes. I didn't think...' She seemed slightly flustered by his father's admittedly louche lifestyle. 'So where does Italy come in? The Lancia?' she prompted.

'My father bought a palazzo in Portofino when he was wooing a contessa. It didn't last—she quickly realised that he wasn't a man for the long haul—but he decided to keep the house. As he said, when a man has as many ex-wives and mistresses and children as he has, he needs a bolt-hole. Not true, of course. It's far too tempting a location. He's never alone.'

He expected her to laugh. Most people took what he said at face value, seeing only the glamour.

'From his history, I'd say he's never wanted to be,' Rose

said, her smile touched with compassion. 'It must have been difficult. Growing up.'

'Life was never dull,' he admitted with rather more flippancy than he felt. Without a country, a purpose, his grandfather had become rudderless, a glamorous playboy to whom women flocked, a lifestyle that his father had embraced without question. His family were his world but after one relationship that had kept the gossip magazines on their toes for eighteen months as they'd followed every date, every break up, every make up, he'd realised that he had no wish to live like that for the rest of his life.

'You didn't mention Ramal Hamrah,' she said, ignoring the opportunity he'd given her to talk about her own grandfather. Her own life.

Rare in a woman.

Rare in anyone.

Most people would rather talk about themselves.

'Do you have a home there?'

'There is a place that was once home,' he told her because the apartment overlooking the old harbour, bought off plan from a developer who had never heard of Kalil al-Zaki, could never be described as the home of his heart, his soul. 'A faded photograph that hangs upon my grandfather's wall. A place of stories of the raids, battles, celebrations that are the history of my family.'

Stories that had grown with the telling until they had become the stuff of legend.

It was an image that the old man looked at with longing. Where he wanted to breathe his last. Where he wanted to lie for eternity, at one with the land he'd fought for.

And Kalil would do anything to make that possible. Not that sitting here, sharing a meal with Lady Rose Napier was as tedious as he'd imagined it would be.

'No one has lived there for a long time,' he said.

For a moment he thought she was going to ask him to tell her more, but all she said was, 'I'm sorry.'

She was quiet for a moment, as if she understood the emptiness, the sense of loss and he began to see why people, even those who had never met her, instinctively loved her.

She had an innate sensitivity. A face that invited confidences. Another second and he would have told her everything but, at exactly the right moment, she said, 'Tell me about your brothers and sisters.'

'How long have you got?' he asked, not sure whether he was relieved or disappointed. 'I have one sister, a year younger than me. I have five half-sisters, three half-brothers and six, no seven, steps of both sexes and half a dozen who aren't actually related by blood but are still family.'

She counted them on her long, slender fingers.

'Sixteen?' she asked, looking at him in amazement. 'You've got sixteen brothers and sisters? Plus six.'

'At the last count. Sarah, she's the English ex, and her husband are about to have another baby.'

Lydia sat back in her chair, stunned. As an only child she had dreamed of brothers and sisters, but this was beyond imagining.

'Can you remember all their names?' she asked.

'Of course. They are my family.' Then, seeing her doubt, he held up his hand and began to list them. 'My sister is Adele. She's married to a doctor, Michel, and they have two children, Albert and Nicole. My mother has two other daughters by her second husband…'

As they ate, Kal talked about his family in France, in England and America. Their partners and children. The three youngest girls whose mothers his father had never actually got around to marrying but were all part of a huge extended family. All undoubtedly adored.

His family, but nothing about himself, she realised. Nothing about his personal life and she didn't press him. How a man talked about his family said a lot about him. She didn't need anyone to tell her that he was a loyal and caring son. That he loved his family. It was there in his smile as he told stories about

his mother in full drama queen mode, about his sister. His
pride in all their achievements.

If he'd had a wife or partner, children of his own, he would
certainly have talked about them, too. With love and pride.

'You're so lucky having a big family,' she told him as they
laughed at a story about one of the boys causing mayhem at a
party.

'That's not the half of it,' he assured her. 'My grandfather
set the standard. Five wives, ten children. Do you want their
names, too? Or shall I save that for a rainy day?'

'Please tell me that it doesn't rain in Ramal Hamrah.'

'Not often,' he admitted.

Neither of them said anything while Atiya cleared the table,
placed a tray of sweet things, tiny cakes, nuts, fruit, before them.

'Can I bring you coffee or tea?' Atiya asked.

'Try some traditional mint tea,' Kal suggested before she
could reply. He spoke to Atiya in Arabic and, after a swift
exchange, which apparently elicited the right answer, he said,
'Not made with a bag, it will be the real thing.'

'It sounds delicious.'

'It is.'

He indicated the tray, but she shook her head.

'It all looks wonderful but I can't eat another thing,' Lydia
said. 'I hope there's a pool in Bab el Sama. If I keep eating like
this I won't fit into any of my clothes when I get home.'

'I don't understand why women obsess about being thin,'
he said.

'No? Have you never noticed the way celebrities who put
on a few pounds are ridiculed? That would be women celebrities,' she added.

'I know. Adele went through a bad patch when she was a
teenager.' He shook his head. Took a date, but made no attempt
to push her to eat. Instead, he bestowed a lazy smile on her and
said, 'Now you know my entire family. Your turn to tell me
about yours.'

Lydia waited while Atiya served the mint tea.

Completely absorbed by his complex relationships, the little vignettes of each of his brothers and sisters that had made them all seem so real, she had totally forgotten the pretence and needed a moment to gather herself.

'Everyone knows my story, Kal.'

Kal wondered. While he'd been telling her about his family, she'd been by turns interested, astonished, amused. But the moment he'd mentioned hers, it was as if the lights had dimmed.

'I know what the press write about you,' he said. 'What Lucy has told me.'

That both her parents had been killed when she was six years old and she'd been raised by an obsessively controlling grand-father, the one who'd taken a newspaper headline literally and turned her into the 'people's angel'.

'What you see is what you get,' she replied, picking up the glass of tea.

Was it?

It was true that with her pale hair, porcelain skin and dazzling blue eyes she could have stepped out of a Renaissance painting.

But then there was that mouth. The full sultry lips that clung for a moment to the small glass as she tasted the tea.

A tiny piece of the crushed leaf clung to her lower lip and, as she gathered it in with the tip of her tongue, savouring the taste, he discovered that he couldn't breathe.

'It's sweet,' she said.

'Is that a problem?'

She shook her head. 'I don't usually put sugar in mint tea, but it's good.' She finished the tea, then caught at a yawn that, had she been anyone else, he would have sworn was fake. That she was simply making an excuse to get away. 'If you'll excuse me, Kal, it's been a long day and I'd like to try and get a couple of hours' sleep before we land.'

'Of course,' he said, easing her chair back so that she could stand up and walking with her to the door of her suite, unable to quite shake the feeling that she was bolting from the risk that he might expect the exposure of her own family in return for his unaccustomed openness.

Much as he adored them, he rarely talked about his family to outsiders. He'd learned very early how even the most innocent remark to a friend would be passed on to their parents and, in a very short time, would appear in print, twisted out of recognition by people who made a living out of celebrity gossip.

Rose, though, had that rare gift for asking the right question, then listening to the answer in a way that made a man feel that it was the most important thing she'd ever heard.

But then, at the door, she confounded him, turning to face him and, for a moment, locked in that small, still bubble that enclosed two people who'd spent an evening together, all the more intimate because of their isolation as they flew high above the earth in their own small time capsule, neither of them moved and he knew that if she'd been any other woman, if he'd been any other man, he would have kissed her. That she would have kissed him back. Maybe done a lot more than kiss.

She was a warm, quick-witted, complex woman and there had, undoubtedly, been a connection between them, a spark that in another world might have been fanned into a flame.

But she was Lady Roseanne Napier, the 'people's angel'. And he had made a promise to his grandfather that nothing, no one, would divert him from keeping.

'Thank you for your company, Rose,' he said, taking her hand and lifting it to his lips, but his throat was unexpectedly constricted as he took a step back. He added, 'Sleep well.'

It was going to be a very long week.

CHAPTER FOUR

TIRED as she was, Lydia didn't sleep. Eyes closed, eyes open, it made no difference.

The hand Kal had kissed lay on the cover at her side and she had to press it down hard to keep it from flying to her mouth so that she could taste it.

Taste him.

His mouth had barely made contact and yet the back of her fingers throbbed as if burned, her body as fired up as if she'd had a faint electric shock.

In desperation she flung herself off the bed, tore off her clothes and threw herself beneath the shower, soaping herself with a gel that smelled faintly of lemons. Warm at first, then cooler until she was shivering. But still her skin burned and when Lydia lifted her hand to her face, breathed in, it was not the scent of lemons that filled her head.

It was nothing as simple as scent, but a distillation of every look, every word, the food they'd eaten, the mint tea they'd drunk. It had stirred the air as he'd bent over her hand, leaving her faint with the intensity of pure sensation that had rippled through her body. Familiar and yet utterly unknown. Fire and ice. Remembered pleasure and the certainty of pain.

Distraction.

She needed a distraction, she thought desperately as she wrapped herself in a fluffy gown, combed out her damp hair, applied a little of some unbelievably expensive moisturiser in an attempt to counteract the drying effects of pressured air.

She could usually lose herself in a book—she'd managed it earlier, even dozed off—but she'd left her book in the main cabin and nothing on earth would tempt her back out there until she had restored some semblance of calm order to her racketing hormones.

She chose another book from the selection Rose had packed for her and settled back against the pillows. All she had to do now was concentrate. It shouldn't be hard, the book was by a favourite author, but the words refused to stay still.

Instead they kept merging into the shape of Kal's mouth, the sensuous curve of his lower lip.

'Get a grip, Lydie!' she moaned, abandoning the book and sliding down to the floor where she sat cross-legged, hoping that yoga breathing would instil a modicum of calm, bring her down from what had to be some kind of high induced by an excess of pheromones leaking into the closed atmosphere of the aircraft.

Combined with the adrenalin charge of confronting the newsmen, tension at the prospect of facing airport security with Rose's passport, then the shock of Kalil al-Zaki arriving to mess up all their carefully laid plans, it was scarcely any wonder that the words wouldn't stay still.

That he was astoundingly attractive, took his duty of care to extraordinary lengths, had flirted outrageously with her hadn't helped.

When they'd sat down to their dinner party in the sky, she'd been determined to keep conversation on the impersonal level she employed at cocktail parties, launches.

Kal had blown that one right out of the water with his reply to her first question and she'd forgotten all about the 'plan' as he'd in turn amused, shocked, delighted her with tales of his family life.

And made her envious at the obvious warmth and affection they shared. His might be a somewhat chaotic and infinitely extendable family but, as an only child with scarcely any close relations, she'd been drawn in by the charm of having so many people who were connected to you. To care for and who cared back. Who would not want to be part of that?

And that was only half the story, she realised. Sheikh Hanif was his cousin and there must be a vast Ramal Hamrahn family that he hadn't even mentioned, other than to tell her that he and his family were personae non gratae at the Ramal Hamrahn court.

More, she suspected, than he told most people. But then Rose had that effect on people. Drew them out.

Instead, he had turned the spotlight on her, which was when she'd decided to play safe and retire.

There was a tap on the door. 'Madam? We'll be landing in fifteen minutes.'

'Thank you, Atiya.'

She reapplied a light coating of make-up. Rose might want her picture in the paper, but not looking as if she'd just rolled out of bed. Brushed out her hair. Dressed. Putting herself back together so that she was fit to be seen in public.

The seat belt sign pinged as she returned to the cabin and she shook her head as Kal half rose, waved him back to his seat and sat down, fastening her seat belt without incident before placing her hands out of reach in her lap. Not looking at him, but instead peering out at the skein of lights skirting the coast, shimmering in the water below them.

'Landing holds no terrors for you?' Kal asked and she turned to glance at him. A mistake. Groomed to perfection he was unforgettable, but after eight hours in the air, minus his tie, in need of a shave, he was everything a woman would hope to wake up to. Sexily rumpled, with eyes that weren't so much come to bed, as let's stay here for the rest of the day.

As if she'd know...

Quickly turning back to the window as they sank lower and the capital, Rumaillah, resolved from a mass of lights into individual streets, buildings, her attention was caught by a vast complex dominated by floodlit domes, protected by high walls, spread across the highest point of the city.

'What is that?' she asked.

Kal put a hand on the arm of her chair and leaned across so that he could see out of her window, but he must have dialled down the pheromone count, or maybe, like her, he was tired because, even this close, there was no whoosh of heat.

'It's the Emiri Palace,' he told her.

'But it's huge.'

'It's not like Buckingham Palace,' he said, 'with everything under one roof. The Emir's palace is not just one building. There are gardens, palaces for his wives, his children and their families. The Emiri offices are there too, and his Majlis where his people can go and see him, talk to him, ask for his help, or to intercede in disputes.'

'I like the sound of that. The man at the top being approachable.'

'I doubt it's quite as basic as it was in the old days,' he replied. There was an edge to his voice that made her forget about the exotic hilltop palace and look more closely at him. 'We've come a long way from a tent in the desert.'

We.

He might be excluded but he still thought of himself as one of them. She resisted the urge to ask him. If he wanted her to know he would tell her.

But, fascinated, she pressed, 'In theory, anyone can approach him?'

'In theory.'

There was something in his voice, a tension, anger, that stopped her from saying more.

'And you said "wives". How many has he got?'

'The Emir? Just one. The tradition of taking more than one wife began when a man would take the widows, children of brothers slain in battle into his family. Then it became a sign of wealth. It's rare these days.' Then, with a curl of his lip that could have been mistaken for a smile if you hadn't seen the real thing, 'My family are not typical.'

'And even they take only one at a time,' she replied, lifting her voice a little so that it was gently teasing.

'Legally,' he agreed. 'In practice there tends to be some overlap.'

'And you, Kal?'

'How many wives do I have?' And this time the smile was a little less forced. 'None, but then I'm a late starter.'

That she doubted, but suddenly the runway lights were whizzing past and then they were down with barely a bump.

Before she left the aircraft she visited the cockpit—now that it was safely on the ground—to thank the crew for a wonderful flight and, by the time she stepped outside into the warm moist air of the Gulf, her luggage had already been transferred to the waiting helicopter.

'Ready?' Kal asked.

She swallowed, nodded.

She'd been bold enough when the reality of committing her safety to what seemed to be a very small, fragile thing beside the bulk of the jet had been a distant eight hours away.

Now she was afraid that if she opened her mouth her teeth would start chattering like a pair of castanets.

Apparently she wasn't fooling Kal because he said, 'That ready? It's not too late to change your mind.'

She refused to be so pathetic and, shaking her head once in a *let's get this over with* gesture, she took a determined step forward. His hand at her back helped keep her moving when she faltered. Got her through the door and into her seat.

He said something to the pilot as he followed her—what, she couldn't hear above the noise of the engine.

He didn't bother to ask if she needed help with the straps, but took them from her and deftly fastened them as if it was something he'd been doing all his life. Maybe he had.

Then he gently lowered the earphones that would keep out

the noise and allow the pilot to talk to them onto her head, settling them into place against her ears.

'Okay?' he said, not that she could hear, but she'd been sent on a lip-reading and signing course by the supermarket and had no problem understanding him.

She nodded and he swiftly dealt with his own straps and headset before turning in his seat so that he was facing her.

'Hands,' he said, and when she lifted them to look at them, not knowing what she was supposed to do with them, he took them in his and held them as the rotor speed built up.

She tried to smile but this was far worse than in a passenger aircraft. Everything—the tarmac, the controls, the reality of what was happening—was so close, so immediate, so in your face.

There was no possibility of pretence here.

No way you could tell yourself that you were on the number seven bus going to work and, as the helicopter lifted from the ground, leaving her stomach behind, she tightened her grip of his hands but, before the scream bubbling up in her throat could escape, Kal leaned forward and said, 'Trust me, Rose.'

And then he kissed her.

It wasn't a gentle kiss. It was powerful, strong, demanding her total attention and the soaring lift as they rose into the air, leaving the earth far behind them, was echoed by a rush of pure exhilaration that flooded through her.

This was flying. This was living. And, without a thought for what would follow, she kissed him back.

Kal had seen Rose's momentary loss of courage as she'd looked across the tarmac from the top of the aircraft steps to the waiting helicopter, followed by the lift of her chin, an unexpectedly stubborn look that no photographer had ever managed to capture, as she'd refused to back down, switch to the car.

It didn't quite go with the picture Lucy had painted of the gentle, biddable girl—woman—who'd lovingly bowed to the dictates of her grandfather. Who was desperate for some quiet time while she fathomed out her future.

That was a chin that took no prisoners and, certain that once she was airborne she'd be fine, he hadn't argued. Even so, her steps had faltered as they'd neared the helicopter and as they'd boarded he'd told the pilot to get a move on before she had time for second thoughts.

This was not a moment for the usual round of 'Lady Rose' politeness, handshakes, introductions. All that could wait until they arrived at Bab el Sama.

And he'd done his best to keep her distracted, busy, her eyes on him rather than the tarmac.

But as the engine note changed in the moment prior to take-off, her hands had gripped his so hard that her nails had dug into his palms and he thought that he'd completely misjudged the situation, that she was going to lose it.

Hysterics required more than a reassuring hand or smile, they needed direct action and there were just two options—a slap or a kiss.

No contest.

Apart from the fact that the idea of hitting anyone, let alone a frightened woman, was totally abhorrent to him, letting go of her hands wasn't an option.

His 'Trust me' had been a waste of breath—she couldn't hear him—but it had made him feel better as he went in for the kiss, hard and fast. This wasn't seduction, this was survival and he wanted her total attention, every emotion, fixed on him, even if that emotion was outrage.

He didn't get outrage.

For a moment there was nothing. Only a stunned stillness. Then something like an imperceptible sigh breathed against his mouth as her eyes closed, the tension left her body and her lips softened, yielded and clung to his for a moment, warm and sweet as a girl's first kiss. Then parted, hot as a fallen angel tempting him to sin.

At which point the only one in danger of losing anything was him.

How long was a kiss? A heartbeat, minutes, a lifetime?

It seemed like all three as his hands, no longer captive, moved to her waist, her back, drawing her closer. A heartbeat while he breathed in the clean, fresh scent of her skin; minutes as the kiss deepened and something darker, more compelling stirred his senses; a lifetime while his hormones stampeded to fling themselves into the unknown without as much as a thought for the consequences.

Exactly like his grandfather. Exactly like his father.

Men without a purpose, without a compass, who'd put their own selfish desires above everything.

That thought, like a pitcher of cold water, was enough to jar him back to reality, remind him why he was here, and he drew back.

Rose took a gasping, thready little breath as he broke the connection. Sat unmoving for long moments before her lids slowly rose, almost as if the long, silky lashes were too heavy to lift.

Her lips parted as if she was going to speak but she closed them again without saying a word, instead concentrating on her breathing, slowing it down using some technique that she'd probably learned long ago to manage nerves.

When she raised her lashes again, she was sufficiently in control to speak.

He couldn't hear what she was saying, but she mouthed the words so carefully that he could lip-read enough to get the gist, which was, as near as damn it, 'If you were that scared, Kal, you should have told me. We could have taken the car.'

It was the response of a woman who, with ten years of interaction with the public behind her, knew exactly how to rescue an awkward moment, who could put anyone at ease with a word.

It put a kiss that had spiralled out of hand into perspective, allowing them both to move on, forget it.

Well, what had he expected?

That she'd fall apart simply because he'd kissed her?

She might—or might not—be a virgin princess, but she'd already proved, with her dry and ready wit, that she was no shrinking violet.

He knew he should be grateful that his rescue mission had been recognised for what it was. Received with her legendary good humour, charm.

But he wasn't grateful. Didn't want to forget.

He wanted to pull her close, kiss her again until that classy English cool sizzled away to nothing, her 'charm' shattered in a pyrotechnic blaze that would light up the night sky and this tender Rose, nurtured under glass, broke out and ran wild.

It wasn't going to happen.

Even if had been an appropriate time or place, their destinies were written. Even if she rejected the Earl in waiting her grandfather had lined up to walk her down the aisle and chose someone for herself, it was never going to be the scion of a disgraced and dispossessed exile.

And when he took a bride, it would not be in response to carnal attraction, the sexual chemistry that masqueraded as love, stealing your senses, stealing your life. His marriage would be an affair of state that would cement an alliance with one of the great Ramal Hamrahn families—the Kassimi, the Attiyah or the Darwish. The surrender of one of their precious daughters an affirmation that he had restored his family to their rightful place.

Had brought his grandfather home.

But time was running out. He had been infinitely patient and he no longer had years. His grandfather was already on borrowed time, stubbornly refusing to accept the death sentence that had been passed on him until he saw his grandson married as a Khatib should be married. Could die in peace in the place where he'd been born.

An affair that would cause scandalised headlines worldwide would do nothing to help his cause. He had to keep himself focused on what was important, he reminded himself, even while he held Rose, could feel her corn silk hair tumbling over his hands, her soft breath upon his cheek.

Fight, as he'd always fought, the demanding, selfish little gene he'd inherited, the one telling him to go for it and hang the consequences. The knowledge that she wanted it as much as he did. The pretence that it would just be a holiday romance, wouldn't hurt anyone.

That wasn't true. You could not give that much and walk away without losing something of yourself, taking something of the other with you. Already, in the closeness of the hours they had spent together, he had given more than he should. Had taken more. He concentrated on the clean, vast infinity of the night sky—diamonds against black velvet—until it filled his head, obliterating everything else.

Lydia wanted to curl up and die with embarrassment. Not because Kal had kissed her. That had been no more than straightforward shock tactics, designed to prevent her from doing something stupid.

And it had worked.

She hadn't screamed, hadn't tried to grab the pilot and make him stop.

Why would she when the minute his lower lip had touched hers, she'd forgotten all about the fact that they were rising from the ground in a tiny glass bubble?

Forgotten her fear.

Forgotten everything as the warmth of his mouth had first heated her lips, then curled through every part of her body, touching the frozen core that had remained walled up, out of reach for so long. As it felt the warmth, whimpered to be set free, he'd drawn her close and the kiss had ceased to be shock tactics and had become real, intense.

A lover's kiss, and as her arms had wrapped themselves around his neck she hadn't cared who he thought she was. He was kissing her as if he wanted her and that was all that mattered, because she wanted him right back.

She hadn't cared that he thought it was Rose who'd reacted so wantonly. Who'd wanted more. Who would still be kissing him as if the world was about to end if he hadn't backed off.

He was still holding her, still close enough that she could feel him breathing. Close enough that when she was finally brave enough to open her eyes she could see the *what-the-hell-happened-there?* look in his eyes. She wanted to explain that it was okay. That she wasn't Rose, just some dumb idiot girl who was having a very strange day.

That he could forget all about it. Forget about her.

But that was impossible.

She had to put things right, restore Rose's reputation. Instead, she closed her eyes again and concentrated on her breathing. Slowing it down. And, as her mind cleared, she realised that the answer was simple. Fear.

She could put it all down to her fear. Or his, she thought, remembering how he'd pretended to be the one who was scared as they'd lifted off.

If she could make him laugh it would be all right. They would be able to move on, pretend it had never happened.

But he hadn't laughed; there was no reaction at all and she realised that just because she could lip-read didn't mean that he could, too. He hadn't a clue what she was saying.

She took her hands from his shoulders, tried to concentrate on what he was saying as he looked up, beyond her. Shook her head to indicate that it hadn't got through.

He turned, looked straight at her as he repeated himself. 'And miss this?'

What?

She didn't want to take her eyes from him. While she was looking at him, while he was still holding her, she could forget that there was nothing but a thin wall of perspex between her and the sky.

But he lifted one of his dark brows a fraction of a millimetre, challenging her to be brave, and she finally tore her gaze from him, turned her head.

In the bubble of the helicopter they had an all round view of the sky which, away from the light pollution of the airport, the city, she could see as it was meant to be seen, with the constellations diamond-bright, the spangled shawl of the Milky Way spread across the heavens.

It was an awe-inspiring, terrifying sight. A reminder of how small they were. How vulnerable. And yet how spectacularly amazing and she didn't look away. But, although she wanted to reach back, share the moment with Kal, she remembered who she was supposed to be.

Not the woman on the checkout who anyone could—and did—flirt with. Not Lydia Young, who had a real problem with leaving the ground, but Lady Rose Napier, who could handle an unexpected kiss with the same natural charm as any other minor wobble in her day.

Instead, she concentrated on this unexpected gift he'd given her, searching for constellations that she recognised until she had to blink rather hard because her eyes were watering. At the beauty of the sky. That was all…

Kal must have said something. She didn't hear him, just felt his breath against her cheek, then, as he pointed down, she saw a scatter of lights below, the navigation lights of boats riding at anchor as they crossed a wide creek.

As they dropped lower, circling to land on the far bank, Lydia caught tantalising glimpses of the domes, arches of half a dozen or more exotic, beautiful beach houses. There was a private dock, boats, a long curve of white sand. And, behind it all, the dramatic, sharply rising background of jagged mountains, black against a sky fading to pre-dawn purple.

While she had not been fooled by the word 'cottage', had anticipated the kind of luxury that few people would ever experience, this was far beyond anything she could have imagined.

It reminded her of pictures she'd seen of the fantasy village of Portmeirion, more like a film set, or something out of a dream than anything real, and by the time the helicopter landed and she'd thanked the pilot, her heart was pounding with excitement, anticipation.

She'd been so determined to keep her reaction low-key, wanting to appear as if this was what she was used to, but that wasn't, in the end, a problem. As Kal took her hand and helped her down, she didn't have to fight to contain a *wow*. The reality was simply beyond words.

There was an open Jeep waiting for them, but she didn't rush to climb in. Instead, she walked to the edge of the landing pad so that she could look out over the creek. Eager to feel solid earth beneath her feet. To breathe in real air laden with the salty scent of the sea, wet sand, something else, sweet and heavy, that she did not recognise.

It was still quite dark, but all the way down to the beach lights threaded through huge old trees, shone in the water.

'I don't think I've ever seen anything so beautiful,' she said as Kal joined her. 'I expected sand, desert, not all this green.'

'The creek is in a valley and has a microclimate of its own,' he said. 'And Sheikh Jamal's father began an intensive tree planting programme when he took the throne fifty years ago.'

'Well, good for him.'

'Not everyone is happy. People complain that it rains more these days.'

'It rains more everywhere,' she replied, looking around for the source of the sweet, heady fragrance filling the air. 'What is that scent?' she asked.

'Jasmine.' He crossed to a shrub, broke off a piece and offered it to her with the slightest of bows. 'Welcome to Bab el Sama, Lady Rose,' he said.

CHAPTER FIVE

LYDIA, holding the spray of tiny white flowers, didn't miss the fact that he'd put the 'Lady' back in front of her name. That his voice had taken on a more formal tone.

That was good, she told herself. Perfect, in fact.

One kiss could be overlooked, especially when it was purely medicinal, but it wouldn't do to let him think that Lady Rose encouraged such liberties.

'The luggage is loaded.'

He might as well have been done with it and added *madam*.

'The pilot won't take off until we're clear of the pad. If you are ready?'

It was right there in his tone of voice. It was the one he'd used before he'd started flirting. Before she'd started encouraging him.

She turned to look at the Jeep, where a white-robed servant was waiting to drive them to the cottage. She'd been sitting for hours and, now she was on her feet, wasn't eager to sit again unless she had to.

'Is it far?' she asked. 'I'd like to stretch my legs.'

He spoke to the driver, who answered with a shake of his head, a wave of the hand to indicate a path through the trees.

Lydia watched the exchange, then frowned.

Kal wasn't telling the man that they'd walk, she realised, but asking the way. He'd seemed so familiar with everything that

he'd assumed he had been here before, but clearly this was his
first time, too.

She hadn't taken much notice when he'd said his family
were personae non gratae at the Ramal Hamrahn court.

Court, for heaven's sake. Nobody talked like that any more.
But now she wondered why, for three generations, his family
had lived in Europe.

What past crime was so terrible that he and his siblings had
never been invited to share this idyllic summer playground
with their cousins? It wasn't as if they'd be cramped for space.
Even if they all turned up at the same time.

'There's a path through the gardens,' he said. Then, 'Will
you be warm enough?'

'You're kidding?'

Rose had warned her that it wouldn't be hot at this time of
year and maybe it wasn't for this part of the world. Compared
with London in December, however, the air felt soft and balmy.

Then, as a frown creased Kal's brows, she realised that her
response had been pure Lydia. Not quite on a scale with Eliza
Doolittle's blooper at the races, but near enough.

She was tired and forgetting to keep up the Lady Rose act.
Or maybe it was her subconscious fighting it. Wanting to say
to him *Look at me, see who I really am...*

'The temperature is quite perfect,' she added. And mentally
groaned. She'd be doing the whole, *How kind of you to let me
come* routine if she didn't get a grip.

Didn't put some distance between them.

In a determined attempt to start as she had meant to go on—
before he'd taken her hand, made her laugh—she said, 'You
don't have to come with me, Kal. Just point me in the right direction and I can find my own way.'

'No doubt. However, I'd rather not have to explain to Lucy
why I had to send out a search party for you.'

'Why would she ever know?'

'You're kidding?'

She ignored the wobble somewhere beneath her midrif as he repeated her words back to her as if he was mocking her, almost as if he knew. 'Actually, I'm not,' she said knowing that it was only her guilty conscience making her think that way.

'No? Then let me explain how it would happen. At the first hint of trouble the alarm would be raised,' he explained. 'The Chief of Security would be alerted. The Emir's office would be informed, your Ambassador would be summoned—'

'Okay, okay,' she said, holding up her hands in surrender, laughing despite everything. 'I get it. If I go missing, you'll be hauled up before the Emir and asked to explain what the heck you were doing letting me wander around by myself.'

There was a momentary pause, as if he was considering the matter. Then he shrugged. 'Something like that, but all you need to worry about is the fact that Lucy would know what had happened within five minutes.'

Not something she would want to happen and, while she didn't think for one moment she'd get lost, she said, 'Point taken. Lead the way, Mr al-Zaki.'

The steps were illuminated by concealed lighting and perfectly safe, as was the path, but he took her arm, presumably in case she stumbled.

Rose wouldn't make a fuss, she told herself. No doubt someone had been holding her hand, taking her arm, keeping her safe all her life. It was what she'd wanted to escape. The constant surveillance. The cotton wool.

As he tucked her arm beneath his, she told herself that she could live with it for a week. And, as she leaned on him a little, that he would expect nothing else.

The path wound through trees and shrubs. Herbs had been planted along the edges, spilling over so that as they brushed past lavender, sage, marjoram and other, less familiar, scents filled the air.

Neither of them spoke. The only sound was the trickle of

...ater running, the splash of something, a fish or a frog, in a ...ark pool. She caught glimpses of mysterious arches, an ornate ...ummer house, hidden among the trees. And above them the ...omes and towers she'd seen from the air.

'It's magical,' she said at last as, entranced, she stored up ...he scents, sounds, images for some day, far in the future, when ...he would tell her children, grandchildren about this *Arabian Nights* adventure. Always assuming she ever got to the point ...vhere she could trust a man sufficiently to get beyond arm's ...ength flirting.

Meet someone who would look at her and see Lydia Young ...nstead of her famous alter ego.

The thought leached the pleasure from the moment.

She'd been featured in the local newspaper when she'd first ...ppeared as Lady Rose, had even been invited to turn up as Rose and switch on the Christmas lights one year when the ...local council were on a cost cutting drive and couldn't afford a real celebrity.

Even at work, wearing an unflattering uniform and with her ...name badge clearly visible, the customers had taken to calling her 'Rose' and she couldn't deny that she'd loved it. It had made her feel special.

Here, now, standing in her heroine's shoes, she discovered that being someone else was not enough.

That, instead of looking at Lydia and seeing Rose, she wanted someone, or maybe just Kalil al-Zaki, to look at Rose and see Lydia.

Because that was who she'd been with him.

It was Lydia who'd been afraid of taking off, whose hand he had held. Lydia he'd kissed.

But he'd never know that. And she could never tell him.

He was silent too and once she risked a glance, but the floor level lighting only threw his features into dark, unreadable shadows.

Then, as they turned a corner, the view opened up to reveal

that while behind them, above the darker bulk of the mountains
the stars still blazed, on the far side of the creek a pale edge o
mauve was seeping into the pre-dawn purple.

'It's nearly dawn,' she said, surprised out of her momentar
descent into self-pity. It still felt like the middle of the night
but she'd flown east, was four hours closer to the day than he
mother, fast asleep in London.

She was on another continent at sunrise and, to witness it
all she had to do was stand here and wait.

Kal didn't even ask what she wanted to do. He knew.

'There's a summer house over there,' he said, urging her in
the direction of another intricately decorated domed and col-
onnaded structure perfectly situated to enjoy the view. 'You can
watch in comfort.'

'No…'

It was open at the front and there were huge cane chairs piled
with cushions. Total luxury. A place to bring a book, be alone,
forget everything. Maybe later. Not now.

'I don't want anything between me and the sky,' she said,
walking closer to the edge of the paved terrace where the drop
was guarded by a stone balustrade. 'I want to be outside where
I can feel it.'

He let her go, didn't follow her and she tried not to mind.

Minding was a waste of time. Worse. It was a stupid con-
tradiction. Distance was what she had wanted and the old lady
with the wand was, it seemed, still on the job, granting wishes
as if they were going out of fashion.

She should be pleased.

It wasn't as if she'd expected or needed to be diverted,
amused. She had a pile of great books to amuse her, occupy
her mind, and exploring the garden, wandering along the shore
should be diversion enough for anyone. If the forbidden
delights of Kal al-Zaki's diversionary tactics hadn't been such
a potent reminder of everything she was missing. The life that
she might have had if she hadn't looked like Lady Rose.

But then, as the mauve band at the edge of the sky widened, became suffused with pink, she heard a step behind her and, as she half turned, Kal settled something soft around her.

For a moment his hands lingered on her shoulders, tense and knotted from sitting for too long, and without thinking she leaned into his touch, seeking ease from his long fingers. For a moment she thought he was going to respond, but then he stepped back, putting clear air between them.

'You will get cold standing out here,' he said with a brusqueness that suggested he had, after all, been affected by their closeness. That he, too, was aware that it would be inappropriate to take it further.

'And you don't want to explain to Lucy how I caught a chill on your watch?' Light, cool, she told herself.

'That wouldn't bother me.' He joined her at the balustrade, but kept his eyes on the horizon. 'I'd simply explain that you stubbornly, wilfully insisted on standing outside in the chill of dawn, that short of carrying you inside there was nothing I could do about it. I have no doubt that she'd agree with me.'

'She would?' The idea of Rose being wilful or stubborn was so slanderous that she had to take a breath, remind herself that he was judging Rose on her behaviour, before she nodded and said, 'She would.' And vow to try a little harder—a lot harder—to be like the real thing.

'His Highness, the Emir, on the other hand,' Kal continued, 'would be certain to think that I'd personally arranged for you to go down with pneumonia in order to cause him maximum embarrassment.'

He spoke lightly enough, inviting amusement, but she didn't laugh, sensing the underlying darkness behind his words.

'Why on earth would he think that?' she asked, but more questions crowded into her head. Without waiting for him to answer, she added, 'And why do you always refer to him as His Highness or the Emir?' She made little quote marks with her fingers, something else she realised Rose would never do, and let her hands drop. 'Sheikh Jamal is your uncle, isn't he, Kal?' she prompted when he didn't answer.

'Yes,' he said shortly. Then, before she could say another word, 'Someone will bring tea in a moment.'

'This is your first visit here, too,' she said, ignoring the abrupt change of subject. 'Why is that?'

'Watch the sunrise, for heaven's sake,' he practically growled at her.

In other words, Lydia, mind your own business, she thought, unsure whether she was pleased or sorry that she'd managed to rattle him out of his good manners.

Here was a mystery. A secret.

That she wasn't the only one hiding something made her feel less guilty about the secret she was keeping for Rose, although no better about lying to him, and without another word she did as she was told.

Neither of them spoke or moved again while the darkness rolled back and the sun, still below the horizon, lit up bubbles of cloud in a blaze of colour that was reflected in the creek, the sea beyond, turning them first carmine, then pink, then liquid gold. As it grew light, the dark shapes against the water resolved themselves into traditional dhows moored amongst modern craft and beyond, sprawling over the steep bank on the far side of the creek, she could see a small town with a harbour and market which were already coming to life.

'Wow,' she said at last. 'Double wow.'

She caught a movement as Kal turned to look at her and she shrugged.

'Well, what other word is there?' she asked.

'Bab el Sama.' He said the words softly. 'The Gate of Heaven.'

She swallowed at the poetry of the name and said, 'You win.'

He shook his head and said, 'Are you done?'

'Yes. Thank you for being so patient.'

'I wouldn't have missed it,' he assured her as they turned and walked back towards the summer house—such an ordinary word for something that looked as if it had been conjured up by Aladdin's djinn—where a manservant was laying out the contents of a large tray.

The man bowed and, eyes down, said, '*Assalam alaykum, sitti. Marhaba.*'

She turned to Kal for a translation. 'He said, "Peace be upon you, Lady. Welcome."'

'What should I say in return?'

'*Shukran. Alaykum assalam,*' Kal said. 'Thank you. And upon you peace.'

The man smiled, bowed again, when she repeated it, savouring the words on her tongue, locking them away in her memory, along with Bab el Sama. He left them to enjoy their breakfast in private.

As she chose a high-backed cane chair and sank into the vivid silk cushions, Kal unwrapped a napkin nestled in a basket to reveal warm pastries.

'Hungry?'

'I seem to have done nothing but eat since I left London,' she said. 'I'll have to swim the creek once a day if I'm going to keep indulging myself this way.'

Maybe it was the thought of all that effort, but right now all she wanted to do was close her eyes and go to sleep. Tea would help, she told herself, just about managing to control a yawn.

'Is that a yes or a no?' he asked, offering her the basket.

'Breakfast *is* the most important meal of the day,' she said, succumbing to the enticing buttery smell. 'I suppose it is breakfast time?'

'It's whatever time you care to make it,' he assured her as he poured tea into two unbelievably thin china cups. 'Milk, lemon?'

'Just a touch of milk,' she said. Then, 'Should you be doing this?' He glanced at her. 'Waiting on me?'

Kal frowned, unable, for a moment, to imagine what she meant.

'Won't it ruin your image?'

'Image?'

He hadn't been brought up like his grandfather, his father to believe he was a prince, above the mundane realities of the world. Nor, despite his Mediterranean childhood, was he one of those men who expected to live at home, waited on by a doting mother until he transferred that honour to a wife. Even if he had been so inclined, his mother had far more interesting things to do.

As had he.

His image was not about macho posturing. He had never needed to work, never would, but once he'd fallen in love with flying he had worked hard. He'd wanted to own aircraft but there was no fun in having them sit on the tarmac. He'd started Kalzak Air Services as a courier service. Now he flew freight worldwide. And he employed men and women—hundreds of them—on their qualifications and personal qualities first, last and everything in between.

'Hanif nursed his first wife, nursed Lucy, too, when she was injured,' he said.

'He did?'

'Lucy has not told you?'

'Only that he loved her.'

'He loved his first wife, too.' The girl who had been chosen for him. A traditional arranged marriage. 'He has been twice blessed.'

'Maybe he is a man who knows how to love,' she said.

Was that the answer?

It was not a concept he was comfortable with and, remembering what Lucy had said about Rose not being able to lift a finger without someone taking a photograph of her, he carried his own cup towards the edge of the promontory and leaned against the parapet. A man enjoying the view. It was what anyone would do in such a place.

The sun was in the wrong direction to reflect off a lens that would betray a paparazzo lying in wait to snatch a photograph. Not that he imagined they would ever be that careless. The only

bvious activity was on the dhows as their crews prepared to
ead out to sea for a day's fishing.

As he scanned the wider panorama, the distant shore, he saw
only a peaceful, contented community waking to a new day,
going about its business. He let the scene sink into his bones
the way parched earth sucked up rain.

As a boy, his grandfather would have stood in this same spot,
looking at the creek, the town, the desert beyond it, certain in
the knowledge that every drop of water, every grain of sand
would, *insh'Allah,* one day be his.

Except that Allah had not willed it. His grandfather had
followed his heart instead of his head and, as a result, had been
judged unworthy. A lesson he had learned well.

He drained his cup, took one last look, then returned to the
summer house.

Sparrows, pecking at a piece of pastry, flew up at his
approach and a single look was enough to tell him that Rose
had fallen asleep, tea untouched, croissant untasted.

And, now that the sun had risen high enough to banish the
shadows from the summer house and illuminate her clear, fair
skin, he could see the faint violet smudges beneath her eyes.

Clearly sleep had eluded her aboard the plane and a long
day, a long flight, had finally caught up with her. This was no
light doze and he did not attempt to wake her, but as he bent
and caught her beneath the knees she sighed.

'Shh,' he said, easing her arm over his shoulder, around his
neck. 'Hold on.'

On some level of consciousness she must have heard him
because, as he lifted her out of the chair, she curled her hand
around his neck and tucked her head into the hollow of his
shoulder.

She wasn't anywhere near as light, as ethereal as she looked,
he discovered as he carried her along the path to Lucy and
Han's seaside retreat. Not an angel, but a real, solid woman and
he was glad that the huge doors stood wide to welcome her.

He walked straight in, picking up a little group of women who, clucking anxiously, rushed ahead to open doors, circled round them tutting with disapproval and finally stood in his way when he reached her bedroom.

'Move,' he said, 'or I'll drop her.'

They scattered with little squeals of outrage, then, as he laid her on the bed, clicked his fingers for a cover in a manner that would have made his grandfather proud—and he would have protested was utterly alien to him—they rushed to do his bidding.

He removed her shoes but, about to reach for the button at her waist to make her more comfortable, he became aware of a silence, a collectively held breath.

He turned to look at the women clustered behind him, their shocked faces. And, remembering himself, took a step back.

That he could have undressed her in a completely detached manner had the occasion demanded it was not in question. But this was not London, or New York, or Paris. This was a world where a man did not undress a woman unless he was married to her. He should not even be in her room.

'Make her comfortable,' he said with a gesture that would have done his grandfather proud. Maybe it was the place calling to his genes, he thought as he closed the door behind him, leaving the women to their task.

Then, to an old woman who'd settled herself, cross-legged, in front of the door like a palace guard, 'When she wakes she should have a massage.'

'It will be done, sidi.'

Lord…

'Don't call me that,' he said, straightening, easing his own aching limbs.

'You don't want to be given your title, Sheikh?' she asked, clearly not in the slightest bit in awe of him. 'Your grandfather wanted to be the Emir.'

About to walk away, he stopped, turned slowly back to face her.

'You knew him?'

'When he was a boy. A young man. Before he was foolish.'

She was the first person he'd met in Ramal Hamrah who was prepared to admit that. He sat before her, crossing his legs so that the soles of his feet were tucked out of sight.

'Here? You knew him here?'

'Here. In Rumaillah. At Umm al Sama. He was the wild one. Headstrong.' She shook her head. 'And he was stubborn, like his father. Once he'd said a thing, that was it.' She brushed her palms together in a gesture he'd seen many times. It signalled an end to discussion. That the subject was closed. 'They were two rocks.' She tilted her head in a birdlike gesture, examining him closely. 'You look like him,' she said after a while. 'Apart from the beard. A man should have a beard.'

He rubbed his hand self-consciously over his bare chin. He had grown a beard, aware that to be clean-shaven was the western way; it would be something else the Emir could hold against him.

'My grandfather doesn't have a beard these days,' he told her. The chemo baldness hadn't bothered him nearly as much as the loss of this symbol of his manhood and Kal had taken a razor to his own beard in an act of solidarity. It had felt odd for a while, but he'd got used to it.

'They say that he is dying,' she said. He did not ask who had said. Gossip flowed through the harem like water down the Nile.

'But still stubborn,' he replied. 'He refuses to die anywhere but in the place he still calls home.'

She nodded, 'You are stubborn, too,' she said, reaching up to pat his hand. 'You will bring him home, *insh'Allah*. It is your destiny.'

'Who are you?' he asked, with a sudden sinking feeling, the certainty that he had just made a complete fool of himself.

'I am Dena. I was found, out there,' she said with the wave of an elegant hand, the rattle of gold on her skinny wrists. 'Your great-grandmother took me into her house. Made me her daughter.'

Oh, terrific. This woman was the adopted child of the Khatib and he'd spoken to her as if she were a servant. But from the way she'd settled herself in front of Rose's bedroom door...

He'd been brought up on his grandfather's stories, had studied his family, this country, clung to a language that his father had all but forgotten, but he still had so much to learn.

He uncurled himself, got to his feet. 'My apologies, *sitti,*' he said with a formal bow.

'You have his charm, too,' she said. 'When you speak to him tell him that his sister Dena remembers him with fondness.' Then, 'Go.' She waved him away. 'Go. I will watch over your lady while you sleep.'

His lady...

Dena's words echoed in his mind as he stood beneath the shower, igniting again the memory of Rose's lips, warm, vital as they'd softened beneath him, parted for him. His mouth burned but as he sucked his lower lip into his mouth, ran a tongue over it, he tasted Rose and, instead of cooling it down, the heat surged like a contagion through his body.

Do you want me to protect her or make love to her...?

Lucy had not answered his question, but it would have made no difference either way. He was not free. He flipped the shower to cold and, lifting his face to the water, stood beneath it until he was chilled to the bone.

And still he burned.

CHAPTER SIX

LYDIA woke in slow gentle ripples of consciousness. Blissful comfort was the first stage. The pleasure of smooth, sweet-smelling sheets, the perfect pillow and, unwilling to surrender the pleasure, she turned over and fell back into its embrace.

The jewelled light filtering through ornate wooden shutters, colours dancing on white walls, seeping through her eyelids, came next.

She opened her eyes and saw an ornate band of tiny blue and green tiles shimmering like the early morning creek. She turned onto her back, looked up at a high raftered cedar wood ceiling.

It was true then. Not a dream.

'Bab el Sama.' She said the name out loud, savouring the feel of it in her mouth. The Gate of Heaven. '*Marhaba...*' Welcome. 'Kalil al-Zaki...' Trouble.

'You are awake, *sitti?*'

What?

She sat up abruptly. There was a woman, her head, body swathed in an enfolding black garment, sitting cross-legged in front of a pair of tall carved doors, as if guarding the entrance.

She rose with extraordinary grace and bowed her head. 'I am Dena, *sitti.* Princess Lucy called me, asked me to take care of you.'

'She seems to have called everyone,' Lydia said.

So much for being alone!

She threw off the covers, then immediately grabbed them back, clutching them to her chest, as she realised that she was naked.

Realised that she had no memory of getting that way. Only of the sunrise with Kal, soft cushions, the scent of buttery pastry. Of closing her eyes.

'Bin Zaki carried you here, *sitti*. We made you comfortable.'

Lydia swallowed, not quite sure how she felt about that. Whether it was worse that an unknown 'we' had undressed her sleeping body or Kal.

The woman, Dena, picked up a robe, held it out so that she could turn and slip her arms through the sleeves, wrap it around her, preserve a little of her modesty before sliding out of the bed.

It clung to her, soft and light as the touch of a butterfly wing, leaving her feeling almost as exposed as if she was wearing nothing at all. The kind of thing a pampered concubine might have worn. With a sudden quickening of something almost like fear, laced through with excitement, she said, 'Where is Kal?'

'He went to the stables.' The woman's eyes, as she handed her the glass of juice she'd poured from a flask, saw the flush that heated her skin and smiled knowingly. 'He took a horse,' she said. Then, 'I will bathe you and then you will have a massage.'

What?

'That won't be necessary,' she said.

'Bin Zaki ordered it so. Princess Lucy always needs a massage when she comes home.'

'Really?'

But the woman had opened a door that led into a bathroom that was out of a fantasy. A deep sunken tub. A huge shower with side jets. A seat big enough for two.

'Which?' Dena asked.

'The shower,' Lydia said, dismissing the disturbing image of sinking into the huge tub, sharing it with Kal.

She really, really needed something to clear her head, wake her up.

Dena turned it on, adjusted the temperature, apparently oblivious of the fact that her floor length black dress was getting wet. Apparently waiting for her to shed the robe and step into the shower so that she could wash her.

No, no, no…

Lydia swallowed, said, 'I can manage. Really.'

She nodded. 'Come into the next room when you are ready and I will ease the ache in your shoulder.'

Lydia stared after her. Raised her left hand to her right shoulder, the one that ached when it was cold or damp. After a long shift on the checkout. The legacy of years of lifting other people's groceries across a scanner.

How did she know? What had given her away?

She shook her head.

Nothing. Dena couldn't know that she was a fake. If she did, the whole house of cards would be tumbling around her ears by now, she told herself as she slipped out of the wrap, stepped under the warm water.

If she was a trained masseuse she would be observant, that was all, would notice the slightest imbalance. It didn't mean anything.

She might have slept awkwardly on the plane or strained it in a hundred ways.

She turned up the heat and let the water pound her body, easing an ache which, until that moment, she'd been scarcely aware of herself.

Lathered herself in rich soap.

Washed her hair.

Putting off, for as long as possible, the moment when, wrapped in a towel that covered her from breast to ankle, her hair wrapped in a smaller one, she would have to submit herself to the ministrations of the slightly scary Dena.

But as she lay down and Dena's hands found the knots in her muscles, soothed away the tension of the last twenty-four hours, all the stress floated away and she surrendered to total pampering.

Wrapped tenderly in a robe, seated in a chair that tilted back, her hair was released and unseen hands massaged her scalp, gently combed out her hair, while a young girl did miraculous things to her feet, her hands.

Painted her nails, drew patterns with henna.

By the time they were finished, she was so utterly relaxed that when one of the girls held out a pair of exquisite French knickers she stepped into them without a flicker of embarrassment.

Slipped into a matching lace bra and left it for someone else to fasten.

Held up her arms as Dena slipped a loose silk kaftan over her head that had certainly not been part of the wardrobe packed by Rose.

It floated over her, a mist of blue, then settled over her shoulders, her arms, falling to the floor before nimble fingers fastened the dozen or more silk-covered buttons that held it together at her breast.

Then she stepped into a pair of soft thong sandals that were placed in front of her.

A week of this and she'd be ruined for real life, she thought, pulling her lips back against her teeth so that she wouldn't grin out loud.

Wow! Wow! Wow!

Thank you, Rose! I hope you're enjoying every second of your freedom. Having the most wonderful time.

And, with that thought, reality rushed back as she looked around for the clutch bag she'd been carrying.

A word and it was in her hand and she took out her mobile phone to send the agreed 'arrived safely' message, followed by another more detailed message to her mother. Not just to let her know that she'd got to her destination without mishap, but that the apartment was great and she was having a great time.

So far, so true. Unless… Did kissing Kal count as a mishap?

She looked at the message doubtfully, then, with a rueful smile, hit 'send', grateful that her mother had insisted that overseas mobile calls were too expensive, that the occasional text was all she expected. She would never be able to bluff her way through an entire week of this, not with her mother. With Kal...

She looked up and realised that everyone was waiting to hear what she wanted to do next.

She slipped the phone into a pocket in the seam of the kaftan and said, 'May I look around?'

Dena led the way, down a series of steps to a lower level entrance lobby with a two-storey domed ceiling richly decorated in floral designs with tiny ceramic tiles, her helpers following, all anxious to see her reaction. Clearly wanting her to love this place they called home.

They waited patiently while she stopped, turned slowly, looking up in awe at the workmanship.

'This is a holiday cottage?' she asked in amazement. 'It's so beautiful!'

Dena was unreadable, but the two younger women were clearly delighted.

The tour took in a formal dining room where ornate carved doors had been folded back to reveal a terrace and, below it, set in a private walled garden, a swimming pool.

More steps and then Dena said, 'This is the room the family use when they are here.'

Furnished with richly coloured sofas and jewel-bright oriental rugs that softened the polished wooden floor, Lydia might have been totally overwhelmed by its sheer size, but then she spotted a fluffy yellow toy duck half hidden amongst the cushions.

It was a reminder that this was someone's holiday home, a place where children ran and played. She picked it up and held it for a moment and when she looked up she saw that Dena was smiling.

'It is Jamal's,' she said. 'He left it there to keep his place while he was away.'

'Bless,' she said, carefully tucking it back where she'd found it and, looking around, saw the touches that made this unbelievably grand room a home.

The box filled with toys. A pile of books that suggested Lucy's favourite holiday activity was reading. A child's drawing of the creek, framed as lovingly as an old master. Children's books in English and Arabic.

'You like children?' Dena asked as she picked up an alphabet colouring book similar to one she'd had as a child. Except that the alphabet was Arabic.

She nodded. 'Even the little monsters…'

Even the little monsters who whined and nagged their stressed mothers for sweets at the checkout. Their soft little mouths, big eyes that could be coaxed so quickly from tears to a smile with a little attention.

She was so relaxed that she'd completely forgotten to guard her tongue but, while Dena regarded her thoughtfully, the younger women giggled, repeating 'little monsters' as if they knew only too well what she meant.

She managed a shrug and Dena, making no comment, folded back doors similar to the ones in the dining room, opening up one side of the room to the garden so that Lydia could step out onto a wide terrace that overlooked the creek.

'All children love Bab el Sama,' she said. 'You will bring your children here.'

It sounded more like a statement than a question and Lydia swallowed.

She had two careers and no time for romance, even if she could ever trust a man again sufficiently to let him get that close.

Maybe Kal was the answer. He, at least, wouldn't be pretending…

She, on the other hand, would be.

Since the one thing she demanded of a man was total honesty, to kiss with a lie on her lips was not something she could live with, no matter how alluring the temptation.

'I'm sure they have a wonderful time,' she said, responding to her first comment, ignoring the second as she walked quickly to the edge of the terrace as if to take a closer look at the beach.

They were much lower here than on the bluff where she'd watched the sunrise, not more than twenty feet above the beach. And, looking around, she thought that the adults must love it too.

There were pots overflowing with geraniums, still flowering in December, the rustle and clack of palm fronds in the light breeze, a snatch of unfamiliar music carrying across the glittering water.

It was peaceful, beautiful, with a delicious warmth that seeped into the bones and invited her to lift her face to the sun and smile as if she were a sunflower.

Even as she did that, a movement caught her eye and below, on the beach, she saw a horseman galloping along the edge of the surf, robes streaming out behind him.

The horse, its hooves a blur in the spray, seemed to be almost flying, elemental, a force of nature. Lydia's breath caught in her throat and she took a step closer, her hand lifting towards him as if reaching to catch hold, be lifted up to fly with him.

'It is Bin Zaki,' Dena said, but Lydia knew that.

He might have shed his designer suit, donned a robe, hidden his dark curls beneath a *keffiyeh,* but his chiselled face, the fierce hawkish nose were imprinted on her memory and, as he flashed by in a swirl of cloth, hooves, spray, the profile was unmistakable.

'He is chasing his demons. So like his grandfather.'

For a moment she didn't respond, scarcely registered what the woman had said, but Kal had gone, lost from sight as the beach curved around massive rocks, the final fling of the mountain range behind them. And already the sea was smoothing away the hoof prints, rubbing out all trace of his passing.

She turned to discover that Dena was watching her and, suddenly coming back to reality, she dropped her hand self-consciously.

'Demons? What demons?'

'He will tell you in his own good time. Do you need anything, *sitti?*'

Only to be held, enfolded, caressed, but not by some anonymous, faceless figure. All the longings and desires that haunted her had become focused on one man and she turned back to the empty beach as if his spirit was still there for her to reach out and touch.

'I think I'll take a walk,' she said, suddenly self-conscious, certain that Dena knew exactly what she was thinking. 'Explore a little. Is there anywhere I shouldn't go?'

'Bab el Sama is yours, *sitti.*'

Dena left her alone to explore and she skirted the terrace, noticing how cleverly it was shielded from the creek by the trees so that no one from below would be able to see the royal family at play.

Taking a path, she found steps that led invitingly downwards in the direction of the beach but, conscious of the silk kaftan flowing around her ankles, she turned instead along a path that led upward through the garden.

After the crash that had killed her father and left her mother in a wheelchair, she and her mother had moved from their small house with a garden into a ground floor flat that had been adapted for a wheelchair user.

She'd missed the garden but, ten years old, she'd understood the necessity and knew better than to say anything that would hurt her mother. It was the hand that life had dealt but even then she'd used her pocket money to buy flowering pot plants from the market. Had grown herbs on the windowsill.

This garden was like a dream. Little streams ran down through the trees, fell over rocks to feed pools where carp rose at her appearance.

There were exquisite summer houses tucked away. Some were for children, with garden toys. Some, with comfortable chairs, were placed to catch a stunning view.

One, with a copper roof turned green with verdigris, was laid with rich carpets on which cushions had been piled, and looked like a lovers' hideaway. She could imagine lying there with Kal, his lips pressed against her throat as he unfastened the buttons...

She lifted her hand to her breast, shook her head, trying to rid herself of an image that was so powerful that she could feel his hands, his mouth on her body.

As she backed away there was a scuffle near her feet as a lizard disappeared in a flurry of emerald tail. For a moment she stared at the spot, not sure whether she'd imagined it. Then she looked up and saw Kal standing just a few feet away.

The *keffiyeh* had fallen from his head and lay gathered about his neck. His robes were made of some loosely woven cream material and the hem was heavy with sea water and sand. As they stood there, silent, still, a trickle of sweat ran from his temple into the dust on his cheek.

After what seemed like an age he finally moved, lifting his elbow to wipe his face on his sleeve.

'I've been riding,' he said wearily.

'I saw you. You looked as if you were flying,' she said.

'That's me,' he said, the corner of his mouth lifting in a self-mocking smile. 'Addicted to the air.' He took a step forward but Lydia, almost dizzy with the scent of leather, of the sea clinging to his clothes, of tangy fresh sweat that her body was responding to like an aphrodisiac, didn't move.

Hot, sweaty he exuded a raw sexual potency and she wanted to touch his face. Kiss the space between his thumb and palm, taste the leather; lean into him and bury her face in his robes, breathe him in. Wanted to feel those long, powerful hands that had so easily controlled half a ton of muscle and bone in full flight, on her own body.

She cooled her burning lip with the tip of her tongue, then, realising how that must look, said, 'Maybe my problem with flying is that I didn't start in the right place.'

He frowned. 'You don't ride?'

'No.' Having studied every aspect of her alter ego's life, she knew that while most little girls of her class would have been confidently astride her first pony by the time she was three, Rose was not one of them. 'But, if I had to choose, I think I'd prefer it to fishing.'

His smile was a lazy thing that began in the depths of his eyes, barely noticeable if you weren't locked in to every tiny response. No more than a tiny spark that might so easily have been mistaken for a shaft of sunlight finding a space between the leaves to warm the darkness. Then the creases that fanned out around them deepened a little, the skin over his cheekbones tightened and lifted. Only then did his mouth join in with a slightly lopsided *gotcha* grin.

'Here's the deal,' he said. 'You let me take you fishing and I'll teach you to ride.'

His voice, his words seemed to caress her so that it sounded more like a sexual proposition than a simple choice between this or that outdoor activity. Standing there in the dappled sunlight, every nerve-ending at attention, sensitized by desire, she knew that if he reached out, touched her, she would buckle, dissolve and if he carried her into the summer house and laid her amongst the cushions, nothing could save her.

That she wouldn't want to be saved.

This powerful, instant attraction had nothing to do with who they were. Or weren't. It was pure chemistry. Names, titles meant nothing.

She lowered her lids, scarcely able to breathe. 'Is that your final offer?'

His voice soft, dangerously seductive, he said, 'How about if I offered to bait your hook for you?'

Baited, hooked, landed…

She swallowed, cooled her burning lower lip with her tongue. 'How could I resist such an inducement?'

A step brought him alongside her and he took her chin in

his hand, ran the pad of his thumb over her mouth in an explora-tory sweep as if to test its heat.

'It is a date, Rose.'

He was so close that she could see the grains of sand thrown up by the flying hooves which clung to his face and, as she closed her eyes to breathe in the pure essence of the man, his mouth touched hers, his tongue lightly tracing her lower lip, imitating the route her own had taken seconds before, as if tasting her.

Before she could react, clutch at him to stop herself from collapsing at his feet, it was over.

'You will fish with me this afternoon. I will ride with you at dawn.'

'Perfect,' she managed through a throat that felt as if it was stuffed with cotton wool. Through lips that felt twice their normal size.

Then, as she opened her eyes, he stepped back and said, 'You might want to wear something a little less...distracting.'

Before she could respond, he strode away in a swirl of robes and she did not move until she was quite alone.

Only when the path was quite empty, the only sound—apart from the pounding of her heart—was the rattle of palm fronds high above her, did she finally look down, see for herself how the light breeze was moulding the thin blue silk to her body so that it outlined every contour. Her thighs, the gentle curve of her belly. The hard, betraying, touch-me peaks of her breasts.

CHAPTER SEVEN

KAL stood beneath the pounding icy shower. He did not need hot water; the heat coming off him was turning the water to steam.

He closed his eyes but it didn't help. Without visual distraction, the image of Rose Napier, silk clinging to every curve, filled his head, obliterating everything from his mind but her.

If he had ever doubted her innocence, he was now utterly convinced of it. No woman who had a scintilla of experience would have let a man see such naked desire shining out of her eyes, been so unconscious of the *come-and-take-me* signals her body was semaphoring in response to his nearness. Given him such power over her.

But maybe they were both out of their depth.

Preoccupied with his own concerns and apparently immune to this pale beauty that the entire world appeared to be in love with, his guard had been down.

Knocked sideways from his first sight of her and, knowing that he wouldn't sleep, he'd gone to the stables, determined to blow away the demands of his body in hard physical activity.

But as hard as he'd ridden he could not shake loose the image of those blue eyes. One moment *keep-your-distance* cool, the next sparkling with life, excitement. A touch of mischief.

Almost, he thought, as if she were two women.

The adored, empathetic public figure—as flawless and beautiful as a Bernini marble, as out of reach as the stars.

And this private, flesh and blood woman whose eyes appealed for his touch, for him to take her, bring her to life.

Living with those eyes, those seductive lips that drew him to her, would not make for a comfortable week. And he'd just made it a thousand times worse.

He'd ridden off the sexual energy that had built over their long flight. Had been totally in control, with the self-discipline to keep his hands off her.

All he'd had to do was keep his distance, leave it to her to initiate any outings. He had his own agenda and it certainly didn't include getting involved with a woman, especially one who was a national icon.

Until he'd taken a turn in the path and saw her standing before him, her hair hanging like silk around her shoulders. Wearing an embroidered silk kaftan that exactly matched eyes shining like a woman on her wedding night.

And he'd been the one insisting that the two of them should spend time alone together on a boat.

Offering to teach her to ride.

Unable to resist touching her lip with his thumb, his tongue, wanting to test the heat, knowing that it was for him.

It had taken every ounce of self-discipline to stop himself from carrying her into the pavilion hidden in the trees behind her. Making her his.

To force himself to step back, walk away.

He flipped off the water, stepped from the shower, grabbed a towel and wrapped it round him.

His clothes had been pressed and hung up but someone, Dena, probably, had added an array of casual and formal robes for his use while he was at Bab el Sama.

The kind of clothes that Hanif would wear. A sheikh, relaxing in the privacy of his own home, with his children around him.

It was Dena, undoubtedly, who'd dressed Rose in that silk dress, had painted her hands with henna. He frowned, wondering what she thought she was doing.

He shook his head. Rose was on holiday in an exotic location and no doubt Lucy had ordered that her friend be totally pampered.

She certainly looked a great deal more rested. Unlike him. He lifted his shoulders, easing them, then reached for his cellphone and called his grandfather at the clinic.

After he'd asked how he was, as if he didn't know—in desperate pain but stubbornly refusing palliative care until he was permitted to return home to die—and getting the same answer, he said, 'I met someone today who knew you.'

'And is prepared to admit it?'

'She said that you were stubborn, *Jaddi*. But charming—'

There was a short harsh laugh, then, 'She?'

'She said, "Tell him that his sister Dena remembers him with fondness."'

'Dena?' There was a rare catch in the old man's voice. 'She is well?'

'She is well,' he confirmed. 'She said it was time you were home.'

'Tell her… Tell her I will be there, *insh'Allah*. Tell her that I will not die until I have kissed her.'

'It will be so, *Jaddi'l habeeb*,' Kal said softly. 'I swear it.'

He put down the phone, spent a moment reminding himself why he was here, gathering himself.

Then he pulled out the jeans he'd brought with him, chose a loose long-sleeved white shirt from the wardrobe and pulled it over his head and stepped into thong sandals that seemed more suitable than any of the shoes he'd brought with him.

As he picked up the phone to stow it in his pocket, it rang. Caller ID warned him that it was Lucy and he said, 'Checking up on me, Princess?'

She laughed. 'Why? What are you up to?' Then, not waiting for an answer, 'I just wanted to be sure that Rose arrived safely.'

'So why not call her?'

'She wants to cut herself off from everyone while she's

away. She wants to think about the future without anyone else offering their opinions, clouding the picture.'

'Instead, she got me,' he said. 'Tell me, was there a single word of truth in what you told me?'

'Absolutely. Cross my heart,' she swore. 'Why do you think her grandfather was so desperate to stop her? He doesn't want her doing anything as dangerous as thinking for herself, not without someone on hand to guide her thoughts in the right direction.'

'And that would be in the direction of the marriage he's arranged?' he asked casually enough, despite the fact that the thought of another man touching her sent a shaft of possessive heat driving deep into his groin.

'She's longing for a family, children of her own, Kal, and I think she's very nearly desperate enough to marry Rupert Devenish to get them.'

'What other reason is there for a woman to marry?' he asked.

Or a man, for that matter.

Far better to have people who had known you all your life, who understood your strengths and weaknesses, to seek a bride whose temperament, expectations matched your own, than rely on unbridled passion that, no matter how intense the heat, would soon become ashes. He'd seen it happen. His grandfather, his father...

'Oh, pish-posh,' Lucy said with the impatience of a woman who'd found a rare love and thought he should be making an effort to do the same. 'How is she?'

'Rose? She slept for a while, but now she's exploring the garden.'

'On her own?'

'I have no doubt that your Dena has someone within call.' Someone who would have seen him kissing her? 'She's safe enough,' he said abruptly. 'And we're about to have lunch.'

'Maybe when you've eaten you'll be in a better mood. Perhaps I should call you then?'

'No. Really. I've just spoken to my grandfather. And, as for your Rose, well, she isn't quite what I expected. I imagined un-ruffled serenity.'

'Oh? In what way is she not serene?'

In the quick blush that warmed her pale skin, in her eyes, a mouth, a body that gave away too much.

'Well,' he said, pushing away the disturbing images, 'I would have welcomed a warning that she's a nervous flyer.'

'Rose? I never knew that. How did she cope with the heli-copter?' Her concern was genuine enough, Kal decided, giving her the benefit of the doubt.

'I managed to keep her distracted.' Before she could ask him how, he added, 'I was surprised to discover that she doesn't ride.'

'I think a pony bolted with her when she was little.' He could see the tiny frown as she tried to remember. 'Something like that.'

'Well, she appears to be willing to give it another go.'

'You're going to take her riding?'

'Amuse and entertain her, that was the brief.'

'Absolutely. I'm glad you're taking it so seriously. But the reason for my call is to give you advance warning that Rose should be getting a courtesy visit from Princess Sabirah later in the week. The household will be warned of her arrival, but I thought you might welcome a little extra time to prepare yourself.'

'Thank you, Lucy. If I haven't sufficiently expressed my grat—'

'It's little enough in return for everything you've done for my charity, Kal. Just do me one favour. Don't tell Rose that I was checking up on her.'

'I won't. Lucy…'

He hesitated. He knew his doubts were foolish. Lady Rose Napier had been hand delivered to him by her security guard…

'Yes?' she prompted.

'Nothing. Take care.'

He disconnected, pushed the phone into his back pocket and, bearing in mind that it was his duty to keep her safe, he went to find Rose.

Lydia resisted the urge to fling herself into the nearest pool to cool herself down. Instead, she walked the winding paths, swiftly at first, outrunning feelings she could not control, until her breath was coming in short gasps and she almost collapsed into a seat that seemed to have been placed precisely for that purpose.

She sat there for an age while her breathing returned to normal and the heat gradually faded from her skin, attempting to make sense of what had happened.

She might as well try to catch mist in her hand.

There *was* no sense in it. Love—or just plain lust—as she knew to her cost, made fools of everyone.

'Get a grip, Lydie,' she said intently, startling a bird from the tree above her. 'Rose is depending on you. This madness will go away.' Then, after a long time, 'It will go away.'

By the time she returned to the terrace her flush might easily have been put down to nothing more than a brisk walk on a sunny day.

Just as well, because one of the girls who'd taken care of her was sitting cross-legged in the shade, embroidering a piece of silk.

'You will eat, *sitti?*' she asked, rising gracefully to her feet.

Food was the last thing on her mind, but it had been a long time since the croissant that she'd barely tasted and eating was a proven distraction for heartache.

'Thank you… I'm sorry, I don't know your name.'

'It is Yatimah, *sitti.*'

'Yatimah,' she repeated, rolling the word around her mouth, tasting the strangeness of it. 'Thank you, Yatimah. Your English is very good.'

'Princess Lucy has taught me. She speaks Arabic as if she

was born here, but her mother comes sometimes. From New
Zealand. And her friends from England.'

'And they do not,' Lydia said.

'A few words,' she said with a smile.

'Will you teach me?'

'*Nam,*' she said. And giggled. 'That means yes.'

'*Nam,*' she repeated. Then, remembering the word Kal had
taught her, she said, '*Shukran.* Thank you.' And received a delighted clap. Encouraged, she asked, 'What is "good morning"?'

'Good morning is *sabah alkhair* and the reply is *sabah alnur.*'

Lydia tried it and got the response from Yatimah who, an
eager teacher, then said, 'Good afternoon is *masa alkhair* and
the reply *masa alnur.* And goodnight is—'

'*Leila sa'eeda.*'

Startled by Kal's voice from the doorway, Yatimah scuttled
away, leaving Lydia alone with him.

The last time he'd kissed her, she'd managed to dismiss it
as if it was nothing. They both knew that wasn't going to happen
this time and for a moment neither of them moved, spoke.

'Lucy called,' he said at last, stepping onto the terrace.

He'd showered and changed into a loose white collarless
shirt that hung to his hips. Soft faded jeans. Strong, bare feet
pushed into thong sandals. The clothes were unremarkable but
with that thin high-bridged nose, polished olive skin, dark hair
curling onto his neck, he looked very different from the man
in the suit who'd met her at the airport. More like some desert
lord surveying his world.

'She wanted to be sure you'd arrived safely.'

'Then why didn't she call me?' Lydia asked, brave in the
knowledge that if she'd rung Rose, by the magic of the cellphone, she'd have got Rose, wherever she was. Except, of
course, that Rose didn't know anything about Kal. She'd need
to send a message, she thought, her hand going to the phone
in her pocket, warn her…

'My own reaction,' he replied, 'but she seemed to be under

he impression that you'd rather not talk to anyone from home. That you did not want to be disturbed.'

...or maybe not.

He turned to her in expectation of polite denial.

Being a lookalike was an acting role, stepping into the shoes of another person, copying the moves, the gestures, the facial expressions. Practising the voice until it became her own. But nothing that Rose had ever done had prepared her for this.

In a situation like this, all she had to fall back on was the supermarket checkout girl with the fast mouth.

And that girl wouldn't let him off with a polite anything. That girl would look him in the eye, lift an eyebrow and say, 'She should have thought about that before she invited you to my party.'

Just like that.

If she'd hoped to raise a smile, she would have been sadly disappointed.

Apart from the slightest contraction of a muscle at the corner of his mouth—as if she needed any encouragement to look at it—his expression didn't alter for so long that, but for that tiny giveaway, she might have wondered if he'd actually heard her.

Then, with the merest movement of his head, he acknowledged the hit and said, 'No doubt that's why she asked me not to tell you she'd called.'

'So why did you?' she demanded, refusing to back down, play the lady. She might not know what Rose would do under these circumstances, but she jolly well knew what she should do after that very close encounter in the garden.

That had gone far beyond simple flirting. Far beyond what had happened in the helicopter, where his kiss had been simple enough. It had been her own reaction that had turned into something much more complex; fear, strangeness, the need to cling to something safe would do that and it was easy enough to dismiss as an aberration.

But what had happened in the garden was different.

He'd touched her mouth as if marking her as his, taken her lower lip into his mouth as intimately as a lover, certain of his welcome.

And she had welcomed him.

That moment had been an acknowledgement of the intense attraction that had been bubbling beneath the surface from the moment she had walked into the airport and found him waiting for her.

It was a dance where they circled one another, getting closer and closer. Touching briefly. Moving apart as they fought it but, like two moths being drawn closer and closer to a candle, totally unable to resist the fatal attraction, even though they both knew they would go down in flames.

Except that she had no choice. She had to withstand the temptation or tell him the truth, because she knew how it felt to be made love to by someone who was acting. Knew how betrayed she'd felt.

And she couldn't tell him the truth. Couldn't betray Rose for her own selfish desires. Not that he'd want her if she did. He was not a man to accept a fake. A copy. If he knew the truth he'd lose interest, turn away.

And if he didn't…

'Kal…'

'You are hungry?'

Her life seemed to be happening in slow motion, Lydia thought. Neither of them moved or made a move to answer Dena's query for what seemed like forever.

It did not matter. Apparently oblivious to the tension between them, she bustled across the terrace to a table set beneath the trees, issuing orders to the staff that trailed after her.

A cloth was laid, food was set out.

'Come, eat,' she said, waving them towards the table.

Kal moved first, held out a chair for her, and she managed to unstick her feet from the flagstones and join him at the table.

'This looks wonderful, Dena,' she said, trying very hard to ignore his hands grasping the back of her chair, the beautiful bones of his wrists, the dark hair exposed where he'd folded back the sleeves of his shirt, the woody scent of soap and shampoo as she sat down and he bent over her to ease the chair forward.

It was like living inside a kaleidoscope of the senses. Everything was heightened. The food glowed, gleamed with colour, enticed with spices. The arm of her chair, worn smooth by many hands. The starchy smell, the feel of the damask cloth against her legs. A silence so intense that she could almost feel it.

Then a bird fluttered down, anticipating crumbs, and gradually everything began to move again and she realised that Dena was speaking. That both she and Kal were looking at her.

'What?' she asked.

Dena excused herself, leaving Kal to pass on the message, but he shook his head as if it was nothing important and instead took her on a culinary tour of the table.

Rice cooked with saffron and studded with pine nuts and sultanas. Locally caught fish. Chicken. Jewelled salads. Small cheeses made from goats' milk.

'It's a feast,' she said with every appearance of pleasure, even though alarm bells were going off in her head, certain that she'd missed something. That somehow they knew... 'I just hope Dena does not expect me to eat it all. I usually have a sandwich for lunch.'

'And here I was thinking that you spent every day at a lavish lunch, raising money for charity.'

His words were accompanied by a wry smile and the bells quietened a little, the tension seeping away beneath the honeyed warmth of his voice, his eyes.

'Not more than once a week,' she assured him. Then, managing a smile of her own, 'Maybe twice. But I only taste the food.'

'A taste will satisfy Dena. None of the food will be wasted.' He took her plate. 'Rice?'

'A spoonful,' she replied, repeating the same word each

time he offered her a new dish. He put no more than a morsel of each on her plate but, by the time he had finished, it was still an awful lot of food to eat in the middle of the day and she regarded it doubtfully.

'It will be a long time until dinner, Rose. We eat late. And you're going to need plenty of energy before then.' She looked up. 'We're going fishing, remember?'

'Is it hard work? I thought you just sat with a rod and waited for the fish to bite.' She picked up a fork. 'Was that what you were arranging with Dena?'

He hesitated for a moment, as if he had some unpleasant news to impart, and the bells began jangling again.

'Kal?'

He shook his head. 'It was nothing to do with this afternoon. She's had a message from Rumaillah. It seems that the Emir's wife has decided to pay you a courtesy call.'

The fork in Lydia's hand shook and the waiting sparrows dived on the scattered grains of rice.

'The Emir's wife?'

'I know that you hoped to be totally private here, Rose, but I'm sure you understand that Princess Sabirah could not ignore your presence in her country.'

Lydia felt the colour drain from her face.

When Rose had asked her to do this it had all seemed so simple. Once she was out of the country there would be nothing to do but indulge herself in one of those perfectly selfish holidays that everyone dreamed about occasionally. The kind where you could read all day and all night if you wanted to. Swim. Take a walk on the beach. Do what you wanted without having to think about another person.

And, like Rose, do some serious thinking about the future.

She'd had ten good years as Rose's lookalike and had no doubt that she could go on for ten more, but now she'd met Kal and the only person she wanted to be was herself.

No pretence.

No lies.

Not that she was kidding herself. She knew that if, in the unlikely event that he'd ever met her as 'herself', he wouldn't have even noticed her.

Everything about him was the real deal, from his designer suit to the Rolex on his wrist—no knock-offs for this man. Including women.

The pain of that was a wake-up call far louder, the argument for reality more cogent than any that her boss at the supermarket could make, even using the in-store announcement system.

She had been coasting through her own life, putting all her energies into someone else's, and she would never move on, meet someone who wanted her, the real Lydia Young, unless she started building a life of her own.

'When?' she asked, ungluing her tongue. 'What time?'

Maybe she could throw a sickie, she thought a touch desperately, but instantly rejected the idea as she realised what kind of fuss *that* would cause. This wasn't some anonymous hotel where you could take to your bed and no one would give a damn. And she wasn't some anonymous tourist.

If Lady Rose took to her bed, panic would ensue, doctors would be summoned—probably by helicopter from the capital. And Kal or Dena, probably both, would call Lucy, the Duke of Oldfield and then the game would be up.

No, no, no…

She could do this. She had to do it.

'Relax. She won't be here for a day or two and she won't stay long,' Kal said, not looking at her, but concentrating on serving himself. 'Just for coffee, cake. Dena will arrange everything,' he added, that tiny muscle in his jaw tightening again.

What was that? Tension?

What was his problem?

'Does she speak English? What will we talk about?'

'I believe her English is excellent and I imagine she'll want to talk about your work.'

'Really?' Lydia had a flash image of herself politely explaining the finer points of the checkout scanner to Her Highness over a cup of coffee and had to fight down a hysterical giggle as the world began to unravel around her.

'Play nice,' he said, 'and you'll get a generous donation for one of your good causes.'

Kal's flippancy brought her crashing back to reality. This was not in the least bit funny and her expression must have warned him that she was no more amused by his remark than Rose, whose parents had been killed on a charity mission, would have been.

'I'm sorry, Rose,' he said immediately. 'That was unforgivable.' He shook his head and she realised that for some reason he was as on edge as she was. 'I'm sure she'll just want to talk about Lucy and her grandchildren. It's a while since she's seen them.'

As if that was better!

She'd assumed that being at Bab el Sama would be like staying in a hotel. Great service but everything at a distance. She hadn't anticipated having to live with the pretence of being Rose in this way. This minute by minute deception.

She'd come dangerously, selfishly close to confessing everything to Kal before Dena had interrupted her but she could not, no matter how desperately she wanted to, break Rose's confidence.

She had made this offer with a free heart and couldn't, wouldn't let her down just because that heart wanted to jump ship and fling itself at someone else.

'I appear to have spoiled your appetite,' Kal said, and she took a little heart from the fact that he didn't seem particularly comfortable to hear of their unexpected visitor either.

'I'm good,' she said, picking up her fork and spearing a piece of chicken so succulent that, despite her dry mouth, she had no trouble swallowing it. 'So tell me what, exactly, is your problem, Kal?'

CHAPTER EIGHT

EXACTLY? Kal took a piece of bread, tore it in two.

'Why would you think I have a problem?' he asked, playing for time in the face of Rose's unexpected challenge.

'There's a muscle just by the corner of your mouth that you'd probably be wise to cover when you play poker,' she replied.

She reached out and touched a spot just below the right hand corner of his mouth.

'Just there.'

As their eyes locked, he kept perfectly still, knowing that if he moved an inch he would be tasting those long, slender fingers, sliding his tongue along the length of each one, and food would be the furthest thing from his mind. That the only thing he'd be eating would be her.

As if sensing the danger, she curled them back into her palm, let her hand drop.

'Should I ever be tempted to gamble, I'll bear that in mind,' he said. Took a mouthful of bread before he blurted out the real reason he had been foisted on her by Lucy and she sent him packing.

Rose made no move to eat, but continued to regard him. 'Well?' she prompted, refusing to let the matter drop. 'I recall that you mentioned your family were personae non gratae at court and presumably, as a royal residence, Bab el Sama is an extension of that. Will Princess Sabirah's visit be awkward for you?'

The breath stopped in his throat. Not suspicion, concern. She was anxious for him…

'This was originally the site of the Khatib tribe's summer camp,' he told her, not sure where exactly he was going with this, but wanting her to understand who, what he was. 'The mountains provided not only water, grazing for the animals, but a fortress at their back in troubled times.' He looked up at the barren peaks towering above them. 'They are impassable.'

'So is that a yes or a no?' she asked, refusing to be diverted by history.

'Good question.'

And the answer was that, far from awkward, Lucy was using court etiquette for his benefit, putting him in a place where his aunt could not, without causing offence to an honoured guest, ignore him.

In London, in her elegant drawing room, it had all seemed so simple. Before he'd met Rose. Now nothing was simple and if this had been for him alone he would have stepped back, taken himself out of the picture for the morning. But this was for his grandfather.

'Maybe you'd better tell me what happened, Kal,' she said when he didn't offer an answer. 'Just enough to stop me from putting my foot in it.'

'Your foot?'

'I'm sorry. You speak such perfect English that I forget that it isn't your first language.' She frowned. 'I'm not even sure what your first language is. Arabic, French…?'

'Take your pick,' he said. 'I grew up speaking both. And quickly added English when my father married for the second time. I know what "putting your foot in it" means. But, to answer your question, the court is wherever the Emir happens to be, so I'm safe enough unless he decides to accompany his wife.'

'And if he does?'

He couldn't get that lucky. Could he? Or was the Emir, like

everyone else, fascinated by this English 'Rose' who'd been orphaned so tragically as a little girl. Who, from the age of sixteen, had taken up her parents' cause, devoted her whole life to the charity they'd founded, adding dozens of other good causes over the years.

'I'm wherever you happen to be, Rose. And you are an honoured guest in his country. Who knows,' he said with a wry smile, 'he might be sufficiently charmed by you to acknowledge my existence.'

'Whoa, whoa...' She put down her fork, sat back. 'Back up, buster. I need to know what I'm getting into here.'

'"Back up, buster"?' he repeated, startled out of his own concerns. 'Where on earth did Lady Rose Napier pick up an expression like that?'

She blinked, appeared to gather herself, physically put the cool façade back in place. 'I meet all kinds of people in my work,' she said. Even her voice had changed slightly, had taken on a hint of steel, as if she was drawing back from him, and he recalled his earlier feeling that she was two separate people. The formal, untouchable, unreadable 'Lady'. And this other woman whose voice was huskier, whose lush mouth was softer, whose eyes seemed to shine a brighter blue. Who used unexpectedly colloquial expressions.

The one he couldn't seem to keep his hands off.

The selfish gene, the one he'd been fighting all his life, urged him to reach out, grasp her hand, stop that Rose from slipping away.

Instead, like her, he took a moment to gather himself, take a step back before, control restored, he said, 'What happened is no secret. Google my family and you'll find enough gossip to fill a book.'

'I'd rather save that for when I've run out of fiction,' she replied crisply. 'The edited highlights will do.'

'I wish it was fiction,' he said. 'My grandfather was hardly a credit to his family.'

He reached for a pitcher of water, offered it to her and, when she nodded, he filled both their glasses.

'Kalil al-Khatib, my grandfather, was the oldest son of the Emir and, although a ruler is free to name his successor, no one ever doubted that it would be him.'

'You have the same name as your grandfather?' she asked.

'It is the tradition. My first son will be named Zaki for my father.' If he achieved recognition, a traditional marriage, a place in the society that had rejected his family.

'That must become rather confusing.'

'Why?'

'Well, if a man has two or three sons, won't all their first-born sons have the same name?' Then, 'Oh, wait. That's why Dena calls you "bin Zaki". That's "son of", isn't it?'

He couldn't stop the smile that betrayed his pleasure. She was so quick, so intelligent, eager to learn.

The curl of desire as, equally pleased with herself for 'getting it', she smiled back.

Then her forehead puckered in a frown as she quickly picked up on what else he'd told her. 'But I don't understand. Why do you call yourself al-Zaki and not al-Khatib?'

'It's a long story,' he said, forcing himself to concentrate on that, rather than the curve of her cheek, the line of her neck. The hollows in her throat that were made for a man's tongue.

'I have all afternoon.'

He sought for a beginning, something that would make sense of tribal history, the harshness of the life, the need for a strong leader.

'My grandfather was his father's favourite. They both loved to ride, hunt in the desert with their falcons. They were, people said, more like twins than father and son. They were both utterly fearless, both much respected. Loved.'

He thought of Dena. She'd called herself his sister, but she was not related to him by blood. Had she loved him, too?

Then, realising that Rose was waiting, 'He was everything that was required of a ruler in those simpler times.'

'Everything?'

'Strong enough to hold off his enemies, to protect the summer grazing, the oases. Keep his people and their stock safe.'

'That would be before the oil?'

He nodded. 'They were still the qualities admired, necessary even in a charismatic leader, but it is true that once the oil started flowing and money began to pour into the country, the role needed a greater vision. Something beyond the warrior, the great hunter, the trusted arbitrator. A man to take the international stage.'

'And your grandfather couldn't adapt?'

'Oh, he adapted,' Kal said wryly. 'Just not in the right way. He was a big man with big appetites and wealth gave him the entire world in which to indulge them. He spent a fortune on a string of racehorses, enjoyed the gaming tables, never lacked some beauty to decorate his arm and, as the heir apparent to one of the new oil rich states, his excesses inevitably attracted media attention. None of it favourable.'

'I bet that went down well at home,' she said with a wry look and he caught again a glimpse of the inner Rose. The one she tried so hard to keep suppressed.

'Like a lead balloon?' he offered.

She laughed, then clapped her hand to her mouth.

'That is the correct expression?' he asked.

'You know it is, Kal.' She shook her head. 'I'm sorry. It's not funny.'

'It all happened a long time ago. My grandfather has long since accepted that he has no one but himself to blame for what happened.'

'So what did happen?' she asked, concentrating on her food rather than looking at him, as if she understood how difficult this was for him. He, on the other hand, watched as she successfully negotiated a second forkful of rice and knew that he could sit here and watch her eat all day.

Instead, he followed her example, picking up a piece of fish, forcing himself to concentrate on the story.

'In an attempt to remind Kalil of his duty,' he went on, 'encourage him to return home and settle down, his family arranged his marriage to the daughter of one of the most powerful tribal elders.'

'Arranged?' He caught the slightly disparaging lift of her eyebrows, the sideways glance.

'It is how it is done, Rose. To be accepted as the husband of a precious daughter is to be honoured. And an alliance, ties of kinship between families, adds strength in times of trouble.'

'Very useful when it comes to hanging on to land, I imagine. Especially when it lies over a vast oilfield. Does the girl get a say at all?'

'Of course,' he said.

'But who would refuse the man who was going to be Emir?'

'Marriage binds tribal societies together, Rose. I'm not saying that ours is an infallible system, but everyone has a stake in the partnership succeeding. No one wants to match two young people who will be unhappy.'

'Yours?'

She sounded sceptical. He could see why she might be. He was the second generation to be born and live his entire life in Europe. But at heart...

'There's no place for love?'

'That would be the happy-ever-after fairy tale perpetrated by Hollywood?' he responded irritably.

He'd hoped that she would understand. Then, remembering Lucy's concern that she was being guided towards marriage not of her own choice, he realised that she probably did understand rather more than most. And found himself wondering just how much choice a girl really had in a society where being married to a powerful man was the ideal. When her family's fortune might rise or fall on her decision.

'Hollywood came rather late in the story, Kal. Ever heard

of Shakespeare? "Love is not love, Which alters when it altera-
tion finds, Or bends with the remover to remove: Oh, no! it is
an ever-fixéd mark, That looks on tempests and is never shaken;
It is the star to every wandering bark…"'

She said the words with such passion, such belief, that a stab
of longing pierced him and for a moment he couldn't breathe.
Wanted to believe that out of an entire world it was possible
for two people to find one another. Reach out and with the
touch of a hand make a commitment that would last a lifetime.

Knowing it for nonsense, that anyone who believed in it was
going to get hurt, he shook his head.

'It's the same story for the same gullible audience,' he
replied. That kind of attraction is no more than sexual chemistry. Powerful, undoubtedly, but short-lived. 'I've lived with
the aftermath of "love" all my life, Rose. The hurt, the disillu-
sion. The confused children.'

She reached out, laid her hand over his. 'I'm sorry.' Then,
as swiftly she removed it. 'I didn't think.'

He shrugged. 'I admit that my family is an extreme case,'
he said, but how could he ever put his trust in such here today,
gone tomorrow feelings? He'd much rather leave the matter to
wiser heads. 'Not that it was a problem in my grandfather's
case. His response to the summons home for the formal be-
trothal was a front page appearance on every newspaper with
his new bride, a glamorous British starlet who was, he swore,
the love of his life.'

'Ouch!' she said. Then, her face softening, 'But how romantic.'

'The romance was, without doubt, intense…' 'Like a
rocket', was the way his grandfather had described it. Hot,
fast, spectacular and gone as quickly as the coloured stars
faded from the sky. 'But the reason for the swift marriage was
rather more prosaic. She was pregnant.'

'Oh.'

'He knew his father would be angry, his chosen bride's
family outraged, but, universally popular and always a favour-

ite, he was confident that the birth of a son would bring him forgiveness.'

'I take it he was mistaken.'

'When a favoured son falls from grace it's a very long drop, Rose.'

'So his father disinherited him.'

'Not immediately. He was told his new bride was not welcome in Ramal Hamrah, but that when he was prepared to settle down he could come home. My grandfather wasn't a man to abandon his bride and return like a dog with his tail between his legs.'

'I like him for that.'

'Everyone likes him, Rose. That was part of the problem.'

'And you,' she said gently. 'You love him.'

'He is my *jaddi'l habeeb*,' he told her. 'My beloved grandfather. While my own father was following in his father's footsteps, *Jaddi* taught me to speak Arabic, the stories of my people. Their history.'

'And he gave it all up for love.'

'While his studious, dutiful younger brother soothed outraged sensibilities and rescued his father's tattered pride by marrying the girl chosen for the heir. Within a year he had a son with blood that could be traced back a thousand years and was visibly putting all this new found wealth to work for his father's people.'

'A new man for a new age.'

'Smarter than my grandfather, certainly. When his father had a stroke *Jaddi* raced home, but he was too late. The Emir had slipped into a coma and was beyond extending the hand of forgiveness. There was to be no feast for the prodigal.'

'Poor man.'

He glanced at her, uncertain who she was referring to.

'I wonder if there was a moment when he knew it was too late. The Emir. Wished he had acted differently? You think that you have all the time in world to say the words. When my father was killed I wanted to tell him…'

She broke off, unable to continue, and it was his turn to reach out for her hand, curl his fingers around it, hold tight as she remembered the family that had been torn from her.

After a moment she shook her head. 'I'm fine, Kal.'

Was she? He'd never lost anyone close to him. Rose had only her grandfather and he wished he could share his many grandparents, parents, siblings with her.

'What did you want to tell him, Rose?' he pressed, wanting to know about her. How she felt. What her life had been like.

'That I loved him,' she said. And for a moment her eyes were noticeably brighter. 'He used to take me for walks in the wood on Sunday mornings. Show me things. The names of trees, flowers, birds.'

'Your mother didn't go with you?'

She shook her head. 'She stayed at home and cooked lunch but we'd always look for something special to take home for her. A big shiny conker or a bird's feather or a pretty stone.'

The Marchioness slaving over a hot stove? An unlikely image, but Rose's mother hadn't been born to the purple. She'd qualified as a doctor despite the odds, had met her polo playing Marquess in A&E when he'd taken a tumble from his horse.

Such ordinary domesticity must evoke a genuine yearning in the breast of a young woman who'd been brought up by a starchy old aristocrat who probably didn't even know where the kitchen was.

'I should have told him every day how much I loved him. That's all there is in the end, Kal. Love. Nothing else matters.'

'It's tragic that you had so little time to get to know him. Be with him. With both of them,' he said. 'To lose a mother so young... What do you remember about her?'

She started, as if brought back from some distant place, then said, 'Her bravery, determination. How much she loved my father.'

She looked at her hand, clasped in his, reclaimed it.

'Go on with your story, Kal,' she urged.

He didn't want to talk about his family. He wanted to know more about her. His six-year-old memories of his mother were of stories, treats, hugs. Were Rose's most abiding memories really of her mother's bravery? Or was that the result of years of media brainwashing?

'What happened after your great-grandfather died?' she pressed.

There was definitely something wrong here, he could sense it, but Rose Napier was no more than a means to an end, he reminded himself. She was not his concern.

'When *Jaddi* learned that his father had named his younger brother as Emir his heart broke, not just with grief,' he told her, refocusing himself on what was important, 'but with guilt, too. For a while he was crazy.'

He stared at the plate in front of him. Somehow, he'd managed to clear it, although he hadn't tasted a thing.

'What happened?' she pressed. 'What did he do?'

'He refused to swear allegiance to his younger brother, raised disaffected tribes in the north, attacked the citadel. He thought that the people would rise to him, but he'd been away for a long time. While they'd once adored the dashing young sheikh, in his absence they had grown to admire and respect his brother.'

'Was anyone hurt?'

He shook his head. 'When it was obvious that he lacked popular support, his allies were quick to make their peace with the man holding the purse strings.'

'It's like something out of a Shakespearean tragedy,' she said.

'I suppose it is. But it was of his own making. Even then, if he'd been prepared to acknowledge his brother as ruler, publicly bow the knee, he would have been allowed to stay. Play his part. When he refused to humiliate himself in that way, his brother exiled him from the tribe, stripped him of his name, title, banished him. All he was left with was the financial settlement that his father had hoped would compensate him for being supplanted by his younger brother.'

'And your father? Was he included in this punishment?'

'Banishment was for *Jaddi* alone, but the rest followed. If a father does not bear the name of his tribe, the title owed to him by birth...'

'So you are al-Zaki.'

'A name without history,' he said. Without honour. 'My father and I are free to come and go, as is my sister. I have an office, an apartment in Rumaillah but, without a family, I remain invisible.' His letters returned unanswered. Barred from his place in the *majlis*. Forbidden any way of appealing for mercy for a dying man. Reduced to using this woman.

'What do you think will happen when Princess Sabirah comes here? Will she "see" you?' she asked.

'Don't worry about it,' he said, angry with himself, angry with the Emir, angry with her for making him feel guilty. 'Her Highness won't do anything to embarrass her distinguished guest.'

That was what Lucy was relying on, anyway. If she acknowledged him, he would beg her to intercede with the Emir for his grandfather. That was all that was left, he thought bitterly. A chance to plead with the woman who shared the Emir's pillow to show pity on a dying man.

Lydia felt the emptiness in Kal's words, the loss, an underlying anger too, but to say that she was sorry would be meaningless and so she said nothing—she'd already said far too much, come close to blowing the whole deal.

The silence drifted back, broken only by the clink of dishes when Yatimah appeared to clear the table, loading everything on to the tray.

Having come—in a moment of high emotion—perilously close to letting slip the truth about her own father's death, she took the chance to gather herself before turning to Yatimah to thank her for the meal.

'*La shokr ala wageb, sitti.* No thanks are due for duty.'

'Will you say that again?' Lydia begged, grabbing the

chance to move away from dangerous territory. Listening carefully and repeating it after her self-appointed teacher.

'I will bring coffee?'

'*Nam. Shukran.*'

When she'd gone, Kal said, 'You listen well, Rose.'

'I try to pick up a few words of the local language when I'm on holiday. Even if it's only hello and thank you.' The truth, and how good that felt, but before he could ask where she usually went on holiday, 'So, what time are we going fishing?'

'Maybe we should give that a miss today,' he said. 'Wait until you're really bored.'

She tried not to look too happy about that.

'You might have a long wait. I've got the most beautiful garden to explore, a swimming pool to lie beside and a stack of good books to read. In fact, as soon as we've had coffee I'll decide which to do first.'

'*Qahwa.* The Arabic for coffee is *qahwa.* You make the q sound in the back of your throat.'

'*Ga howa?*'

'Perfect.' Then, with one of those slow smiles that sent a dangerous finger of heat funnelling through her, 'Maybe we should add Arabic lessons to the schedule.'

Doing her best to ignore it, she said, 'You do know that I had planned to simply lie in the sun for a week?'

'You can listen, speak lying down, can't you?'

Lydia tried to block out the image of Kal, stretched out on a lounger beside her at the pool she'd glimpsed from the dining room, his skin glistening in the sun while he attempted to teach her the rudiments of a language he clearly loved.

Did he really believe that she would be able to concentrate?

'Lying in the sun resting,' she elaborated swiftly, all the emphasis on *resting.* 'You seem determined to keep me permanently occupied. Rushing around, doing stuff.'

'It won't be hard work, I promise you.'

His low honeyed voice promised her all kinds of things,

none of them arduous, and as he picked up her hand the heat intensified.

'We can begin with something simple.' And, never taking his eyes from her face, he touched his lips to the tip of her little finger. *'Wahid.'*

'Wahid?'

'One.'

'Ithnan.' His lips moved on to her ring finger, lingered while she attempted to hold her wits together and repeat the word.

'Ithnan. Two.'

'Thalatha.'

Something inside her was melting and it took her so long to respond that he began to nibble on the tip of her middle finger.

'Thalatha!'

'Arba'a.' And he drove home the message with four tiny kisses on the tip, the first joint, the second joint, the knuckle of her forefinger.

'Arba'a.' It was her bones that were the problem, she decided. Her bones were melting. That was why she couldn't move. Pull free. 'Four.'

'Khamsa.' He looked for a moment at her thumb, then took the length of it in his mouth before slowly pulling back to the tip. 'Five.'

He was right. This was a language lesson she was never going to forget. She mindlessly held out her other hand so that he could teach her the numbers six to ten, already anticipating the continuation of a lesson involving every part of her body.

He did not take it and, catching her breath as she came back to earth, she used it to sweep her hair behind her ear, managing a very creditable, *'Shukran,* Kal.'

Yatimah placed a tray containing a small brass coffee pot and tiny cups on the table beside her.

Feeling ridiculously light-headed as she realised that he must have seen her coming, that he had not rejected her but chosen discretion, she said, 'Truly, that was a huge improvement on Mrs Latimer's Year Six French class.'

'Mrs Latimer?' Lucy had been saying something about Rose not being allowed to go to school when he'd interrupted her. He wished now he'd been less impatient...

For a moment Lydia's mind froze.

'A t-tutor,' she stuttered as Kal continued to look at her, a frown creasing that wide forehead.

She longed to tell him everything. Tell him about her brave mother who'd lost her husband and her mobility in one tragic moment on an icy road. Tell him about school, how she'd left when she was sixteen because what was the point of staying on when she would never have left her mother to go away to university? Tell him everything...

She was rescued from his obvious suspicion by the beep of a text arriving on her mobile phone.

'Excuse me,' she said, retrieving it from her pocket. 'It might be...' She swallowed, unable to say the word *grand-father*, turned away to check it, assuming that it was simply a 'have fun' response from her mother to her own text.

But it wasn't from her mother. It was from Rose.

Vtl you b on frnt pge am!

Vital you be on the front page tomorrow morning...

Lydia swallowed. Had she been recognised? Clearly she had to convince someone that she really was in Bab el Sama.

She quickly keyed in *OK* and hit 'send', returning the phone to her pocket. Realised that Kal was watching her intently.

'Is there a problem?' he asked as Yatimah offered them each a cup, then filled them with a thin straw-coloured aromatic liquid that was nothing like any coffee she'd ever seen.

'Good heavens, no!' she said with a nervous laugh which, even to her own ears, rang about as true as a cracked bell.

Only him.

Only her guilt that she was lying to a man who made her feel things that needed total honesty. And she couldn't be ιonest. The text was a timely reminder just how deeply she was embedded in this pretence. She was doing this for Rose and ight now only she mattered...

They were four hours ahead of London, plenty of time to make the morning papers, but to accomplish that she had to get into the open in daylight. On her own. Wearing as little as possible.

She and Rose both knew that what the paparazzi were really hoping for was a picture of her in a private 'love nest' scenario with Rupert Devenish.

That was never going to happen, so in order to keep them focused, they'd planned a slow striptease to keep those lenses on her for the entire week.

First up would be a walk along the beach in shorts with a shirt open over a bathing suit.

After that she was going to discard the shirt to reveal a bathing suit top beneath it. Rare enough to excite interest, but nothing particularly sensational—it was a very demure bathing suit. Finally she'd strip down to the swimsuit. That should be enough to keep the photographers on their toes, but there was a bikini in reserve in case of unforeseen emergencies.

Rose's text suggested they were in the 'unforeseen emergency' category. What she didn't, couldn't know was that her good friend Lucy al-Khatib had provided her with a 'protector'. Kal was relaxed about letting her wander, unseen by the outside world, in the shelter of the gardens, but she very much doubted that he'd sit back and let her take a walk along the beach without her minder.

While it was true that his presence would absolutely guarantee a front page spot, she also recognised that the presence of some unknown man in close attendance would cause more problems than it solved.

She was going to have to evade her watchdog and get down to the beach and she had less than an hour in which to manage it.

Kal watched Rose sip gingerly at the scalding coffee. Clearly, whatever had been in the text had not been good news.

The colour had drained from her face and a man didn't have to be fluent in body language to see that she was positively twitching to get away.

Which begged the question, why didn't she just say, *Great lunch, see you later...* and walk away? Or tell him that something had come up that she had to deal with?

Why was she sitting there like a cat on hot bricks, doing her best to pretend that nothing was wrong?

A gentleman would make it easy for her. Make an excuse himself and leave her to get on with whatever it was she wanted to do.

A man who'd been charged with her safety, in the face of some unspecified threat, would be rather less obliging. Lucy might have disparaged the Duke's concerns, but she hadn't dismissed them entirely.

She hadn't elaborated on them, either. Could it be that she was more worried about what Rose might do than what some imaginary assailant had in mind?

Maybe he should give her a call right now. Except that would leave Rose on her own, which didn't seem like a great idea.

'This is desert coffee,' he said conversationally. 'The beans are not ground but boiled whole with cardamom seeds. For the digestion.'

'Really? It's different. Very good,' she said, although he doubted she had even tasted it.

As she put the cup down, clearly eager to be away, he said, 'Traditionally, politeness requires that you drink two cups.'

'Two?'

She scarcely managed to hide her dismay and his concern deepened. What on earth had been in that text?

'They're very small. If you hold out the cup, like this,' he said, holding out his own cup, 'Yatimah will refill it for you.'

Obediently she held out the cup. Drank it as quickly as she could without scalding her mouth, handed the cup back to the girl.

And it was refilled a third time.

'She'll refill it as often as you hold it out like that,' he explained. 'When you've had enough you have to shake the cup from side to side to indicate that you have had enough.'

'Oh. Right.' She swallowed it down, shook the cup the way he told her, thanked Yatimah who, at a look from him, quickly disappeared. Rose, looking as if she wanted to bolt after her, said, 'If you'll excuse me, Kal, I'll go and get my book. Find somewhere quiet to read. You don't have to stand guard over me while I do that, do you?'

'Not if you stay within the garden,' he said, rising to his feet, easing back her chair.

'What about the beach?' she asked, so casually that he knew that was where she would be heading the minute he took his eyes off her. 'That's private, isn't it?'

'It's private in that no one will come ashore and have a picnic. Local people respect the privacy of the Emir and his guests, but the creek is busy.' He glanced across the water. 'There are plenty of boats where a photographer hoping to catch a candid shot of you could hide out.' He turned back to her. 'Lucy said you found the intrusion stressful but if you want to risk a walk along the shore, I'll be happy to accompany you.'

'Lady Rose Napier plus unknown man on a beach? Now, that really would make their day.' Her laughter lacked any real suggestion of amusement. 'I'll stick to the garden, thanks.' Then, 'Why don't you take yourself off on that fishing trip you're so keen on? Give me a break from the maggots.'

Give her a break? Where on earth had the secluded Lady Rose picked up these expressions?

'The maggots will be disappointed,' he said, coming up with a smile. 'I'll see you at dinner?'

'Of course.'

Her relief was palpable at the prospect of an entire afternoon free of him. He would have been offended but, from the way she'd responded to his kisses, he knew it wasn't personal.

'Although I'd better put in a few laps at the pool, too, or at this rate none of the clothes I brought with me will fit.'

'There's an upside to everything,' he replied.

His reward was a hot blush before she lifted her hand in a small, oddly awkward, see-you-later gesture and walked quickly towards the cottage.

Kal, getting the message loud and clear, didn't move until she was out of sight.

CHAPTER NINE

LYDIA's luggage had been unpacked and put away and she quickly hunted through drawers, doing her best not to linger and drool over silk, cashmere, finest linen, as she searched for a swimsuit.

She had refused to accept a penny from Rose for this assignment. This was a labour of love, gratitude, respect and she'd insisted on taking a week of her paid holiday entitlement. But Rose had found a way to reward her anyway. She'd raided her wardrobe for more clothes than she could possibly wear in a week at the beach. Clothes she had never worn. Insisting that Lydia keep them.

The half a dozen swimsuits that she'd packed, each bearing the name of a world famous designer, were uniformly gorgeous. Each, inevitably, had the 'pink rose' theme and Lydia chose a striking black one-piece costume with a single long-stemmed rose embroidered across the front from the right hip, with stem and leaves curling diagonally across the stomach, so that the bud bloomed above her heart.

It was clearly a one-off that had been made especially for her and, with luck, the delighted designer would call the gossip pages and claim whatever PR was going. Which would help to establish that it could be no one but Rose on the Bab el Sama beach.

It fitted her like a glove, holding, lifting in all the right places. She didn't waste any time admiring her reflection,

however, but threw the kaftan over it, ran a brush through her
hair, freshened her lipstick and grabbed a book.

All she had to do now was find her way down to the beach
unobserved and, avoiding the exit through the garden room to
the terrace where Kal might still be lingering, she slipped out
through the dining room.

Kal stood in the dark shadows at the top of a rocky outcrop,
sweeping the water with a pair of powerful glasses, hoping to
pick up anything out of place. Anyone who didn't have business
on the water.

It was as peaceful a scene as a bodyguard could hope for.
Fishermen, traders, local people pottering on their boats.

He glanced at his watch, wondering how much longer Rose
would be. Because she'd come. He'd put money on it. But
why?

He took out his BlackBerry and put Rose's name into the
search engine. There was a picture of her leaving the lunch yesterday, '…radiant…' as she left for a week in Bab el Sama.
Raising the question of whether she'd be alone.

There were other photographs. One of her with Rupert
Devenish a couple of weeks earlier. Not looking radiant.

Maybe she had just been tired. Or perhaps the hollows in
her cheeks, around her eyes were the result of a cold or a
headache. Perhaps the camera angle was unflattering. Whatever
it was, she had none of the glow that had reached out, grabbed
him by the throat and refused to let go.

In fact she looked like a pale imitation of his Rose. He continued his search for answers until the soft slap of leather
thongs against the stone steps warned him that she was on her
way. He could have told her that to be silent she would need
to remove her shoes. But then she hadn't expected him to be
there.

She paused in a deep patch of shade at the bottom of the
steps that led from the garden, a book in one hand, presumably

an alibi in case he hadn't done as she'd suggested and conveniently removed himself from the scene, but instead taken his promise to Lucy seriously enough to stick around and keep an eye on her.

He kept very still as she looked around, checking that the beach was empty. Even if she had looked up, he was well hidden from the casual glance, but she was only concerned that the beach was empty and, having made certain the coast was clear, she put the book on the step. Then she took the mobile phone from her pocket and placed it on top.

No...

The word stilled on his lips as she reached back and pulled the kaftan over her head to reveal a simple one-piece black swimsuit that displayed every curve, every line of her body to perfection. A slender neck, circled with a fine gold chain on which hung a rosebud pendant. Wide, elegant shoulders, an inviting cleavage that hadn't appeared on the photograph of her in the evening gown. A proper waist, gently flared hips and then those endless legs, perfect ankles, long slender feet.

For a moment she stood there, as if summoning up the courage to carry on.

Don't...

The thought of his Rose appearing on the front page of tomorrow's papers in a swimsuit, her body being leered at by millions of men, was utterly abhorrent to him and he knew that the rush of protectiveness he felt had nothing whatever to do with the charge that Lucy had laid on him.

He'd spent much of his life on beaches, around swimming pools with women who would have raised their sophisticated eyebrows at such a puritan reaction and he knew his response was the very worst kind of double standard.

By modern standards, the costume she was wearing was modest.

Before he could move, do anything, she draped the kaftan over a low branch and she stepped into the sun. Shoulders

back, head high, she walked towards the water, where she
paused to scan the creek.

The light breeze caught her hair, lifting tiny strands that
caught the light, lending her an ethereal quality.

Dear God, she was beautiful.

As cool and mysterious as a princess in some *Arabian
Nights* story, escaped from some desperate danger and washed
up on an unknown shore, waiting for Sinbad to rescue her,
restore her to her prince.

'That's enough,' he whispered. 'Turn back now. Come
back to me.'

She glanced round, looking up, as if she'd heard him, but it
was a bird quartering the air that had caught her attention and,
having watched it for a moment, she turned, then took a step…

'No!'

…bent to pick up something from the sand. It was a piece
of sand-polished glass and, as she held it up to the light, he
caught an echo of the flash out on the creek.

He lifted the glasses, scanned the water and this time found
the telltale glint as the sunlight dancing on the water was reflected off a lens hidden beneath a tarpaulin on an anonymous-
looking motor launch. It was anchored amongst half a dozen
or so boats on the far side of the creek, its name obscured, deliberately, he had no doubt, and he had to fight the urge to race
after Rose, drag her back.

But the one thing they were in complete agreement about
was that she must not be photographed with him.

It would provoke a feeding frenzy among the press and it
wouldn't take them five minutes to uncover his identity. His entire
history would be rehashed in the press, along with the playboy
lifestyle of both his grandfather and father, to fuel innuendo-laden
speculation about why he was in Bab el Sama with Rose.

And no one was going to believe that the millionaire CEO
of an international air freight business had accompanied Lady
Rose Napier to Bab el Sama as her bodyguard. The million-

...ire grandson of an exiled sheikh, son of an international ...layboy, he hadn't been exactly short of media coverage ...imself before he'd stopped the drift. Found a purpose in life.

The fallout from that would cause a lot more embarrassment ...han even the most revealing photograph.

Worse, her grandfather, the Duke, would be apoplectic and ...blame Lucy for embroiling her in such a mess. Not to mention ...the fact that the Emir would be so angry that Kalil could kiss ...goodbye forever to any chance of *Jaddi*'s banishment being lifted so that he could die in peace at Umm al Sama.

His sole remit was to protect Lady Rose from danger. Shooting her with a camera didn't count, especially when she was going out of her way to make it easy for whoever was laid up in that boat.

He watched her as, apparently oblivious to scrutiny from both sea and shore, she wandered along the shoreline, stopping now and then to pick up a shell or a pebble. Lifting a hand to push back her hair. It was a classic image, one he knew that picture editors around the world would lap up, putting their own spin on it in a dozen headlines, most of them including the word *alone*.

So who had sent the message that had her scurrying to expose herself to the world's press?

He looked down at the shady step where she'd left her phone.

Lydia stood for a moment at the edge of the water, lifting her face to the sun, the gorgeous feeling of wet sand seeping between her toes taking her back to childhood holidays when her father had been alive, memories of her mother laughing as the waves caught her.

She remembered one holiday when she'd collected a whole bucket full of shells. By the end of their stay, they had smelled so bad that her father had refused to put them in the car. To stop her tears at the loss of her treasures, her mother had washed the most special one, given her a heart-shaped box to keep it in.

She still had her memory box. It contained a picture of

her father, laughing as she splashed him with a hosepipe. Her mother with the world famous couturier she'd worked for before the accident. The newspaper picture of her in the very first 'Lady Rose' outfit her mother had made when she was fifteen.

There had been a rush of additions in that brief spell when she'd thought she was in love. All but one of those had been tossed away with many more tears than the shells when she'd realised the truth. She'd kept just one thing, a theatre programme, because all memories were important. Even the bad ones. If you didn't remember, you didn't learn…

After that the memories had nearly all involved her lookalike gigs. Her life as someone else.

Looking around, she saw the edge of an oyster shell sticking out of sand washed clean by the receding tide.

She bent to ease it out, rinsed it off in the water, turned it over to reveal the pink and blue iridescence of mother-of-pearl. A keepsake to remind her of this moment, this beach, Kal al-Zaki kissing her fingers as he taught her Arabic numbers. A memory to bring out when she was old and all this would seem like a dream that had happened to someone else.

The last one she'd ever put in that old box, she vowed. She was never going to do this again, be Rose. It was time to start living her own life, making her own memories. No more pretence.

She stood for a moment, holding the shell, uncertain which way to go. Then, choosing to have the wind in her face, she turned right, towards the sea, wishing that Kal was walking with her to point out the landmarks, tell her the story behind a crumbling tower on the highest point on the far bank. To hold her hand as she turned through the curve that had taken Kal out of sight that morning.

Until now Kal had been able to dismiss the turmoil induced by his charge as nothing more than the natural response of a healthy male for a woman who had hit all the right buttons.

He was thirty-three, had been surrounded by beautiful women all his life and was familiar with desire in all its guises, but as he'd got older, become more certain what he wanted, he'd found it easy to stay uninvolved.

That he'd been knocked so unexpectedly sideways by Lady Rose Napier, he'd been convinced, no more than the heightened allure of the unobtainable.

All that went out of the window in the moment she stepped out of his sight.

Lydia continued for as long as she dared, scanning the creek, hoping for some sign that there was someone out there.

Then, because she doubted it would be long before someone realised that she wasn't where she was meant to be and start looking for her, she turned back, relieved to be picking her way across the soft sand to the shade, the anonymity of the giant rock formation near the foot of the steps.

She'd half expected to find Yatimah standing guard over her book, her phone, her expression disapproving, but her escapade had gone unobserved. Relieved, she pushed her feet into the leather thong sandals, then turned to carefully lift the kaftan from the branch.

It wasn't there and she looked down to see if it had fallen.

Took a step into the shadows behind the rocks, assuming that it had been caught by a gust of wind and blown there.

And another.

Without warning, she was seized from behind around the waist, lifted clear of the sand, her body held tight against the hard frame of a man.

As she struggled to get free, she pounded at the arm holding her, using the edge of the shell as a weapon, opened her mouth to scream.

A hand cut off the sound.

'Looking for something, Lady Rose?'

She stilled. Kal…

She'd known it even before he'd spoken. Knew that woody scent. Would always know it…

As soon as she stopped struggling he dropped his hand and, knowing he was going to be mad at her, she got in first with, 'I thought you were going fishing.'

'And I thought you were going to curl up by the pool with a good book.'

He set her down and, with the utmost reluctance, she turned to face him.

'I am.' Head up. And Lady Rose, the Duke's granddaughter at her most aristocratic, she added, 'I decided to take a detour.'

'And give one of your paparazzi army tomorrow's front page picture?'

She instinctively glanced at the phone lying defenceless on top of her book. 'Have you been reading my messages?' she demanded.

'No need. You've just told me everything I need to know.'

'No…'

'What is it, Rose?' he asked. 'Are you a publicity junkie? Can't you bear to see an entire week go by without your picture on the front page?'

She opened her mouth to protest. Closed it again.

His anger was suppressed, but there was no doubting how he felt at being deceived, made a fool of, and who could blame him? Except, of course, he hadn't. He'd been ahead of her every step of the way. Instead, she shook her head, held up her hands.

'You've got me, Kal. Bang to rights.' She took a step back. 'Can I have my dress back now?'

As he reached up, lifted the kaftan down from the place he'd hidden it, she saw the blood oozing from his arm where she'd slashed at him with the shell she was still clutching.

She dropped it as if it burned, reached out to him, drew back without touching him. She'd lied to him and he knew it.

'I hurt you,' she said helplessly.

He glanced at the wound she'd made, shrugged. 'Nothing that I didn't ask for.'

'Maybe, but it still needs cleaning.' Ignoring the dress he was holding out to her, she began to run up the steps. 'Sea shells have all kinds of horrible things in them,' she said. 'You can get septicaemia.'

'Is that right?'

Realising that he hadn't followed her, she stopped, looked back. 'Truly.' Then, realising that perhaps that wasn't the best choice of word, 'I've been on a first aid course.' She offered her hand but, when he didn't take it, said, 'Please, Kal.'

Relenting, he slung the dress over his shoulder, stooped to pick up the book and phone she'd abandoned in her rush to heal, adding the number of his mobile phone to her contact list. Adding hers to his as he followed her up to the house, the bedroom where he'd left her sleeping a few hours earlier, into the huge, luxurious bathroom beyond.

'I've put my number in your phone,' he said, putting them on a table. 'In case you should ever need it.'

She rolled her eyes. 'Sit there!'

He obediently settled himself on a wide upholstered bench while she took a small first aid box from a large cupboard that was filled with the cosmetics and toiletries she'd brought with her and searched through it for sachets containing antiseptic wipes.

'Why did you do it?' He addressed the top of her head as she bent over him, cleaning up the scratches she'd made.

'This is nothing,' she said. 'I did a self-defence course and you're really lucky I wasn't wearing high heels.'

'I wasn't referring to your attempt to chop my arm off. Why did you strip off for that photographer?'

'I didn't strip off!' she declared, so flustered by the accusation that for a moment she forgot what she was doing. Then, getting a grip, 'I took a walk on the beach in a swimsuit. A very modest swimsuit.'

Modest by today's standards, maybe, but this close, clinging

like a second skin, revealing perhaps more than she realised
as she bent over him—suggesting more—the effect was far
more enticing than an entire beach filled with topless lovelies.

She looked up. 'Did you say "photographer"?'

'I did.'

She straightened abruptly as she saw exactly where his eyes
were focused.

'You saw him?'

'He was in a launch out on the creek and well camouflaged
from above. He forgot about the sun reflecting off the water.'

The tension went out of her shoulders, her neck. Relief, he
thought. That was sheer relief.

'So why did you do it?' he persisted.

'I thought we'd established that,' she said, concentrating
once more on his arm.

The speed with which she'd grabbed at the insulting explanation he'd offered suggested desperation to hide the real
reason for her exhibitionism. While he had his own suspicions,
he was beginning to wish he'd overcome his squeamishness
about plundering her phone for the answer.

'Maybe you'd better run it by me again.'

Apparently satisfied with the clean up job on his arm, or
maybe just wanting to put a little distance between them, she
gathered up the used wipes, dropped them in a bin.

'It's a game, Kal,' she said, busying herself, filling a marble
basin with warm water. Looking anywhere but at him. 'We
need each other. Celebrities need headlines, the media have an
insatiable appetite for stories. The trick is to give them what
they want and then hope they'll leave you alone.'

She plunged her hands in the water, then looked around for
soap.

He took a piece from a crystal bowl but did not hand it to
her. Instead, he put his arms around her, trapping her as he
leaned into her back, his chin against her hair as he dipped his
hands into the water and began to soap her fingers.

'Kal!' she protested, but feebly. They both knew she wasn't going anywhere until she'd told him what was going on.

'What, exactly, do they want from you?' he asked.

'Right now?' The words came out as a squeak and he waited while she took a breath. 'Right now,' she repeated, 'they'd give their eye teeth for a picture of me here, in flagrante with Rupert Devenish.' She tried a laugh, attempting to ignore the way his thumb was circling her palm. The way she was relaxing against him. 'He's—'

'I read the newspapers,' he said, not wanting to hear the words on her lips. Or that it was Lucy who'd filled him in on the marriage mania in the gossip columns. 'But that isn't going to happen, is it?'

Unless he'd got it totally wrong and the text had been from Devenish announcing his imminent arrival, urging Rose to convince the paparazzi that she was alone before he joined her.

In which case her eager response to him, the way she had softened in the circle of his arms, surrendered her hands for him to do with what he would, was going to take a little—make that a lot of—explaining.

'It's not going to happen,' she confirmed. 'I'm afraid they're going to have to make do with the clichéd Lady Rose, alone on a beach, how sad, picture.'

And it was his turn to feel the tension slide away from his shoulders.

But only halfway.

According to Lucy, Rose was falling apart because of the constant intrusion into her life. Ten years without being able to lift a finger unobserved, she'd said.

He wasn't getting that impression from Rose. Far from it. She seemed totally relaxed about what could only be construed as a unwarranted intrusion into her private life.

'And if they aren't?' he asked.

A tiny tremor rippled through her and he knew that there was a lot more to this than she was telling him.

'Trust me, Rose,' he said. 'The picture will be a sensation. He reached for a towel, taking her hands, drying them one finger at a time. Then, because he was still angry with her, 'And if I'm wrong you can always go for the topless option tomorrow.'

'Tomorrow will be too late…'

She caught herself, no doubt realising that she should have objected to the 'topless', not the 'tomorrow'. But he had the answer to at least one of his questions.

For some reason she wanted a picture of herself on the front page and for some reason it had to be tomorrow. And he went straight back to that mysterious threat.

Was this what it was all about? Give me a photograph or… Or what?

What on earth could anyone have over the universally loved and admired 'people's angel'?

Except, of course, that the woman in his arms was not Rose Napier.

On some subconscious level he'd known that from the moment she'd walked into the VIP lounge at the airport. Right from the beginning, he'd sensed the split personality, the separation between the woman playing a role—and occasionally slipping—and the woman who shone through the disguise, lighting him up not just like a rocket, but the whole damn fourth of July scenario. Whoosh, bang, the sky filled with coloured stars.

He didn't trust it, knew it was a temporary aberration, nothing but chemistry, but he finally understood why his grandfather had lost his head, lost his country over a woman.

He was here on a one-off last-chance mission and from the moment she'd appeared on the scene this woman had attacked all his systems like a virus taking over a computer memory, supplanting herself in place of everything that was vital, important, real.

Lucy had obviously told him a pack of lies—he was only here to inveigle his way into a meeting with Princess Sabirah, so why would he be bothered with something as important as the truth?

Presumably the real Rose was holed up in some private love nest with Rupert while this woman, this lovely woman who was superficially so like her, was nothing but a plant to keep the press focused on Bab el Sama.

So what had gone wrong? Had someone found out? Threatened to expose the switch? Directing his own personal photo shoot by text?

In which case he had no doubt that the topless scenario would be the next demand. Because, even if she was a fake, that picture would be worth millions to the photographer who delivered it to a picture agency.

'You've got nothing to worry about,' he said, tossing the towel aside, not sure who he was most angry with, Lucy or this woman, whoever she was, for putting at risk his own mission.

No, that was wrong. Lucy had used the situation to give him a chance. This woman had lit him up, responding to his kisses as if he was the last man on earth. Lies, lies, lies…

'I guarantee you that there won't be a picture editor in London who won't grab that picture of you for their front page tomorrow.'

Her all too obvious relief flipped something in his brain and he stroked the pad of his thumb over the exquisite rose that curved invitingly across her breast in an insultingly intimate gesture, opened his mouth over her all too obvious response as the bud beneath the costume leapt to his touch.

Her throat moved as she swallowed, doing her best to ignore the intimacy of his touch, but the tiny shiver that rippled through her betrayed pleasure, desire, need and her response was not to pull away but buckle against him.

Too late, he discovered that he was the one caught in a lie, because it didn't matter who she was, he desired her as he had never desired any other woman. Not just with his body, but with his heart, his soul and simply holding her was not enough.

Nothing could disguise from her how very much it wasn't enough but, as the wildfire of desire swept through him, he was not alone. Her seeking lips found his neck, trailed moist kisses across his chin, touched his lips, her need as desperate as his.

'Whoever you are,' he murmured, looking down at her, 'you can trust me on that…'

For a moment she looked at him, her mouth soft, her lids heavy with desire and the slow-burning fuse, lit in the moment their eyes had first met, of that unfinished kiss, lay between them.

The air was heavy with the desire of two people for whom the need to touch, to explore, to be one, blotted out memory, bypassed hard-learned lessons, destroyed reason.

Lydia heard him, understood what he was saying, but wrapped in the powerful arms of a man she desired beyond sense, this was not a time for questions, answers. Time was suspended. There was no past, no future. This was for now. Only the senses survived—scent, taste, touch—and she reached out and with her fingertips traced the perfection of Kal's profile.

His wide forehead, the high-bridged nose, lingering to trace the outline of those beautifully carved lips.

The thin clothing pressed between them did nothing to disguise the urgent response of his body and she was seized by a surge of power, of certainty that this was her moment and, leaning into him so that her lips touched his, she whispered, 'Please…'

As her fingers, her lips touched his, took possession of his mouth, Kalil al-Zaki, a man known for his ice-cold self-control, consigned his reputation to oblivion.

His arms were already about her and for a moment he allowed himself to be swept away. To feel instead of think.

Drink deep of the honeyed sweetness of a woman who was clever, funny, heartbreakingly lovely. Everything a man could ever want or desire.

Forget, just for a while, who he was. Why he was here.

Her mouth was like silk, her body eager, desperate even, but it wasn't enough and, lost to all sense as he breathed in the scent of her skin, the hollows of her neck, her shoulders, he slowly peeled away the swimsuit to taste the true rosebuds it concealed.

Her response was eager, as urgent as his own, and yet, even as he offered him everything, he could not let go, forget the lies...

How she'd played the virgin, acted the seductress. Was this just another lie to buy his silence?

She whimpered into his mouth as he broke free, determined to regain control of his senses, yet unable to let go as she melted against him.

'Who are you?' he demanded helplessly. 'Why are you here?' When she didn't answer he leaned back, needing to look her in the face, wanting her to see his. But her eyes were closed, as if by not seeing, she would be deaf to his words. 'What do you want from me?'

'Nothing!' Then, more gently, 'I'm sorry.' And, without looking at him, she slowly disentangled herself and, shivering, clutched her costume to her and said, 'You can g-go fishing now, Kal. I promise I'll g-go and sit by the pool like the well behaved young woman I'm supposed to be.'

Torn between wanting her to behave and wanting her to be very, very bad indeed, he reassembled the shattered pieces of his cast-iron self-control, picked up his shirt and, taking her hands, fed them into the sleeves, buttoning it around her as if she were a child.

'I'm going nowhere until you tell me the truth,' he said. Then, with a muttered oath, 'You're shivering.' She couldn't be cold... 'What can I get you?'

'A proper cup of tea?' She sniffed and he lifted her chin, wiped a tear from beneath her eye.

Shivering, tears... He wanted to shake her, hold her, yell at her, make love to her...

'Tea?' he said, trying to get a grip.

'Made in a mug with a tea bag, milk from a cow and two heaped spoons of sugar.' She managed a rueful smile. 'Stirred, not shaken.'

'I'm glad your sense of humour survived intact,' he said.

'My sense of humour and everything else.' She lifted her

shoulders in a simple up and down shrug. 'I've only come tha▮ close to losing my virginity once before, Kal. I'm beginning to think I'm destined to be an old maid and the really bad new▮ is that I'm allergic to cats.'

Better make that two cups of hot, sweet tea, he thought picking up the phone.

CHAPTER TEN

'WHO are you?'

Lydia, her hands around the mug of tea he'd rustled up for her, was sitting in the shuttered balcony of her room, bars of sunlight slanting through into a very private space and shimmering off Kal's naked shoulders.

'What are you?'

'Lydia. Lydia Young. I've been a professional lookalike pretty much from the moment that Lady Rose made her first appearance.'

'Lydia.' He repeated her name carefully, as if memorising it. 'How old were you?'

'Fifteen. I'm a few months younger than Rose.' She sipped at the hot tea, shuddering at the sweetness. 'How did you know?' Then, because it was somehow more important, 'When did you know?'

'I think that on some level I always knew you weren't Rose.' He glanced at her. 'I sensed a dual personality. Two people in the same body. And you have an unusual turn of phrase for a young woman with your supposedly sheltered upbringing. Then there was the Marchioness slaving over Sunday lunch. And Mrs Latimer.'

'Year Six French.' She took another sip of tea. 'I knew you'd picked up on that. I hoped I'd covered it.'

'You might have got away with it but once that text arrived

you were in bits. It wasn't difficult to work out that you'd be heading for the beach as soon as you'd got rid of me so, while I waited for you to show up, I took a look at the Internet, hoping to pick up some clue about what the hell was going on.'

'What was the clincher?' she asked. Not a Lady Rose word, but she wasn't pretending any more.

'You made the front page in that cute little hat you were wearing. The caption suggested that after recent concerns about your health you appeared to be full of life. Positively glowing, in fact. Fortunately for you, they put it down to true love.'

She groaned.

'I should have done more with my make-up, but we were sure the veil would be enough. And it was all going so well that I might just have got a bit lippy with the photographers. What an idiot!'

'Calm down. There was nothing in the stories to suggest that you were a fake,' he assured her. 'Just a recent photograph of Rose with Rupert and some salacious speculation about what you'd be doing here.'

'But if you had no trouble spotting the difference—'

'Only because I've become intimately acquainted with your face, your figure,' he said. 'I don't pay a lot of attention to celebrity photographs, but the "people's angel" is hard to miss and I expected someone less vivid. Not quite so…' He seemed lost for an appropriate adjective.

'Lippy?' she offered helpfully.

'I was going to say lively,' he said, his eyes apparently riveted to her mouth. 'But lippy will do. One look at the real thing and I knew you were someone else.' Then, turning abruptly, he said, 'So what's going on? Where is Rose Napier? With Rupert Devenish?'

'Good grief, I hope not.'

'Strike two for Rupert. Lucy isn't a fan either. I take it you've met him?'

'I've seen him with her. He's an old style aristocrat. Her grandfather,' she explained, 'but thirty years younger.'

'Controlling.'

She thought about it for a moment, then nodded. 'Rose and I met by chance one day. I'd been booked for a lookalike gig, a product launch at a swanky hotel. I had no idea Rose was going to be a guest at a lunch there or I'd have turned it down, but as I was leaving we came face to face. It could have been my worst nightmare but she was so sweet. She really is everything they say she is, you know.'

'That's another reason I saw through you.' He reached out, wiped the pad of his thumb across her mouth. 'You're no angel, Lydia Young.'

She took another quick sip of her tea.

'How is it?'

'Just what the doctor ordered. Too hot, too sweet. Perfect, in fact.'

'I'll remember the formula.'

She looked at him. Remember? There was a future?

Realising just how stupid that was, she turned away. Just more shocks, she decided, and concentrated on getting through her story.

'Rose spent a little too long chatting with me for Rupert's liking and when he summoned her to heel she asked me how much I charged. In case she ever wanted an evening off.'

'How much do you charge?' he asked pointedly.

'This one is on the house, Kal. I owe Rose. My father was killed in a car accident when I was ten years old. My mother was badly injured—'

'Your brave, determined mother.'

'She lost the man she loved, the use of her legs, her career in the blink of an eye, Kal.'

'I'm sorry.'

She shook her head. It was a long time since she'd cried for the loss and when he reached out as if to take her hand, offer comfort, she moved it out of reach. Right now, comfort would undo her completely and she was in enough trouble without that.

'Is this what you do? I mean, is it a full-time job?'

'Hardly. Two or three gigs a month at the most. The day job is on the checkout at a supermarket. The manager is very good about me swapping shifts.' She was going to tell him that he wanted her to take a management course. As if that would make any difference... 'The money I earn as Rose's lookalike has made a real difference to my mother's life.'

The electric wheelchair. The hand-operated sewing machine. The car she'd saved up for. And the endless driving lessons before she'd eventually passed her test.

'So, like Rose, you have no other family?'

She shook her head.

'And, like her, no lover? You are a beautiful, vivid woman, Lydia. I find that hard to believe.'

'Yes, well, I live a rather peculiar life. My day job is in a supermarket, where staff and customers alike call me Rose despite the fact that I wear a badge with my real name on it. Where most of them can't quite decide whether I'm fish or fowl. The rest of the time I'm pretending to be someone else.'

'And taking care of your mother. I imagine that takes a chunk out of your time, too. Who is with her while you're here?'

'A friend stays with her sometimes so that I can take a holiday. And I'm not totally pathetic. I do get asked out. Of course I do. But I'm never sure exactly who they think they're with.'

'Someone must have got through. If we... If I... If that was the second time.'

She nodded. 'He said he was a law student. He always came to my checkout at the supermarket. Chatted. Brought me tiny gifts. Wooed me with sweet words and posies, flattery and patience. Endless patience. It was weeks before he asked me out.'

Months before he'd suggested more than a kiss. So long that she'd been burning up with frustration. Ready to go off like a fire-cracker.

'It was the patience that did it,' she said. 'The understanding.

How many men are prepared to put up with the missed dates, always coming second to my mother, the job, the gigs? To wait?'

'A man will wait for what is precious,' Kal said.

'And who could resist that?' Not her. She'd fallen like a ton of bricks. 'It was that flash, bang, wallop love thing that you so distrust, Kal. In this case with good reason because when I say precious, I do mean precious. My worth, it seems, was above rubies.'

She could have made a lot of money selling the story to the newspapers but she'd never told anyone what had happened. Not her mother. Not her friends. Not even the agency that employed her. But, sitting here in this quiet space above a beautiful garden carved out of the desert, nothing but the truth would do. She had lied to Kal, hidden who she was, and if she was to win his trust now, win him over so that she could fulfil her promise to Rose, she had to strip herself bare, tell him everything.

'When he asked me to go away for the weekend I felt like the sun was shining just for me. He made it so special, booked the honeymoon suite in a gorgeous hotel in the Cotswolds. I suppose I should have wondered how a student could afford it, but I was in love. Not thinking at all.'

'So what went wrong?'

'Nothing, fortunately. The "Lady Rose" effect saved me.'

He frowned. Well, why wouldn't he? Unless you'd lived it, how would anyone know?

'An elderly chambermaid—a woman who'd seen just about everything in a long career making beds—thought I was Rose and she waylaid me in the corridor to warn me, told me where to find the hidden cameras.'

She swallowed. Even now the memory of it chilled her.

'When I confronted my "student" he confessed that he was an actor who'd been hired to seduce me by a photographer who intended to make a fortune selling pictures of "Lady Rose" losing her virginity with some good-looking stud. Someone who worked in the hotel was in on it, of course. He even offered me a cut of the proceeds if I'd go ahead with it since, as he so eloquently put it, "I was gagging for it anyway". I declined and since then...' she shrugged '...let's say I've been cautious.'

'And yet you still believe in love?'

'I've seen it, Kal. My parents were in love. They lit up around each other and my mother still has a dreamy look whenever she talks about my dad. I won't settle for less than that.' She looked at him. 'I hope that Rose won't either. That this week away from everyone, being anonymous, will help her decide. Will you let her have that?'

'She's safe?' Kal asked, reserving judgement.

'She's been wrapped in cotton wool all her life. I've loaned her my car and right now she's as safe as any anonymous woman taking a few days to do something as simple as shopping without ending up like the Pied Piper of Hamelin, or appearing on the front page of next day's newspaper eating a hot dog.'

'So what was the panic this morning?'

'I think someone must have said something that panicked her. She's not as used to people commenting on the fact that she looks like Lady Rose as I am.' She used her free hand to make little quotes, put on a quavery voice. '"Has anyone ever told you you look a bit like Lady Rose, dear?"'

Kal smiled, but wondered what it must be like to always be told you look like someone else. Whether she sometimes longed for someone to say that Lady Rose looked like her.

'I'll bet that gets old. How do you cope?'

'It depends. If some old biddy whispers it to me in the supermarket, I whisper back that I really am Lady Rose and I'm doing undercover research into working conditions. Warn her not to tell a soul, that she's spotted me. Then wait to see how long it takes before she points me out to someone.'

'That's really bad.'

'You said it, Kal. I'm no angel.'

And for a moment he thought only about the touch of her

ips beneath his fingers, the taste of them beneath his mouth. Then forced himself to remember that she had deceived him. Put his own mission in jeopardy. If the Emir, the Princess ever discovered the truth…

'Sometimes I do a flustered "good heavens, do you really think so, no one has ever said that before" routine,' she said, distracting him with the whole surprised expression, fluttery hand to chest routine.

'I like that one,' he said, which brought that light-up-the-day smile bubbling to her face.

'My favourite is the one where I put on a slightly puzzled smile…' she did a perfect version of the world famous luminous smile that was about a hundred watts less bright than her natural one '…and say "Only a bit?" and wait for the penny to drop.'

'You're a bit of a clown on the quiet, aren't you, Lydia Young?'

'Quiet?' she repeated.

He'd caught glimpses of this lively woman beneath the Rose mantle, but in full flood she was irresistible. Now that she'd stepped out of the shadows, was wholly herself, he knew that it was the lippy woman desperate to break out of the restraints of being Lady Rose that he desired, liked more and more. Her laughter lit him up, her smile warmed him. Even when he was furious with her he wanted to kiss her, wrap her up in his arms and keep her safe, love her…

'Maybe that wasn't the most appropriate word,' he said quickly. 'Did you never consider a career as an actress?'

'No.'

One minute they were laughing, the next they weren't.

'No more,' she said. 'I can't do this any more, Kal. I shouldn't be here. Rose shouldn't be hiding and I shouldn't be living a pretend life.'

'No.' Then, 'You've stopped shivering.'

'Nothing like tea for shock,' she said.

'I'm sorry if I frightened you.'

'Only for about a millisecond. Then I knew it was you.'

'I was angry,' he said.

Lydia swallowed, nodded. Of course he was angry. He'd been charged with protecting her—protecting Rose—and she had sneaked off the minute his back was turned.

'You had every right,' she said. 'But you stuck around to look out for me, even when you knew I wasn't Rose.'

Long after her momentary fear had been forgotten, she'd still feel his strong, protective arm as he'd held her against him. She recalled the warm scent of his skin.

She wouldn't need a shell or anything else to remember that. Remember him.

'So,' she said, sensing the weight of unspoken words between them and, recalling his earlier tension, she repeated the question she'd asked him then, 'what's your problem, Kal? What aren't you telling me?'

'Not just lovely, not just cool under pressure and a loyal friend, but smart, too,' he said, not looking at her. 'You're right, of course. I have a confession to make.'

'You got me at lovely,' she said. Then, because when a man needed to confess, it was never going to be good news, she summoned up all the flippancy at her command and said, 'Don't tell me. You're married.'

No one would have guessed that, in the time it took him to answer, her heart had skipped a beat. Two. Maybe he was right. She should take up acting.

'No, Lydia, I'm not married.'

'Engaged?' This time the pause was longer, but he shook his head.

'That wasn't totally convincing,' she said.

'I am not in a relationship of any kind.'

Better, but there was something he wasn't telling her. Maybe if she shut up and let him get on with his 'confession' in his own way it would all become clear.

It took another half a dozen heartbeats before he said, 'I want you to understand that Lucy was truly concerned for

Rose. Her grandfather tried to talk her into withdrawing the invitation, said there had been a threat of some kind.'

'A threat? What kind of threat?' she asked, alarmed.

'Lucy was certain there was nothing, that it was just a ploy to keep her under his control, but she had to do something to pacify the Duke so she told him that the Emir's nephew would be in charge of his granddaughter's security.'

'That would be you. And he was happy with that?'

'No, but he couldn't object without offending the Emir.'

'And what about the Emir? Wasn't Lucy afraid of offending her father-in-law?'

'She saved Hanif. She can get away with things that no one else would dare to. Even be my friend. My grandfather is dying, Lydia. He lives only to return to Ramal Hamrah to die in the house where he was born.'

Her hand found his and she squeezed it, knowing how much he loved the old man.

'Lucy knew that Princess Sabirah would want to pay her respects to Rose and she seized the chance to put me where I could make a personal appeal to her, beg her to intercede with her husband.'

'And?'

'That first. Above everything...'

'But, once he has been allowed home, you hope the rest will follow. That you can become a Khatib again. With everything that entails.' His name, his title...

'It is as if I have been cut off from half my life. I have the language, I have property here, can study the culture, the history, but without my family...'

The metaphorical clock struck twelve. Time for the coach to turn back into a pumpkin, for Cinderella to go back to the checkout and check out the alternatives to getting a cat. Maybe a rabbit or a guinea pig, she thought. Or half a dozen white mice. Just in case the fairy godmother ever dropped in again.

'Not just your name, your title, but you want the ultimate prize of an arranged marriage to one of the precious daughters of a powerful Ramal Hamrahn family.'

His silence was all the answer she needed.

'That was why you stopped.' She swallowed. 'Would not make love with me.'

'Honour would not allow it,' he agreed.

Honour. What a rare word, but this man who'd been raised in the west was steeped in the culture that had excluded him.

'Absolutely,' she agreed. The kitchen telegraph would be humming to news of an affair before they disturbed the sheets. Princess Sabirah would suddenly find herself too busy to call and all Kal's hopes and dreams would fly right out of the window. 'Good call.'

Lydia stood up, pushed open one of the shutters, looked out over the garden, needing a little space to recover, put the smile back on.

'I'm glad that we were able to be honest with one another, Kal.'

Honest.

This was honest?

This was honour?

Lydia was pretending to be someone she was not, while he was about to collude with her deception, not just of the world's press but the Emir of Ramal Hamrah.

She turned to him.

'Will you take me to the souk tomorrow? I'd like to buy a gift for my mother.'

The request was simple enough, but that wasn't the question she was asking. They both knew it and when, after the briefest pause, he responded in the affirmative with a slight but formal bow, he was confirming that there would be a tomorrow for 'Lady Rose' at Bab el Sama.

What choice did he have?

He had been prepared to be patient, wait for those precious things he wanted for himself, no matter how long it took. But for his grandfather time was running out, leaving him with no choice but to seize the chance Lucy had given him.

She wasn't sure that honour had much to do with it, but love was there in abundance.

'You should believe in love, Kal,' she said. 'You are living proof of its existence. Your love of your family shines through when you talk of them. You yearn with all your heart for this country, for everything that you have lost here and yet you would risk it all on this chance to bring your grandfather home. That's love at its finest. Unselfish, pure, the real thing.'

'I am asking a great deal of you, Lydia. I would understand if you said you could not go through with it.'

'We both have debts, Kal, and to pay them we need each other.' Then, 'You'll excuse me if I ask you to leave now? I need to change.'

Kal watched her wrap herself in the figurative mantel of Lady Rose Napier. Stand a little taller, inject the crispness back into her voice as she distanced herself from him. And where he had been warmed by her smile, her presence, a touch as she'd reached out without thinking, there was now an icy chill.

'Will you come to the stables in the morning?' he asked.

He saw her neck move as she swallowed, glimpsed a momentary longing for the closeness that would give them as he lifted her to the saddle, fitted her feet in the stirrups, placed her hands just so on the reins.

Then she shook her head just once and said, 'Lady Rose is afraid of horses.'

'And Lydia?'

'It's safer to stick to Rose, don't you think?'

He wasn't thinking. That was the problem. He'd set out on a quest that he'd believed nothing in the world could distract him from. How wrong could one man be?

He leaned forward, kissed her cheek. 'I'll send Yatimah to you.'

* * *

When Yatimah arrived, Lydia was filling the huge sunken bath.

'*Sitti!*' she declared. 'I must do that for you.' Then, 'Bin Zaki says that you are going to the souk tomorrow. I will bring you an *abbayah* to keep the dust from your clothes,' she said as she ladled something into the bath that foamed magically, filling the air with an exotic, spicy fragrance. 'Would you like me to wash your hair?'

'Not tonight. I'm really tired so I'll just take a bath and then go to bed.'

She closed the bathroom door, locked it. Leaned back against it. Lifted her hand to her cheek.

Flash, bang, wallop...

Kal walked along the shore that she had walked, but went much further before sitting on a rock and calling his grandfather in London. He didn't ask how he was feeling. He knew he would be in pain because he refused to slide into the morphine induced coma that would lead to death.

Instead, he described the scene before him. The lights along the far shore, the boats riding on the water, the moon rising, dripping, from her ocean so that he could, in his heart, be here with him.

He called his mother, who'd complained of a cold the last time they'd spoken, listened to her news, her happiness at becoming a grandmother again. She demanded to know when he was going to settle down and add to her joy.

Talked to a brother who was struggling at university. Made a promise to go and see him soon.

This was what Lydia called love, he thought. Joint memories that needed only a word to bubble to the surface. Shared connections, history. To know that you could reach out and there would be a hand waiting.

Without that, how would you ever know how to see beyond the fireworks and make a marriage?

How could you ever know for sure?

He was still holding the phone and he scrolled through his contact list until he found 'Rose'.

'Kal?'

Was that it? When just the sound of her voice made your heart sing?

'Where are you, Kal?'

'On the beach, watching the moon rise. I called my grand-father so that he could share it.'

'And now you're sharing it with me?' she asked, still distant, still 'Rose'.

'I'm making a memory, Lydia.' One that, for the rest of their lives, whenever either of them looked at the rising moon would bring back this moment. 'Go onto your balcony and you will see it rise above the trees.'

He heard her move. A door opening. A tiny breath that was not quite a gasp, not quite a sigh. 'It's there,' she said. 'I can just see the top of it.'

'Be patient…'

Was it when you could sit miles apart watching the same spectacle and words weren't necessary?

'Thank you, Kal,' she said, minutes later when it was high enough to have cleared the trees around Bab el Sama. Her voice softer. Pure Lydia.

'*Afwan ya habibati, hada mussdur sa'adati,*' he replied. Then, when she'd broken the connection, 'It is the source of my pleasure, beloved.'

Lydia stood on the terrace at dawn, sipping the orange juice that Dena had brought her, staying to watch Kal ride along the beach.

'He is faster this morning,' Dena said enigmatically. 'The demons must be getting closer.'

'Yes,' she replied without thinking. 'They are.'

She'd scarcely slept—at this rate she would soon look

exactly like Rose—and had watched the sky grow light, barely able to stop herself from going to the stables, just to be near him.

'Come, *sitti*, I will prepare you.'

Two hours later, resolved to keep her distance and wearing a feather-light black silk wrap, she and Kal crossed the creek to visit the souk.

It started well enough. They'd kept a clear foot between them and the conversation safely on topics such as the weather, Arabic vocabulary, followed by a whole lot of incoherent babbling as she'd seen the amazing array of colourful spices that came in dustbin-sized containers instead of tiny little glass jars.

Neither of them had mentioned the full moon they'd watched rising from the far ends of Bab el Sama. Apart and yet more intensely together than if they had been in each other's arms.

'Would you like the full tour?' he asked, 'or shall we go straight for the good stuff?'

She gave him a 'Lady Rose' look and said, 'The full tour. I want to see everything.'

Maybe that was the wrong answer. The area where the blacksmiths worked was noisy, hot and sparks flew everywhere. There were tinsmiths hammering away too and carpenters repairing furniture.

Once they turned into an area where tailors were waiting to run her up a dress in an hour or two things improved. There were tiny shops containing all kinds of strange and wonderful foods that weren't on the shelves of the supermarket that was her second home. She tasted Turkish delight flavoured with cardamom, a glass of tea from a man wandering about with an urn, little sticky cakes from a stall.

It was a different world and she sucked up every experience, her guard dropping long before they reached the stalls piled high with gorgeous silks.

Once there, she realised that she was not alone in wearing western clothes beneath the *abbayyeh*. There were plenty of woman who, when they leaned forward to look at the goods on display, revealed business suits, trousers, simple dresses beneath them. And although her pale hair and blue eyes made her an obvious foreigner, no one took much notice.

'They're used to Lucy and her friends,' Kal said. 'And another cousin, Zahir, is married to an English woman, too. A redhead in his case.'

'I read about it,' she said. 'It caused quite a sensation but I had no idea he was your cousin. Do you know him?'

'Our paths have crossed,' he said. 'We're in the same business.' He shrugged. 'My planes carry freight. His carry passengers.'

'Air freight? When you said you'd hadn't quite broken the habit of acquiring planes, you weren't joking, were you?'

'I ran out of room, so I had to keep some of them in the air,' he said. Joking, obviously. He had to be joking. 'Have you decided what you want?' he asked.

'It's impossible, but I've narrowed it down to three,' she said.

'I thought you were looking at this one?' He lifted the edge of a rich, heavy cream silk that would be perfect for a wedding dress.

'It's lovely,' she said, 'but I have no use for it.'

'Why do you have to have a use for something?' With a gesture that took in all four fabrics, he spoke briefly to the stall-holder. Moved on.

'Kal,' she protested. 'I haven't paid. I haven't told him how much I want. And what about my parcels?'

'He'll deliver them. And Dena will settle with him. Unless you want to haggle?'

Giving it up as a lost cause, she said, 'No, thanks. I'd rather hear more about this air freight business of yours. Does it have a name?'

'Kalzak Air Services.'

'Kalzak? That's your company?' Even she'd heard of them. Everybody had heard of them. 'I…um…hadn't made the connection. It's not exactly a hobby, then?'

'No,' he admitted. 'It's not a hobby. But I wasn't interested in the family business.'

She frowned. He hadn't mentioned a family business but there must be one or how else had they supported all those wives, children?

'Exiled playboy?' he prompted.

'I'm sorry—'

He stopped her fumbling apology with a touch to the elbow. 'It's okay. My grandfather lost his throne, but his father made a generous financial settlement—probably out of guilt.'

'And his brother didn't take that away?'

'He couldn't have, even if he'd wanted to, but I imagine he thought he was less dangerous playing with his race-horses and women than taking to the hills and fermenting more trouble.'

'You said he was the clever one.'

She thought that Kal was a lot more like his great-uncle, with his work ethic and philanthropy, than the grandfather he adored.

'Well, you and your cousin have something in common. Isn't that a starting place?'

'I help Lucy out when she needs to move disaster relief supplies. Zahir al-Khatib suggested I was taking advantage of her and offered to carry anything she needed so that she wouldn't have to turn to me for help.'

'Oh…'

And then, just when she was feeling desperately sorry for him, he gave her one of those slow smiles calculated to send her hormones into a dizzy spin.

'She probably shouldn't have told him that I had more aircraft, fewer family commitments. That I could afford to bear the cost more easily. His airline is very new,' he explained. 'But he wanted him to understand that my participation wasn't a matter for discussion.'

'Honestly,' she declared, 'I was just about to open up my heart and bleed for you.'

'I know.' And he touched the spot just by her mouth where she had pointed out his own giveaway muscle. 'You probably shouldn't ever play poker unless you're wearing a full face mask, Lydia,' he said softly. Then, as if nothing had happened, 'Gold next, I think.'

She followed him on rubbery legs to the glittering gold souk where the metal shone out of tiny shop windows and the air itself seemed to take on a golden glow.

It was a stunning spectacle and she could have spent hours there, but she quickly chose a pair of earrings, a waterfall of gold and seed pearls for her mother—who wore her hair up and adored dangly earrings—and a brooch set with turquoise for Jennie for looking after her.

'You will not choose something for yourself?'

He lifted the heavy rose pendant she was wearing at her throat. 'I imagine you'll have to give this back?'

'You imagine right.' But she could read him too, and she shook her head. 'Don't!' Then, 'Please, don't even think it...' she said, and walked quickly away in the direction of the harbour and the launch that had brought them across the creek, knowing that he had no choice but follow.

But later that afternoon four bolts of cloth were delivered to her room. And when she asked about paying for them Dena simply shrugged and suggest that she ask 'bin Zaki.'

Lydia didn't know much about the protocol in these things, but she was fairly certain that a man on the lookout for a bride was not supposed to buy another woman anything, let alone something as personal as cloth she would wear next to her skin.

Easy to see, in retrospect, that the spark that flared between them had been lit in the first moment they had set eyes on one another and for a moment it had burned so intense that, even while he was single-mindedly focused on his future, he had still come close to losing control.

There could be nothing 'little' between them and she was holding herself together with nothing but willpower.

CHAPTER ELEVEN

LYDIA wanted this over. Was desperate for Princess Sabirah to pay her call and the week to be over so that she could just stop pretending and go home.

Stop pretending to be Rose. Stop pretending that she felt nothing for Kalil. Not that that worked. He'd only had to call in the darkness. She only had to hear his voice. If she hadn't cared she would have hung up, not stood there with her phone pressed to her ear, imagining she could hear him breathe while that huge moon rose above them.

Why had he done that?

He was the one who'd stepped back from the brink, broken the most intense, the most intimate connection there could ever be between a man and a woman even when it was obvious he'd wanted her as much as she'd wanted him.

Trapped, like her, committed to a course from which there was no escape but unable to stop himself from touching her. Calling her. Making love to her with words.

Breaking her heart.

She had taken lunch alone, keeping her nose firmly in a book until the words all ran together in a smeary blur, swam fifty lengths of the pool just to stop herself from thinking about him.

Except that when she emerged, slightly dizzy with the effort, he was waiting to wrap a towel around her.

'You shouldn't be here,' she said.

'I am your bodyguard. It is my duty.'

'I'm not in any danger.'

Only from falling in love with a man who didn't believe in love. Who thought marriage was no more than a convenient contract arranged by two families for their advantage. Maybe the girls did have some say, but the pressure had to be intense to make a 'good' marriage. Scarcely any different from the way that medieval barons gave their daughters to men whose land marched with theirs, or who could bring them closer to the King.

'Please…' She grabbed the towel and ran from the poolside to her room. Sat with it pressed to her face.

'Be strong, Lydie. You have to be strong…'

But, no matter how she ignored him, Kal's presence permeated the house.

Everywhere she went, she was sure he'd been there a second before. She couldn't escape the woody scent that clung to him, the swish of freshly laundered robes, the gentle flapping sound of leather thongs against marble floors.

The thrumming beat of hooves against sand.

It was all in her head, she knew, but she retreated to her room, allowing Yatimah to pamper her with facials, massage the tension out of her shoulders, paint more ornate patterns on her hands and feet with henna.

She caught sight of them as she reached for the phone, hoped they would wear off before she went back to work or they'd cause a few comments from the regulars as she swished their weekly shop over the scanner.

She checked the caller ID and, when she saw it was Kal, considered not answering. But then he'd come looking for her.

She took a deep breath, composed herself.

'Kal?' she queried, ice-cool.

'Just checking. I haven't seen you all day. Are you hiding from me?'

Reckless, bold, dangerous Bagheera, whose skin shimmered like watered silk, whose mouth tasted like wild honey—only a fool wouldn't hide.

'Just putting my feet up, taking it easy while I plan my future,' she said.

'Oh? What did you have in mind?'

'Well,' she said, her fingers lingering on the bolt of cream silk on the table beside her, 'now I'm giving up the lookalike business I thought I might set myself up in the rag trade,' she said. 'Costing is tricky, though. I need to know how much to budget for material.'

'Oh, I see. This is about the silk…'

'I can't wear it all myself,' she pointed out. Not unless she made a wedding dress with a thirty foot train. 'I need to know how much it cost.'

'You must ask Dena. She dealt with the merchant.'

'She told me to ask you.'

'Then it's a mystery,' he said with an infuriating hint of laughter in his voice that undid all her good intentions, all her cool.

'Kal!' she exploded. 'I just wanted a few metres for a suit or dress. I can't take all that home with me.'

'No problem.' Now he was enjoying himself. 'I'll deliver.'

'Deliver them to your bride,' she snapped. 'Yatimah was telling me that's what a groom is supposed to do. Send jewels, cloth, carpets, the biggest flat screen television you can afford.'

'Yatimah has altogether too much to say for herself,' he snapped back and she rejoiced in having rattled him out of his teasing. He had no right to tease her. No right to call her and make her want him… For a moment neither of them spoke and the only sound was of raised breathing. Then, after a moment, his voice expressionless, his manner formal, Kal said, 'Lucy phoned to check up on how well I've been looking after you, *sitti*.'

'Tell her what you like,' Lydia replied, not even trying for cool. 'I won't tell tales. And cut out the *sitti*.' It was one thing having Dena or Yatimah calling her 'lady', quite another from Kal.

'I can't tempt you to come on a picnic?'

Oh, the man knew how to tempt.

She refused without having to think twice. Well, maybe twice, but she knew the attraction between them was too great to risk another close encounter. And that even while he was paying lip service to honour, his frustrated libido was refusing to quit.

'Sorry, Kal, but I'm planning a walk on the beach this afternoon and, unlike you, I'm happy with my own company,' she said, knowing how much that would infuriate him. But she was angry with him for putting her through this, with herself for aching for something so far out of reach. For bringing tears stinging to her eyes. 'But you're welcome to stand and watch if you like. Just remember how handy I am with a shell.'

She didn't wait for him to command her not to do it, but hung up. Then had to hold herself together. Physically wrap her arms around herself, holding her breath, just to stop herself from falling apart.

Kal took himself to the stables in the foulest, blackest mood.

He was behaving like a man who didn't know his own mind. Who had lost control of his senses.

It wasn't true. When he could have taken Lydia, he had known it was wrong. That, without commitment, honour, such an act was beneath him, could only hurt her.

He'd hurt her anyway.

She could hide nothing from him and he'd seen her eyes in the moment she had realised why he had refused the greatest gift a woman could bestow on any man. Had seen her pain in the way she'd moved as she'd taken herself away from him in the souk, when all he'd wanted to do was shower her with gold, pearls. Put diamonds in her ears, on every one of the fingers he had taken to his lips. When, seeing that in his face, she had begged him not even to think it.

He was furious because, even as he weakened, unable to stay

away, she grew stronger, keeping him at arm's length when he needed them around her.

A nagging, desperate need that came from somewhere deep inside, from a place he hadn't, until that moment, known existed. All he knew was that he was ready to consign common sense, five years of patient planning along with everything he had learned about the fleeting nature of 'love' from his grandfather, his father, to the deep blue sea.

And still she had turned him down. Not because she didn't want to go. He was attuned to every nuance in her voice, every hesitation and he'd heard the unspoken longing in a whisper of a sigh before she had said no to his picnic.

But, even when he was losing control, she was strong enough to save him from himself.

Lydia Young might not be a princess, but she had all the attributes of one. Courage, dignity that would become a queen. A spirit that was all her own. He wanted her with a desperation that was driving every other thought from his head.

At home he would have taken up the small biplane he used for stunting, shaken off his mood in a series of barrel rolls, loops. Here, the closest he could get to a release in the rush of power was on one of Hanif's fine stallions but, as he tightened the girth, the horse skipped edgily away from him, sensing his frustration.

But it wasn't simply his out of control libido, the sense of being too big for his skin. This was a need that went much deeper, challenging everything he believed in.

He'd spent the last five years planning the perfect life but Lydia was forcing him to face the fact that life wasn't something that you could plan. It happened. Some of it good, some of it bad, none of it 'safe'.

He had arrogantly assumed that his grandfather, his father had wasted their lives but, while their families were scarcely conventional, their quivers were full of the children of their youth and they were, he realised with a shock, happy men.

That, wherever his grandfather died, he would be surrounded by his children, grandchildren, people who loved him.

He lay his hand on the neck of the horse, gentling him with soft words, even while he yearned for the sound of Lydia's voice. The sweet scent that clung to her, as if she had been brushing her hands over jasmine. The touch of her hands against his skin.

Wanted to see her face, her eyes lighting up, her mouth softening, her hands describing what her lips were saying. Her quickness with a tender touch to show that she understood. Her laugh. The swiftness with which she melted to his kisses.

While he kept the world at bay, carefully avoiding the risk, the pain that was an inevitable part of what Lydia called 'love', she held nothing back.

She had answered every question he had asked of her with not just her body, but her heart and her soul and he wanted to shower her with gifts, buy her every bolt of cloth in the market, heap up gold, pearls, gems in a dower that she could not ignore.

Except, of course, she could and would. She had told him so. Her price was above rubies. Only his heart, freely given in an avowal of love, without negotiations, conditions, guarantees would win her acceptance.

She would not settle for less and neither, he knew now, would he. Because the nearest a man could come to perfection was to take every single moment and live it to the full. With love. And she was right. He was not a stranger to the emotion. Love for his family was part of who he was.

But this was new. This love for a woman who, from the first moment he had set eyes on her, had made the lights shine more brightly.

He'd lost the perfect moment, had hurt her. Now, to show her how he felt, he had to give her not just his heart but his world. Everything that made him who he was. And there was only one way he could do that, could win her trust.

The horse snorted impatiently, eager to be off, but he left the groom circling the yard as he made the calls that would change his life.

Lydia stepped onto the beach, kicking off her sandals. It was cooler today and she was wearing cotton trousers, a white shirt, a cashmere sweater knotted at her waist.

There were clouds gathering offshore and the wind coming off the sea was sharper, whipping up little white horses on the creek and, as she strode along the beach, hanging onto her temper by a thread, she glowered at the photographer's launch, bobbing on the waves, hoping that he was seasick.

She doubted that. There hadn't been pictures in the papers for a day or two. A sighting of Rupert Devenish at a business meeting in the States had downgraded interest in Bab el Sama and he would have packed up his telephoto lenses and gone in search of more lucrative prey.

It hadn't been a great week for anyone, she thought, her hand tightening around the note from Princess Sabirah's secretary that Dena had delivered to her as she'd left for her walk.

It was brief and to the point, informing her, regretfully, that the Princess had a cold and was unable to travel this week. Wishing her a pleasant stay and the Princess's sincere hope that they would meet soon in London.

Somewhere where there was no chance that Kal al-Zaki would pop out of the woodwork, presumably.

That the illness was diplomatic, she had no doubt, and she let out a very unladylike roar of outrage that all Kal's hopes and dreams had been crushed without even a chance to put in a plea for his grandfather.

What on earth was the matter with these people? It had all happened fifty years ago, for heaven's sake.

'Get over it!' she shouted to the sky, the seabirds whirling overhead.

He had to know. She would have to tell him and the sooner the better. Maybe there was still something he could do. She could do...

If she really had been Rose, she could have gone to Rumaillah by herself, taken some flowers to the 'sick' Princess. On her own, she would have been admitted. Could have pleaded for him.

She stopped, stood for a moment staring at the phone in her hand as she realised something else. That with his mission dead he would turn to her for comfort, would be free to love her...

She stopped the thought dead, ashamed even to have given it room in her head, and quickly scrolled down the contact list and hit 'dial'. Unexpectedly, it went straight to voicemail...

'Kal,' she began uncertainly, hating to be the bearer of such bad news. Then, as she hesitated, above the buffeting of the wind she heard another sound. The pounding of hooves. She swung round and saw him riding towards her astride a huge black horse, robes flying behind him, hand outstretched. Before she could think, move, there was a jolt as he swooped low, caught her round the waist, lifted her to his saddle.

It was the dream, she thought crazily as she clung to him, her face pressed against his pounding heart.

She'd reached out to him as she'd watched him from above, wanting to be lifted to the stars.

There were no stars and she knew that at any moment he would slow down, berate her for taking unnecessary risks.

But he didn't stop, didn't slow down until Bab el Sama was far below them, the horse rearing as he brought it to a halt, turned, slid to the ground with her.

'Did your English heart beat to be swept onto my horse, *ya habibati*?' He smiled as he curved his hand around her face. 'Did you feel mine, beloved?' He took her hand and placed it against his chest. 'Feel it now. It beats for you, Lydia Young.'

Beloved...

He had called her his beloved and as his lips came down on hers she was lost.

* * *

'This is kidnapping,' she said when he carried her to a waiting four-by-four. 'Where are you taking me?'

'You will see,' he said as he fastened the seat belt and climbed in beside her. 'Then I will ask you if you wish me to take you back.'

'But what about…?'

He silenced her protest with a kiss.

'The groom will take him back,' he said and she realised that this had not been a spur of the moment escapade but was a carefully arranged assault on her defences by a man who when he offered a treat refused to take no for an answer. No doubt there would be a picnic waiting for her at the side of the river, or some archaeological treasure.

But when he stopped there was nothing but a distant view.

'There,' he said. 'Do you see it?'

She could see something shimmering through the dust haze like a mirage. A tower, a shimmer of green above high walls, and she knew without doubt that she was looking at Umm al Sama.

'I see it,' she said. Then, turning to him, 'I see you, Kalil bin Zaki.'

'Will you go there with me?'

He had brought her to the place where his grandfather had been born. The place he called home. Not home as in the place where he lived, like the apartments in Rumaillah, London, New York, but the home of his heart. The place that an exile, generations on, still carried deep in the memory, in his soul.

That he would keep for a woman who meant more than a brief affair. This was the home he had been preparing not just for the return of his grandfather, but for the bride he would one day bring here and, even though he knew who she was, Lydia Young, he was offering it to her.

Words for a moment failed her, then a phrase came into her head, something from long ago Sunday School…

'Whither thou goest, I will go; and where thou lodgest, I will lodge...'

Kal knew this was a perfect moment. He had offered the woman he loved all that he was and she had replied with words that touched his soul and as he reached for her, embraced her, sealed their future with a kiss, he knew he owned the world.

Kal led her through Umm al Sama by the hand, through gardens that had run wild, but were being tamed. Beside pools that had been cleaned and reflected the blue of a sky that had magically cleared above them. Through arched colonnades decorated with cool blue and green tiles.

Showed her a wind tower that funnelled the air down to a deep cooling pool below ground. Buildings that had been beautiful once and would be beautiful again when he had finished restoring them.

One building, smaller than the rest, was finished. Kal watched her from the doorway as she walked around an exquisite sitting room touching fine tables, running a finger over the smooth curves of fine porcelain.

'This is so beautiful, Kal. So special.' She looked at him. 'What was this?'

Kal had not touched Lydia since they'd arrived at Umm al Sama. Outside, in the garden, where they might be seen, he'd kept a discreet distance between them. Showing her respect. He had not brought her here to make love to her, but to give her his heart. To give her this.

'My great-grandfather's wife lived here before they moved to the new palace at Rumaillah.'

'Leaving it to the heir apparent?'

'No one has lived here since my grandfather was banished. If you go upstairs, there should be something to eat on the balcony.'

'All this and food too?'

'I invited you on a picnic,' he reminded her, leading the way to a wide covered balcony with carved shade screens that ran the length of the building.

She stared for a moment at the distant view of the mountains, then pushed open a door to reveal the private apartment of a princess.

The polished floor was covered with rare carpets, the walls hung with vivid gauzy silk, as was the great bed at its heart.

Lydia looked back at him. 'Are you expecting Scheherazade?'

'Only you. Come, *ya habibati*,' he said, extending his hand to her. 'You must be hungry.'

'I'm starving, Kal.' As she raised her hand to meet his, she came into his arms, lifted her lips to his. 'Feed me.'

As she breathed the words into his mouth he shattered. The man who had been Kalil al-Zaki no longer existed. As he shed his clothes, fed Lydia Young, the wife of his heart, with his touch, his mouth, his body, she rebuilt him with her surprise, her delight, tiny cries of pleasure at each new intimacy and finally with her tears as they learned from each other and finally became one.

'I have to go back to Bab el Sama, Kal,' she protested the following morning as she lay in bed while he fed her pomegranate seeds and dates for breakfast. 'I have no clothes here.'

He kissed her shoulder. 'Why do you need clothes?'

'Because otherwise I can't leave this room.'

He nudged the edge of the sheet, taking the kiss lower. 'I repeat, why do you need clothes, *ya rohi, ya hahati?*'

He'd showered her with words she did not understand as he'd made love to her, but she refused to be distracted.

'Dena will be concerned.'

'Dena knows that you are with your bodyguard. Am I not guarding your body?' And his smile, his touch, made everything else go away.

Thoroughly and completely distracted, it was gone noon

when she stirred again. She was alone in the great bed they'd
shared and, wrapping the sheet around her, she went to the
balcony, expecting to find him there waiting for her to wake.

The balcony was deserted but her clothes, freshly laundered, were waiting for her on a dresser with a note from Kal

> *Ask for whatever you want. Umm al Sama is yours. I
> will back soon.*

She held it to her breast, smiling. Obviously he'd gone to
fetch her clothes, explain their absence, and she bathed, washed
her hair, dressed. The note from the princess's secretary, forgotten in the wild excitement of her abduction, of Umm al
Sama, of Kal, was at the bottom of the pile. That had been
ironed, too.

She should have told him about that. As she put on Rose's
watch she wondered what time he'd left. How long it would be
before he returned.

Maybe he'd rung. She checked her messages but there was
nothing. Tried his number but it went straight to voicemail but
this wasn't news she could dump on him that way. And leaving
a *When will you be back?* message seemed so needy…

A servant brought her food. She picked at it. Took a walk
in the garden.

Checked her phone again. With nothing to read, no one to
talk to, she switched to the Net and caught the urgent flash of
a breaking news story and her blood ran cold.

Lady Rose kidnapped…

Rose…

But it wasn't Rose.

Of course it wasn't. It was her in the picture.

Make that a whole series of pictures.

Alone on the beach. Kal riding her down. Lifting her to his
saddle. Disappearing into the distance.

The photographer hadn't gone anywhere, she realised. Or had he been tipped off because he'd had all the time in the world to get the whole story in pictures...?

No question by whom.

There was only one person at Bab al Sama who wanted to be visible.

Well, two. She had wanted to be visible and maybe she'd given Kal the idea. Because when he'd realised that the princess wasn't coming—Dena had no doubt had her own note from the palace and would certainly have told him—he must have been desperate.

Not for himself. Whatever happened, he'd thrown away his own hopes and dreams the minute he'd picked her up from the beach. The family name, the title, the bride. Five years of quiet diplomacy, of being invisible.

He'd done this solely out of love for his grandfather.

For love, she reminded herself as she stared at the pictures for one last moment.

One thing was certain—with the world's press on the case, he was no longer invisible. The Emir could no longer pretend he did not exist. On the contrary, he had probably sent his guard to arrest him, lock him up. That would explain his lengthy absence. Why his phone was switched off.

And only she could save him.

She resisted the temptation to leave him to cool his heels for a night in the cells and went to find someone to take her to Rumaillah.

All he'd planned was a photo opportunity followed by a picnic. She was the one who'd got completely the wrong end of the stick, responding to his polite invitation to visit his family home with a declaration of eternity. Led all the way with her desperate *'I'm starving...feed me'*. What on earth was a man to do faced with that? Say no, thanks—again?

Once she was on her way—and had stopped blushing long enough to think straight—she called Rose. She couldn't have picked up the story yet, or she'd have been on the phone herself. She growled with frustration as her call went straight to voice-mail and she left a reassuring message.

Then she called her mother, not because she'd be worried, but because she really, really needed to hear her voice.

Kal left his beautiful Lydia sleeping. He could have asked for her things to be sent to Umm al Sama, but he wanted to visit the souk.

While she had clearly understood the significance of his taking her to Umm al Sama, that no one but his bride would ever sleep in that bed, he wanted to buy her at least one of the diamonds that he would shower on her.

He left Yatimah to pack their bags while he crossed the creek in search of a perfect solitaire. A stone that would say the things that words could never say. A pledge. A promise of forever.

Then he called his grandfather to tell him that he must not be in such a hurry to die. That, if he was patient, he would see not only a wedding at Umm al Sama but a great-grandson born there, too.

It was after lunch before he arrived home to be told that the *sitti* had insisted on being taken to Rumaillah. To the palace.

Rumaillah…

Had there been a call? A summons from the Princess? No. She would not have made a formal visit wearing a pair of cotton trousers and a shirt. This was something else. He took the stairs two at a time as he raced to the room where they had spent the night in blissful discovery of each other, certain that she must have left a message.

There was nothing.

Only the message he had left for her.

And a note from the palace with Princess Sabirah's regrets…

Dena had told him that she'd been unwell; it was why she

hadn't come earlier. This must have been in Lydia's pocket
when he'd taken her from the beach. It couldn't have anything
to do with her racing off to Rumaillah.

Unless…

He flipped to the Net, saw the breaking news story. And
swore long and inventively in several languages. He'd had the
photographer warned off but he'd either come back or this was
another one. It made no difference.

He knew exactly what Lydia must be thinking.

She'd assume that he'd known that the Princess was not
coming and that he had used her to force the Emir to notice him.

That she'd trusted him with all that she was, given him her
most precious gift, and he had betrayed her.

Lydia stood at the door to the *majlis*. She'd borrowed an
abbayeh from one of the women at Umm al Sama but she was
the only woman in the group of people who had arrived to
petition the Emir. She was aware of a rumbling of disapproval,
a certain amount of jostling, but she stood tall, refused to turn
tail and run, and waited her turn.

The room was vast. At one end the Emir sat with his
advisors. Along each wall men, drinking coffee from tiny cups,
sat on rows of sofas.

As she kicked off her sandals, stepped forward, the *abbayeh*
caught—or maybe someone was standing on it—and slipped
from her hair and every sound died away.

The Emir rose, extended a hand in welcome and said, 'Lady
Rose. We were concerned for your safety. Please…'

He gestured her forward.

She walked the length of the room. Bowed. Said, 'Thank
you, Excellency, but as you see I am safe and well. If you have
seized Kalil al-Zaki, have him locked in your cells, I must ask
you to release him.'

There was a buzz, silenced by a look from the Emir.

'Who is Kalil al-Zaki?' he asked.

She gasped, snapped, 'Who is he? I don't believe you people! It's been fifty years since his grandfather was exiled. Was stripped of everything he cared about. Your nephew has an apartment in this city, yet you treat him as if he did not exist.'

Now there was silence. Pin drop silence, but she was too angry to care that she was flouting royal protocol. Even an Emir needed to hear the truth once in a while.

'Kalil al-Zaki is a man of honour, a man who cares for his family, who has built up an international business that would grace any nation. He wants nothing from you but to bring his grandfather home to die. You would grant that to a dog!' Then, in the ringing silence that followed this outburst, 'And, by the way, my name is Lydia Young. Lady Rose has taken a holiday in a place where she won't be photographed twenty-four hours a day!'

Then, because there was nothing left for her, she sank to her knees before him.

'The son of your great-grandfather is dying, Excellency. Will you not let him come home?'

Kal was too late to stop her. He was blocked at the doorway by the Emiri guard, forced to watch as she berated the Emir.

But, in the deathly silence that followed her appeal for mercy, even they were too stunned to stop him and he pushed the man aside, lifted her to her feet, then touched his head, his heart and bowed to her.

'*Ya malekat galbi, ya rohi, ya hahati.* You are beautiful, my soul, my life. Ahebbak, ya tao'am rohi. The owner of my heart. *Amoot feeki.* There is no life without you.' Then, 'I did not know, Lydia. Please believe me, I did not use you. I did not know.'

She would have spoken, but the Emir stepped forward. 'I have listened to your appeal, Lydia Young.'

That she was dismissed, neither of them were in any doubt, but as he turned to leave with her, caring only that she should believe him, the Emir said, 'I have not heard from you, Kalil al-Zaki.'

She touched his hand, said, 'Stay.'

'No…'

'For heaven's sake, Kal. This is what you wanted. Your chance. Don't blow it now.'

Then she turned and walked away.

Lydia had been taken to the Princess's quarters. She'd been fed and given a change of clothes and then, having asked to be allowed to go straight home, the British Consul had been summoned to provide her with temporary papers since her passport was with her belongings and only Kal knew were they were.

She arrived home to a dozen messages from newspapers wanting her story and one from a famous publicist who warned her to sign nothing until she'd talked to him. And reporters knee-deep on the footpath outside her mother's flat.

Her mother didn't say a word. Just hugged her.

Numb until then, she finally broke down and cried.

Rose called to make sure she was really all right. To apologise for the publicity. To thank her.

'You've changed my life, Lydia. Words cannot express my gratitude. You should sell your story, make a mint.'

'There is no story, Rose.' Then, 'Is there any chance of getting my car back soon? I'm due back at work the day after tomorrow.'

'That's a bit of a bad news, good news story, I'm afraid. The bad news is that I had a little bit of an accident,' she confessed.

'Oh.' The car had been her pride and joy. It had taken her forever to save up for it… 'Is it in the garage?'

'Er…a little bit more of an accident than that,' she admitted. 'It's nothing but a cube of metal in a scrapyard, but the good news is that George has arranged a replacement for you. A rather jolly red Beetle. I'll make sure it's delivered tomorrow.'

'Thank you. And Rose. Congratulations. I hope you will be really happy.'

'I'll send you and your mother an invitation to the wedding.'

There was nothing from Kal and, since she didn't want to

hear from the reporters, the newspapers or the publicist, she un-plugged the phone and turned off her mobile.

She sent an email to the lookalike agency, informing them that she would no longer be available and asking them to take her off their books.

Deleted dozens from newsmen offering interviews, and weirdos who just wanted to be weird.

She didn't open the door to the manager of the local garage who came to deliver a brand-new red VW Beetle, which she knew cost about three times what she'd paid for her car, until he put a note through the door explaining who he was.

There was no missing the black and gold livery of the Kalzak Air Services courier who pulled up outside and delivered her luggage. All those lovely clothes, the cosmetics, the scent, the four bolts of silk.

She gave her mother and Jennie their gifts.

And then, in the privacy of her room, she cried again all over the cream silk.

The Emir had given Kal a hard time. Made him wait while he consulted his brothers, his sons, his nephews. Hanif had sup-ported him and so, unexpectedly, had Zahir and all the time he had been berating himself for letting Lydia walk away. Fly away.

She had thought he was in trouble and had come to help. Had begged for him.

Only her 'stay' had kept him here while members of a family he did not know video-conferenced from all over the world, deciding the fate of his grandfather, eventually deciding that compassion required that he should be allowed to return to Umm al Sama. And that, after his death, his family could use the name Khatib.

Kal told the Emir that he would bring his grandfather home but under those terms they could keep their name. He didn't want it. Lydia deserved better from him than acceptance of such a mealy-mouthed offer.

And the Emir smiled. 'I remember him. You are just like him.'

'You honour me, Excellency.'

At which point His Excellency had thrown up his hands and said, 'Let the old man have his name and his title.'

'Will you permit Dena to return to London with me to fetch him, travel back with him and his nurses?'

'If she is agreeable.' Then, with heavy irony, 'Is there anything else you want, Kalil bin Zaki al-Khatib? One of my granddaughters as a bride, perhaps, now that you are a sheikh?'

'I am very conscious of the honour you bestow, Excellency,' he replied, 'but, like my grandfather, I have chosen my own bride. You have had the honour of meeting her.'

And this time the Emir laughed appreciatively.

'She is all fire, that one. You will have your hands full.' He did not appear to believe that this was a bad thing.

Since there was no other way to get rid of them, Lydia finally faced the newsmen, standing on the pavement outside her home giving an impromptu press conference, answering their questions.

'Who was the horseman?'

'A bodyguard rescuing me from intrusive photographers.' Laughter.

'Lady Rose has cut her hair. Will you do that?'

'No.'

'When did you meet?'

'Will you be seeing her?'

'Have you met her fiancé?'

No. No. No.

She kept a smile pinned to her face, didn't lose her temper, even at the most intrusive questions, and eventually they ran out of things to ask.

And since she wasn't Lady Rose, it didn't take long for the madness to die down. One moment the pavement in front of their flat had been mobbed, the next there was no one.

The agency was still pleading with her to reconsider her

decision. They'd been inundated with requests for appearances since Rose had announced her engagement. But the publicist who'd been so keen to negotiate a contract for her to 'write' the story of her career as Rose's lookalike—with the titillating promise to reveal who had really swept her away on that black stallion and what had happened afterwards—finally accepted that she meant it when she said 'no'.

With the excitement of Rose's engagement to occupy the gossip pages, she quickly became old news.

The story about the exiled Sheikh who had been pardoned by the Emir and allowed to return home to die probably wouldn't have made the news at all, except that Ramal Hamrah was where that very odd incident had taken place, when everyone thought Lady Rose had been kidnapped.

She had heard nothing from Kalil.

No doubt he had his hands full taking care of his grandfather, transferring him to Umm al Sama. Getting to know a whole new family.

She winced as *White Christmas* began to play for the fiftieth time that week on the seasonal tape. Turned to smile at yet another harassed mother doing her Christmas shop. Reached for yet another turkey.

Kal quietly joined the checkout queue.

All his duties done, he had come straight from the airport to find Lydia. Had gone to her home. He'd met her mother and, with her blessing, he had come to claim his love publicly, in her real world. Wanted her to know that there was no misunderstanding between them. That he knew who she was. That it was not some icon he had fallen in love with but Lydia Young.

Not the aristocrat in the designer suit, but the ordinary girl on the supermarket checkout wearing an overall and a ridiculous hat.

She looked exhausted. There were dark shadows beneath her eyes, her cheeks were hollow and had lost their glow, but the smile never faltered.

She greeted regular customers as friends. Asked what they were doing for the holiday and, as she listened with every appearance of interest, they lost a little of their tension as she swiftly dealt with their purchases. He watched her pack the shopping for one old lady whose hands were crippled with arthritis, helped her count out the money.

He made an instinctive move forward to help as she heaved a heavy bag of potatoes over the scanner, got a glare from the woman in front who was fiddling with a mobile phone. She was trying to take a picture of Lydia, he realised, and he leaned forward and said very quietly, 'Don't do that.'

About to tell him to mind his own business, she thought better of it and, muttering something about forgetting something, melted away.

Next in line was a woman with a toddler and a small baby who was grizzling with exhaustion.

Lydia whizzed the goods through, packed the bags, then took the baby, put it to her shoulder as the woman searched helplessly for her wallet. Reassuring the woman, patting the baby. The baby fell asleep, the wallet was found.

'Can I take you home with me?' the woman asked as she retrieved her baby.

He'd seen her dressed in designer clothes, every inch the lady with a capital L.

He'd seen her sweetness with Yatimah, her eyes hot with passion, soft with desire. Seen her berate the Emir in a room filled with hostile men. Seen her on her knees begging for him...

Beauty was a lot more than skin-deep and with each revelation he'd fallen deeper in love with Lydia. And as he watched her kindness, her compassion, her cheerful smile even though she was exhausted, he fell in love with her all over again.

She lifted her hands to her face and rubbed it, turned as someone came alongside her. 'Your shift is nearly up. Just this last one and then I'll take over.'

His cue to place the basket he was carrying on the shelf, take out the single item it contained and place it on the conveyer.

He saw her gather herself for one last effort. Put the smile back in place, turn to wait for the goods to reach her. Saw the smile falter, the frown pucker her brow as she watched the tiny dark blue velvet-covered box move slowly towards her. The diamond solitaire at its heart sparking a rainbow of light.

Confused, she looked up. Saw him standing at the far end of the conveyer as, behind him, half a dozen shoppers stared open-mouthed. Rose slowly to her feet.

'Kal…'

'The ring was in my pocket when I returned to Umm al Sama, Lydia. I was sure that you knew, understood that the only woman I would take there would be my bride. But I wanted to give you a tangible token of my love. Something more than a dream.'

'I am not what you wanted.'

'Until I met you I didn't know what I wanted, but love is the star to every wandering bark, Lydia. You taught me that. I had been wandering all my life, without a star to guide me…' He sank to his knees. '*Ahebbak,* Lydia. I love you. I am begging you to marry me, to be my princess, my wife, my lover, the mother of my children, my soul, my life.'

The growing crowd of onlookers broke out into a spontaneous round of applause but it was Lydia who mattered.

'How is he?' she asked. 'Your grandfather?'

'Happy to be home. Thanks to you.'

'Then you have everything.'

'Everything but you.' He stood up, took the ring from the box, held it up, then touched it to each finger of her left hand, counting slowly in Arabic… '*Wahid, ithnan, thelatha, arba'a, khamsa…*

'*Ithnan, ya habibi*—my beloved,' she said. '*Ahebbak,* Kalil, I love you.'

He slipped the ring onto the ring finger of her left hand, then walked around the checkout, took her in his arms and kissed her.

By this time they had brought the entire row of checkouts
to a standstill. And the entire store was clapping.

'Maybe we had better leave, my love,' he said. 'These good
people need to finish their shopping. And we have a wedding
to arrange.'

Daily Chronicle, 2nd March 2010

LADY ROSE LOOKALIKE MARRIES HER LORD

Lydia Young, who for ten years made regular appearances as a Lady Rose lookalike, was married today at Umm al Sama in Ramal Hamrah to Sheikh Kalil bin Zaki al-Khatib, nephew of the Emir.

Sheikh Kalil, who founded the international air freight company Kalzak Air Services, met Miss Young before Christmas and proposed after a whirlwind romance.

The bride's mother Mrs Glenys Young, who was formerly a seamstress for a London couturier, made her daughter's wedding dress from a bolt of cream silk that was a gift from the groom.

Four of the groom's sisters were attendants and his brother was best man. Family members and guests flew in from all over the world to be present at the ceremony, amongst them Lady Rose Napier and her fiancé billionaire businessman George Saxon. The groom's grandfather, who is gravely ill, rallied sufficiently to make a short speech at the reception.

The couple will spend their time between homes in London, Paris, New York and Ramal Hamrah.